Praise for *Cascadia Rising*

"Kevin's done it again with *Cascadia Rising*! An intricately crafted story that takes the reader through a slow burn before erupting into a high-speed revolution, *Cascadia Rising* combines old and new characters to bring you an action-packed sequel. His cast covers a wide range of relatable characters, and provides an eye-opening view of what a new society could look like after a country's collapse."

—Charley Hogwood, author and survival consultant

Praise for *Big Sky Fallen*

"If you enjoy apocalyptic literature, you will enjoy this one. The storyline is riveting and keeps the reader engaged."

—Mark Lawley, prepper author and podcaster

"Well-written and maybe prophetic. I read a lot of post-apocalyptic fiction, and this is one of the best."

—Amazon review

CASCADIA RISING

THE UNRAVELING: BOOK TWO

Kevin Craver

ISBN e-Book: 979-8-9882166-4-3

ISBN Paperback: 979-8-9882166-1-2

Library of Congress Control Number: 2024903846

First Edition, 2024

Printed in the United States of America

Cover design by Christian Bentulan

Created with Atticus

For the record, this book was proudly written by a human being. No AI software was used at any time to develop, write, or edit this work. By buying this book, you support actual *homo sapiens* authors who do honest work. Buy human—don't give your money to douchebags who ask an AI to write a book for them and get paid because they're too lazy or stupid, or both, to do it themselves.

Books By Kevin Craver

The Unraveling Series

Big Sky Fallen

Cascadia Rising

Contents

Disclaimer

Thank you very much for buying this novel and kicking a pittance of your hard-earned money into the Grace and Logan Craver College Fund. This novel is the second in my Unraveling series; several of its characters are introduced, and their backstories established, in the first novel, *Big Sky Fallen*. While *Cascadia Rising* can stand on its own, reading *Big Sky Fallen* will increase your understanding and enjoyment of this book.

However, before we get to the story, we need to get some things out of the way in order to cover my posterior in this humorless and litigious society in which we find ourselves trapped.

Cascadia Rising is a work of fiction. Aside from the mention of a handful of historical figures, politicians, and celebrities, none of the characters in this novel are based on anyone, either living or dead. Sorry to disappoint those of you who know me personally or served with me in the military, but you're not in here.

The novels in my Unraveling series tell the story of a societal collapse, brought about by a deadly flu pandemic and a worldwide economic crash, that results in the breakup of the United States. I wrote these books to entertain you, and if they get you thinking about how you and your family can prepare for the day this house of cards we call modern civilization goes belly-up, so much the better.

Cascadia Rising centers on an armed rebellion against a state government that embraces tyranny in the wake of the collapse. While I'm not shy about my belief that our federal government is utterly broken, and that our garbage institutions like the FBI and DOJ have been outright weaponized against us by garbage people, this book is in no way a call to take up arms against the federal government, state government, or any other lawful authority. If you happen to be a member of some anti-government militia group reading this right now, let me do you a great big favor—the fellow on your left is actually an undercover federal agent, and the fellow on your right is an undercover reporter for *The New York Times*. In short, you're compromised, so for your sake and your family's sake, quit and join a bowling league instead—it's less stressful, you don't have to camp out in the rain, and the uniforms are cooler.

The Unraveling timeline also involves a number of states seceding from a shattered Union; in *Cascadia Rising*, the conservative eastern half of Washington State fights to split from the liberal western half. As I started writing this book in earnest, I became aware of a grass-roots movement in Washington to seek this very partition. While I understand the deep frustration that Washington residents east of the Cascades must feel over their rights and values being trampled by their State Legislature—having been born and raised in the People's Republic of Illinois, believe me, I get it—this book is neither an endorsement nor a condemnation of their efforts. I'll also reiterate that none of the characters in this novel are meant to bear any resemblance to individuals, living or deceased, who are involved with the Liberty State movement or any other state partition effort.

(For the record, unlike secession, the US Constitution allows the creation of new states from existing ones, provided it gets approval from the affected state legislatures as well as Congress; the language can be found in Article IV, Section 3, Clause 1.)

In the disclaimer for my first novel, *Big Sky Fallen*, I cordially invited any corporate regime media journalist or social justice warrior who alleges that my work contains any racist or sexist undertones to play hide and go screw yourself. My position on this remains the same for this second novel.

While *Cascadia Rising* is set in a world without law and order, we live in a nation where law and order are still in effect, even though it's become glaringly obvious that we have a two-tiered justice system that appears far more eager to go after red voters than blue ones. With that in mind, there are a number of activities described in this book that will get you in very deep doo-doo with the authorities, including but not limited to owning an unlicensed automatic weapon, raising a guerrilla army and taking over your small town, broadcasting pirate radio transmissions on amateur radio bands, shooting down aircraft with surface-to-air missile launchers, sabotaging government equipment, practicing medicine without a license, and other no-nos. Likewise, there are activities in this book, such as the use of medical marijuana and the ownership of "assault-style rifles" or high-capacity magazines, that are legal in some jurisdictions, but not in others, so please consult your applicable laws.

In conclusion, you and you alone are solely responsible for your own actions, and the consequences of your own carelessness or stupidity. The author is in no way culpable if this work of fiction inspires you to do something that hurts you, hurts other people, breaks their stuff, lowers your credit rating, or ruins your ability to get laid.

I have spoken.

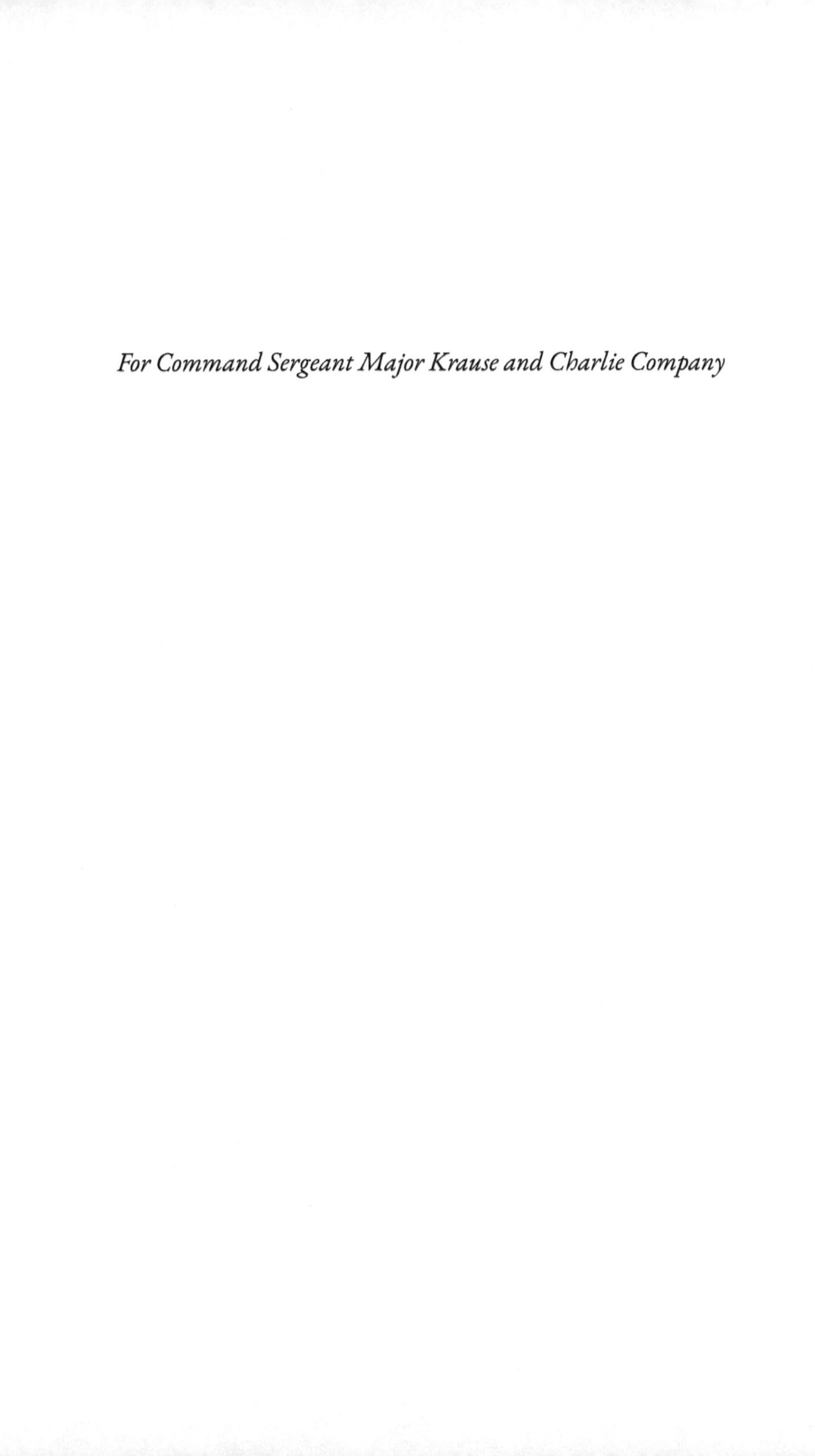

For Command Sergeant Major Krause and Charlie Company

It was not well to drive men into final corners; at those moments they could all develop teeth and claws.

—Stephen Crane

PART ONE

As yourselves your empires fall, and every kingdom hath a grave.

—William Habington

CHAPTER 1

OLYMPIA, WASHINGTON

"The New York Stock Exchange halted trading again. Third straight day," State Senator Rebecca Stevenson read from her smart phone over the nervous conversations and shuffling papers marking the adjournment of the State Legislature's special session.

"God, I hate being right," James Rand, her neighbor on the Republican minority side of the Senate, said as he angrily shoved his iPad into his black executive bag and rose from his padded leather chair. "I don't think we're gonna borrow, tax, and spend our way out of this one—that is, not for lack of trying," he quipped to his close friend and legislative ally.

Governor Alicia Embrey had recalled lawmakers to the capitol in the final days of a hot and muggy July for the emergency session when it became obvious that the nation's rapidly worsening economic crisis would blow a megaton-sized hole in the new two-year state budget that had taken effect at the beginning of the month. She and her fellow Democratic legislative leaders submitted a raft of emergency measures aimed at raising revenues, which of course meant raising taxes. Bills hiking the state sales tax, excise taxes, and the gross receipts tax on Washington businesses—as well as a slew of legislation creating new taxes and fees—sailed through the tightly controlled House and Senate over the futile objections of James, Rebecca, and other fiscal conservatives. The constant stream of grim financial news, not to mention consecutive days of halted trading as the plummeting Standard & Poor's 500 tripped the circuit breakers within hours of the opening bell, didn't help their arguments.

James shook his head at the absurdity of the legislation now headed to Governor Embrey's desk. The underlying problem wasn't shrinking revenues, but rather that *the dollar itself* would soon lose its value as a currency if things didn't turn around, and fast. *These fools who can't see past opinion polls and the next election will learn the hard way soon enough,* he thought.

The relative quiet of the carpeted Senate chamber gave way to the roar of voices echoing off the Alaskan marble of the Rotunda and the Capitol Building's massive masonry dome. James lowered Rebecca's smart phone from her face to stop her from texting as they reached the edge of the polished marble stairs. "Watch your step—you're no good to me if you fall and break your neck."

"No touching, James," Rebecca teased, shoving her phone in her purse. "That's how rumors get started."

James knew that all too well; he and Rebecca were unusual legislative bedfellows. Rebecca, a human resources executive and graduate of the United States Naval Academy who won election four years prior to the district covering her hometown of Kennewick, was the textbook example of a pragmatist. James, on the other hand, was a conservative firebrand and leader of the Cascadia statehood movement, which argued that the disconnect between the rural eastern half of Washington and the urban coastal west was so great that the only solution was to partition the twenty counties east of the Cascades into a new state. It didn't take long for the gossip mill to churn when Rebecca became fast friends with James, a successful lawyer and veteran four-term lawmaker. He was married with three children, she was a single mother, and both were athletic and stunningly good-looking, but the rumors were just that.

"Texting Carleigh?" James asked as they started down the stairs. "What's she want to major in this week?"

"Journalism," Rebecca groaned—her eighteen-year-old daughter was set to start her freshman year at the University of Washington in the fall.

"My condolences," James said with a smirk—they, like many conservative lawmakers, learned early on in their legislative careers that reporters held them and their beliefs in about as high a regard as athlete's foot.

James waved to his legislative assistant, Jenn Maxwell, who awaited them at the bottom of the stairs. She nervously pushed away a lock of blonde hair that stubbornly refused to stay pinned back. "Stock market tanked again," she said over the echoing din, holding up her smart phone as if to back up her statement.

"Old news," James said, adjusting black-framed glasses that matched hair just starting to go gray.

"So you also heard the president's gonna close all the banks for a week?"

Rebecca's eyes went wide. *"What?!"*

"Fox Business just reported it. And Bloomberg's reporting that Japan's probably gonna dump its US debt. Like the stock market needs any more reasons to nosedive, on top of worries about a repeat of COVID-19 with that nasty flu bug China's supposedly dealing with."

"I need a drink. It's been one of those days," James muttered and motioned the ladies to follow him; *this is bad*, he said to himself as they passed the velvet ropes protecting the brass state seal embedded in the center of the Rotunda floor. He noticed Rebecca's face etched with similar concern—they both knew how ugly things would get if the worst-case scenario they had endlessly discussed came to pass.

Rebecca's expression quickly tightened into a scowl at the sight of the two men at the bottom of the stairs leading to the statuary hall at the Capitol Building's north entrance. "Ugh—no way I'm dealing with those two assholes today," she told James. "I'll save you a stool at the bar. We may as well run up one last tab while our fiat currency is still worth something."

James understood Rebecca's aversion to Senate Majority Whip Michael Kelso and Dan McTaggart, statehouse reporter for the *Olympia Statesman*. The former, who represented an affluent sliver of Seattle, was a hyper-partisan who wouldn't say a nice thing about a Republican if one saved his family from a burning building. The latter reserved his poison pen solely for attacking anything conservative, especially James and Cascadia. While James proudly bore the muck Dan routinely raked his way, it infuriated him that he also flung it at Rebecca for merely associating with him.

Rebecca strode past the duo and out the main doors, Dan sneaking a not-so-subtle glance at her backside as James walked over, with Jenn in tow. "Way out of your league, buddy," James chided, his voice dripping contempt.

Michael snorted. "How goes establishing your little Christian caliphate? Not too well, I'm hearing."

"Cascadia's going great, actually," James retorted. "Matter of fact, the steering committee is meeting next week to nominate you as the official state parasite."

"What's that supposed to mean?" Michael snapped as Dan started furiously scribbling in his notebook.

James felt Jenn's hand fall on his shoulder to silently advise restraint. *Not this time, Jenn—sorry*, James silently apologized to his aide as a wicked grin crossed his face. "Sorry I forgot to preface my remarks with a trigger warning for your feels, Mikey. It means you're a douchebag. But I don't mind—your contempt for my half of the state does more to advance Cascadia's cause than any speech I could ever write."

Dan whistled. "Wow, Jim, none of this bile for me?"

James's grin of satisfaction disappeared—while he disliked Michael, he truly loathed Dan, whose fawning coverage of the senator during his participation in the Capitol Hill Autonomous Zone protests in Seattle years prior had kickstarted the ambitious politician's rise. "No, Dan, because you're not important enough. In a couple of years, your newspaper will be out of business, even if Mikey here manages to pass that quid-pro-quo media bailout your publisher's been screaming for. When that day comes, the only way I'll be exposed to your worthless opinions is when you give me a lift to the airport—that was an Uber sticker I saw on your car to supplement your paycheck, wasn't it?"

Dan stared daggers at James. Jenn's fingernails dug into her boss's shoulders with a vise-like grip, but James couldn't help himself as anger over the special session, and the economic catastrophe about to destroy the nation he loved, engulfed him. "What, no witty remark? No snappy comeback? You've lost your edge. Happens to every hack who spends his time kissing the asses of fellow travelers. And no one, Dan, kisses ass like you."

"Hope you had fun being powerless today," Dan petulantly retorted, face flushing crimson.

"You see, buddy? Now you're getting the hang of it!" James said and slapped Dan's flabby left bicep. "And I hope you have fun surviving your newsroom's next round of cutbacks and layoffs—I wouldn't give up that

Uber gig, If I were you. Then again, I always thought that learning to code was your, uh, 'profession's' fallback."

James broke away and hustled down the Capitol Building's granite steps, breezing by the legislative leaders setting up for a news conference. "That wasn't very smart," Jenn admonished with an edge to her voice—she would be the one dealing with the fallout once Dan wrote his inevitable hit piece.

"No, it wasn't," James said, his stride slowing as the adrenaline and anger began to subside. "Sure felt good, though."

The ubiquitous leaden skies of northwest Washington threatened rain as James partook in a ritual he had ended every legislative session with since his freshman term. He walked past the capitol's flag circle, cutting through the ornate Temple of Justice where the Washington Supreme Court deliberated, to the outdoor law enforcement memorial overlooking Puget Sound. James set his hands on the black polished granite ledge, deeply breathed the moisture-laden air, and gazed at the panoramic view of Capitol Lake and the start of the picturesque waterway's hundred-mile northward track to the Pacific Ocean.

The buzzing of Jenn's smart phone and a muttered curse snapped James out of his brief, and all too rare, moment of zen. "Aidan's canceling on me tonight," she said of her on-again, off-again boyfriend who worked in the governor's office. "Governor Embrey's gonna be burning the midnight oil."

"Sorry about your plans, but that's not surprising, given the fiscal catastrophe bearing down on us like Juggernaut's carriage," James said as Jenn's phone buzzed with another text message.

"It's not that," Jenn continued, eyebrows furrowing with worry as she read. "Embrey got some sort of urgent call from the State Department of Health and the CDC office in Spokane. Said they needed to talk to her right away. She . . . she cleared her schedule. Aidan doesn't know any more than that."

James sighed. "Don't come in tomorrow. I'm cutting you loose."

"What?!" she exclaimed, jaw dropping. "Do you have any idea how much I have to do? How much we have to go over?"

"Yes, I do. And none of it's gonna matter. None of any of this is gonna matter," James said, waving his arms at the Temple of Justice and the Capitol Complex behind them. "Jenn, how many times have we talked—or rather, how many times have I rambled and forced you to listen against your will—about the US heading for a collapse?"

Jenn smiled wanly. "Too many times."

"I think this one's for real, kid. You can see with your own two eyes that things are going south very fast. This isn't gonna be like the Great Recession or COVID-19, where the feds can just pull trillions of fake dollars out of their asses to get us out of this fix—I got a gut feeling our debtors are finally gonna cut up Uncle Sam's credit cards." James stabbed his finger toward the Capitol Building. "When these jokers run out of other people's money," he said, then pivoted to point up the sound toward Seattle, "and when the middle class watches their life savings get vaporized by inflation, and the poor's EBT cards stop working, a hard rain's a-gonna fall on everyone." The senator put his hands on Jenn's shoulders and looked her squarely in the eyes. "The center isn't gonna hold. This is the final act, and we're far too hopelessly divided—red versus blue, rural against urban, people who want to live free versus loyal subjects who want to be ruled—to band together and stop it."

James paused and took a deep breath. "I want you to set the plan we talked about into motion—just in case. You understand?" Jenn nodded and bit her lip; she was to cram as many supplies as she could into her car, top off her gas tank, and wait for the word to leave her Olympia apartment and cross the state to James's summer home an hour north of Spokane. "Start today. Not tomorrow, not after the weekend. Today," James sternly said. "If it turns out I'm Chicken Little, and the sky doesn't end up falling, I'll reimburse you for whatever you spend, plus an extra 10 percent in punitive damages for the mental anguish I caused you." Jenn chuckled through the tears that started to run down her cheeks. "But if I'm right, what you do in the next twenty-four hours could determine whether you live or die. Now go."

Jenn grabbed a tissue from her purse and blew her nose. "I hope you're wrong," she said and headed toward the stairs back through the Temple of Justice.

"So do I," James said and waved goodbye until she was out of earshot. "But I'm not." He pulled his smart phone from his suit coat pocket, selected his wife and four other contacts, and fired off a terse text: ROME IS FALLING. He would tell Rebecca in person when he met her for drinks.

James turned back to the granite ledge as a drop of rain stung his cheek. He smirked at how apropos it was that a storm was coming before he cleared his mind to admire the view that centered him after every session. James knew in his bones it would be the last time he would ever enjoy it.

SPOKANE

"Aaaaand, that's it for me this morning, folks!" Alexandra Chase's contralto voice purred from radios throughout the Spokane area over the opening riffs of Van Halen's "You Really Got Me." "Have a great weekend, and I'll see you in two weeks to get you through the morning when I return from my staycation!" She pushed back her chair in the KHTF broadcast studio, peeled off her Bose headphones, and shook loose brunette locks colored with a single streak of pink in honor of her victory over breast cancer, and in memory of her mother, who wasn't so lucky.

Alexandra rose to stretch and grabbed her lukewarm half-empty mug of honey tea as newsreader Brian Bierhaus marched into the studio and flipped open his laptop to prepare for the hourly news break. "Brian, I just wished everyone a happy weekend, so don't you go ruining it for them."

"Don't shoot the messenger 'cause the world's going to shit," Brian grumbled, brushing doughnut crumbs and granulated sugar from the blue station t-shirt covering his ample belly. "Stock market's in free fall—I wouldn't look at your retirement portfolio anytime soon."

Alexandra strolled down the hall to the office of Paul García, the station manager and her husband of twenty years. News of the slumping economy, urban unrest, and lawmakers in DC and Olympia scrambling to do something, had them both genuinely worried. But they were survivors.

Paul and Alexandra had first met as DJs for arch-rival FM stations in Kansas City. They fell head over heels for one another almost instantly, and carried on a Romeo-and-Juliet romance behind their bosses' backs for almost a year until an alt-weekly newspaper published a picture of them kissing at a party. They were both unceremoniously fired the next day, and the day after that jumped into Paul's beater sports car and eloped to Las Vegas. They spent the next decade bouncing across the West from one radio job to another as conglomerates gobbled up station after station and either changed formats or slashed staff; on one occasion, they came to work to find the locks changed and a burly but apologetic security guard telling employees that they had fifteen minutes to clean out their desks. Then they came to Spokane and everything fell into place. *Alex in the Morning*—her ebullient personality delivering the hits of the '80s through the aughts—rocketed to the top of the ratings and stayed there. Even though KHTF's ownership had changed twice since, the corporate suits didn't touch the goose that laid their ratings golden eggs.

Alexandra found Paul glued to his computer as Brian led the news brief with the Federal Reserve scheduling an emergency meeting and the Dow plunging fifteen hundred points within minutes of the opening bell.

"Penny for your thoughts, hon?" she asked, sauntering next to his chair.

"Sure, if money'll even be worth anything the way things are going," Paul groused as Brian transitioned to a story about the president and Governor Embrey appealing for calm. "My great-grandparents escaped Cuba on a wooden raft—now it looks like Cuba's comin' to us."

"You really think it'll get that bad?"

Paul wordlessly handed his wife two wrinkled printouts. The first was an email from corporate that ominously warned of the likelihood of companywide layoffs should the financial situation continue to deteriorate. The other was a memo from the Federal Communications Commission imploring all radio, television, and cable operators to ensure that their Emergency Alert System equipment was in good working order, and advising that an impromptu nationwide test would take place later in the day.

Alexandra raggedly sighed and eased herself into Paul's lap, a wave of melancholy washing over the chill that had crept down her spine. "I don't wanna lose my show again because the goddamn suits can't stomach the idea of getting a measly ten-million-dollar bonus instead of twenty."

Paul clicked off the office stereo, cutting off a news clip about reports of a new influenza strain in China sickening tens of thousands of people. "Honey, if we lose our jobs, it looks like we're gonna have lotsa company."

She ran a hand through Paul's thinning black hair. "We're still gonna enjoy our vacation together, the rest of the world be damned."

"I wanna talk to you 'bout that," Paul said, slipping his hands around her waist. "You know how Uncle Guillermo and Aunt Maria have been bugging us about driving up to Sandpoint to visit? I think we should take 'em up on it, given, uh, everything going on right now."

Alexandra thought for a moment. She had been looking forward to working on the home and in the garden, but they could do a lot worse for a vacation than two weeks in the Idaho Panhandle, enjoying the beauty of the convergence of three mountain ranges and three national forests around Lake Pend Oreille—and if things did get ugly, the fact that Sandpoint was at least an hour and a half northwest of the more than half a million souls in Spokane County was an added bonus.

"Go ahead and call them."

Paul kissed his wife and smiled. "I already did. Let's go home and pack."

CHEWELAH

Jed Schmidt's eleven-year-old twins, Mikey and Beth, squealed in tandem and cannonballed into their in-ground pool in a futile attempt to soak their parents and uncle on the deck.

Jed's deep belly laugh rolled across the spacious backyard. "That was weak, kids!" he bellowed from his comfortable recliner under the burgundy canvas umbrella shielding the adults from eastern Washington's merciless summer sun. His loud baritone barely roused Archie, the family's geriatric black Labrador retriever, who slept at his master's feet—his days of leaping in the pool with the kids had long passed. Jed sipped his rum and Coke and grimaced at the watered-down taste from the melting ice cubes.

"Drink faster, Big Brother, and it won't taste so bad," Allan Schmidt joked as he leaned back on the wicker couch and polished off his lemonade. His thin, wiry frame kept him from holding his liquor; one beer would mean that his girlfriend, Julie Eddington, would be driving them home.

"Honey?" Jed called for his wife through the kitchen screen door. "Could you bring me the Captain Morgan? And Hercules over here needs another Shirley Temple!"

Jed was three years old when his parents adopted Allan, whom God had gifted with a razor-sharp intellect and an aptitude for math and electronics. He became hooked on amateur radio at an early age, and at fourteen had achieved the ham radio pinnacle of successfully calling each of the more than three hundred radio prefixes on Earth recognized by the American Radio Relay League. However, God had dealt Allan a lousy hand when it came to physique—he was thin as a reed and weak as a kitten. That weakness, combined with his book smarts, would have made him a prime target for bullies had it not been for Jed, a state champion wrestler; Jed had worn the detentions and suspensions he had racked up for dispensing bloody noses and black eyes to anyone who messed with his kid brother as badges of honor.

Mary Ellen Schmidt set down the rum bottle, which Jed grabbed with a muscular arm. "So, how was Montana?" she asked Allan as he held out a pale, spindly arm to accept a refill of his lemonade.

"Great. Julie and I had a good time visiting friends," he answered with a forced smile; he had managed for a few minutes to forget about current events until his sister-in-law brought up the trip. Allan and his girlfriend belonged to a survival group, and the main purpose of their annual trip to Helena was to ferry supplies and install a software upgrade for the ham radio that would be waiting for him at the leader's rural home in the event the shit hit the fan. He wondered how long it would be until they had to beat feet back to Big Sky Country.

Julie climbed out of the pool and headed for the diving board, adjusting a bikini that almost matched her naturally red hair before executing a can opener dive to the delight of the twins. She hit the water with an unimpressive splash, given that she was only slightly less lanky than Allan was.

"You two've been dating, what, three years now?" Mary Ellen asked, easing herself into the chair next to Jed. "So, what's your plan? Women don't wait around forever—I'd hate to see this great catch slip out of your net."

"Plan?" Jed laughed before Allan could respond. "Forget marriage—I'd give my left nut to see Allan actually come up with any kind of plan for his life!" While Jed loved his kid brother, it frustrated him to no end that Allan was content with drifting on the wind when he was capable of so much more. Jed was twenty-one when he took over the family's auto body shop in Spokane after their parents died in a car crash. He married Mary Ellen a year later, the twins arrived the year after that, and by twenty-eight the family had bought their dream home on the outskirts of Chewelah, which sat an hour north of the city. Allan dropped out of Gonzaga University after his sophomore year, and worked for Amazon when he wasn't fiddling with radios or attending video game and comic book conventions with Julie, who lived with him in a small two-bedroom rental home in Spokane. Their financial security came from Julie's job as a software coder.

"We're good—we have no complaints," Allan answered, running a hand through sandy blonde hair matted from his earlier dip with his niece and nephew.

Jed frowned and lit a cigar. "The rest of your life'll be here faster than you think, Little Brother," he scolded. "Seems like yesterday I was changing Mikey's and Beth's diapers, and I'll be sendin' 'em off to college before I know it. I know I sound like a broken record, but you got potential, and we hate to see it wasted. That, and the twins really love Julie—it'll break their hearts the day she wisens up and dumps you on your ass." He laughed as Mary Ellen punched his beefy arm, and laughed louder as she clutched her wrist and pretended to grimace in agony as if she had punched a brick wall.

Allan sipped his lemonade. "I don't mean to change the subject—actually, yes I do—but how're all these new taxes the Legislature just slapped on us gonna affect the body shop?"

Jed took a long pull from his cigar and dabbed the ash in a glass tray that Mary Ellen slid to him in the nick of time. "Too early to tell. Those commie dipshits in Olympia already treat me like an ATM that can walk and talk—I don't wanna think about what else they've cooked up. I sure hope the feds figure out how to fix this mess—my own livelihood aside, I'd hate to have to let anyone go."

A jet of ice cold water from Mikey's squirt cannon splashed across Jed's shirtless chest. "Oh, that's *it*! You asked for it, pal!" He set his cigar in the ashtray and galloped toward the pool, landing in a cannonball that soaked Mary Ellen, Allan, and Archie, who woke with a start and rose on wobbly legs to shake himself dry.

Allan pulled off his wire-rimmed glasses with a grin and dried them with his t-shirt. He, too, hoped that things would turn out all right. But if they didn't, he and Julie indeed had a plan for their lives. He hoped that Jed and his family had one, too.

SEA-TAC AIRPORT

At least it's not raining, Li Guan thought as he rode the crowded elevator to the third floor of Seattle-Tacoma International Airport's massive main parking garage to catch a ride home. While his two-week trip to visit his grandparents in Chengdu was delightful—to say nothing of two weeks of authentic Sichuan cuisine—his return flight was anything but. Twenty hours in economy class was hell in and of itself, but the added twelve-hour delay in Taipei because of a passing typhoon was enough to grind a man's soul to powder.

And on top of that, I think I'm catching what the person three seats back had, Li said to himself after sneezing loudly into his left hand. He wanted to get back to his Seattle apartment so bad he could taste it, but he would have to wait until dark to go to sleep—hitting the hay at noon wouldn't help his jet lag. He sneezed again and jostled his way out of the elevator the moment the door slid open.

Li reached the ride-sharing area and whipped out his smart phone to hire one of the Uber drivers waiting for a fare through the airport's first-in, first-out system. Five minutes later, a blue Prius slid into a nearby diagonal parking space and popped open its trunk; Li tossed in his two bags and tiredly plopped into the rear passenger-side seat.

"*Ni hao*," Dan McTaggart greeted his fare.

"Hello to you, too, but English is fine—I was born and raised in Kirkland," Li replied in a standard American accent, stifling a yawn before sneezing twice into his hand.

"*Gesundheit*—hope you don't mind German, because 'hello' is the extent of my Chinese," Dan joked, offering Li a tissue before checking his phone to learn where his passenger needed to go as he backed out to navigate the winding maze of turns out of the airport to I-5 North. He had been waiting more than forty minutes for a customer, and was eager to get out and grab some weekend fares; his need for extra income brought back the angry memory of James Rand's cheap shot at the end of the emergency legislative session. Dan couldn't wait to get to work Monday and write a column sticking it to the right-wing Nazi and the toothless country bumpkins of eastern Washington who kept re-electing him.

Dan lost count of the number of times his passenger sneezed at thirty in the forty-five minutes it took to drive to his apartment; he shuddered at the memories of the COVID-19 pandemic and chastised himself for leaving his mask on his kitchen counter before making a mental note to pop an extra vitamin C pill when he got back to his Lakewood home.

In the weeks that followed, journalists nationwide did their best to cover the collapse of the United States of America from the one-two punch of economic meltdown and the global outbreak of a vicious new strain of H7N9 avian flu that cut a deadly swath around the world. However, the single greatest tragedy to ever strike humanity would go unreported by the *Olympia Statesman*.

Li Guan, by way of the hapless Dan McTaggart, killed the entire newsroom.

CHAPTER 2

JOINT BASE LEWIS-McCHORD

Army Sergeant Tom Ngo craned his helmeted head skyward at the twin AH-64E Apache Guardian helicopter gunships tearing overhead toward the innumerable pillars of smoke rising like black tentacles across the northern horizon.

Toward what was left of Seattle.

I'm not even supposed to be here, Tom groused over the chopping thunder of helicopter blades echoing through the South Tacoma Way overpass under which his unit blocked off I-5. *Then again, I'd probably be dead had I ETSed as scheduled.* He grabbed the plastic straw attached to his non-firing shoulder and sipped from the CamelBak bladder on his back, its water nauseatingly warmed by the hot August afternoon sun beating down on him and his comrades in arms.

Charger Company, Second Battalion, Third Infantry Regiment—"The Patriots"—had returned from three weeks of maneuvers at Yakima Training Center just before the shit started hitting the fan. Tom had paid scant attention to news of the economic downturn—he was busy counting down the days until his discharge after four long years in the Army, and was set to attend the University of Alabama in the fall. When the downturn spiraled into a full-blown economic crash, Tom and the other short-timers in the company were told by their sympathetic but firm commander that their discharges were postponed "for the duration of the emergency." Their brigade of Stryker armored combat vehicles fought an uphill battle to keep the peace in the Seattle metro area until the H7N9 flu made their efforts as futile as stopping the tide. Tom's memory of the weeks since had consisted of stop-motion snippets of dead bodies, burning buildings, and hysterical refugees—all seen through the smudged plastic lens of his rubber protective mask.

The Army had pulled back from the city to form a defensive cordon around Joint Base Lewis-McChord and the Washington Army National-al Guard headquarters at Camp Murray, blocking off I-5 and several other nearby state routes—and by the authority granted them under the emergency orders approved by the president and the governor, blowing up several bridges and ramps. While most survivors who still had the means to escape were fleeing east on I-90 toward the Cascades, or south toward rural southwest Washington, the roadblock Tom and his platoon guarded just south of the State Route 512 cloverleaf still got plenty of refugees who needed to be turned away under threat of deadly force.

"We got company!" Sergeant First Class Marcos Vasquez, Tom's platoon sergeant, bellowed from down the line; the platoon's cherry second lieutenant had gone AWOL after the withdrawal from Seattle. "Those Apaches just overflew a large mob headin' down I-5 straight for us! Mask up! Grenadiers, load gas!"

Tom slammed his Enhanced Combat Helmet on the concrete barrier in front of him and ripped his jet black M50 protective mask out of the burlap pouch on his left thigh. He slapped it on his face, yanked the straps over the back of his head, and looked to his flanks as he cleared and sealed the mask to ensure that the three soldiers in his fire team were following suit.

"How you holdin' up, soldier?" Tom asked Specialist Allie Monahan, a personnel clerk thrown into his fire team to replace a wounded private.

She turned her head, unrecognizable behind her "Darth Vader" mask, so nicknamed for the M50's vague resemblance to the Sith lord's faceplate. "Doing all right, sergeant, except for wishing I'd joined the Navy instead!"

Tom looked past her to Private First Class Ron McNeilly, who had taken his time to mask. "This is fucked up," McNeilly yelled, angrily sliding a 40-millimeter CS gas shell into the grenade launcher mounted underneath the barrel of his M5 rifle. "Why can't the Apaches just light these bastards up?"

"That's enough, private!" Tom admonished, his mask muffling the edge in his voice. "You wanna call an airstrike on fellow Americans, you got no business wearing that uniform. Let's hope the gas scares 'em off like that group the other day. Stay icy, soldier!"

Boots pounded on the interstate's concrete deck as Vasquez brought up his remaining two squads so that the entire platoon, save for his two machine-gun teams on the overpass itself, was on line behind the concrete barriers hastily delivered the week before by what was left of the Washington State Department of Transportation. A summer breeze caressed the back of Tom's neck, his mask sparing him from the septic stink of the portable toilets that had reached capacity with no service willing or able to come pump them out.

"Here they come!" Specialist Edwin Warren, the team's automatic rifleman, yelled from behind the scope of his belt-fed M250 light machine gun.

Tom assumed a firing position against the barrier—the magazine pouches strapped along the length of his Modular Lightweight Load-Carrying Equipment tactical vest awkwardly pressing into him—and cocked his head to prevent a rivulet of sweat under his sweltering rubber mask from running into his firing eye. He peered through his rifle scope just as the first bodies, shimmering from the oppressive heat rising from the road, weaved around and climbed over the barriers set up to stop incoming vehicles. In seconds, the trickle became a deluge of dirty, ragged, and desperate civilians heading straight for them.

The order to disperse, blared with a squeal from a loudspeaker mounted to one of the imposing eight-wheeled Strykers lined up behind the platoon, was met with catcalls, jeers, and hurled rocks and bricks that fell far short of the soldiers. "Fuck that!" hollered a masked man clad in a black hoodie and jeans and brandishing an AK-47. "These warmongering pigs are sittin' on a mountain of food, water, and medicine! Why won't they share? They can't stop us all!" The mob roared in support.

"Come and get some, you little Evergreen College punk!" McNeilly screamed through his mask, referring to the infamously radical college northwest of Olympia.

"*Shut up*, private!" Tom snapped.

The mob surged toward the overlapping strands of concertina wire strung across the highway. "Grenadiers, on my mark!" Vazquez hollered and raised his arm. Several masked rioters armed with large bolt cutters pushed their way through the crowd to go to work on the wire. "*Fire!*"

The hollow *thunks* of grenade launchers were followed by the skittering of shells down the road and the hiss of CS gas. Coughing, gagging, and retching rioters quickly faded to gray silhouettes floundering in the billowing, dirty white clouds. Several wild shots from a lone high-powered rifle rang out from the crowd, one of which pinged off a Stryker's armor. It had the effect of striking a match to gasoline; McNeilly let loose a three-round burst, prompting the entire platoon to rain copper-jacketed death into the crowd.

"Cease fire, goddammit! *Cease fire!*" Vasquez screamed, running down the line and smacking soldiers' helmets as they one by one repeated his order. The machine guns on the overpass were the last to fall silent.

A gust of wind blew back the thinning gas long enough to reveal a bloody sea of mutilated civilians sprawled across the pavement and lying tangled in the razor wire, their dying screams and moans strangled by the CS shells still releasing their noxious payloads. Tom stared blankly at the slaughter, his mind almost incapable of processing what they had just done.

"Oh my God oh my God oh my God . . ." Allie chanted in horror, her rifle trembling in her shaking hands as Vasquez grabbed the radio handset from the platoon radiotelephone operator to call for instructions.

"Private, *no!*" Edwin shrieked. Tom spun to see McNeilly, his helmet and mask at his feet, shove his burning hot rifle barrel into his mouth and pull the trigger.

"Medic!" Tom hollered as the young private crumpled to the concrete, the top of his head a red, spurting mess. *This isn't real,* Tom's mind screamed as he and Edwin sprinted to the private's twitching body to go through the motions of trying to save a dead man. *I'm in hell. I've died and gone to hell.*

CHAPTER 3

CAMP MURRAY

"**M**adam Governor?"

Alicia Embrey fought to remain in the comforting nothingness of her dreamless and all too brief slumber. *Governor—yes, that's me, isn't it*, she told herself before slowly returning to reality like a deep-sea diver rising toward the sunlight dancing on the ocean surface.

She lifted her head from her folded arms and squinted at her chief of staff, David Hampton, her eyes adjusting to the sterile overhead lighting of the State Emergency Operations Center at Camp Murray, just across I-5 from Joint Base Lewis-McChord. The EOC had been her home for the past two weeks; at last report, the governor's mansion, along with the Capitol Complex and much of Olympia, was ransacked and burning.

"Wha . . . whatizzit?" she mumbled, wiping a rivulet of drool from her chin.

"You told me to come get you when it was time for the next briefing. They're ready."

Oh, that's right—the world is ending. Alicia reluctantly embraced consciousness and massaged the crick in her neck from her twenty-minute power nap as she followed David, and the two State Patrol troopers assigned to protect her, past harried and overworked faces. Barely two months prior, she had visited the EOC to participate in a disaster exercise based on a simulated 9.0-magnitude earthquake and tsunami—a horrific scenario, she realized with dread, that would have been far preferable to the nightmare Washington now faced.

Alicia's small entourage entered the cavernous operations room and made its way toward her briefers. The state's emergency nerve center, which had the floor space of a four-bedroom home, was packed with clusters of desks and flat-screen computers. Two of the three large projection screens at the front of the windowless room displayed scenes of carnage—one from a still-functioning highway camera on I-5 near Seattle, the other from CNN's nonstop coverage of civilization's disintegration. The third pinpointed the ongoing mass jailbreaks from state prisons at Walla Walla, Monroe, Shelton, and elsewhere. Alicia breathed a silent prayer of thanks that her husband and their two grown children were under military protection at a secure location.

State Emergency Management Director Antonio DiBernardi wiped his sweaty hands on his large paunch and nervously rubbed his balding head. "Madam Governor, I wish we had some tiny scrap of good news for you, but we don't. At this point, there's no way we're going to regain control of the Seattle metro area. We're standing on the one island of calm, courtesy of the Army and Air Force units surrounding us and JBLM with shoot-to-kill orders."

Alicia angrily slammed her hand on the cheap wood finish of a nearby conference table. "So that's our plan, gentlemen? Hunker down and wait for everyone to *die*?!"

"Madam Governor, there's nothing more we *can* do," Major General Jack Westman, commander of I Corps, flatly responded—the imposing, gray-haired deputy commander had inherited the mantle of leadership when the three-star general above him died of the flu. "We were fighting a losing battle just dealing with the rioting once the economy tanked and the president closed the banks—and that was with I Corps, the entire Washington Army National Guard, and the reservists vectored here from neighboring states. Then the damned flu hit. For every soldier and first responder we've lost to violence or the pandemic, we've lost another to desertion as people abandon their posts to protect their own families."

Alicia's skin crawled as she flashed back to her closed-door briefing from her visibly frightened state health department director and a CDC epidemiologist following the Legislature's emergency session. The H7N9 avian flu strain brewing in China was the deadliest anyone had ever seen, the ladies had said as Alicia stared at grainy, clandestinely shot photos of mass graves filled to the brim with thousands of men, women, and children. The flu's victims drowned in their own hemorrhagic fluid as their bodies pulled out all the stops to fight it off—a "cytokine storm," the older lady from the CDC had called it. The healthier a person was, the greater the odds that their own immune system would kill them fighting the virus; and just like the COVID-19 pandemic, the state health director had warned with haunted eyes, it was only a matter of time until an infected traveler flew into Sea-Tac. Her warning was prophetic; the virus took advantage of the nationwide disorder over the collapsing economy and ripped through Seattle and other West Coast cities with dizzying speed—by the time harried state governments had dusted off their emergency plans, the bodies already were piling up.

Westman pointed to the screen showing abandoned cars jamming I-5 as thick black smoke began obscuring the highway camera's view. "Ma'am, we're barely able to hold our perimeter—we're in no shape to engage in pacification operations, and our available supplies wouldn't put a dent in the humanitarian catastrophe out there." The young lieutenant Westman had secretly tasked out of desperation to get his only daughter, Kara, flown from London to JBLM tried to get the general's attention. *Not now*, he sternly mouthed.

Alicia looked to DiBernardi, who raised his hands to cut her off. "If you're gonna ask about FEMA, don't bother," he said, shaking his head. "We've lost contact with Region Ten headquarters up in Bothell. We managed to get a hold of the Bothell police about an hour ago. It's gone. They're . . . uh . . . the building is . . ." He turned away and wiped his bloodshot eyes with his thumb and forefinger—Alicia suddenly remembered that his wife worked at the FEMA complex.

Westman broke the uncomfortable silence. "It gets worse, ma'am. We're . . ." He paused and glanced around before continuing *sotto voce*. "We're having trouble reestablishing contact with USNORTH-COM in Colorado—or the Pentagon, or any command in the DC Military District, for that matter. Naval Base Kitsap across the sound from us can't raise anyone, either. Our equipment and our satellites are working fine—they're just not responding. The entire chain of command from the president on down could be incapacitated." Westman looked around again. "Last we heard, DC's on fire. The whole city." Alicia's mouth went agape.

"I'll be blunt, Madam Governor," DiBernardi said, his composure regained. "You asked if our plan was to hold in place and wait for people to die. That's exactly what we're proposing, because we're powerless to do anything else. The only course of action left is to sit tight, wait for the pandemic to burn itself out, and then do our best to help whoever's left with whatever local resources we can scrounge. Outside help won't be coming."

Alicia nervously stroked her chin as she grappled with the enormity of her situation. They needed their remaining military and law enforcement personnel, but had nothing to pay them with because money had become worthless. Millions of her constituents would survive, but would need to be housed, fed, and clothed. And while Seattle was experiencing an uncharacteristically hot and dry summer like the climate east of the Cascades, winter would descend on the weak, homeless, and malnourished survivors before they knew it.

"We don't have the resources."

Westman's steely glare bore into Alicia. "Then, Madam Governor, we have to take them."

CHAPTER 4

ARDEN

Rebecca reached down to grab the remote for the wall-mounted flat-screen television in the living room of James Rand's summer home.

"We interrupt our programming at the request of the White House," the creepy computer-generated voice repeated. *"This is the Emergency Alert System. All normal programming has been discontinued during this emergency..."*

"Don't bother changing the channel, Mom," Carleigh said dejectedly, hugging a pillow on the plush couch and staring at the spartan flashing text on the blackened screen. "It's on every one."

"I know, honey," Rebecca said, thumbing the off button to end the repeating announcement of the president's declaration of martial law and a nationwide dusk-to-dawn curfew; Governor Embrey had done the same more than a week earlier, when Rebecca and Carleigh pulled into James's rural retreat in a forest outside the tiny unincorporated town of Arden. Rebecca sat next to her only daughter, who with her wavy brunette hair and athletic build was a spitting image of her. "How're you doing?"

Carleigh yanked a Kleenex from a half-empty box and looked down at her outfit—a University of Washington tank top and dolphin shorts she had bought during her orientation visit. "Today was supposed to be the day you moved me into the dorms. I was so excited, Mom. And now . . ." Carleigh stopped to blow her nose as Rebecca rubbed her back. "Now, it's all gone. Everything's all gone."

Rebecca carefully pondered her next words—Carleigh never tolerated being mollycoddled. "Honey, we're gonna have to get used to things being very different from now on. But we're safe, and we have a plan. A lot of people didn't, and I'm sorry to say that they're going to pay with their lives. We have enough supplies to last us a very long time, and we're far away from where the trouble is." She jerked her thumb at the four lethal-looking men studying maps at the dining room table with James. "And you're surrounded by people who will die to protect you." A sizzle from the kitchen was followed seconds later by a mouth-watering aroma as James's wife, Diane, sautéed vegetables for the venison medallions that their eldest child, James Jr., was grilling for lunch. "And look on the bright side," Rebecca said, forcing a smile. "Their cooking beats the heck outta mine."

A laugh escaped Carleigh through her latest round of tears. "You think Dad's OK?"

"I'm sure he's safe, honey," Rebecca answered with more conviction than she felt. He had moved back to his native San Diego after the divorce a decade ago, and southern California by all accounts—when there were accounts to be had—had become a giant fiery graveyard. He hadn't responded to any of their calls or texts, even before the cell phone towers overloaded. What's more, Rebecca and Carleigh had been forced to surrender their smart phones at the insistence of their imposing houseguests, who Rebecca learned were former members of First Special Forces Group out of JBLM.

James stepped into the living room. "Lunch'll be ready in a couple of minutes, so I hope you two are hungry."

Carleigh stood. "If you want, Mr. Rand, I can go get Candace and Emily."

"That'd be great. And it's 'James,' please—my dad was Mr. Rand," he said with a smile. Carleigh headed downstairs to shepherd his young daughters, who were playing games in the entertainment room—James kept them far away from any talk of the collapse.

Rebecca watched out of the corner of her eye until Carleigh disappeared. "Any word from Jenn?" she quietly asked.

James bowed his head and offered a quick prayer for his legislative aide. "Haven't heard from her since I texted everyone to drop everything and get out here. We've been monitoring the frequency of the handheld radio I packed in her bug-out bag—nothing."

Rebecca's lower lip momentarily quivered before the Navy officer in her commanded it to stop for her daughter's sake. "We're in real trouble, aren't we?"

James nodded. "We always knew the economy would collapse when Uncle Sugar finally spent us into the poorhouse. I planned for that. But I didn't anticipate we'd simultaneously end up in a real-life adaptation of *The Stand*. We're looking at a full-blown collapse of civilization with this H7N9 flu thrown into the mix. We're OK for now—we're in a secure and well-stocked hidey-hole with four Green Berets watching our backs—but only time will tell if we make it or not. This, believe it or not, is the easy part."

Rebecca cocked her head. "What do you mean?"

"Tyrants will rise to fill the power vacuum. They always do. Maybe it'll be some local warlord, but I'm betting it'll be what's left of our fellow lawmakers back in Olympia sending in their goons to plunder eastern Washington to feed all the surviving big-city folks who don't know what end of the shovel goes into the ground. They got a taste of wielding absolute power during the COVID-19 pandemic, and believe me, they absolutely loved it." He pointed at the proposed Cascadia flag pinned to the far wall—a large evergreen tree and a mountain on a dark blue background. "And like our Founding Fathers before us, as sure as God made green apples, we're gonna have to choose whether to sit back and take it, or send the tyrants packing. Trust me."

"I hope you're wrong," Rebecca said as Carleigh, Candace, and Emily bounded up the wooden stairs.

"If I had a dollar for every time Jenn said those very words to me, I'd have a lot of kindling for the fireplace, seeing as how the dollar's worthless now," James said as they fell in behind the girls toward the dining room table where James Jr. had just set down a tray of grilled venison. "I'd tell her that I hoped I was wrong, too."

Rebecca sighed. "But you're not."

CHEWELAH

Jed threw out his large, calloused hands just in time to stop him from face-planting in the dirt.

With maximum effort, he pulled himself to his knees and leaned back against the large oak tree in his backyard—and almost immediately hunched forward to cough up another glob of blood, almost falling face down again before righting himself. The setting sun shone on his face, which was filthy save for the two tracks kept clean by tears as he struggled against the virus ravaging his body to bury his wife and children.

He wanted to die more than anything. A Bible verse bubbled up through his delirium as his ears started ringing a high C—the fever he thought he had finally licked had returned with a vengeance.

In those days, men will seek death and will not find it. They will long to die, but death will flee from them.

Jed squinted against the sunset at the unmarked graves that took him three days to dig. The tears flowed again as his fevered mind flashed back to gingerly lowering Mary Ellen, Mikey, and Beth into the earth—his son with the baseball glove with which they had played innumerable games of catch, and his daughter with her unicorn Squishmallow that she still innocently slept with at the foot of her bed. His sobs quickly gave way to a raspy, wet cough.

"I'm so sorry," Jed croaked, wiping away frothy blood with the back of his wrist. "I killed you all."

As the economic slide became an avalanche, Jed made the hard decision to close the body shop for the duration of what he naïvely thought would be a temporary disruption. Against Mary Ellen's advice, he drove back to Spokane, where four of his six loyal employees helped him pack his truck to the gunnels with whatever tools and equipment they could fit. *That's when I caught this. I took a stupid fucking trip I didn't need to take and delivered you all a death sentence*, Jed berated himself.

Jed coughed again, his thoughts drifting to his sole remaining family—he had received a single terse text from Allan that he and Julie were high-tailing it to their friends in Montana. *Please, Lord, let them have made it*, he prayed. *Someone has to live. Don't take us all.*

The evening breeze nudged the worn tire dangling from the tree with a creak of hemp rope. Jed closed his eyes and for a second could hear the twins' laughter from being pushed on the swing, but the memory of happier times was shoved away by the future memories of which he would be forever robbed. Tossing Mikey the keys to the truck and asking him to return it with a full tank of gas. Cleaning his shotgun on the living room table to scare the hell out of the first boy who came to pick Beth up for a date. Growing old with Mary Ellen and rocking on the front porch to admire sunsets like this one.

Jed numbly stared at the plume of smoke that had been rising from downtown Chewelah, and wondered what was burning before he began shivering uncontrollably. He stared down at the .45-caliber handgun he had more than once put into his mouth, and tried one more time to work up the courage to die next to his family, but couldn't go through with pulling the trigger. The handgun fell to his side, the raw emotion of attempting suicide sapping what little strength he had left.

"Lord, I'm not gonna kill myself—I don't have the guts," Jed chattered, barely conscious. *But I'm not gonna try to save myself, either*, his talk with the Almighty continued in his thoughts. *I'm not crawling back to a dark house and an empty bed. I'm staying right here. It's Your will if I wake up tomorrow, but please take me—I don't deserve to live.*

Jed wrapped his large arms around his freezing body and closed his eyes, which he hoped would be for the last time.

CHAPTER 5

YAKIMA

Army Captain Demetrius Mathers raised his head from his stained pillow with the *click-clack* of the key unlocking his cell door at the Yakima County Correctional Center.

"Wait here—I'll be fine," Major Robert McAndrews ordered his accompanying MP before stepping through the peeling pea-soup-green metal doorway into the temporary quarters of his former company commander. The handsome black captain slowly sat up and stretched, not bothering to reach for his camouflage blouse draped over the wall shelf that passed for a desk.

"You stand when being addressed by a superior officer," the gray-haired battalion commander growled.

A defiant grin spread across Demetrius's face. "With all due respect, what're you gonna do—lock me up more? Besides, you may outrank me, but those illegal orders you've been passing along hardly make you superior . . . sir."

McAndrews angrily threw a small mesh bag of toiletries that Demetrius intercepted one-handed before it smacked him in the face. "You may not want to act like a soldier, but you're sure as hell gonna look and smell like one. So, *captain*, what made you think I wouldn't find out that you were secretly countermanding my orders?"

Demetrius tossed the bag on the mattress and ran a hand over his high-and-tight haircut. "I dunno, sir—because I'm smarter than you, I guess."

The men of Battle Company, Fifth Battalion, Twentieth Infantry Regiment, had breathed a collective sigh of relief when they were re-deployed from the burning, bloody rubble of Seattle to the Yakima Valley to restore order to the major agricultural region that was key to feeding Washington's remaining population. However, Demetrius's relief quickly turned to disgust with the orders of the governor turned *de facto* commander-in-chief that McAndrews obediently passed down without question. Forced relocation and compulsory labor for agriculture. Forced quartering of Seattle-area refugees. Door-do-door gun confiscation. His protests to McAndrews went nowhere.

Demetrius had swelled with pride when his soldiers unanimously agreed to disobey the unconstitutional edicts. Battle Company quickly became very crafty at conducting sham patrols and submitting fudged reports to deceive battalion headquarters. One night, as the company refueled its Strykers at the fuel point at the spacious Yakima Training Area north of the city, a hand-picked squad led by the company's trusted executive officer, First Lieutenant Deion Carver, stole six duffel bags' worth of illegally confiscated civilian firearms, then turned them in over the following days as proof of their nonexistent sweeps.

It was Demetrius himself who had inadvertently given them away. He had been visiting one of First Platoon's squads on checkpoint duty when an Alpha Company convoy of Light Medium Tactical Vehicles—the boxy armored trucks that had replaced the venerable Army deuce-and-a-half—pulled to a halt. Two dozen disheveled and flex-cuffed civilians rode in the back of the lead LMTV; most of the women and children were crying, save for a few who sat glassy-eyed with shock. The young second lieutenant leading the detail told Demetrius that the citizens had been arrested for violating curfew or possessing banned firearms. When the lieutenant refused Demetrius's order to release the prisoners, the six-foot-three captain flattened him with a haymaker—the convoy's soldiers promptly freed the civilians and unceremoniously loaded their unconscious butterbar into the back instead. Demetrius found the MPs waiting for him when he returned to the abandoned tire store that was serving as Battle Company's command point.

"Do you understand the gravity of your crimes under the Uniform Code of Military Justice during time of war?" McAndrews demanded.

"What war would that be?" Demetrius shot back. "The war you're waging against civilians, or the war against the Constitution you swore to protect?"

McAndrews turned for the cell door. "Don't get too comfortable, captain—we're taking you back to Fort Lewis to face a court martial," he said over his shoulder.

"I don't have to do nothin' but eat, drink, stay black, and die," Demetrius sneered. The MP slid an MRE—Demetrius's chow for the day—across the small cell's vinyl tile floor before closing and locking the door with a jingling of keys.

Demetrius scooped up his meal and peered through the grimy window that stretched the length of his cell, his view greatly diminished by the vertical concrete slabs running up the side of the building. He admired the Cascades and snow-capped Mount Rainier—the view beat the hell out of his native Biloxi, Mississippi—before looking down on Yakima's westward sprawl. The city had taken a beating, but was in much better shape than other cities its size nationwide, and the lights were still on, thanks to Washington's abundance of hydroelectric power—and if the rumors were to be believed, thanks to Governor Embrey's emergency orders keeping plant workers and linemen on the job at gunpoint. While Demetrius hoped the rumors were untrue, he was very thankful to be incarcerated in a climate-controlled cell and not slowly roasting to death in a dark hotbox.

He glanced at his MRE and grimaced at the thought of eating his third straight day of creamy spinach fettuccine—his jailers had been ratfucking all the good rations. He absentmindedly ripped open the plastic pouch and sat at the foot of his cot, promising himself that, one way or another, he would not be taken alive to JBLM.

SANDPOINT, IDAHO

Uncle Guillermo swiveled in his chair the moment Alexandra hit the creaky spot in the wood floor at the entrance to his small ham radio room.

The silver-haired man held up his index finger without turning around and keyed his microphone to wrap up his latest successful mission. "You don't need to thank me, ma'am—I'm just tryin' to keep some Christian charity alive in this messed-up world. I'm glad your family's safe. Redoubter Charlie Delta Four Eight out." With a flourish, Guillermo crossed out a handwritten line on a legal pad filled top to bottom, and pages deep, with desperate survivors trying to reach loved ones. He looked to see his beloved nephew's wife holding a glass of apple juice and a plate of chicken, rice, and fresh garden greens.

"Oh, that's right—I need to eat, don't I?" he said, slipping his Bose headphones down around his neck.

Alexandra set his dinner on his wood-carved desk, which matched the shade of the beautiful wood-finish home. "Aunt Maria asked me to ask you if you still remember who she is and what she looks like," she quipped.

"It's Labor Day weekend—I woulda been doin' this all day anyway if the world hadn't ended," Guillermo said. "Maria knows what I'm doin' is important. Ham radio used to be my hobby, but now, I'm a candle in the dark—I just told that sweet old lady outside of Enid, Oklahoma that her son and his family in North Dakota are OK." He reached under his glasses and wiped his eyes. "One of these happy endings negates a hundred sad ones."

The walls of Guillermo's "ham shack" were wallpapered with maps and QSL contact cards from amateur stations around the world. The card from his successful long-ago contact with the International Space Station caught Alexandra's eye—she shuddered as she remembered Guillermo briefly pulling in a desperate attempt by its crew to reach the Johnson Space Center as its supples of food, water, and oxygen dwindled to critical levels.

The maps, particularly his National Geographic map of the Pacific Northwest, were plastered with fluorescent notes summarizing the intelligence Guillermo had gleaned. Boise was a shambles, and Coeur d'Alene was struggling with an influx of refugees from Spokane, but Idaho as a whole was faring much better than its neighbors, courtesy of the leadership of Governor Jed Curtis. The Seattle metro area and Spokane were devastated, and the rest of Washington wasn't faring much better. Montana was an absolute mess with no functioning state government whatsoever.

Alexandra read the yellow Post-it Note that Guillermo asked her to stick to the national map anywhere in the Gulf of Mexico. *"Secession?!"* she asked incredulously.

"Yup," he said, fiddling with the controls on his transceiver to monitor another band. "The governors of Alabama and South Carolina are talkin' about it after the federal government shit the bed with the economy and the flu response. The governor of Texas—a real ballsy lady who gave blanket amnesty to anyone killin' a criminal or looter—is actually convening the Legislature to discuss going back to bein' their own country. You be gentle stickin' that note—I got a feeling that map of fifty United States is gonna become a collector's item real soon." He turned back to the computer screen and keyed his mike. "This is Redoubter Charlie Delta Four Eight, lookin' for a caller."

Alexandra gestured to an espresso-stained wood carving of Guillermo's actual FCC-assigned callsign. "What's this 'Redoubter' callsign you're using? I've been meaning to ask."

"Top secret—I could tell you, but then I'd hafta kill you," Guillermo joked, shoveling a forkful of food into his mouth. "I'm part of somethin' called the Redoubt Radio Network—I stumbled on it by chance right after Maria and I got into doomsday prepping after retirin' from the Air Force. We're a national network of ham operators who relay news and information whenever the manure hits the oscillatin' air cooling unit—like now. The Pacific Northwest over the years has become something of a redoubt for conservative and God-fearin' people who saw what was comin', hence the name. Federal law forbids usin' code names on ham frequencies, but seein' as how the FCC is all but past tense, we can use our super-secret James Bond handles."

Paul's voice crackled from the Multi-Use Radio Service walkie-talkie on the desktop charger for his hourly radio check with the house down the street. The six homes in their isolated cul-de-sac had banded together to rotate armed twenty-four-hour security at their intersection with their lonely country road—his six-hour shift ended at midnight.

"We got enough beans, bullets, and Band-Aids to last us to the Second Coming—not like those poor souls on the space station," Guillermo said before scarfing another bite of food. "Maria and I picked our hideaway well. Sandpoint had its act together; there's only three roads in or out, and the cops an' townspeople roadblocked 'em the moment things started fallin' apart. Boise's still a mess, but things here in the Gem State could be a lot worse. You need to get on your knees tonight and thank God you an' Paul had the common sense to come here—Washington State's fallin' apart, and what's left of its government's goin' full Third Reich."

The setting sun peeked in through the corner window, painting the forested mountains where Guillermo and Maria had built their tiny slice of retirement paradise. "A fight's comin', Alex. I feel it in my bones," Guillermo tiredly said, leaning back in his chair. "I'm too old to pick up a rifle an' play soldier, but this radio of mine is just as deadly, and I plan to put it to work fightin' for what's right. Fightin' not just the bona fide bandits and predators roamin' the countryside, but also the despots wrappin' themselves in the sheep's clothing of government authority."

Alexandra smiled and took Guillermo's hands. "Uncle, aside from pulling guard duty every couple days with an AR-15 I just learned how to shoot, I'm going nuts passing the time. You gave me an idea as to how I can help, if you'll hear me out."

Guillermo smiled back. "And what, Miss Radio DJ, would that be?"

CHAPTER 6

CHEWELAH

The convoy of military vehicles and buses slowed to a halt in front of the hundred-strong welcoming committee blocking US Route 395 at the south end of town.

"Nice to see the locals rolled out the red carpet for us," Captain Harold Pratt said as he alit from the lead armored Humvee and made a slashing motion across his throat for the twelve-vehicle convoy's drivers to kill their engines; even though the military in Washington had plentiful fuel reserves, courtesy of the huge fuel depot at Naval Base Kitsap, they had to make every drop count.

A nine-man infantry squad scrambled from the rear of the trailing Stryker and sprinted toward Pratt, weapons at the ready. First Sergeant Kirk Orland grimaced at the unintended show of force and gave them the hand signal to slow to a walk before Pratt ushered them into a school circle around him.

"These people are scared—we've all been through a lot, and as you can see, the good citizens of Chewelah aren't cottoning very well to our being here," Pratt said, cocking his head back at the crowd and the bumper-to-bumper pickup trucks parked across both lanes behind them to form a primitive barricade. "Those Cascadia and Gadsden flags some of 'em are flying, and the rifles they're carrying, should tell you that this'll get ugly fast if we lose our cool. Stay ten steps behind me, and keep your hands off your weapons. Do not—*do not*—fire unless fired upon. Understand?" The squad nodded as one.

The townspeople nervously watched the huddled soldiers at the head of the halted convoy. "Whaddya think they're talkin' about?" a rifle-toting man with a gray beard and overalls asked no one in particular.

"Pro'bly rehearsin' their lines for how they're gonna blow rainbows and unicorns up our asses before they screw us over," a middle-aged man armed with an AR-15 answered.

A young lady with a 9-millimeter Glock on her hip looked up at the dark gray sky and felt for rain with an outstretched palm. "Beautiful day for a standoff."

"Hush that kind of talk. All of you," Anita Edmunds, the city's five-term mayor, sternly admonished without taking her eyes off the soldiers now walking toward them. The city council had convened an emergency meeting after the acting police chief received word from Camp Murray informing the town of two thousand people—Chewelah's population before the flu had been three thousand—that it would receive four hundred refugees from Spokane and Seattle. The council put the word out on the city's small public radio station for as many able-bodied people as possible to meet the soldiers and do their best to talk them out of it.

Jed took his hand off the pump of his twelve-gauge shotgun and nervously scratched his beard—there were almost no clean-shaven men among them two months into the collapse. The bent blue sign proudly proclaiming Chewelah home of the state champion Cougars girls' golf and track teams brought back the pain of losing Mikey and Beth, and he shook his head as if to physically drive it away.

Anita raised her hand in salutation to Pratt and Orland; her right arm cradled a Remington .30-06 bolt-action hunting rifle with which she had personally executed several out-of-town looters. She launched the opening salvo before Pratt could even tip his helmet to the wiry old lady. "Good morning, gentlemen. Thank you for your service to our country. And the answer is no."

"You must be Mayor Edmunds—your reputation precedes you," the captain said with a forced smile he hoped looked sincere. "Captain Harold Pratt, Alpha Company, Third Battalion, 161st Infantry. Well, you see, ma'am, I'm sorry to say you're not in any real position . . ."

A well-dressed bald man with glasses and a salt-and-pepper beard held up a lambskin Bible. "If it's all the same, ladies and gentlemen, we need the Lord's wisdom and guidance. May I offer a prayer?" The townspeople and the infantrymen nodded and bowed their heads.

"Amen," Pratt murmured as his first sergeant, the mayor, and a number of townspeople crossed themselves. "Let's get down to brass tacks, folks. I don't need to tell you we're facing a tribulation of historic proportions. Seattle and Spokane are in ruins, and our state is swarming with refugees—fellow Americans—with no place to stay. The federal government's non-op, and under the emergency orders approved by Governor Embrey, Chewelah has been designated to host a small number of displaced persons until the crisis has passed."

The mayor knitted her brow. "We know all about crisis, young man. The flu killed one person in three here—my son and granddaughter among them. We burned most of the diesel we had left to dig a mass grave at the soccer field behind the hospital, and I'm burning the midnight oil trying to figure out how we're gonna feed who's left through the winter! You're the first we've seen of the government since this started, and instead of bringin' aid," she yelled, stabbing her finger at the half dozen school buses in the middle of the convoy, "you're bringin' us even more mouths to feed!"

A young Native American woman in filthy scrubs stepped forward. "Sir, my name is Carol Price—I'm one of a handful of nurses left at Providence St. Joseph's Hospital. We're cleaned out. We got nothing. I just left the bedside of an eight-year-old boy who's septic and burning a 103-degree fever because he cut his knee playing, and we got no antibiotics—he's gonna be dead by tomorrow." Price wiped her eyes. "There's not so much as an aspirin to be found, thanks to hoarding and all the damn druggies that looted every pharmacy this side of the Cascades. Do you got any medicine with you? Or any food, water, or clothes? Anything at all?"

"No, we don't, and I'm sorry," Pratt answered to jeers. "But I understand that relief will be coming soon, once things get sorted out."

Carol scowled. "And I hope you understand, given the government's track record of its dealings with my people, that your word don't mean squat."

Shouts of "Amen!" and "Tell 'em, ladies!" rippled behind Anita and Carol. Several townspeople pumped their rifles in the air, prompting some of Pratt's soldiers to slowly place their firing hands on their rifle grips. Pratt realized he had to assert control before he lost it for good.

"Ladies and gentlemen, we've been civil, but orders are orders. I need you to move these trucks and let us through." The crowd's anger grew as Pratt gestured at several citizens carrying AR-15s and at least one AK-47 in defiance of Governor Embrey's emergency order banning possession of most civilian firearms; while Washington before the collapse had passed an assault weapons ban, state's attorneys and sheriffs in most rural counties had outright refused to enforce it. "As a token of our goodwill, on top of the supplies that'll be forthcoming, we'll overlook the illegal weapons many of you own in violation of the governor's emergency declaration."

"The only illegal things here are your orders!" James Rand's voice boomed from the center of the crowd, which burst into applause once people realized who he was through the goatee and the Seattle Mariners baseball cap covering his head.

A strong hand grabbed James's shoulder. "Jim, this is a really bad idea," Sean "Hawk" Mitchell, one of the former Green Berets who now guarded James and his family, yelled in his ear over the cheers. The four special ops soldiers had chosen predatory birds for their callsigns, with James jokingly designated "Rooster" for his inability to stand down and be quiet—a trait that could get him killed in situations like the one he was about to dive into head first.

"I got this, Hawk. Watch my back!" The crowd parted to let James through—even though he didn't represent Chewelah's district in the Washington Senate, he knew the area well through his many trips to generate support for the Cascadia movement.

"And who are you, sir?" Pratt asked.

"A patriot standing up to tyranny," James answered, his hands off the black AR-15 he carried on a chest harness. "Your unit's from Spokane, I assume?"

Pratt nodded. "What's left of it."

"You city folks have always had this misconception that country folks are armpit-deep in food. We're not. Like the good mayor here said, these people don't even have enough for themselves." James gestured to the crowd. "Half these folks might be gone by the spring thaw—and if you're even remotely observant, you'll see that quite a few of them are swimming in loose clothes that were snug two months ago." Murmurs rose from the townspeople, their enthusiasm over James's presence dimmed by the thought of a winter die-off. "And now you wanna dump hundreds more people here? You're not helping your refugees—you're condemning them to death by starvation!"

Pratt opened his mouth to respond but was cut off as James continued. "And then you have the unmitigated gall to tell us that our Second Amendment right to protect ourselves from the lawlessness erupting everywhere now exists solely at your *pleasure*?" The crowd roared in approval of James's audacity. "Let's cut the crap, captain. You and I both know that either your unit or another will be back soon enough to disarm us on Empress Embrey's orders so the government can push us around and rob us blind! I have no doubt that you'd also be confiscating stuff from these people today, or maybe even rounding them up, if it wasn't for our arms."

"That is *not* true!" Pratt hollered over the unruly crowd.

"Isn't it? Your masters want us disarmed so they can do whatever they want to us, whenever they want to do it! Captain, you tried to appeal to our better nature—now I'll appeal to yours. You and your soldiers took an oath to uphold and protect the Constitution! Don't obey these unlawful orders! Turn around, go home, and *let these people be*!"

Sean's laser focus on James, who was sandwiched between intransigent soldiers and an increasingly rowdy crowd, was interrupted by a buzz in the radio bud tucked in his left ear. "Hawk, we got a problem!" the agitated voice of their sniper overwatch reported; Sean pressed the bud deeper, his heart beginning to pound as he tightened his grip on his custom FN SCAR-H battle rifle.

Cade "Eagle" Laine, lying on a rooftop two thousand feet away, watched through the large Leupold scope of his mammoth M107 Barrett .50-caliber sniper rifle as Pratt's executive officer studied James against the display screen of his OtterBox-clad tablet. "Rooster's on some sorta government shit list! Get him outta there!" Cade reported, silently cursing the stiffening breeze as he mentally calculated his firing adjustments—one of the things he missed about his sniper days in Second Battalion, First Special Forces Group, was having a spotter to give range and wind speed.

The executive officer cautiously walked to Pratt and showed him the tablet as James pontificated. "They made him, Hawk!" Eagle hissed into the small microphone of his hands-free radio.

Pratt held out his hands in a show of harmlessness. "Sir? There's gotta be a way we can work this out," he said, beckoning James with a jerk of his head. "Let's step back to the Humvee and talk this over."

"Boss, get back *now*!" Sean screamed, body-checking the old man in overalls who had inadvertently stepped in his way. The man, who had carelessly laid his finger on the trigger of his .308 Winchester rifle with the safety off, fired a round into the elevated rock berm of the Burlington Northern Santa Fe tracks running parallel to the road. The match had been lit, and Sean tackled James as the spooked National Guard soldiers opened fire. Sean looked up just in time to see Captain Pratt's head disappear in a spray of gore, disintegrated by one of the monster two-and-a-half-inch-long rounds from Cade's rifle. The thunderclap of the shot boomed over the withering gunfire seconds later as Cade's second shot sliced Pratt's executive officer in half.

"*Cease fire! Cease fire!*" Orland screamed, wildly waving his arms. The dead executive officer's tablet had landed barely a foot away from Sean, who lunged to snatch it up.

"Get off . . . can't . . . can't breathe . . ." James gasped. Sean rolled off of James to discover to his horror that a round had caught him under the left armpit, just past the body armor he wore underneath his windbreaker.

"God-*dammit*!" Sean yelled. "Rooster down! I say again, Rooster *down*! Evac Plan Alpha! Out!" Sean screamed into his mike as he slung his groaning friend over his shoulder in a fireman's carry and dashed down Route 395 into town, hurdling over bloody bodies to blend in with the fleeing survivors.

Carol scrambled to the mayor on all fours to staunch the blood fountaining from the bullet wound in her neck. *"Are you happy now?!"* she screamed at Orland, blood gushing in spurts between her fingers as the first drops of cold rain patted the gore-covered highway.

Orland spun to his soldiers, who still had their weapons aimed at the high ready. "Get the fucking medics up here, now!"

"You've done *enough*!" Carol shrieked as the mayor's life slipped away on the wet macadam. The rain became a downpour that drowned out the moans of the wounded and washed their blood like red rivers into the roadside drainage ditches. "Get out of here! If you're stupid enough to force your way through and resettle your refugees, how many of them do you think'll still be alive come sunrise? *Get out of here, you bastards!*"

It took Orland two seconds to decide to fold his hand. The convoy's engines revved up as the squad piled back into their Stryker, save for the unlucky, dry-heaving privates ordered to carry the bodies of their headless captain and eviscerated executive officer. Several minutes of three-point turns against the railroad berm later, the convoy sped back to their operating base at Fairchild Air Force Base southwest of Spokane.

North of town, an olive drab pickup truck tore down Route 395 in the driving rain toward Arden, sacrificing the stealth of back roads and old logging trails for speed as its very important passenger clung to life.

CHAPTER 7

CHEWELAH

Jed scanned his surroundings for the hundredth time the moment he and Archie reached the woodline at the uphill edge of his property just after midnight. Archie weakly growled at a great horned owl hooting its disapproval of their presence from its perch atop a dead fir.

"Shh. It's OK, boy. Come," Jed whispered, pulling his steel utility cart over an exposed root and into the protective shroud of the forest, confident they had not been spotted by any remaining nosy neighbors. He stopped fifty feet into the woods, in front of the spade he had stabbed into the soft earth to mark the edge of the hole he had dug; just enough of the first-quarter moon's chalky white light filtered through the conifers to allow Jed to finish his work without a lantern.

Archie slowly circled three times on aching joints and curled up on a bed of pine needles. Jed sat on a fallen evergreen with a groan and grabbed a rag from his pocket to wipe the rivers of sweat running down his face; the flu and his much leaner diet since the collapse had sapped much of his vitality. He glanced at his father's old wind-up wristwatch, which he had scrounged out of his junk drawer once his smart phone became useless—his new friends would come to pick him up in four hours.

Jed unscrewed his Schmidt Auto Body & Repair water bottle and eagerly guzzled it as his mind flashed back twelve hours to the National Guard opening fire on him and the other townspeople at their hastily mustered roadblock. His mad dash for dear life had brought him to a woman's home, where he huddled with her and her brother in the small living room, gasping and retching as the adrenaline drained from them. Even though the community radio station had reported that the Army had retreated to Spokane, Jed and his new acquaintances realized they'd be back, and in a much nastier mood. They agreed to scrounge whatever supplies they could and hunker down at the woman's hunting cabin just outside Kaniksu National Forest.

He had gathered his remaining food, his half a dozen firearms, and the camping gear and warm clothes he would need to survive the mountain winter in the garage, next to the pile of unsorted tools from the body shop. Jed then grabbed his fuel transfer pump from the wall and siphoned the remaining gas from his truck and Mary Ellen's sport utility vehicle into two five-gallon jerrycans to ensure they'd have enough for the trip to their hideout. He worked swiftly, exploiting the daylight before night wrapped his empty house in spooky darkness; the power, unreliable as it had been since the collapse, snapped off in Chewelah an hour after the convoy left, and he had no doubt the government in Olympia had thrown the switch in retaliation. Jed had no idea why God had spared him from the flu and the massacre, but he knew it wasn't so that he could waste away behind a prison camp's barbed wire.

The owl hooted again, snapping Jed's attention back to the task at hand. Jed hoisted a heavy-duty plastic tub from the utility cart and set it into the hole with a grunt. He remembered little of wrapping his photo albums and family heirlooms in bubble wrap and packing them to be cached, as if his brain had set itself on autopilot to spare him painful memories of everything he had lost. With a grunt, Jed slid a large, flat rock on top of the filled hole to help him find his priceless cache if he ever returned; he eased himself back onto the fallen tree and stared vacantly at his handiwork for several minutes before realizing he was stalling—he had one last job to do before he left.

Jed swallowed the lump in his throat and woke Archie from his slumber with a scratch behind the ears. "Hey, boy," he said in a quivering voice. "Let's go home."

Archie slowly raised his head from his folded paws and lovingly gazed at his master, his moist and tired black eyes gleaming with moonlight. "Good dog," Jed croaked as he laid the exhausted retriever on the cart, yanked the spade out of the ground, and trudged downhill to his darkened home, and the other hole he had dug that long day for his final act of mercy for an old friend.

A lone gunshot echoed through the valley fifteen minutes later. The owl flew away with silent flaps to search for a new hunting ground.

CHAPTER 8

ARDEN

Something resembling a smile crossed James's pale, clammy face as Rebecca gently held his hand in the Rands' guest room turned operating room.

"How you feeling?" she sheepishly asked, red-eyed from exhaustion and the emotional toll since his Green Beret protectors barged into the house with her wounded friend eight hours earlier.

"Like a piñata," James whispered, grimacing as he shifted in the upright bed, his left abdomen covered with bandages and tape.

"Take it easy, boss—you're not outta the woods by a long shot," warned their Special Forces medic, Grant "Osprey" Reid, as he adjusted the IV drip. Concluding on the drive back to Arden that James would die without immediate aid, Grant ordered Sean to pull into the woods so he could drain the air that had collapsed James's left lung with a fourteen-gauge needle in the bed of the pickup truck. That had bought Grant enough time to remove the bullet and insert a chest tube to allow James's lung to inflate.

Sean, his tactical vest stained with James's blood, stepped to the corner to check in on his shoulder radio with their communication specialist,

Miguel "Caracara" Lopez, who was watching the lone dirt road leading to the Rands' summer home. Sean's pulse quickened with a glance at his watch—time was becoming more and more their enemy with each passing minute.

Grant examined the battered 6.8-millimeter round between his thumb and trigger finger with blood-streaked nitrile gloves. "I can't explain this short of divine intervention. Even as a ricochet, this shoulda had enough energy to slice right through you. You should be dead—although you're gonna wish you were for the foreseeable future."

Rebecca rounded the bed to kiss Grant on the cheek. "God may have intervened, but He had help," she whispered. "Thank you for saving my friend's life."

"All part of the service, ma'am," Grant said, slightly embarrassed. "Saving this guy from himself is a full-time job."

It was a job James's friends took very seriously. Sean had first met James at an outdoor gun range practicing drawing and firing his concealed .45-caliber Glock handgun. The senator was a regular, courtesy of the politicized Washington State Patrol having zero interest in investigating the steady stream of death threats levied against him and his family by angry leftists, and the two became fast friends. Sean took it upon himself to give James intense and realistic firearms training, and soon introduced him to Grant, Cade, and Miguel—three of his buddies from Washington's community of former Green Berets, courtesy of the presence of First Special Forces Group at JBLM.

Cade entered the room, carrying the aroma of rifle oil and bore solvents from cleaning his sniper rifle. "Diane and the kids are all right," he reported, trying to forget the cacophony of James's screams of agony and his family's wailing. "If it's all the same to you, Sean, I'm gonna grab an hour of rack before I relieve Miguel on watch." Sean dismissed Cade with a nod and a grunt. "Carleigh really kept her head tonight comforting the kids—they're all zonked out on Emily's bed. You got one helluva daughter, ma'am," Cade told Rebecca before making a beeline for the living room couch.

Rebecca turned back to James. "Want me to wake the kids up to see you?"

"Let 'em rest," Sean answered for him, shutting the creaky wooden door behind Cade. "We'll be giving 'em a rude awakening soon enough to bug outta here."

"We're leaving?!" Rebecca blurted in shock. "What about Jenn? What if she finally gets here and we're gone? It's not like we can leave her a forwarding address!" Rebecca's outburst was met with stone-faced silence from Sean and Grant—silence that told her they didn't expect to ever see James's aide again.

"It's not safe here anymore—we'll get to that in a minute," James groaned. "I have something very important to ask of you."

Rebecca pulled a folding wooden chair to James's side. "I have a feeling I'll wanna be sitting down for this."

"Not a bad idea," James said and hissed—Grant had given him just enough morphine to stay lucid, which made the pain only a touch less excruciating. "Rebecca, we need you to pick up the torch and lead the fight to create the State of Cascadia and boot these goons back to what's left of Seattle."

Rebecca shot up like she had sat on a tack, the wooden chair legs screeching across the hardwood floor. *"What?!"*

"I went to Chewelah to light the spark when we heard the Army was gonna forcibly resettle refugees and disarm the townspeople. Unfortunately, the spark lit me," James whispered, his eyes flicking down at his chest tube. "Doc here says I'm gonna live, but I won't be playing pickleball or leading revolutions anytime soon." He paused to catch his breath with a gasp. "They slaughtered those innocent people, Rebecca. And that's just the latest atrocity committed by Governor-for-Life Embrey. Cascadia needs you."

"Like hell!" Rebecca yelled before lowering her voice to keep from waking the children. "I've always thought this whole Cascadia thing was stupid—the only flattering writeup I ever got from that asshole Dan McTaggart was the day I said that to your face on the Senate floor! Now you're asking me to take over as Don Quixote and tilt at your windmills?! Absolutely not! Maybe you haven't noticed, but America's dead, and politics died with it. All I care about now is ensuring that Carleigh survives and has a mother, and if that makes me a self-centered bitch, guilty as charged."

"Funny you should mention 'guilty as charged'," James said and nodded to Sean, who handed Rebecca a tablet from the corner table. Her jaw dropped the moment she laid eyes on the glowing cracked screen, wrapped by a scuffed and blood-spattered olive-drab OtterBox.

"Where did you get this?" she gasped.

Sean encouraged her to keep reading with a nod. "A little souvenir from our field trip, ma'am. The rightful owner has no further need of it, thanks to terminal ballistics."

Rebecca read, aghast, her two-page entry on a PDF list of "known and potential subversives." Her profile included her official portrait as a state lawmaker, a photo of her debating on the Senate floor, and another from her campaign Facebook page of her and Carleigh handing out candy and stickers at a parade.

REBECCA STEVENSON IS WANTED FOR TREASON AND SEDITION FOR ACTIVELY SUPPORTING THE CASCADIA STATE MOVEMENT. SHE IS MOST LIKELY HIDING IN HER HOME DISTRICT AND/OR SOUTH-

EASTERN WASHINGTON (SPECIFICALLY THE TRI-CITIES AREA) OR IN THE COMPANY OF SUBJECT JAMES RAND (SEE EARLIER ENTRY). SHE IS A FORMER NAVY OFFICER AND GRADUATE OF THE US NAVAL ACADEMY; CONSIDER HER ARMED AND DANGEROUS. DEADLY FORCE IS AUTHORIZED IN APPREHENSION OR PREVENTING ESCAPE. DAUGHTER, CARLEIGH STEVENSON (THIRD PICTURE FROM LEFT), IS TO BE APPREHENDED IF FOUND—DEADLY FORCE IS AUTHORIZED TO PREVENT ESCAPE.

James coughed weakly and grimaced with pain. "Congratulations, Rebecca—you're an enemy of the state, guilty of the dual crimes of being conservative and having shitty taste in friends. And apparently, having you for a mother now constitutes a capital offense." Rebecca, jaw clenched in fury, scrolled through the rest of the document. The governor's fugitive roster, aside from a handful of bone fide criminals, was a who's who of Washington's conservative and libertarian movements that included other elected officials, bloggers, free-market advocates, and in one case, an outspoken homeschooling mother.

"Motherfuckers," she growled, shoving the tablet back to Sean with disgust.

"James is number two on Big Sister's shit list—you and Carleigh made it into the top ten, though," Sean said. "That's why we gotta pop smoke, most rikki-tik. They wanna snatch him up and finish him off, and we can't risk staying on a fool's hope that they won't find out about this place."

"They want you and Carleigh dead, whether you wanna get involved or not," James said. "They see their golden opportunity, like so many other two-bit commissars throughout history . . ." James again paused to catch his breath, ". . . to create their dream totalitarian socialist state, and they're gonna hunt down those of us who wanna live free."

Rebecca ran her fingers through her hair. "Don't get me wrong—if Alicia wants a piece of me, I'd love for her to try. But leading your revolution? One, wars require an army, which we don't have, and two, there's the teeny little issue that I have no clue how to lead one."

James glanced at Sean and Grant. "Well, for starters, you got four Green Berets at your disposal who specialize in turning pissed-off natives into trained killers. Secondly, don't sell yourself short." He nodded toward Rebecca's left hand. "Unless, of course, you got that Annapolis ring from the claw machine at Chuck E. Cheese. Wrap yourself in Cascadia's flag and stand up to tyranny, and your army will come out of the woodwork to follow you."

Rebecca's boots clacked on the hardwood floor as she stepped to the corner table to study the tablet again.

"Things happen for a reason, Rebecca," James whispered to her back. "I wanted to lead this fight, but God has other plans for me, which fortunately for the time being don't include meeting Him in person. And like it or not, I was a political lightning rod—people either loved me to death or hated my guts."

Grant swiftly leaned in to check James's carotid pulse with two fingers as his patient coughed twice more and winced again with pain. "Boss, if you don't take it easy, you're gonna finish the job those asshole weekend warriors started."

"People like you, Rebecca," James continued, the little strength he had left slipping away. "You're straightforward, you're honest, and you proudly served your country. You ran for office because you hate seeing the little guy getting stomped on—and that's exactly what the government's doing right now to everyone who's left."

Sean cautiously put his hand on Rebecca's shoulder. "We know we're asking a lot of you. If you want no part of this, we'll smuggle you and Carleigh over the border to Idaho. You two'll probably be safe there—their governor sounds like he's one of us, and no one will think you a coward. But the bad guys you'll be running from, the ones who want to hurt you and your daughter, will still be here doing all sorts of bad things to good people—the good people you once swore an oath to protect. Whatever choice you make for yourself could mean the difference between freedom and slavery for many others."

Rebecca stared for what seemed like an eternity at the PDF before handing it back to James with a resigned smile. "Of course, my change of heart would have nothing to do with the PSYOPS training you quiet professionals get at Fort Liberty, right?"

Sean swiped his index and middle finger in front of her face. "These aren't the droids you're looking for, ma'am."

"All right, James, I'll do it," Rebecca said with an exasperated sigh. "Dammit, you had me over a barrel the moment you forgot to duck. But listen up, mister, and you listen good," she admonished, jabbing her finger at James's battered chest. "The moment Doc Grant here clears you for duty, you and I are having a *long* talk about passing this cup back to your lips."

"Fair enough," James whispered and weakly shook Rebecca's hand. "I'll make sure Dan McTaggart spells your name right."

Rebecca turned to Sean. "I assume you guys have an alternate hideout picked for us?"

"Roger that, ma'am."

"My first order is that, come sunrise, we bug out—lock, stock, and barrel. My second order is that you stop calling me 'ma'am,' for the love of God. I'm gonna be gray by the time this is all over, provided I live through it—I don't need you making me feel old."

Sean nodded. "Got it. You need a callsign—that'll help. James got his because he loudly draws attention to himself like a rooster, hence the hole in his side. Got any ideas?"

Rebecca thought for a second. "Mama Bear," she said with conviction. "No one—and I mean no one—messes with my daughter."

CHAPTER 9

YAKIMA

Sergeant Tom Ngo balanced a styrofoam cup of hot coffee on top of the paper plate keeping Allie's late dinner warm as he made his way from the chow point at Yakima Air Terminal to his squad's parked Stryker. The vast tarmac, devoid of aircraft with the end of civilian and commercial air traffic, made it the perfect place to stage the eight-wheeled fighting vehicles that were the mainstay of JBLM's and the Washington Army National Guard's armor.

He found Allie sitting on the lowered ramp of the olive drab war machine and gazing at Ahtanum Ridge, which marked the city's far southern limits just past the airport. During the day, the barren and brown mountains contrasted with the green of the Yakima Valley, but they turned a beautiful deep purple each evening as the sun disappeared behind the Cascades.

"Here you go, soldier," Tom said, gingerly setting the coffee and the plate of lo mein noodles, green beans, and a mushy red apple beside her. "Doesn't taste like much of anything, but it's hot."

Allie removed her helmet, revealing dark black hair tied up in a bun; her bloodshot eyes revealed that she had had yet another good cry while

Tom snagged her some chow. "Thanks, sergeant," she said, her voice leaden with pain. "You can have what I don't eat—I'm not that hungry."

Another fine morale-building exercise by our fucking S-2 shop, Tom thought as Allie unbuckled her rifle harness and unzipped her MOLLE tactical vest. Earlier in the day, their squad had run across battalion intelligence and proceeded to bombard them with questions regarding their hometowns. Tom knew his rural corner of northeastern Alabama was faring all right, although it floored him to learn his home state was considering leaving the Union. However, the S-2 personnel, frustrated from constant interrogations from soldiers starving for any news of the outside world, bluntly confirmed the rumors Allie had heard—her native Indianapolis was charred rubble, and those who survived the collapse and the flu were almost certainly overwhelmed by the swarms of refugees streaming from Chicago, Detroit, and Cleveland.

"You gotta keep your strength up, specialist," Tom said and sat next to her. "You know how many desperate people out there would give anything for a hot meal? Even that slop?"

Allie half-heartedly spun a plastic fork in her noodles, politely smiling at Tom's attempt to cheer her up. "I didn't imagine you to be a gourmet, sergeant."

"My mom and dad owned . . . I mean, *own* a Vietnamese restaurant," Tom quickly corrected himself. "Spaghetti, ground beef, and mixed vegetables is *not* lo mein."

"I also would never have guessed that you hail from Alabama."

"Born and raised—y'all come back now, ya heah?" Tom said in an over-the-top Southern accent. "I was set to ETS right before the shit hit the fan—was registered for fall semester at Bama and everything—but Uncle Sam stop-lossed my ass. I should be at a house party right now, drunk as a monkey and hoarse as hell from the Crimson Tide game."

Allie stabbed at her green beans. "You'd be dead, sergeant. Bama's gone, just like Indy. Just like my parents and my younger sister."

Tom unbuckled his helmet and ran a hand over sweaty, jet-black hair that hadn't been visited by clippers in weeks. "You gotta have something to live for, soldier. I gotta believe that my family's OK, and you have to, too. For your own sake, and for all of ours."

"I hope you're right, sergeant—not like all those dead flu victims we buried in that mass grave over yonder," Allie said, nodding at the open field on the other side of the runway. She sighed and set down the plate, her appetite a casualty of the memories of the sights and smells from the gruesome task. "I don't know how much more of this I can take."

Tom was about to respond when he spotted two soldiers out of the corner of his eye heading straight for them from the direction of the air terminal. In the deepening darkness, Tom could make out captain's bars on one, and the lone bar of a first lieutenant on the other.

"Look alive, high-speed—incoming brass," Tom said, both of them hopping off the ramp and snapping to attention as the two black officers stopped in front of them.

"You two alone?" Deion Carver nervously asked.

"Yes, sir!" Tom barked—Edwin, his automatic rifleman, was on KP, and they were still awaiting a replacement for the late Ron McNeilly.

"Outstanding," Demetrius Mathers said. "I need a ride. You're hired."

Tom cleared his throat. "Sir, with all due respect, our company has a presence patrol coming up at 2200—we got our orders."

"You got new orders!" Demetrius growled, raising his M5 rifle with a snap and leveling it at Tom's chest. Tom's and Allie's jaws dropped; their rifles were leaned inside the Stryker and out of arm's reach, and with the captain getting the drop on them, they may as well have been leaning against what was left of the Taj Mahal.

The duo nervously started to raise their hands before Demetrius stopped them with a flick of his rifle. "Don't put your hands up, you dumbasses—this isn't a stick-up!" he hissed, glancing around. "May as well plug in a neon sign announcing you're being carjacked!" Demetrius had no intention of killing two innocent soldiers, but it was only a matter of time until his former jailers raised the alarm; he knew he had to improvise the sales pitch of his life, and fast, if he wanted to live to see sunrise. "I'm not a deserter, or a murderer, rapist, looter, or any combination thereof. The Army locked me up because my men and I refused to follow all these unlawful orders we've been getting." He pointed his rifle to the ground as a gesture of goodwill. "You two've seen and heard what's being done to civilians, right?"

Tom and Allie nodded.

"Do you like what's happening? Is this what you two signed up for?"

They shook their heads.

"Good. Neither did I, hence this fine mess I got myself into." Demetrius motioned with his rifle for Allie to move closer to Tom, and strode to the Stryker to grab both of their rifles by the slings and toss them, one-armed, over his shoulder. "Here's the deal—I'm not gonna hurt you, unless you do something stupid like try to jump me or get me caught. You're gonna drive me somewhere safe. After that, you're free to do whatever—rejoin your unit, or go AWOL from this godawful shitty mess and start new lives. Or you can stick with me, because I'm gonna grab every soldier I can get my hands on who remembered their oaths and start kicking the shit out of the ones who forgot."

Deion nervously looked around. "You got this, sir?"

Demetrius nodded, not taking his eyes off Tom and Allie. "I got a good feeling about these two. Scram. *Imshi.* And be ready when I call for you and Battle Company—may be next week, may be next year, but be ready."

"God be with you!" Deion whispered without saluting and jogged for the front gate.

Demetrius glared at Tom. "You're driving. No funny business. Let's go." He shepherded his hostages into the Stryker and kicked Allie's cold dinner onto the asphalt. Tom gave Allie a reassuring nod and crawled over the vehicle commander's seat into the cramped driver compartment. Allie sat down in the black padded folding seat across from the commander's station, which Demetrius promptly occupied.

Tom brought the Stryker to life. "Where you wanna go, sir?" he yelled back over the idling engine and the mechanical whine of the raising ramp.

Demetrius slipped the station's combat vehicle crewman helmet onto his head and plugged it into the vehicle's comms system. "East. The Tri-Cities—I got a friend stationed in Richland who can help me out." He cleared Tom's and Allie's rifles and flipped on the computer monitor displaying the periscope view. "I'll guide you onto the back roads so we can skirt I-82 and avoid any checkpoints. Once we get outta town, kill your headlights and switch to thermal, unless you wanna get picked off by any of those bandit groups roaming around!"

The Stryker lurched forward as Demetrius furiously yanked out the power cable and wires connecting its "blue force" battlefield intelligence GPS system, in the hope of denying pursuers the ability to track them—it wouldn't take the Army long to connect his escape with a missing Stryker.

"You hurt, sir?" Allie yelled over the engine, pointing at the rusty red stains covering both of his sleeves and his left breast.

Demetrius shook his head. "Blood's not mine, soldier."

Tom killed the interior lights, illuminating the fugitive officer and the frightened enlisted woman in the ghostly glow of the monitor screens.

CHAPTER 10

CHENEY

"**A**re you *shitting me*?!"

Derek Nealon fought the urge to lunge over his large metal serving pan of mashed potatoes and punch the four-eyed twerp who had just pushed him to the breaking point with the stupidest question in the history of stupid questions.

"No, asshole, your fucking food *isn't* certified organic!" Derek screamed at the scrawny twenty-something refugee, spiking his serving spoon to the asphalt of the Roos Field parking lot with a loud metallic *clang*. The lot, which on a normal sunny Saturday in early October would be packed with drunken tailgaters waiting for the Eastern Washington University Eagles football game, now served as the feeding center for Cheney's large refugee population, most of them from Spokane ten miles northeast.

"There's no need to get angry. I was just asking," the bespectacled young man haughtily responded in a reedy voice as his wife nervously balanced her plastic tray with one hand and pulled their young son close with the other.

"If you don't like it, don't fucking eat it!" Derek hollered, crimson-faced. "Go to what's left of Seattle and see if you can find a refugee camp serving organic mashed goddamned potatoes!"

Two of Derek's fellow servers stepped to him and laid plastic-gloved hands on his shoulders. "Calm down—it ain't worth makin' a scene," one muttered into his ear.

"You're damned right it isn't worth it! None of these people are!" Derek spat, veins bulging in his neck. "These freeloaders come pouring in from Spokane and Seattle like a plague of locusts, eatin' us outta house and home, stealin' everything that isn't nailed down, bringin' the damned flu with 'em—"

One of the servers discretely jerked a thumb at the four Army soldiers guarding the chow point who had begun to step their way. "Buddy, you're attractin' the wrong kind of attention. I think you need a break before you get yourself in a whole lotta hot water."

Another kitchen volunteer took Derek's place on the line as he stepped out from the protective shade of the pole tent shielding the servers and the mess line from the noontime sun. "Oh, and while I'm at it, on behalf of the remaining people of the great city of Cheney, thanks to all you assholes for bringin' head lice, too!" Derek hollered at the serpentine of hungry refugees, angrily pointing to his shaved head. "I love looking like Captain fucking Picard and nicking my head every day with my dull-ass razor. Thanks a lot!"

He stormed northward up the stadium parking lot, past the oddly-designed twin dorm towers of Pearce Hall across the street, where displaced persons milled about on its adjacent basketball courts. The university's six residence halls—the seventh, which had a complicated Salish name, had burned to the ground—were packed with refugees, and horror stories had abounded amongst Cheney's residents that the conditions inside were supposedly vile beyond description.

The smell of bland cooked food from the open-air mess immediately gave way to the stench from the hundreds of refugees encamped on the football field itself, sheltered in tents and camping gear appropriated from local businesses and townspeople. Their arrangements would become untenable with the quickly approaching winter cold, and the townspeople, with growing resentment, knew it would be weeks at most until the Army began forcing people to quarter refugees in their homes.

Derek's neighbor, Camila, greeted him with a wave as he reached the open-air kitchen where locals prepared the refugees' food. She wiped her brow with her filthy apron while her friend, a young Latino shaved bald like Derek, tuned a solar-powered radio.

"Bad day at the office, Mr. Clean?" Camila asked, motioning Derek to an adjacent stack of orange milk crates.

He plopped down without answering and watched the rest of the kitchen detail, under guard by more armed soldiers, unload bags of staple foods from the back of a trailer truck; rumors abounded that the farmers of eastern Washington weren't giving up their crops willingly.

"Just my friends saving me from myself again," he sighed, rubbing his bald head. "When you're paid in food and your pantry's empty, telling the hand that feeds you to take this job and shove it is a really lousy idea. The First Amendment died right along with the USA, I guess."

A wicked smile crossed the Latino man's face as rock music burst from his Kaito Voyager radio. "I wouldn't count free speech out just yet, amigo—you're gonna like this lady," he said with a conspiratorial turn of his head to ensure that any soldiers or quislings were too far away to listen.

SANDPOINT

"Good afternoon! You're listening to *The Alexandra Chase Show*, coming to you loud and proud from a safe and secure location in the great state of Idaho!"

Alexandra flashed a pearly white smile at Paul from Uncle Guillermo's cozy swivel chair as he turned down the background music with which she had always started her KHTF morning show. She had taken to amateur radio like whiskey takes to soda, and her impromptu program had quickly become the crown jewel of the Redoubt Radio volunteer network, which subsequently made sure it got blasted out on AM bands as well.

"Keep it right here for an hour of news and inspiration as we all work to rise from the ashes. I know my show breaks pretty much every rule the FCC has, but seeing as how there's no internet, no phones, and probably no more FCC, good luck filing a complaint." Aunt Maria, who sat in the corner by the window, held her hand to her mouth and chuckled—Uncle Guillermo, who did his best to never miss an episode, was pulling guard duty at the end of the cul-de-sac.

"Today, we'll update you on the newly reconstituted legislatures of Oklahoma and Arkansas debating whether to join the newly independent Republic of Texas, as well as the secession conversation taking place right here in Idaho. The federal government—from some unknown 'safe location' since Washington, DC, burned to ash—is rattling the saber, just as it did when Texas seceded, but we're still not sure who's in charge, or at this point whether we even have a president or a Congress. But our top story this hour is the situation in neighboring Washington, where a full-on rebellion against their tyrannical governor is brewing east of the Cascades . . ."

KANIKSU NATIONAL FOREST

Jed gritted his teeth in anger as the lady on the radio described the Chewelah Massacre for her listeners—the trauma of the slaughter competed against the death of his family for top billing in his nightmares.

He turned his attention from the portable radio on the tree stump back to the tarp teepee under which he patiently smoked strips of venison from the deer he had shot and dressed earlier in the week. Making jerky had been practically his sole job in the month since his small group fled Chewelah for Autumn Nielsen's hunting cabin. It was tedious but vital work—they needed to stock up enough food and firewood to survive the winter, and the dusting of snow that had fallen two days prior was a kick in the pants from Mother Nature reminding them that time would not be on their side much longer. Jed gazed up at Kaniksu's tall ponderosa pines reaching for the blue sky, and did his best to savor the sun warming his back and the cool mountain breeze carrying the aromas of wood smoke and wild game.

Gabe Culver, Autumn's neighbor and former manager of one of Chewelah's three gas stations, spread mashed huckleberries from a pot fresh off the campfire onto a large, flat rock to dry into fruit leather—with a diet that would be heavily meat-based for the foreseeable future, having a steady supply of dietary fiber would be crucial to their health. The younger man leaned back and adjusted a ponytail holding shoulder-length brown hair. "Man, am I glad we got the hell outta Dodge—that lady on the radio said the Army came riding back into town, and they were pissed. Wonder what happened to the people they took away?"

"Ixnay on that kind of talk around the kids," Jed murmured, nodding his head toward the Taylors—Autumn's twin brother Bruce, his wife, Min-ji, and their children, Ronan and Lona—as they stepped out of the woods.

Lona set down a colander full of freshly picked huckleberries and blackberries next to Gabe. "Are they gonna come after us?" she asked, nodding at the radio.

Gabe shook his head. "I don't think you have anything to worry about, kiddo. They're not lookin' for us, and even if they were, they'd never find us. There's a reason why the Air Force runs its SERE school for downed pilots in eastern Washington—this state is one big hiding place."

"SERE?" Lona asked.

"Survival, evasion, resistance, and escape—getting back to friendly lines."

Jed cocked his head quizzically at the out-of-place remark from a gas station manager; he still knew little about his new roommates, but that would change, he thought with dread, once all seven of them were trapped together in a hunting lodge through a mountain winter in which the snow would be measured in feet. Bruce set down a sloshing plastic office water cooler jug with a grunt—it had held the family's spare change before Bruce repurposed it by dumping the now-useless fiat currency in a tinkling cascade on the concrete floor of their garage. The small stream flowing near Autumn's cabin would fulfill their water needs, but without a commercial filter to ensure its potability, boiling at least ten gallons a day for drinking, cooking, and bathing would be a major hassle requiring a small mountain of firewood.

Ronan stooped to grab split wood from their stockpile to throw on the withering fire before Jed stopped him. "Don't use the maple for fire—that's for smoking meat. Use the pine."

The boy tossed the wood back onto the pile with a hollow wooden *clonk* and grabbed two split logs of sticky, sappy pine. "What's it matter, Mister Schmidt?"

"Smoking with coniferous wood is great if you wanna barf all over the place because the meat ends up tasting like Pine-Sol," Jed said, eliciting a giggle from Lona. "You gotta use deciduous, and only certain kinds. Maple isn't the best for smoking venison, but it'll have to do." He slapped the section of maple tree he was siting on. "Besides, it took me forever to find this bad boy in a pine forest, to say nothing of chopping it down and haulin' it back here in pieces, so I'd rather this last us a while."

Autumn carried a bucket of hot water out the cabin's squeaky back door to a tarp wrapped around a copse of young pine trees that served as a makeshift shower stall; she smiled as Jed jokingly lowered his head and covered his eyes. The two shared the common bond of loss—Autumn's husband, Brandon, was one of the thousand victims of the H7N9 flu interred in Chewelah's mass grave.

Silence fell across the group as they listened, mesmerized, to Rosa Linn's "Snap" wafting from the radio. Autumn's flannel shirt flopped over the top edge of the tarp, followed by the horn-rimmed black glasses that matched her curly black hair; she had more than once chided herself for not having the foresight to order a backup pair, and fretted about what she would do if they broke.

Min-ji snapped her fingers when the announcer returned to the air. "I remember her!" she exclaimed in Korean-accented English. "Alexandra Chase! The DJ!"

Eyes went wide with cheers and laughter at the lifeline of normalcy that Alexandra had thrown them—a musical reminder of a lost civilization. But Jed's fleeting moment of happiness evaporated as he remembered his loyal workers listening to her show while sharing the rare privilege of earning a living through their passion for rebuilding cars and trucks; he fought back tears with the memory of Mary Ellen, Mikey, and Beth throwing him a surprise birthday party at the body shop just before the collapse.

Jed stoked the dim embers under the tarp and snuck an envious glance at the Taylors, who didn't realize how fortunate they were to be together as a family. His wife and children were dead—killed by the pestilence he had brought home—and he had no idea if Allan and Julie were alive, and probably never would.

It's gonna be a long, cold winter, he said to himself.

CHAPTER 11

CAMP MURRAY

"*People aren't taking Olympia's tyranny lying down, and it sounds like they only need a spark to light the flame of liberty. Sources tell us the torch will officially be lit tomorrow morning at the Stevens County seat of Colville by State Senator Rebecca Stevenson, who we're told will declare eastern Washington's independence. And thanks to our friends in the Redoubt Radio network, we'll be broadcasting it live!*"

"That *bitch*!" Governor Alicia Embrey screamed, slamming her palms on the conference table and startling the timid gray-haired volunteer from the government-run Radio Amateur Civil Emergency Service who had punched up Alexandra's show.

"Senator Stevenson, or the announcer?" Chief of Staff David Hampton cautiously ventured as heads rose from the EOC's computer screens with the outburst.

"Both! This is the *last* thing we need right now," Alicia railed at her assembled aides and the officers leading the remnants of the state's military assets for which she now served as commander-in-chief. "Just our luck," she growled, furiously waving a terse report detailing their inability to track down surviving state legislators, "that the first lawmakers who've popped out of their rabbit holes happen to be Rebecca Stevenson and James fucking Rand! So we've had no luck hunting them down?"

"No, ma'am," answered Major General Chris Kett, the adjutant general of the Washington Army and Air National Guard. "As you know, we're almost certain that Senator Rand was shot during that, um, incident in Chewelah. With I Corps's help," he said, pronouncing the command as "eye corps," "we cordoned off the town and searched every nook and cranny of every home and business. Based on a tip, we located Senator Rand's home east of Arden, but it had been recently abandoned. We can only assume Senator Stevenson and her daughter are with him—they've gone to ground, Madam Governor."

Alicia jabbed her finger at the ham radio and its elderly operator. "Well, according to Little Miss Bubblehead DJ, she's about to come out of hiding to declare independence, and we now know where and when. So what can we do about it?"

General Westman adjusted his camouflage blouse—unlike Kett, he had long ago abandoned wearing his dress uniform—and fidgeted as he skirted the line between legitimate military operations and getting involved in a political pissing match between elected officials. "Madam Governor, we have to be very careful how we proceed if we're talking about engaging in offensive operations against fellow Americans. Things are touchy right now with unit loyalties, especially with that rogue captain sneaking around and encouraging soldiers to rebel or desert."

Kett handed Alicia a tablet with a map of unit locations in northeastern Washington as Alexandra's show droned on in the background, relaying reports of mass death and devastation in the Far East and Australia. "We have no units to spare in the immediate vicinity of Colville. We can't issue movement orders to the garrison in Chewelah and leave it unoccupied, and even if we did, Senator Stevenson would get tipped off by any of a thousand modern-day Paul Reveres with a CB radio. They'd be long gone by the time we got there."

Alicia turned to face Westman. "Don't even ask about First Special Forces Group," he cut her off. "Third and Fourth Batt were elsewhere in CONUS or deployed overseas when the shit hit the fan, and Second Batt's essentially non-op—it suffered the same attrition through deaths and AWOLs that every other unit did." The general left unsaid that the Green Berets, who were trained to operate in failed states and collapsed societies, undoubtedly knew an untenable situation when they saw one and decided to scatter for the hills. "Besides, we'd run into the same problem that General Kett mentioned—the target would almost certainly get tipped off. We know for a fact that Senator Rand, and now Senator Stevenson by proxy, have a security retinue of former operators—they'd smell our boys coming a mile away."

The governor angrily shoved the tablet back to Kett; her temper got shorter with each passing day she was trapped inside their protective concrete tomb. "That leaves an airstrike. And I want options—I've heard 'no' enough times since I got here."

Westman cleared his throat. "Madam Governor, I don't think you want to want to go that route."

"I'll make you a deal, general—if you can get a hold of anyone in DC or the Pentagon for guidance, I'd be happy to reconsider. It's this, or we let the state's breadbasket split off and you can watch your troops and everyone else starve to death. Options, gentlemen." Alicia looked to Kett, whose ingratiating nod of approval to his pre-collapse boss wasn't lost on Westman—if he didn't play ball, he'd be put out to pasture and the reins handed to the two-star who owed his job to the governor.

Westman whispered orders to an aide, who hustled to a nearby phone. "We don't have many options to choose from," he said. "The

142nd Fighter Wing out of Portland is a write-off, because Portland's a write-off. And even if they weren't, they'd be preoccupied—Oregon's having the same problems with their eastern half that we're having with ours. In Idaho, there's the 366th at Mountain Home Air Force Base and the 124th at Gowen Field, but I don't think they'll cotton well to helping us."

"Yeah, 'cause their adjutant is buddies with that right-wing kook of a governor who sealed Idaho's border to keep our refugees out," Alicia interjected. "So what's that leave us?"

Westman's aide dutifully held up a black phone. "I have Kitsap on the line, sir. Patching through to speakers."

"That leaves the Navy," Westman said. "It took a while for her to get back home from the Middle East, but the aircraft carrier USS *Stennis* docked at Puget Sound Naval Shipyard two days ago. Her fighter complement will come in very handy if the situation in eastern Washington comes to blows, and Naval Base Kitsap's in very good shape, thanks to Captain Emrickson." Emrickson—who had never stepped foot in the EOC—wisely decided early into the H7N9 pandemic to cordon off the Kitsap Peninsula across Puget Sound from Seattle. His sailors and Marines blew the State Route 104 bridge over Hood Canal at its northernmost point, blocked off State Route 3 at the far southern tip of Sinclair Inlet, and ordered all assets at the nearby naval bases at Everett and Whidbey Island to consolidate into Kitsap with all possible haste. He deployed three destroyers into Puget Sound and issued a one-time warning that any ferries attempting to cross from Seattle would be sunk—he had to give that unfortunate order twice. No one at Kitsap got sick as a result.

The base commander had more to protect than his sailors and their families. Kitsap was home to more than thirteen hundred nuclear weapons, stored at Strategic Weapons Facility Pacific and mounted atop ballistic missiles in the four Trident submarines that had been recalled to port. And just across Sinclair Inlet sat the Manchester Fuel Depot and its seventy million gallons of fuel that would prove vital to military operations and eventual rebuilding. Kitsap's sailors and Marines were dug in around it to their eyeballs.

"They've got their hands full, but I don't think Captain Emrickson or the *Stennis*'s skipper will make a fuss about parting with a fighter or two for a few hours," Westman told Alicia. "If that's still what you want to do."

"Yes it is, and I want to see a plan ASAP to nip our little problem with Senator Stevenson in the bud," she ordered before staring daggers at the radio from which Alexandra Chase was wrapping up her program. "Then we can deal with her."

CHAPTER 12

COLVILLE

Rebecca gently stroked the sandy blonde hair of a toddler contentedly sucking his fingers in the arms of a pale middle-aged woman at the entrance to the Northeast Washington Fair Grounds. "He's absolutely adorable! What's his name?" Rebecca asked.

"I call him Emmanuel—that means 'God is with us.' I don't know his real name."

Sadness fell across Rebecca's face as she steeled herself to hear yet another tragic story of survival and personal loss. To her flanks, Sean and Miguel scanned the growing crowd for trouble, their presence clearly advertising that Rebecca was not to be messed with.

The woman shifted Emmanuel's weight. "I lived in Kettle Falls 'till everyone started droppin' dead from the flu, thanks to all the people takin' in friends an' relatives fleein' from Seattle. My sister here in Colville begged me 'fore the phones went dead to get to her so's we could be together—strength in numbers, I guess. Packed my beater car with as much as I could and took off. The smell 'n the flies were just . . ." she trailed off.

"I was takin' the back way to Route 395, just past a burnin' house—not a fireman in sight—when I found this little guy toddlin' down the middle of the road cryin' his eyes out, wearin' only a diaper an' red as a lobster from sunburn. I couldn't just leave 'im . . ." The woman's voice caught in her throat. "I was so worried 'bout him givin' me an' Daisy the flu, but . . . but if we leave babies to die, we're all dead already."

Rebecca wiped her eyes as the woman continued. "We got in right before Colville blocked off the roads. Just to be safe, me an' this li'l fella lived in Daisy's toolshed for five days 'till we knew we weren't sick. Didn't matter in the end, 'cause Daisy was diabetic and living on borrowed time—she ran outta insulin an' died two weeks ago." The woman stared at Emmanuel, who playfully tugged at her shirt. "He's all I got now."

"Thank you for sharing your story with me," Rebecca said with a wan smile.

The woman grabbed Rebecca's sleeve with surprising speed, the sadness in her face instantly replaced with desperation. "Ma'am? Can you, you know—can you fix all this? Set things right?"

She let go as Sean discretely caught Rebecca's attention and pointed to his watch. "I'll do my best, or die trying," she said.

Rebecca, Sean, and Miguel followed the men, women, and children descending on the fairgrounds on the sunny and bright autumn morning. Half-built, weather-beaten booths and faded plywood signs advertising a county fair that never took place lay scattered in the overgrown, weed-choked grass. Rebecca stopped just past the vacant horse stalls, the warm breeze carrying their stale manure smell, and stared forlornly at a hand-painted sign of a freckled, smiling redheaded girl eating pink cotton candy. She suddenly burst into tears at the enormity of all that had been lost, and the task that had been laid at her feet.

"Thank goodness I'm not wearing makeup," she joked as Sean handed her a handkerchief.

"You're gonna do great," Sean said. "You're the perfect person to lead these people out of this mess—that poor lady back there, just like James, had you pegged."

Miguel scouted ahead as they continued on the path toward the grandstands. Rebecca sniffled loudly and thumbed for the hundredth time through the handwritten pages of her speech. "I haven't felt this nervous since I was a scared plebe at Annapolis asking myself on I-Day just what in the hell I had gotten myself into. How do you Green Berets do it? What's your secret?"

Sean spun to walk backwards to check their six o'clock. "I was scared shitless my first day of infantry basic," he said nonchalantly. "I was scared shitless my first day of Ranger school and the Special Forces q-course. Don't get me started about airborne school—it blows my mind that some people like to jump outta perfectly good airplanes for fun. You wanna know my secret? I do what I gotta do, and get scared shitless later when no one's looking."

"That's not very reassuring," Rebecca said.

Sean turned back around. "As one of my instructors was fond of saying, if it's stupid but it works, it's not stupid."

Miguel nodded to a slightly overweight soldier standing guard at the entrance to the grandstands and arena. Local veterans, as well as a handful of hometown National Guard soldiers who had deserted and made their way back to Colville, provided security for the event, as well as early warning on the roads leading into town—and on some nearby rooftop, Cade was watching over them with his .50-caliber sniper rifle, ready to pop the head off of anyone who made any threatening move.

The shaded grandstands, which to Rebecca's surprise were almost packed, broke into applause when Rebecca and her guardians stepped foot onto the dirt arena. A lectern, complete with microphone and floor speaker, had been set up for her. *"Buena suerte, Mamá Oso,"* Miguel said as he and Sean headed to their prearranged overwatch positions.

"You'll do fine," Sean said. "Just treat it like any other speech."

"Sean, I've been working crowds since you were watching *Bluey*. It's declaring independence and hanging a big red bull's eye on my butt that's a new experience for me."

"Don't you go knocking *Bluey*—Bandit Heeler's one righteous dude," Sean said. "Remember, Mama Bear—get scared shitless later."

"I already penciled it in."

PUGET SOUND NAVAL SHIPYARD

Lieutenant Callie "Amazon" Harman savored being shoved into her seat on max throttle as Catapult 3 hurled her F-35C Lightning down the deck of the *Stennis* and over the churning blue water of Sinclair Inlet.

She let go of the "towel rack" handles on both sides of the canopy to assume control of the carrier variant of the ultramodern, fifth-generation jet fighter, which had already stabilized its own flight. Grasping the control stick, she reached to raise her landing gear and set the wing flaps to automatic before settling her other hand on the bulky but versatile throttle. She eased the stealth fighter into a gentle ascent, crossing the debris-filled inlet and passing over what was left of the small city of Port Orchard. Her altitude ticked up on the green heads-up display projected directly onto the inner visor of her sophisticated Gen 3 flight helmet, which at four hundred thousand dollars apiece before the collapse cost more than most American homes. Callie glanced to her right at the snow-capped Olympic Mountains and the eponymous national forest carpeting them, beyond which lay the Pacific Ocean the *Stennis* had crossed after being called back to port by US Pacific Fleet Command—that is, before USPACFLT went dark like everything else.

Her plane disappeared around her, as if by magic, as Callie toggled the fighter's six distributed aperture system cameras, which projected the outside world onto her inner visor for unparalleled, 360-degree situational awareness. She gawked at the devastation around and beneath her as she eased into position behind her flight leader, Lieutenant Commander Tanner "Kurgan" Sims, who had taken off on Catapult 1. Their altitude now far above any threat of small-arms fire from looters and criminal gangs ruling over their newfound empires of ash, the duo slowly banked east over Puget Sound, the ugliness of the blackened ruins of Tacoma and the majesty of Mount Rainier lazily drifting across their canopies.

The devastation of the nation Callie had sworn to protect, and to which she had pledged at least a decade of her young life, negated the joy of flying for the first time since the collapse, and without having to follow any visual flight rules or Sea-Tac airspace bullshit. She knew the rest of her fighter wing—Strike Fighter Squadron 97 (VFA-97), the "Warhawks"—would have killed for the opportunity to fly again, if anything to keep their minds off of whether their families were alive or dead. While Kitsap was safe, the Warhawks' home base of Naval Air Station Lemoore, sandwiched in the San Joaquin Valley between the half million souls apiece in Fresno and Bakersfield, never stood a chance. The fertile valley attracted hordes of desperate and hungry survivors streaming from Los Angeles the way an open can of root beer attracts autumn yellowjackets. All of southern California had gone absolutely silent.

The altimeter and compass on Callie's sophisticated visor ticked toward their preplanned altitude and eastward bearing. Her attention briefly shifted to a distant forest fire in Okanogan-Wenatchee National Forest, which left a large, dirty smear across the northern horizon. Callie wondered how long it would burn without a US Forest Service to contain it—she couldn't imagine the rotten luck of surviving the collapse, only to be burned out with cold and snow barely a month away.

She and her fellow Warhawks couldn't help their loved ones, but they could help other innocent people, now at the mercy of the monsters that had slithered from the shadows with the collapse of law and order to prey on them. Marauders had raped and slaughtered the people of the small town of Colville, near the Idaho border, and were massing to pillage what was left of northeast Washington like a modern-day Mongol horde. Whatever was left of Washington's state government needed them blown off the face of the Earth, and Callie was more than happy to oblige.

And her sole regret was that she and Kurgan would only be able to kill them once.

CHAPTER 13

COLVILLE

Rebecca stepped up to the gouged and faded cherry-finish lectern planted in the dirt of the fairgrounds arena. She flashed a humble smile as she adjusted the rust-speckled metal snake holding an old black microphone—she knew the crowd wasn't cheering and applauding for her, but for themselves. They were ecstatic to still be alive; they had made it—at least so far. Winter would surely carry some of them off, particularly the children, Rebecca thought as a chill ran up her spine.

She got two syllables into the most important speech of her life before the skull-splitting screech of feedback whined from the portable speaker, prompting adults to grimace and children to slap their hands to their ears.

"Everybody awake now?" she asked to scattered laughs accompanying the feedback's echo from the sides of Colville's homes and empty businesses. "In all seriousness, if you wouldn't mind, I'd like to start with a moment of silence for all of the people who, um, aren't here with us today." Rebecca bowed her head and snuck a peek at Sean and Miguel, who were watching the crowd like hungry raptors ready to pounce on the slightest twitch of movement. The sounds of muted sobs and parents hushing up their children carried on the light autumn breeze.

Rebecca raised her head and gestured to two rifle-toting men in hunting overalls flanking an older couple at a folding table with a field radio at the arena's edge. "I'd like to thank your local volunteer security detail for keeping us safe, as well as the fine people from Redoubt Radio who are broadcasting this all over the world. And thank you to the nice family who lent their big ol' Goal Zero solar generator to power our speaker and the ham radio. Not that the juice has been very reliable to begin with, but I'm sure it's a coincidence that Colville just so happened to lose power the day of my speech."

The audience chuckled nervously as Rebecca looked them over. "I've never been to Colville before today. The district I represented in the State Senate was clear across Washington—the Tri-Cities area near the Oregon border—but my constituents faced the same problem you folks did. We were ignored. Held in utter contempt by Olympia and Seattle politicians who considered us nothing more than illiterate, backward country bumpkins incapable of making our own decisions." A handful of spectators grumbled in support.

"I never thought I'd ever consider what was going on in Olympia—the constant uphill battle against the never-ending assault on eastern Washington's values and rights—as the good old days. But now, after we survived the worst disaster in human history, we find ourselves trapped in a police state—one that considers all of us, and our children, and our children's children, as nothing more than indentured servants at best, and outright slaves at worst, to serve what's left of Seattle and the Left Coast.

"You all know my good friend James Rand, who for years has advocated for eastern Washington to split off into a new state called Cascadia.

He loves Colville, by the way—he told me you always gave him a warm welcome and an open ear. He should be the one up here extolling the benefits of reclaiming our long lost self-determination. But he isn't." Rebecca's voice caught in her throat. "Because they shot him, and killed two dozen innocent people, just down the road in Chewelah. In cold blood."

SNOQUALMIE PASS

"Billy?" the woman's reassuring voice echoed from the black.

No, his mind answered back. *It's safe here. Go away.*

"Billy?" the disembodied voice asked again. "It's OK. You're OK."

Billy, the man realized as the sensation of a hand gently rubbing his back slowly guided him out of the darkness. *Yes. That's my name.*

He opened his eyes to find himself face down in the black earth of the garden that would help sustain him and his Olivia through the winter, courtesy of the pressure canner boiling on the wood stove in the kitchen. *Olivia. That's my girl. And this isn't Afghanistan. I'm home,* he slowly reminded himself as if awakening from a horrible nightmare.

Billy had been pulling carrots when the twin deafening *booms* roared down the valley and immediately catapulted him back to That Day, when the young private woke up in the Army hospital in Landstuhl, Germany, as the lone survivor of the improvised explosive device that had killed the rest of his team. Billy slowly learned to live with the injuries to his body, but he and Olivia struggled daily with the injuries to his soul. He thanked God every day that he managed to wean himself off his meds prior to the collapse—he couldn't imagine the hell that surviving veterans whose prescriptions had run out were going through.

"What in the Sam Hill was that ungodly noise? What blew up?" Olivia asked, helping Billy struggle to his feet against the needles of pain stabbing into bones shattered by that crude but effective bomb so long ago.

"Those weren't explosions," Billy mumbled, dusting the dirt from his flannel shirt. "That was two fighter jets punching sonic."

"Sonic booms? As in breaking the sound barrier? Why?"

Billy grabbed his nearby binoculars as a glimmer of reflected sunlight revealed the distant but distinctive silhouettes of two F-35s overhead, arcing eastward across the sky—he breathed a silent prayer of thanks that the IED that had taken much of his mobility had spared his eyesight. "Can't be good, whatever the reason—I gotta call this in," he said, shambling up the small dirt path to the modest home his beloved parents had left their only son in their will.

Glass from a shattered picture frame crunched under Billy's worn combat boots the moment he stepped inside. Olivia angrily marched to the kitchen closet to grab a broom and a dustpan. "After you call your buddies, can you call the military and ask 'em to replace the two Mason jars that Maverick and Goose made me drop? It's not like we can drive to Walmart and buy more."

Billy eased himself with a groan into his leather living room chair. He grabbed the handset for the Midland CB base station on the lamp stand, dialed up channel 36, single sideband, and hoped the handler who forwarded his reports to Redoubt Radio's ham network was listening. *At least those fighters are ours and not Chinese,* Billy said to himself. *If the flu hadn't wiped China out along with the rest of the world, they probably would've taken everything on the West Coast that wasn't nailed down as collateral for the trillion-dollar debt Uncle Sam died owing 'em.*

His handler answered on Billy's third try. "If you're callin' in another military convoy crossin' the I-90 bridge you got eyes on, you gotta wait, hoss," the gruff older man responded over the ambient swirl of static. "Net control's busy jugglin' all the people reportin' them sonic booms with the folks tryin' to get outta the way of that damned forest fire in Okanogan."

"The booms are what I'm calling about—I got eyes on the bogeys," Billy responded. "Two fast movers; F-35s—that's foxtrot three fives—tearing ass northeast, probably outta Kitsap or McChord. Need you to pass it up the network."

"Wilco—I'll give this FLASH priority and clear the net so they can shoot it up the ladder fast. I haven't seen a single plane since the world went to hell, and now we got fighters lookin' to scrap. Someone's 'bout to have a real bad day," the old man said and signed off without waiting for a response.

Billy painfully stood and shuffled back to the garden to continue reaping a harvest that would mean the difference between life and death for him and Olivia. He made a mental note, based on his brief chat with the man he knew only by his Redoubt Radio handle, to take a peek later at the assets the Army had parked around the elevated I-90 bridges across Keechelus Lake from his home. Interstate 90 through Snoqualmie was one of only three year-round, all-weather passes through the Cascades, which made it prime tactical real estate.

Olivia stepped out the door into the backyard. "Never thought I'd miss the liberal media, but I'd love to be able to turn on the TV and learn more, even if most of the coverage ends up being wrong," she quipped. "Whaddya think's goin' on?"

"Damnfino," Billy answered and tossed a handful of carrots into a metal bucket with a *clang*.

CHAPTER 14

COLVILLE

"I'll be honest with you—I thought James was certifiably crazy when he first broached the idea of Cascadia with me. I'm not going to say here the words I actually used, but I bet you can guess what some of them were," Rebecca told the crowd.

"But he's *not* crazy. In fact, he's been right about everything. James warned everyone who would listen that the federal government's runaway spending would drive the economy off a cliff. And after he hit *that* nail on the head, he predicted the government would throw what little was left of the Constitution in the trash and terrorize us. He was right about that, too—just ask the next of kin of the peaceful protesters they slaughtered in Chewelah. Ask anyone in town, actually. Two days after the massacre, Alicia Embrey sent the Army rolling back in to drop off truckloads of refugees that Chewelah has no ability to feed or clothe." Rebecca pointed south down Route 395 toward the neighboring town. "Ladies and gentlemen, how much longer until they hop back in their war machines and roll up the road to show all of *you* who's boss?"

Anger crossed Rebecca's face. "Do you know why they killed those people, ladies and gentlemen? They recognized James on the governor's most-wanted list and tried to arrest him for the crime of speaking his mind. Before the collapse, they didn't care one heck of a lot for that in Olympia and Seattle, unless you thought the exact same way that they did—they'd try to cancel you, or sic their media buddies on you, to scare you into keeping your 'dangerous' ideas to yourself. But without the Constitution or rule of law holding them back any longer, they've taken off the gloves. They want to permanently silence James, and anyone else who thinks like him.

"They're hunting for me, too, for the crime of being his friend. And now, I guess, for trying to spark a rebellion." Rebecca paused, struggling to keep composed. "But that's not enough for them! My only child, Carleigh, is on their list, too. She has no politics whatsoever—in fact, she was the strongest voice against my running for re-election! They authorized using deadly force against her. That's right—they're willing to kill an eighteen-year-old girl because she's my daughter. That's how depraved our rulers—no, our overlords—have become."

The crowd hanged on Rebecca's every word. "Ladies and gentlemen, monsters have taken over. They have to be stopped, and the only way to stop them is to send them back where they came from and do what should've been done a long time ago—partition the twenty counties east of the Cascades into our own state . . . or our own nation now, I guess. Many of you are probably thinking that this isn't your fight—that all you can afford to focus on is survival. I don't blame you. But how many of the poor souls killed in Chewelah—how many of the town's survivors now living under the yoke of military occupation—wanted to stay out of it? You may not be interested in what's going on, but I guarantee that it's very much interested in each and every one of you, whether you like it or not."

WARHAWK TWO

The F-135 Pratt & Whitney turbofan engine that had announced to what was left of Washington that Callie had reached Mach 1 hummed behind her as her fighter hurtled toward Colville.

Callie had almost wished she couldn't see through her advanced fighter as mile after mile of post-apocalypse Washington passed underneath en route to her mission objective. Some small towns had burned to the ground, leaving nothing but ugly black gashes surrounded by brown fields and green mountains. Others, thanks to their distance from dense population centers and either divine providence or sheer dumb luck, had fared all right—at least, from the air.

She glanced once again at the black and green stores management display on the right side of her cockpit touch screen, which listed the armament loaded in the fighter's dual storage bays. Like her wingman, her fighter carried two Paveway II GBU-16 thousand-pound precision-guided bombs, and two AIM-120 AMRAAM air-to-air missiles; the missiles, she and Kurgan were told by the mission briefing officer, were insurance in case Idaho got skittish and sortied fighters to intercept them. Callie had looked at the officer like he had sprouted a second head when he shared that tidbit.

In case she had to take the shot instead of Kurgan, Callie thumbed her throttle's cursor control over the fairgrounds on the tactical situation display on the left side of her screen, then thumbed the target designate button in the center of her stick to order the F-35's advanced forward-looking infrared radar and on-board computer to generate a synthetic aperture map of their target—the dregs of society they were about to reach out and touch with thousand-pound crowd pleasers. The grayscale image popped up seconds later where the stores display had been; Callie toggled to air-to-ground mode with the click of a throttle switch, and a blood red triangle appeared smack in the center of the arena.

She glanced straight ahead to examine her updated air-to-ground heads-up display before her gut instinct brought her attention back to the image of the fairgrounds.

Something isn't right about this . . .

COLVILLE

"You've all heard about what's being done on Embrey's orders—Chewelah's FM station was doing a great job of reporting it until the military shut it down," Rebecca told the crowd. "Arrest and detention without counsel. Seizure of food and personal possessions. Forcing people in vital industries to essentially work as slaves. Confiscating firearms and leaving you defenseless in a lawless world. Makes the nonsense we had to put up with from Olympia's legions of unelected bureaucrats and apparatchiks seem trivial by comparison, doesn't it? They're not gonna stop, and no one's gonna swoop in and fix this for us. We have to stand up and fight for ourselves."

Rebecca shook her head. "Good Lord, it's tough talking about the United States of America in the past tense, but that's the harsh reality we face. We don't even know if we have a president or a Congress anymore. The only thing we have now is Miss Embrey, who all but crowned herself queen, with a bunch of military leaders who forgot their oaths to uphold the Constitution acting as her muscle. 'Miss' is the only title I'm giving her from here on out—trust me, others come to mind, but I can't say them with children around. I refuse to call her governor. Because she's not my governor. Or yours." The crowd burst into applause.

"Many others have come to the realization I have, and that I hope you do—we're on our own, and we're better off being the captains of our own destiny. Texas seceded, and Idaho's reconvened Legislature is voting next week whether to follow the Lone Star State out the door. To our south, the counties of both eastern Oregon and northern California—which has wanted partition for more than a century—are having this very same debate about splitting from states that never cared anything for them."

Rebecca gripped both sides of the lectern, her voice rising. "Ladies and gentlemen, eastern and western Washington have been two different states for a *very* long time. Before the collapse, Embrey didn't give a tinker's damn about you if she couldn't see your house from the Space Needle. Now that she and her lackeys have no rules to follow, they're letting their true colors fly with impunity. We've become nothing more than a colony under foreign occupation! Our invaders take food from our children's mouths and ship it to what's left of western Washington, and the only thing that gets shipped our way are refugees and armed thugs who think their uniforms give them legitimacy!

"It's time to stop their wholesale pillage so we can rise from these terrible ashes! It's time to rise up and *fight*!" Rebecca screamed with the swelling applause. "Fight until we kick every last occupier back over the Cascades so we can live free and rebuild!"

Sean had allowed himself the luxury of a few seconds to watch Rebecca make what he hoped would be a speech for the history books when he caught movement out of the corner of his eye. He snapped his SCAR-H rifle with lightning speed at the chest of a tall black man in a flannel shirt and jeans with a military rifle slung on his back; the man was flanked by a young Asian man and an even younger white woman, similarly dressed and armed.

"That's close enough!" Sean warned over the cheers and stomping of feet on the grandstands above.

"You don't have much time!" Demetrius screamed over the cacophony; Tom and Allie stayed deathly still, knowing better than to make any sudden moves in front of a trained killer. "Senator Stevenson and all these people are in danger! You gotta get her outta here!"

CHAPTER 15

WARHAWK TWO

"I'm telling you something stinks!" Callie protested to her flight leader.

"Warhawk Two, I relayed your concerns straight to the CAG," Kurgan replied, Callie's flight helmet broadcasting his tinny response from the direction of his fighter at her ten o' clock. "They stand by their intel. Charlie Mike—stay icy, Amazon."

Callie mouthed a curse and shot a glance at the spooky grayscale image of the fairgrounds. "Trust your eyes, Kurgan! If those are marauders, where are their vehicles? Why aren't there any houses burning? *And why would they be sitting in the grandstands?!* To get a safety briefing before they go raping and pillaging? Topside's giving us textbook mushroom treatment!"

"Warhawk Two, if I wanted a conscience, I would've asked the pork chop to issue me one," Kurgan reprimanded. "You're here to cover my six while I take out the trash before they do to the civvies down there what they did to our families in Lemoore. Now secure your mouth."

Goosebumps crawled under Callie's flight suit as she stared at the air-to-ground display on her flight helmet. The sideways V—the "carrot" at the top of the vertical lime-green line of her air-to-ground display—began creeping downward in a countdown to entering weapons range.

COLVILLE

"What kind of babbling bullshit is this?" Sean demanded of the strangers before him. "Fast movers inbound? What, you got a radar in your pocket?"

Demetrius shook his head. "Wouldn't work if I did—they're stealths outta Kitsap. We don't have time to go over my résumé! We're on your side here, and I'm tellin' you that you gotta evac the senator before it's too late!"

Cade's voice buzzed in Sean's radio earbud. "Hawk, I got a clear shot at your tangos, over," he calmly radioed from his sniper position.

Sean toggled the transmitter switch on his rifle. "Got this under control, Eagle. You see anyone makin' a move on Mama Bear, take 'em out, and any of these three still standing. Out."

"You got a sniper on overwatch—good thinking," Demetrius said. "Speaking of which, don't you think we would've done a scope job on the senator ourselves if we wanted her dead, rather than come face-to-face to a special operator with trust issues? Time's running out—hers and yours!"

"My trust issues are what's kept us alive, friend," Sean shot back. "And right now, your story has my bullshit detector whistling Dixie."

Demetrius cautiously checked his wristwatch over another raucous round of cheers above. "Times' up—Navy's about to deliver its air mail. Don't say we didn't warn you."

The trio took two cautious steps back when Grant's agitated voice blared in Sean's ear. "Redoubt Radio's reporting two fast movers, likely Foxtrot Three Fives from Kitsap—supersonic, heading northeast. Sightings in Snoqualmie Pass and Chelan—straight line for Colville—ETA at any fucking minute!" Grant radioed in. "How copy, over?"

"Shit!" Sean spat. "Good copy, Osprey! We're gonna exfil! Out!" One of the Redoubt Radio ham operators broadcasting Rebecca's speech tore off his headphones and yanked his partner out of her folding metal chair while furiously pointing skyward.

"Told you so!" Demetrius yelled at Sean over the crowd.

Rebecca stopped mid-sentence as Sean leaped over the chain-link fence and sprinted straight for her. Miguel, following hot on the trail of Demetrius and his companions, dashed past the grandstands, kicking up dust as they fled toward the open gate near the animal pens on the arena's south side. Sean roughly pulled Rebecca from the lectern to the agitated chatter of the crowd. "We got an airstrike inbound—we gotta go!"

The senator painfully tore from Sean's vise-like grip to grab the microphone. "Ladies and gentlemen, you're all in danger! Get away from here as fast as you can and get to shelter—" she pleaded before the Redoubt Radio duo violently yanked out the cords connecting their equipment and her mike to the generator.

Sean grabbed her again. *"Now!"*

WARHAWK TWO

"Dammit, sir, you're about to bomb a civilian target!" Callie growled, the carrot on her visor inching downward on her HUD.

The sleepy town, blanketed in a light haze from the cooking and heating fires burned by the surviving townspeople, lay on the horizon just beyond the Columbia River, nestled in a narrow valley carved out of the forest-carpeted Selkirk Mountains. The green triangle on Callie's visor marking the fairgrounds edged closer and closer.

Callie radioed Kurgan again. No response. *"Commander!"* she all but screamed.

"Lieutenant, if you're gonna shoot me down, then do it!" Kurgan thundered. "If not, then *stow* it, goddammit, before I have you busted back down to slick sleeve!"

The carrot reached the vertical box indicating weapons range. Moments later, the sun flashed off the two Paveway bombs that dropped from Kurgan's weapons bays, their nose-mounted seekers and boxy rectangular fins following his fighter's laser to their target with a combined two thousand pounds of explosive power—enough to destroy the fairgrounds and everyone in them a hundred times over.

"Back the way we came for egress, Warhawk Two—I wanna give that forest fire a wide berth," Kurgan curtly ordered. Callie helplessly watched her display flare white with heat as the Paveways found their mark, her distance and the birds' eye view making the monstrous twin explosions appear deceptively puny. The lucky victims, Callie knew, were instantly incinerated. The unlucky ones would die as the blast overpressure ruptured their lungs and butchered their flesh with shrapnel and flying debris.

"Bearing two three zero, angels three zero for Romeo Tango Bravo," Kurgan confirmed.

"Roger that," Callie seethed. "Falcon two two one."

"Say again, over?"

"Disregard," she responded, simultaneously relieved and disappointed that her flight leader didn't know the old-school naval aviator code for telling a fellow pilot on the air to commit an impossible sexual act with himself and the horse he rode in on. She banked left in formation toward their return course, trembling with anger over what they had just done, and what had become of the world.

CHAPTER 16

DOUGLAS FALLS

Sean knew better than to ask Rebecca if she was OK.

He stood silent vigil while she stared in mute sorrow at the small waterfall below, on the opposite side of Colville Mountain from the smoldering remains of the town they had barely escaped with their lives. Their newfound allies scurried in the grassy parking area behind them to pack up and roll out of the secluded Grange park they had temporarily called home.

"Sean? I don't feel so—" Rebecca managed to croak before doubling over and vomiting over the rough-hewn stone ledge. He darted to steady her and hold back her hair, the waterfall's dull roar drowning out the sound of her heaving.

"Why?" she gasped, wiping her mouth with her sleeve.

"Because they're the bad guys," Sean said matter-of-factly. "That's what bad guys do."

"I killed all those people!" Rebecca sobbed, her face twisted with anguish. "They came to hear me pretend to be George Washington, and I killed them! That little orphan boy and the good Samaritan—"

"*They* killed those people, Rebecca," Sean sternly cut her off. "They decided that slaughtering civilians was an acceptable cost if it meant killing you. *They're* the murderers. Not you. Remember that."

Rebecca turned back to the falls cascading down through the autumnal oranges, reds, and yellows of deciduous trees sprinkled among Washington evergreens. She took a deep breath, ripped her hard-earned Annapolis ring off her finger and flung it into the water below with all her might. "I want no part of a Navy that would do something like this," Rebecca said flatly.

Demetrius and Miguel trudged down the small nature path leading to the scenic overview. "Had to climb halfway up the mountain to get a clear signal," Miguel said, "but you'll be happy to know I got a hold of Carleigh to let her know you're not dead, *Mamá Oso*." Rebecca smiled at Miguel, lip quivering. "*De nada,*" he added, heading back for their pickup truck where Cade was standing guard.

Rebecca let out a ragged sigh and offered Demetrius her hand. "And thank you, sir, for saving our lives. I didn't catch your name."

"You don't have to thank us," he said as they shook. "Captain Demetrius Mathers, United States Army—well, formerly, anyway."

Sean took a cautious step toward him. "We figured out for ourselves that you aren't trying to kill us, on account of the fact you would've done it already. How'd you know about the inbounds?"

"We're not much, but we've got a handful of people in the right places. Governor Embrey and her advisers hatched their plan right after that lady on Redoubt Radio announced you were comin' to Colville, and we high-tailed it out here."

"Which brings us to the next burning question," Rebecca said. "Why?"

Demetrius swept his arm to the troops scrambling in the open lot behind him. "To join forces, ma'am. We've been traveling eastern Washington, cautiously cobbling together a ragtag fighting force: local militias, units that'll turn when the time is right, Iraq and Afghanistan veterans who got one helluva education on how to plant bombs and fight dirty—you get the idea. These men and women are ready to fight and die for liberty, but without something to rally around, we'll end up fighting forever, with no end in sight like some Third World shithole. We need a cause—and that, Senator Stevenson, is you and Cascadia." It was Demetrius's turn to offer his hand. "We're at your disposal, ma'am, and with that atrocity Olympia just committed, I have a feeling our ranks are gonna start swelling real soon."

"You need a cause, and Cascadia needs an army. Let's give these bullies a fight," Rebecca said, shaking hands again to officially seal the alliance.

The afternoon sun dipped below Colville Mountain, wrapping the valley in a shadow that magnified the autumn chill. "On that happy note, we need to scram," Sean said. "I don't think we wanna chance waiting 'till sunset to move out this close to town. They may have eyes in the sky, but I think it's a risk we gotta take."

Demetrius nodded his agreement and led his new allies up the steep dirt path to the parking area, where eighteen vehicles—mostly trucks with a handful of armored Humvees—were hidden just inside the surrounding woods. The trio walked to Demetrius's purloined Stryker, where Tom and Allie had finished stowing its camouflage netting.

"We got clear skies, sir," Allie reported. "No chatter on the Redoubt Radio freqs about any more aircraft—and after what just happened, believe me, everyone's watching."

Demetrius smiled at Sean and Rebecca. "Radar without the radar—we're good to go. We'll be in touch about getting out to you or the other way around." He nodded toward Miguel and Cade, who clandestinely studied him from their adjacent truck. "No disrespect to your entourage of pipe hitters, but I think you'd benefit from safety in numbers. Your commo guy over there already exchanged SATCOM protocols with our commo lady. We can talk nice and secure."

Rebecca scratched her head. "Let's you and me connect at, say, 0800 tomorrow, after I get some sleep and inform the world that I'm still alive and kicking. You have a callsign, captain? I'd rather not ask for you by your Christian name, even on a secure uplink."

Demetrius smirked. "Lando. Not my choice, but it stuck." Rebecca stifled a chuckle as Demetrius stabbed his finger at Tom, who hoisted himself over the Stryker's front grip bars into the driver's hatch. "Courtesy of my driver, Sergeant—soon to be Private Fiftieth Class—Tom Ngo, of Bumblefuck, Alabama!"

"My pleasure, sir!" Tom yelled with a smile, donning his combat vehicle crewman's helmet. Demetrius jogged to the center of the open field, prompting his loitering soldiers to immediately pile into their vehicles, with Rebecca, Sean, Miguel, and Cade following suit.

"Hell of a day," Rebecca ventured as she buckled her seat belt. Demetrius held out his arms, slowly turning a circle to make sure every driver could see him.

Sean laid a gloved hand on the keys in the ignition. "Score another win for James—he said people would rally around you, and here we are. Hope they get your likeness right on the statue when this park becomes a historical landmark."

"Yeah. 'Rebecca Stevenson Puked Here,'" she muttered.

Sean laughed. "Cracking jokes in the face of certain death? I knew you'd get the hang of this!"

Demetrius held out his fingers and counted down from five, the convoy's engines revving to life simultaneously so an eavesdropping enemy couldn't estimate their size by counting their starts. He sprinted up the ramp of his Stryker, which led the way out of the park. The convoy headed north out of the valley with Rebecca's truck in the center until Sean split off at a fork in the road several miles later. Behind them, ugly black plumes rose like tendrils from Colville as unabated fires consumed what was left of town.

CHAPTER 17

SANDPOINT

The *tick-tock* rhythm of the song "The Syncopated Clock" echoed from radios all over the Pacific Northwest with a click of Alexandra's mouse.

"If you've lost track of time, ladies and gentlemen, get ready to set your clocks on my mark," she said, staring at the crimson digital readout at Uncle Guillermo's ham radio station. Alexandra and other Redoubt Radio operators did their best to keep some sort of time standard; the destruction of Denver and the I-25 corridor had knocked out the atomic clock maintained by the National Institute of Standards in Boulder, eliminating both its spoken-word beacon and the signal that millions of clocks relied on to keep time—or at least those still functioning with the disruptions to the east, west, and Texas power grids.

"We're coming up on 1830 hours Pacific Daylight Time here in the panhandle of the newly independent Free State of Idaho—that's 0230 Zulu and UTC—so if you need to, set your clocks in five, four, three, two, one, *mark*! And yes, I said daylight time, even though it's November—no more springing forward, falling back, or any combination thereof—that nonsense is one casualty of this terrible tribulation I'm not gonna miss!"

Her hourly time check complete, Alexandra faded out the old pops orchestra ditty and ran a finger down her handwritten script to recap the news of the day. After months of silence, the state government in neighboring Montana announced it was still functioning and was trying to restore order and grid power; however, Redoubt Radio had relayed numerous horror stories from Big Sky Country about the terror of lawlessness being replaced by the trampling of liberties by reemerging authority.

Much of New England, Southern California, the Rust Belt, and the East Coast were silent, and what was left of the Union was unraveling like a threadbare tapestry. The legislatures of Oklahoma and Arkansas, and the surviving northern parishes of Louisiana, were debating joining in a federation with Texas; Missouri, Mississippi, Kentucky, and Tennessee also were talking independence. The federal government insisted from its secret location that it was still in control, that aid would be coming, and that secessionist activity would be crushed by force. However, rumors abounded that the president and much of the chain of succession was dead, and that the few who were left were fighting over who was next in line.

"If you haven't heard, Redoubt Radio now has official competition in the form of government propaganda from the state of Washington—not to be confused with the new and improved State of Cascadia," Alexandra reported. "Olympia managed to get the KOMO AM transmitter up and running—hopefully not at gunpoint like they like to do—so they can cover you with manure. They have yet to mention the Chewelah Massacre or the bombing of Colville, but I'm sure that's just an oversight on their part, right?"

Alexandra glanced at the canvas tarps covering both windows in her father-in-law's ham shack to prevent their lights from making the home what Aunt Maria called a "loot me beacon" in a world without grid power. "It's already dark outside, Thanksgiving is next week, and here in the mountains, we're already snowed in. A lot of you are cold, hungry, and scared. I know many of you don't know where your next meal is coming from, or where your loved ones are. I hope this little program of mine is doing something to lift your spirits, and I want you to know that I'm praying every day for all of you. And if you live in Cascadia, I pray you do whatever you can, no matter how small, to answer Senator Stevenson's call to resist tyranny."

She sipped her honey tea, silently dreading the day she would run out of the supply that Guillermo had lovingly stockpiled for her in anticipation of having her and Paul as long-term house guests. "I'll repeat what I said at the top of the hour about the cholera outbreaks in Cheney and Kalispell—if you don't have a reliable water filter, like a Berkey or Katadyn, you have to boil any water you're gonna use for drinking and cooking. And please, whatever you do, don't go to the bathroom in or near any open water source . . ."

KANIKSU NATIONAL FOREST

"This stuff is *gross*!" Lona gagged after sipping her pine-needle tea, her hands wrapped around the steaming red tin mug for its warmth. "It's like drinking Dad's car air freshener!"

Gabe helped himself to a cup from the top of the wood-burning stove the motley group of Chewelah refugees had huddled around as winter winds roared outside their cabin. "Beats gettin' scurvy, kid—you'd have to drink five glasses of orange juice to get the same amount of vitamin C you're holding right now."

"How do you know this stuff? I mean, really?" Lona asked him for the hundredth time since their arrival.

"Tending a gas station gave me lotsa time to read," Gabe answered, pointing to the *Harry Potter* book in Lona's lap—fortunately for the group's sanity, her brother Ronan had had the forethought before they bugged out to cram every spare nook and cranny of their two-vehicle convoy with books, board games, and other diversions. Lona rolled her eyes, not accepting Gabe's answer.

Jed wiped down his camouflage-patterned Winchester SXP twelve-gauge shotgun with an oil-stained rag. "When this storm lets up, I'll go out and see if I can bag us a tom. Wouldn't be Thanksgiving without a turkey dinner."

"*If* this storm ever lets up, you mean," Autumn moaned and sipped her tea. "I used to love coming up here with Brandon to hunt, but I'm going stir crazy—this makes the COVID-19 lockdown feel like a Caribbean cruise! Spring can't get here soon enough."

Jed picked up the wool-knit comforter that had fallen behind Autumn and gingerly draped it over her shoulders. The first foot of snow had fallen in mid-October, and now, a month later, they had four feet on the ground; aside from bringing in firewood, melting snow for water, and dreaded trips to the outhouse, the group was cabin-bound for the foreseeable future. However, they counted their blessings, knowing that millions of survivors had it much worse than them.

"Be careful what you wish for, big sis—you might just get it," Bruce said; Autumn was the older twin by exactly five minutes. "We got some big decisions to make once spring comes. We can't stay here forever eating meat and berries."

"And wiping our butts with leaves and moss," Lona groused—they had run out of toilet paper several days prior.

Jed set his shotgun behind him. "My mind's already made up. I'm gonna fight. I always told Mikey and Beth to stand up for the little guy—bragged about all the times in school I got in hot water for whaling the tar outta bullies who messed with my kid brother. That's what they'd want me to do."

Bruce slipped his arms around Lona and Min-ji and nodded toward Ronan, who stood by the window, trying to pull in a signal on Gabe's portable radio. "Part of me would love to join you, but I got a family, and they come first."

"Absolutely—you have a Christian duty to care for them," Jed said. "But seeing as how I don't got a family any longer, I'm gonna make these sorry excuses for Americans pay." Jed felt Autumn's reassuring hand on his back.

Gabe patted his black Rock River Arms LAR-15 military-style rifle. "Be sure you relieve the first bad guy you kill of his boomstick—magazines, too. Your long rifles are great for keeping us fed. Fighting a war, not so much."

Jed scratched his beard and stood, the joints in his legs popping as he stepped to the teapot and the plate of trimmed pine needles. "Let's see if today's drink special is as vile as Lona says."

The wooden floor creaked as Ronan excitedly twisted around, holding the radio and its antenna still. "Mom? Dad? Some guy keeps repeating something weird. Where's Kitsap?"

CHAPTER 18

CAMP MURRAY

"*We say again—Naval Base Kitsap is declaring itself neutral in this fight,*" the announcer said in the soulless deadpan style known so well to American Forces Radio listeners. "*We will not participate in any further acts of aggression except to defend ourselves and maintain our cordon of the Kitsap Peninsula—attempts to break through will be met with deadly force. Rest assured that Kitsap's nuclear arsenal, and the non-deployed warheads at Strategic Weapons Facility Pacific, are secured . . .*"

Alicia listened dumbfounded, mouth agape. "What's this mean?" Chief of Staff David Hampton asked no one in particular.

"Ssssh!" Alicia hissed.

"*Our forces from this point forward will only be deployed in self-defense. No words of ours can assuage the pain of the people of Colville, but we would like to say, simply, that we apologize. We were misled.*"

Emergency Management Director Antonio DiBernardi's head rose from a nearby radio terminal. "They're broadcasting in the clear on military and civilian frequencies. Besides Kitsap's local AM station, they somehow pirated KOMO's transmitter on Vashon Island—this is going out all over the place."

The message started repeating.

General Westman strode into the EOC, still buttoning up his camouflage uniform top. "Get Kitsap on the horn right now and punch it up on speakers!" he ordered an aide.

A *chirp* echoed through the concrete edifice, followed a second later by a young woman's cheerful voice. "Good evening! We've been expecting your call. I take it you heard about the change in management?"

"Who the hell is this?" Westman demanded.

"Lieutenant Callie Harman, United States Navy—Strike Fighter Squadron Niner Seven, callsign Amazon. You don't happen to be the dickhead who ordered us to bomb a fairground, are you?" she defiantly asked, smiling in spite of herself. After six weeks of plotting and organizing, she and the *Stennis*'s skipper—with the help of the crew, sympathetic fleet Marines, and a detachment of Navy SEALs who had been training in Puget Sound when the collapse first started—took over Kitsap and relieved Captain Emrickson at gunpoint. Callie had properly avenged her flight leader and the poor souls he was tricked into bombing; telling the people who gave the order to go fuck themselves was the cherry on top of the sundae.

"*Excuse me*, lieutenant?" Westman shot back.

"I'll take that as a 'yes,' then," Callie said. "So, you have a name, or do I just call you 'dickhead'?"

The polo shirt-clad worker bees in the EOC stopped to listen as Callie's insolence echoed throughout the cavernous room. "Is there an adult over there I can talk to, *lieutenant*?" Westman barked, face reddening.

"Affirmative, which is fine by me, because you're boring as hell. Captain!" Callie yelled, her voice fading as she handed off the phone. "Some dickhead from Camp Murray's asking for you!"

"Hello?" an older, tired male voice answered moments later.

"This is Major General Jack Westman, Commander of Forces in Washington. And you are?"

"Captain Gregory Fitzgerald, commanding officer, USS *Stennis*, and I guess Naval Base Kitsap, too, as of today."

"What the hell's going on over there, captain?"

"I should ask you the same question. What in the Sam Hill possessed you and Captain Emrickson to bullshit me and my flight wing into bombing a civilian target for the purpose of assassinating a governor's political rival?"

"If you haven't noticed, captain, we're on our own!" Westman yelled. "The chain of command is gone—we're it! Washington is one of the last bastions of something resembling civilization, and we can't afford to be fighting a civil war!"

"From what they're saying on the radio, it sounds like you officially touched one off," Fitzgerald said. "The lady announcer said at least three hundred men, women, and children died! That doesn't include my pilot, who blew his brains out when he discovered the truth of what he did on your orders. His name was Lieutenant Commander Tanner Sims, and I place responsibility for his death directly at your feet—sir."

Westman paused. "Where's Captain Emrickson?"

"Recovering from the souvenir bullet he caught in the knee from when we relieved him. Piece of advice, general—when a SEAL tells you to get your ass outta your chair, don't refuse."

Alicia leaned over the speakerphone, hands balled into fists. "He saved your families by sealing off Kitsap from the rest of the world, captain!"

"And we'll be forever grateful. That's why he'll be allowed to retire instead of being court-martialed and shot," Fitzgerald said. "Anyway, ma'am, you heard our warning. Stay away. Until legitimate and lawful civilian authority reasserts itself and makes its will known, we're staying out of your little war. We're willing to discuss bartering our fuel reserves for food and other supplies, but be aware we're going to make the very same offer to your enemy. We have highly motivated sailors and Marines—and nukes if you really piss us off. Don't try anything."

"I promise you'll face a firing squad when this is over," Alicia growled.

Fitzgerald laughed. "When this is over?! Best joke I've heard in a while. Good luck, General Westman—both on fighting the insurgency and yanking the governor's hand out of your ass," he said, hanging up before Alicia or Westman could respond. The EOC workers hastily returned to their duties as Westman's aide shut off the speakerphone with another electronic *chirp*.

"Madam Governor, I warned you that trying to eliminate Senator Stevenson was a mistake," Westman said, hands on the conference table. "*Stennis*'s fighter complement would've given us absolute air superiority; we just don't have enough Apache attack helicopters to do the job. But that's not our biggest problem with Kitsap out of the picture. Losing access to Manchester Fuel Depot is really gonna smart unless we secure other sources of POL—petroleum, oil, and lubricants—to replenish our diminishing stocks. I can't be explicit enough—wars have been lost because one side or the other ran out of gas." He turned to DiBernardi. "How's Operation Full Service going?"

DiBernardi was ready for the question. "We have all the pieces in place," he said, setting down a tablet displaying the entirety of Puget Sound, the EOC's lighting shining off his bald head. "Washington State's five refineries before the collapse were capable of processing more than six hundred thousand barrels of petroleum a day. We can't rely on the BP refinery at Cherry Point or the Phillips 66 refinery at Ferndale—they're too far away, and too close to the Canadian border, where we're still dealing with refugees who fled what's left of Vancouver. And as we all know, the US Oil refinery at Tacoma went up in flames and burned down what was left of the city."

"And took one million barrels of refined fuel and its underground pipeline to JBLM with it," Westman groused. Alicia bowed her head, saddened for the umpteenth time by the ecological catastrophe the refinery's destruction had wrought on Puget Sound—huge swaths were choked with millions of gallons of crude. *Damned tree-hugger's shed more tears for the fucking otters than she has for the dead*, Westman thought with a flash of anger.

DiBernardi spread his thumb and forefinger to zoom in on Fidalgo Island at the northernmost edge of Puget Sound, where the Juan de Fuca and Georgia straits split around Vancouver Island. "That leaves us the Shell Oil and Marathon refineries at Anacortes. Both are intact, as are the neighboring towns where most of the refinery employees live. We can scrounge enough people to get the Shell refinery back on line, which at peak capacity would mean one hundred and forty-five thousand barrels a day."

"You wouldn't come close to that," Hampton objected.

"We wouldn't have to—perfect is the enemy of the good," Westman shot back. "We'd be able to refine more than enough to maintain our peacekeeping and humanitarian operations, as well as put down the insurrection in eastern Washington." Hampton opened his mouth as if to respond, but pursed his lips and kept quiet.

"We impounded several dozen full oil tankers when things started falling apart, thanks to the emergency orders the governor signed. Some are already at Anacortes," DiBernardi said. "We'll pay the refinery employees in food and fuel, once the governor gives the OK to go."

"You have it," Alicia consented.

Westman glared at the portly emergency operations chief. "Unleaded only for employees—until further notice, we get every last drop of diesel, and all the JP-8 for our Apaches. We also need to grab every last tanker truck we can find, and shanghai every last driver we can, so we can get the fuel where it needs to go. General Kett," Westman whirled on the state's National Guard commander, "it's your job to continue providing security for our fuel convoys, and to keep I-90 and State Routes 2 and 12 open—especially the Stevens, Snoqualmie, and White passes through the Cascades. With the rail lines through Seattle ripped to shreds—and because one partisan with a stick of dynamite can derail a train anywhere along the line—the roads are all we got." Westman stabbed his finger at the tablet map display. "Those three highways are our lifelines to our forces in the east. If they get cut off, we're done."

Kett accepted his orders with a nod as Alicia grimaced and cleared her sore throat; she was counting down the days until she could leave the EOC and its desert-dry air, and rejoin her family at a home that would serve as a replacement for the governor's mansion, which was smashed along with the rest of Olympia.

"I feel good—and I can't say I've felt that very much since we got here," Alicia told her advisers, her anger over the Kitsap mutiny temporarily subsided. "We'll overcome our fuel setback, and if we clear that hurdle, I have no doubt we can find air support from elsewhere to fill the void those traitors at Kitsap have left." She ran her fingers through her graying hair and told the group to meet again at eight the next morning to discuss food stocks for their soldiers and Washington's refugees.

The yawn that Alicia had kept stifled escaped as she turned to head back to her quarters to catch some sleep. Hampton caught up to her at a trot.

"Can it wait 'till tomorrow, David?" she moaned without stopping her stride.

"More good news—great news, actually," he said with a grin, handing Alicia a small note as she pulled her reading glasses down to her nose. She came to a halt, her eyes going wide.

"Now that's . . . interesting," Alicia said with a grin. "Good catch."

"I thought you'd like that. So, what do we do with them?"

"Bring them here," Alicia said and handed him back the flimsy. "Let's see if they can help us do something about Cascadia's would-be king and queen."

PART TWO

No bastard ever won a war by dying for his country. He won it by making the other poor dumb bastard die for his *country.*

—General George S. Patton

CHAPTER 19

CHENEY

Derek Nealon tallied each gunnysack of staple foods that his crew of workers unloaded from the semi truck backed in the parking lot of Hargreaves Hall.

A reeking man in a stained white foodservice uniform slung the last bag of lentils over his shoulder with a grunt and plodded past Derek down the worn brick path to Tawanka Commons, which had become the feeding point on the Eastern Washington University campus for the refugees who had survived the long winter; dual waves of influenza and diphtheria had swept through their filthy, cramped dormitories to cut them down without mercy. Winter hadn't been much kinder to Cheney's native residents—his friend and neighbor Camila had succumbed to the seasonal flu shortly after the new year. Despite the bad feelings Derek harbored for the "city people" and the problems they had caused the town, his heart ached for them—especially the children, many of whom were now orphaned.

The end of Derek's work day was one signature away—once he signed off on the food shipment, he would grab a plate of rice and beans and get home just in time to catch Alexandra Chase's radio show to keep up with a world that was exploding with change with the spring thaw. Oklahoma and Arkansas had seceded, and banded together with the Lone Star State to create the Texas Federation. Kansas, Nebraska, and the Dakotas also had quit the Union over the long winter. Idaho was in talks with neighboring states, including fledgling Cascadia—which pissed off Olympia to no end—to form some sort of alliance. Cascadia's ongoing fight had inspired similar insurrections; eastern Oregon, now calling itself Pacifica, was fighting a low-intensity civil war against western Oregon, which was now ruled from Eugene following the destruction of Portland and the state capital of Salem. The northern counties of California made their century-old pipe dream of partition a reality and formally split to form the State of Jefferson. And in Montana, an active resistance had risen against the Big Tech billionaire who cajoled or outright forced the surviving Legislature to crown him governor.

The soldier in charge of the food convoy beckoned to Derek for his signature; Derek only knew Sergeant First Class McGreavy's last name, and only because it was sewn to his helmet cover and his MOLLE vest. McGreavy and his soldiers would bed down by their vehicles and leave the following morning, like they always did—bandits and the resistance ruled the roads at night.

McGreavy handed Derek a clipboard and pulled out a pouch of shag and some rolling papers to have himself a smoke. "Shoot, you need something to sign this with, don'cha? I got a pen here somewhere," the sergeant said, handing Derek his box of rolling papers so he could search his pockets. Derek's heart began to pound with the code phrase informing him that McGreavy had a message to pass on to the resistance. *So much for a quiet evening of old-timey radio*, Derek thought; he'd have to spend the evening encoding the message to leave at the drop site so his friend in town could transmit it to the Cascadian Army or whatever the hell the people fighting back were calling themselves.

Derek clandestinely peeked at the message scribbled on the rolling paper in the palm-sized cardboard box. The blood drained from his face as he quickly memorized the terse report, fighting the urge to bug out his eyes like a character in a Tex Avery cartoon.

McGreavy handed Derek a ball-point pen and began sprinkling the note with tobacco. "Got what'cha need, chief?"

Derek nodded as he nervously signed for the food. "You know, I think I'll go home and rest. I'm not that hungry," he lied—he was famished. He nodded at the cigarette between McGreavy's lips as the sergeant whipped out a Zippo and lit it with a flourish. "Those things'll kill you, you know."

"Oh, I'll be dead of lead poisoning long before I get lung cancer—you can bet on that," McGreavy said and took a long drag, the cherry burning away the evidence of his act of treason.

Derek strolled past a four-man team of soldiers guarding the parked convoy and headed for home. It took all his cool to keep from running.

CHAPTER 20

CHEWELAH

"Ten minutes late—very sloppy, boys," Demetrius quietly chided the midnight changing of the guard at the checkpoint blocking off Chewelah's sole road winding east into the Selkirk Mountains and Colville National Forest. The next-generation night vision binoculars mounted to his helmet gave him a crisp, white picture that was a marked improvement from the fuzzy, cathode-ray green of models past.

Demetrius raised the goggles with a *click* and slowly crawled back to Pioneer Cemetery to rejoin his growing army. The lonely graveyard just outside city limits offered a commanding view of the roadblock and a former senior living facility where the occupying garrison was billeted—the H7N9 flu had killed every last pre-collapse resident. He re-entered the perimeter and made a beeline for a red granite headstone, where a camouflage rain poncho on the ground with four legs sticking out from underneath concealed the dim glow of a red-lens flashlight. The flashlight winked off and the poncho flipped up to reveal a sixteen-year-old boy updating Sean on the garrison's locations and movements.

Sean and Demetrius had spent a month wargaming how to liberate Chewelah with the assets they had. Sean had been the voice of restraint, warning they would be outnumbered almost two to one by the company-sized garrison, while Demetrius strongly favored attack, gambling that the town's occupiers were ill-equipped and dispirited. In the end, their battle plan won Sean over—if executed quickly and violently, the bulk of the enemy forces would be killed or pinned down in the opening minutes of the fight.

"Max here says the enemy's disposition hasn't changed," Sean told Demetrius as he pocketed his map of Chewelah. "They still got their north-south roadblocks on US 395, an' their two smaller ones on the east and west roads leading out. They have a twenty-four-hour presence at the hospital, the Safeway, and the Hico gas station on the south side that serves as their fuel point."

"They do a walkin' patrol in town several times a day," Max whispered hoarsely over the graveyard's oppressive silence. "A dozen guys—two groups of four with the leader and a machine-gun team in the middle. They change up their times and routes."

Demetrius mussed the boy's scraggly, sandy hair as Rebecca and Carleigh, dressed in spare fatigues, appeared out of the darkness. "Great work, son. Come sunrise, we're gonna kick these bastards out and give you your town back. I'm afraid you'll have to stay with us tonight, though—we can't risk you getting caught past curfew with our plans rattling around in your head."

Max sat and leaned back on the headstone. "It don't matter. Mom and Dad died of the flu, and they drafted my older brother and hauled him away. I got nothin' in town left to go back to."

"Get some rest, hon. You still have a big part to play," Rebecca sweetly whispered to Max and draped a military surplus wool blanket over him.

She stared into the faces of her two combat leaders in the dim starlight of the new moon. "We still on, gentlemen?"

Demetrius nodded. "At first light, our lone Javelin will take out their lone Stryker fighting vehicle parked in front of their barracks. Then we attack in force with three blended teams of regular Army and irregulars—Alpha, Bravo, Charlie—with Chewelah natives acting as guides."

"And if the Javelin misses?"

Sean pointed east toward Chewelah Mountain and its shuttered ski resort. "Then we turn back that-a-way and run like hell, and you and Carleigh stick to Miguel like glue. I'll say it again, Mama Bear—I don't think your being here is the smartest idea."

"I will not sit in the rear while people fight and die on my behalf. This is where I belong," Rebecca said flatly.

Demetrius grabbed his own map and beckoned the trio underneath Sean's poncho to prevent his red-lens flashlight from giving away their position. His finger fell on Chewelah Municipal Airport two miles north of town—the airport and its surrounding golf club community had become a rich old man's boneyard.

"There's still the issue of those three Black Hawks that arrived a couple days ago," Demetrius said. "Recon says those 'copters and their dismounts have just been sitting on the tarmac."

"I'm thinking they're just passing through—that runway's so run down that it's practically worthless and not even worth holding. They would've arrived in force if they meant to reinforce town, and recon says they don't have door-mounted guns for close-air support, so I'm not worried about 'em getting in the way of what we're about to do," Sean said. "Besides, we've got insurance in the event they start causin' trouble."

"Agreed." Demetrius looked at Rebecca, her face like theirs smeared with light and dark green. "You look good in camouflage paint."

"Thanks. First time I've worn makeup since the collapse," she joked.

He turned to Carleigh, her face similarly painted. "And how're you?"

"Nervous," Carleigh fidgeted. "And I don't think your soldiers like me very much." Rebecca barely managed to stifle a laugh; what Carleigh didn't know was that Demetrius had warned every young man in the outfit that he would personally geld anyone who tried to get fresh with the senator's daughter. His reputation as a grade-A badass—further cemented by the rumor mill embellishing his escape from the Yakima jail into an orgy of blood and explosions straight out of a Jerry Bruckheimer film—made for a comically wide berth around Carleigh at any given time.

"They like you just fine," Demetrius said with a smirk before snapping off the flashlight and throwing off the poncho, the cool night air instantly replacing its stuffy warmth. "In a few hours, we slit throats and hoist the black flag. You two might wanna get some sleep."

Rebecca bit off a disbelieving laugh. "Are you kidding?"

"It's easy if you try," Demetrius said before he and Sean weaved between the headstones into the darkness.

"I think he likes you, Mom," Carleigh mischievously ribbed the moment the duo were out of earshot. "'You look good in camouflage paint'?"

"Don't be ridiculous," Rebecca answered back a touch too fast. "You know, Demetrius—Captain Mathers—has a point. You should try to sleep, hon."

"Are you kidding?"

Demetrius found Tom and Allie sound asleep next to their Stryker, curled up together under Tom's poncho liner. He wrapped himself in his own trusty "woobie"—by far any Army infantryman's most beloved piece of gear—and stared at the starry moonless sky. *Are you a planet?* he tiredly asked a bright point of light overhead. *No, planets don't twinkle—that's Deneb*, he realized, and quickly found Vega and Altair right where they were supposed to be, the stargazing bringing back a pleasant memory of his late father showing him around the night sky during one of their innumerable camping trips. *What did he call those three stars? The Great . . . no, the Summer Triangle.* He grinned as he drifted off to sleep on a bed of grass and pine needles—the cold war that had set in with the long winter was about to burn red hot, and he would be the one striking the match.

CHAPTER 21

CHENEY

*B*am *bam bam.*

Derek pounded on his contact's weathered and peeling white door, nervously scanning for prying eyes down the trash-strewn street and its wild, ratty lawns.

Bam bam bam.

"Ty! Open up, man! It's me!" Derek hissed, squinting into the sunset that heralded the start of the nightly curfew.

The unmistakable *cha-chunk* of a pump-action shotgun being racked—a sound that had made ne'er-do-wells and unwanted guests shit their pants since time immemorial—sounded from behind the door. Derek breathed a sigh of relief a second later with the metallic clicks and clacks of the deadbolt and chain locks coming undone.

An older black man with graying hair grabbed Derek's arm with his free hand and yanked him inside. "Are you fuckin' crazy, comin' to my house?" Tyrone Davis growled and shut the door. "What's so goddamn important that you can't leave it at the drop?!" Derek marched to a notepad and pen on Ty's kitchen table and scribbled furiously as Ty leaned his twelve-gauge against the wall to hastily lock his door. "Answer me, man! Why you riskin' our asses like this?"

Derek thrust the message in Ty's face, letting it answer for him. "Aw, shit," Ty said, jaw dropping.

"Tomorrow's too late. This has gotta go out right now."

"Yeah . . . yeah, I gotcha," Ty stammered, shoving a small Phillips-head screwdriver from the kitchen junk drawer into his overalls and dragging his kitchen step stool into a hallway plastered with photos of family, friends, and his many ports of call from thirty years in the Navy. He stepped up to loosen one of the screws holding up the hall vent screen—careful not to brush off the caked lint and dust he intentionally left on it—and reached into the air duct to retrieve a one-time pad.

Ty shambled back to the kitchen table with the pad and a notebook, scooting in his chair with a squeal of its rubber feet across the yellowed linoleum. "It's gonna take a bit for me to encode this, so how's about you stay outta my hair?" he told Derek. "We'll wait 'till after dark to transmit so's we don't tip off the neighbors."

Derek plopped on the living room couch and thumbed through a well-worn issue of *The New York Times* on the coffee table. Many of its stories were dedicated to the then-ongoing collapse of the American economy as the day of reckoning from decades of overpromising, over-borrowing, and overspending finally arrived. Others chronicled the first reports making it out of China about the deadly new strain of H7N9 flu—which a Johns Hopkins virologist interviewed for one story said could "make the COVID-19 pandemic look like a case of the sniffles." Derek wondered if the issue happened to be the last issue the *Times* ever published.

It took Ty thirty minutes to encrypt the message. The rise of Redoubt Radio and the Cascadia resistance movement had prompted the authorities in Cheney to confiscate all ham radios "as a temporary measure," and the huge Yagi-Uda antenna in Ty's backyard made his house one of their first stops—but Ty, like many ham enthusiasts, had a Plan B. Ty stepped into his musty one-car garage, illuminated by a bare dangling light bulb. He shifted some exposed fiberglass insulation by his corner workbench to reveal the hidden compartment he had built to hide his stash before Washington legalized marijuana, but now hid a palm-sized, battery-operated Morse code transceiver and a small dipole antenna. Returning to his kitchen, Ty opened his junk drawer and grabbed a bright orange iambic Morse code transmitter key; the idiot soldiers who had confiscated his ham rig mistook it for a potato chip bag clip, and Ty had kept it there ever since for good luck.

Ten minutes later, Ty was expertly squeezing away on the key, broadcasting the coded string of random letters from the portable antenna he had set up in the backyard under cover of darkness. Derek paced behind him, running his hands through the thinning hair he had allowed to grow back—Cheney's head lice problem had ended with the refugee die-off.

"They get it?" Derek anxiously asked the moment Ty pulled the black listening bud out of his left ear.

"Yup—said they'll pass it along pronto," Ty answered, unplugging the Morse key from the transceiver. He tore the sheet off the one-time pad and lit it aflame over the kitchen sink, along with Derek's note and the paper on which he encoded the message. "At least these assholes are keepin' the water flowin' and the lights burnin'," Ty said as he washed the ashes down the drain. "Now, please, if you'd be so kind, get the fuck outta my house."

"Listen, I'm sorry about puttin' you at risk, but this was important," Derek said. "I really appreciate this, and I'm sure she will, too."

"Risk ain't the right word," Ty seethed and waved the one-time pad in Derek's face, the smell of burned paper and his repulsive breath assaulting Derek's nose. "This is the third pad I've gotten since I started passin' on your snippets about what unit patches you see on campus, when convoys come and go, and which goddamn private is bitchin' in the chow line about gettin' the clap. That means the previous two codebooks were compr'mised." Ty poked Derek's sternum hard. "And 'compr'mised' means someone like me got caught on account o' someone like you, and sang like a canary while they cracked his motherfuckin' nuts open with a hammer."

Ty killed the lights and quietly slid open the glass door. "Sneak out the back over the fence. You get caught out after curfew, it's *yo'* ass, not mine! You keep yo' mouth shut about me!"

CHAPTER 22

CHEWELAH

Even with her elbows firmly planted in the dirt, Rebecca's shaking hands could barely keep the enemy Stryker parked at the former senior home in her binoculars' field of view in the sepia of morning twilight.

"Any second now, *Mamá Oso,*" Miguel muttered from behind an adjacent pine tree, his eyes on the target and his finger on the transmit button of his black radio handset.

As if on cue, a loud *pow* from the field just outside the cemetery heralded their lone FGM-148 Javelin leaving its launch tube, followed by a *whoosh* as it streaked west on a white-hot jet of rocket propellant, eagerly seeking the prey imaged into its microchipped brain like a police dog unleashed to bring down a criminal. The missile found its mark a second later with an explosion that wrecked the infantry fighting vehicle and peppered the nearby barracks with hot shrapnel.

"Holy shit!" Carleigh screamed as pieces of the Stryker rained down around the rising fireball; Rebecca reflexively pulled her daughter in tight when the deafening *ka-boom* reached them two seconds later.

"All stations, all stations—time to make the doughnuts! I say again, time to make the doughnuts! Go, go, go!" Miguel yelled into his radio, hoping that the shrapnel had taken out some of the billeted soldiers.

A loud *buzz* tore inches above Miguel's head as Max's drone flew straight toward town. "One step ahead of me, boy!" Miguel yelled to the young man with a thumbs-up. "Lemme know the moment you get eyes on that roving patrol!"

"You got it!" Max shouted with barely restrained glee as he eased the drone into a smooth ascent; Chewelah's occupiers had banned drone flights, and the young man savored the opportunity to deal out some payback with his proscribed hobby.

Rebecca anxiously shifted her binoculars to the small manned checkpoint guarding the east road into town barely a mile away; the soldiers had ducked behind their concrete barriers the moment the Javelin rocketed overhead.

"Demetrius and Sean—Team Charlie—just crossed Phase Line Rubicon," Miguel said for Rebecca's and Carleigh's benefit. "They'll hit in five, four, three, two . . ."

The rhythmic *thunk thunk thunk* of a Mark 19 automatic grenade launcher—its rounded shells arcing through the air slow enough to be seen in flight—was followed by explosions as the 40-millimeter high-explosive munitions ripped the checkpoint's soldiers and their nearby Humvee apart. Rebecca's pulse raced the moment Demetrius came into view, swaying behind his cupola-mounted grenade launcher as the Humvee driven by Tom and Allie swerved off-road around the roadblock's concrete construction barriers. A second later, the trailing Stryker commanded by Sean came into view, cutting loose with a burst from its unmanned, roof-mounted M2 Browning .50-caliber machine gun at a more distant target. Both vehicles disappeared into the black smoke billowing from the burning Humvee, the chattering of their weapons fading into the distance.

Rebecca closed her eyes and mouthed a prayer for their fledgling army and the people of Chewelah caught up in the battle. *Stay safe, Captain Mathers*, she said to herself. *I'd miss you terribly if you didn't come back.*

CHAPTER 23

T he crosshairs of Jed's rifle scope bobbed with his pounding heart on the young soldier he was ordered to kill.

Jed had had hours to stew in his anxieties as he and the rest of Team Alpha laid prone in dark, cold, and wet silence along a tree-lined creek cut, three hundred meters west of the Route 395 roadblock at the southern edge of Chewelah. Team Alpha had crawled to the edge of the cut with the rising sun to exploit the fact that the sophisticated thermal imaging systems of the Stryker blocking both lanes of the road were least effective at sunrise and sunset. Grant, the team's leader, had wagered that the squad of soldiers manning the roadblock would be watching south for incoming threats, rather than back their way into town.

The target the Special Forces medic had assigned Jed was leaning against the side of the eight-wheeled vehicle, which was topped by a menacing 30-millimeter turret cannon—*a Stryker Dragoon*, Jed remembered from their mission briefing. If Team Alpha lost the element of surprise, Grant warned them, the cannon would cut them to ribbons before they knew what hit them.

A wave of nausea washed over Jed—the rank smell of overloaded septic tanks and trash from the rickety prefab homes behind them didn't help. *Lord, he's young enough to be Mikey and Beth's big brother*, Jed thought, shifting his weight to steady the aim of his Remington 783

.308-caliber hunting rifle on the young man's chest. *I lost my kids, and here I am, about to send this kid back to his mom and dad in a pine box.*

"Any second now, but keep your safeties on and fingers off the trigger!" an Army sergeant whispered behind him, Autumn, and Gabe. "Wait until the machine gun opens up, then let 'er rip and get ready to mow through!" The sergeant's boots sloshed in the bubbling creek as he crept down the line to repeat the message.

Jed scanned the surroundings of the young man who had no idea he was about to die. The growing trickle of morning light over the mountains revealed a small clump of weathered and wind-bent crosses on the far roadside—the makeshift memorial marking the spot where the National Guard had slaughtered his fellow towns-people the previous fall.

That's how you justify this, Jed said to himself. *An eye for an eye . . .*

Jed went rigid with the roaring *whoosh* of the Javelin in the distance. The soldiers spun toward the noise in disbelief before scrambling behind their concrete partitions with the explosion announcing the destruction of the Stryker at their repurposed barracks half a kilometer away. Jed nervously thumbed off his safety as the squad leader standing in the Stryker's command hatch crumpled with the *boom* of Cade's sniper rifle, his head exploding in a spray of pink mist.

The M240B machine gun to Jed's left opened up with an ear-splitting roar, cutting a bloody swath down the line of cowering soldiers. It took all of Jed's will to pull the trigger, but his shot went high and right, piercing the young soldier's left shoulder and splattering the concrete slab behind him with blood. The boy seemed to look straight at Jed, eyes large as saucers and mouth agape in horror, as he clutched the wound and slid to the ground, leaving a streak of gore.

"I'm sorry!" Jed screamed, furiously yanking back his bolt handle to chamber another round over the ambush's deafening fusillade. He struggled to line up a shot to end the boy's suffering, but jerked the trigger, causing the bullet to go wild and ricochet off the concrete. He quickly chambered the third round from his four-round steel magazine and settled his sights on the writhing soldier's screaming face, but missed again. Autumn's hunting rifle barked to Jed's left, and the boy's forehead below the brim of his helmet flew apart.

"It's OK, Jed! It's OK!" Autumn yelled, chambering another round.

The machine gun fell silent. "Cease fire!" Grant hollered as a formality to a firing line that had run out of targets. "Watch for movement! Johnson! Hernandez! Get those AT-4s ready in case we need to knock out the Stryker!"

Jed fumbled a fresh four-round magazine from his hunting vest and slid it into his rifle with shaking hands. A young buck sergeant lying prone to Jed's right whipped his rifle around to his back and grabbed the sling of the one-shot AT-4 anti-tank rocket tube lying next to him. The Stryker, streaked with the blood of the squad leader and driver slain in its hatches, remained motionless, as did the fallen soldiers around it.

Grant leaped to his feet. "We got 'em! Let's move!" he hollered, the need for noise discipline gone. "Assault across, and don't stop 'til we clear the objective!" Grant blew a long note from the black plastic whistle tied to his MOLLE vest, and Team Alpha rose as one to charge on line across the rutted field. A plume of black smoke from the Stryker demolished by the Javelin missile rose in the distance over the silhouettes of trees and shuttered businesses, growing thicker against the morning light to the chatter of small arms as Team Bravo poured suppressing fire into the garrison's damaged barracks.

Jed struggled to keep pace, his imposing bulk slowing him down. He reached deep to press on, huffing and puffing as Autumn, Gabe, and the soldier with the AT-4 started peeling away.

"Catch up, old timer!" Gabe hollered over his shoulder.

JOINT BASE LEWIS-McCHORD

Second Lieutenant Lorena Torres fidgeted by the Operations Building at Gray Army Airfield as she waited to perform the unenviable duty of giving General Jack Westman shitty news.

A light drizzle—a miserable accompaniment to western Washington's near-constant cloud cover—shrouded the rising sun and Mount Rainier towering on the southeast horizon across the airfield's runway. The general's driver stomped her feet to ward off the morning chill, cursing her rotten luck; Torres had managed to snag a full ten minutes of sleep slumped on the steering wheel of their hard-shell Humvee before its boxy SINCGARS radio transceiver squawked its rude awakening from the EOC at Camp Murray.

The airfield swarmed with troops who had flown in two days prior. All four of its "ramps"—huge parking lots for military aviation—were packed shoulder to shoulder with UH-60 Black Hawk and CH-47 Chinook transport helicopters, their tail markings revealing they were cobbled together from all over the western US. Large canvas tents filled the open grassy spaces on both sides of the runway, which had been appropriated on the dreary morning by thousands of exercising soldiers, their rhythmic counting of repetitions and bellowing of running cadences echoing across the airfield's vast openness.

To Westman's dismay, the soldiers were just passing through, and the general had come that morning in a last-ditch effort to get some of them reassigned to help quell Washington's growing rebellion. The units were on orders from some deputy under-secretary of defense claiming to be next in line for the presidency, Westman had let slip to Torres during the drive—one of at least three surviving Cabinet officials who were jockeying for the office.

Torres snapped to attention as Westman's angry voice boomed from around the corner of the ops building. "Pissants!" he thundered, storming into sight with Chief of Staff David Hampton in tow. "We've got a goddamn insurrection on our hands, and this stupid fucking asshole is sending perfectly good soldiers to reinforce *Montana*?! There's nothing fucking there!"

"Sir!" Torres barked, eyes locked forward, cold mist beading on her glasses.

Westman stopped and eyeballed the young lieutenant. "Do I want to know?"

"The garrison at Chewelah is being attacked in force," Torres reported like a cadet on her first day of Officer Candidate School. "They have at least one Stryker, so it's likely the resistance and not bandits. General Kett ordered their commander to hold in place, but hasn't been able to raise them again, sir." She steeled herself for an explosive outburst that didn't come—Westman wordlessly strode to the Humvee, leaving a surprised Torres to jump behind the wheel. The general grabbed the black plastic SINCGARS handset as Torres pulled onto the access road to hook around the airfield and back to Camp Murray across I-5.

"This can work in our favor if our asset makes it in—but what about Operation Jackal . . ." Hampton interjected from the back seat before Westman cut him off so he could holler at Kett on the other end of the line.

"They just have to hold—we have no reinforcements out that way!" Westman shouted. "And order the Operation Jackal team from Chewelah Airport back to Fairchild. Their mission's still on for tonight—intel says the HVT may be leaving soon, and we may not get another shot. Get your people working on an updated flight plan! Out." The general glared at Torres and jabbed his hand straight ahead with a five-fingered military point. "Floor it, lieutenant."

Two poncho-clad sentries snapped their rifles vertical in salute as the Humvee breezed through their checkpoint. Lieutenant Torres fought the urge to nod off behind the wheel to the rhythmic, hypnotic clicking of the windshield wipers.

CHAPTER 24

CHEWELAH

Demetrius rocked back and forth in his cupola's restraint webbing, tightly gripping the dual aiming handles of his Mark 19 grenade launcher as Allie drove their armored Humvee across an open field leading to the senior apartments turned barracks.

He thumbed the trigger and lobbed a dozen high-explosive grenades the moment the complex came into view past a small cul-de-sac of homes, adding to the steady stream of suppressing fire coming from Team Bravo, which had taken position in a tree farm one hundred meters to the south. The grenades struck in quick succession, ripping the run-down apartments open on balls of flame. A gaggle of soldiers taking cover from Team Bravo's fire had just enough time to realize they were being flanked before Sean's Stryker-mounted machine gun cut them down.

Allie slowed to a halt as Sean's driver wheeled the Stryker in front to shield the Humvee from return fire that never came. Demetrius grabbed his radio and punched the preset for Team Bravo's frequency, reflexively wincing with the *boom* of the burning enemy Stryker's ammunition cooking off.

"You got this, over?" Demetrius asked Team Bravo's leader.

"Roger that—you can continue mission," the former Army lieutenant radioed back. "But give us one more vulgar display of power on the way out just to be safe, if you'd be so kind."

A wicked grin crossed Demetrius's face as he ordered Allie and Sean to their next objective—the gas station that Chewelah's garrison had commandeered as a fuel point. The two vehicles tore northwest, their wheels kicking up huge clumps of weeds and topsoil as they both let loose into the flaming ruins of the apartment buildings before Team Bravo's men and women began advancing by fire teams to give whatever survivors they found one chance to surrender or die.

The Humvee returned to the road with a jolt that slammed its three occupants around like ping-pong balls in a lottery machine. "Well, this is definitely Lower Wacker Drive!" Allie yelled as she straightened the Humvee with a squeal of its tires over the chatter of gunfire. "If my estimations are correct, we should be very close to The Honorable Richard J. Daley Plaza!"

Tom shot her a confused glance. "That's in Chicago! What the hell are you talking about?"

"That's where they got that Picasso!" Demetrius hollered down from the cupola.

"Yes, sir!" Allie barked with a nervous laugh.

***

The soldier lying next to his empty Javelin launcher whooped as Demetrius's volley of grenades tore into what was left of the apartments, the *whump whump whump* of the explosions following at the speed of sound several seconds later. The stink of rocket propellant and burned weeds from the Javelin's backblast still hung in the air.

"How're we doing?" Rebecca asked Miguel. Carleigh sat next to her mother in silence, transfixed by the sights and sounds of battle.

"Muy bien," he answered without looking, headset pressed into his ear. Team Bravo was advancing on the demolished barracks. Team Charlie was advancing on the gas station, where they would link up with Grant and Team Alpha, which had overwhelmed the southern roadblock and claimed its Stryker Dragoon as a spoil of war. In a matter of minutes, the partisan force had pinned down or destroyed the bulk of the occupying garrison.

"I got the roving patrol!" Max hollered, shoving the glowing LCD screen of his drone controls in front of Miguel. "Looks like they're takin' fire from neighbors with the guns we ain't supposed to have!" He stabbed his finger at a dilapidated house with a red car as the soldiers bolted inside to take cover.

"Good job, buddy! Show me exactly where," Miguel said, thrusting his laminated map of Chewelah in front of the teenager, who pointed to a residential block on the northwest side of town.

Footfalls in the dry weeds behind them heralded the runner from the incident command truck the resistance had "liberated" over the winter from the Pend Oreille County Emergency Management Agency, its white façade sloppily camouflaged with a slapdash paint job of olive drab and black. A scrawny teenage boy, swimming in a camouflage top two sizes too big, handed Miguel a note from the radio operator and pushed a mop of sweaty black hair out of his face. "This came in from Redoubt Radio—FLASH priority, whatever that means. Ed over there says it explains why those copters are sittin' at the airport."

The hint of good humor Miguel had allowed himself to feel with the battle's progress drained away. "It sure as hell does," he growled to the confused boy and keyed his mike.

***

Sean ordered his driver to slow to a crawl as they reached the dirt path leading to the back of the Hico gas station. He swiveled the Stryker's machine gun turret with a flick of a squat black joystick and laid the red crosshair on his commander's situational display screen just past the station to watch for the enemy Humvee that Max warned would be guarding it. Sean's tactical situation forced him into a dangerous choice of slow caution instead of speedy violence of action, given that reckless .50-caliber machine gun fire and large quantities of gasoline are not an optimal combination.

The enemy Humvee rolled into view a second later, its machine gunner firing back they way they came on Route 395 at some unseen target while two panicked soldiers flung the rear passenger side door open and tried to scramble inside. Before Sean could engage, the Humvee erupted in a shower of sparks and flame with the muffled *pum-pum-pum* of a vehicle-mounted cannon that echoed through the Stryker's armor. Sean pulled the joystick trigger, catching what was left of the Humvee and its occupants in a crossfire.

"Move on up—the Stryker that's gonna be comin' up on our left is a friendly!" Sean ordered the driver before turning to the nine-man squad crammed into the armored personnel carrier's bay. "Get ready to move! And remember—you get trigger happy around a bunch of gas, and the last thing you'll ever see is gonna be your own flaming nutsack flyin' past your face! You read me?"

"We read you, sir!" they barked in unison.

Sean's driver closed the gap, clearing the Hico station to find a Stryker Dragoon idling on the highway facing north; its new owners had hastily spray-painted black chevrons on its sides and tied a Cascadia flag tied to its left rear antenna to prevent the newest addition to the rebel nation's motor pool from drawing friendly fire. Sean popped the commander's hatch to find Grant standing in his, the hot Bushmaster cannon that had just Swiss-cheesed the Humvee with high-explosive rounds rotated a safe distance from his head.

"Great fucking day to be in the infantry!" Grant hollered as Sean's squad charged down the Stryker's lowered ramp to clear and occupy the gas station.

Demetrius lurched forward as his Humvee skidded to a halt in the gravel seconds later. "Nice set of wheels, Osprey!" he yelled to Grant.

"You'd be amazed at the deals you can find at the Fort Lewis lemon lot!" he retorted.

Allie released her painfully tight grip on the Humvee's steering wheel and tried to work out the stiffness in her hands. She took a deep breath and watched the dismounted squad stack at the gas station's shattered glass door to make entry to sweep for any surviving or cowering enemies.

"You're doing great, soldier," Tom said from the passenger seat, his M5 rifle strapped across his chest. "You wanna switch?"

"Not on your fucking life," she said, wiping her brow under her helmet—the duo had long ago discarded military courtesies with one another. "Our next objective's the Safeway, right?"

Tom pointed north out his window. "Roger that—about a mile up the main drag, smack in the middle of town." From the cupola above, Miguel's agitated and garbled voice echoing from the radio stopped Demetrius's banter with Sean and Grant cold. "They, uh, got a squad guardin' what little food the townspeople have—hopefully they'll surrender once they see two Strykers bearing down on 'em, provided they haven't bugged out already." He slugged Allie's right bicep. "We just may live to see tomorrow."

"Shit!" Demetrius hollered, slamming his hand on the roof hard enough to see stars from the pain.

"You had to hex it, didn't you?" Allie chastised Tom with a grimace as Sean's Stryker wheeled around the burning Humvee and headed toward downtown. "What's goin' on, sir?" she yelled over her shoulder.

"Monahan, get on Sean's ass and stay there! Don't stop for anything!" Demetrius bellowed. Allie floored the accelerator, spraying gravel behind them; Tom caught a brief glimpse of a blackened and twisted figure that had once been a human being roasting in the driver's seat of the engulfed Humvee before the heat forced him to look away.

Demetrius ducked down into the cupola. "You two pay attention in that class a few weeks ago on how to fire a Stinger?"

Tom twisted around and glanced by Demetrius's feet at the two six-foot-long olive-drab cases that each contained a handheld surface-to-air missile launcher. "Yes, sir! Why?"

Demetrius swore as Allie hit a large pothole in the dilapidated road. "Those Black Hawks at the airport are here to slip into Idaho tonight to kill that Redoubt Radio lady with the sexy voice!" he yelled, relaying the vital intelligence that had started as a scribble on a cigarette rolling paper in the college town of Cheney. "I hope you both were a 'go' at the Stinger station, 'cause she dies if you eff this up!"

"No pressure!" Allie exclaimed and swerved around another pothole, silently wondering how she could feel both terrified and exhilarated at the same time.

CHAPTER 25

eam Alpha reflexively ducked and cursed with the *ping* of the bullet ricocheting off the armor of their cramped and sweltering Stryker Dragoon.

"We're the good guys, you dumbasses!" Gabe berated the faceless Chewelah local who had taken a potshot at their liberated armored personnel carrier. "We're flyin' a Cascadia flag, for God's sake!"

The Stryker turned hard left, sliding team members into one another as the driver sped toward the barricaded foot patrol that the team—a mix of Army infantrymen and civilians—had been ordered to destroy. Jed squirmed in the tight quarters next to the driver and commander seats, his bulk a serious disadvantage in a vehicle designed with negligible concern for comfort; he was the largest man in the twelve-person squad, and the Stryker was built to carry nine. Sweat ran down his face in rivers as he fought a queasiness compounded every second by claustrophobia, heat, and terror. *Don't puke, asshole,* Jed commanded himself, staring at the Strkyer's closed ramp as if to force it open by sheer mental will. *Let's get there already and get out of this cracker tin! Come on, come on!*

Cade turned from the commander's seat display screen and held up a finger to Grant, who squatted by the ramp between the two packed rows of inward-facing seats. "One minute!" Grant yelled over the Stryker's diesel engine. "Follow me and haul ass once the ramp drops! Five meters between each of you, just like we practiced—don't bunch up! And stay sharp—last thing we wanna do is accidentally shoot civilians!"

The driver slammed on the brakes, violently sliding the sardine-packed team forward before the ramp dropped, filling their cramped quarters with blinding natural light. Jed scooted along the black cushions as Team Alpha exited and, with a guttural scream, sprinted headlong into the unknown.

***

"Hang on, sir!" Allie yelled to Demetrius, veering off Route 395 onto the country road leading to the airport. She floored the accelerator to catch up with Sean's leading Stryker just as Miguel relayed a report that the Black Hawks were starting up and that the strike team assembled to kill Alexandra Chase was hurriedly boarding.

Through the dust kicked up by the Stryker's gigantic wheels, Demetrius eyed a small patch of woods to their left just past a bend in the road. "Hawk, we're outta time!" he radioed Sean with a cough. "The farm field just past the trees! We'll set up there! Ten bucks says they're slinkin' back to Fairchild—they'll fly right by us!"

He grasped the cupola's rim for dear life as Allie nosed the Humvee into the fallow field and slid to a halt next to the Stryker with a whine of brakes in the loose dirt. Allie and Tom raced to the Humvee's rear hatch and yanked out the heavy Stinger cases, wrestling with the clasps holding them shut as as Demetrius hastily unbuckled himself from his safety harness. Tom yanked the six-foot-long FIM-92J Stinger missile from the foam-padded case onto his shoulder and seated the cylindrical battery coolant unit into its well with a twist, praying it still held its charge and hadn't seeped away the liquid argon needed to cool the missile's infrared seeker warhead before launch.

Demetrius hopped down from the Humvee and grabbed his olive-drab Steiner binoculars. The chop of helicopter blades began to rise from the north.

CHAPTER 26

Cade kept his crosshairs motionless on the cinderblock wall along the side yard of the house where the roving enemy patrol had taken up a hasty defense. A bright muzzle flash flared from the wall's edge, giving away the position of the machine gun that had Team Alpha pinned down.

He fine-tuned the windage and elevation knobs on the telescopic sight mounted to his M107 sniper rifle from the roof of a church three blocks away. "Eagle, I got two wounded!" Grant's voice howled from the bud in Cade's ear as he made his adjustments. "I know you can't rush art—" he managed before he was cut off by another burst, "—but we could use your magic touch, like right fucking now, over!"

Cade settled his aim on the cinderblock he guessed would give him the best chance of killing the entire three-man crew—the machine gunner, assistant gunner, and ammunition bearer—with one of his few specialty rounds for eliminating a target behind a thick barrier. He waited ten seconds, tuning out the world around him, and squeezed the trigger, kicking up a huge puff of dust from the monster weapon.

The Raufoss Mark 211 .50-caliber round struck true. Its tungsten steel penetrator punched through the wall and eviscerated the machine gunner, and its high-explosive component burst through a millisecond later with a white-hot spray of shrapnel that shredded the rest of his gun crew. Through his scope, Cade saw a perfect black hole punch through the cinderblock, instantaneously followed by a shower of sparks and a huge splat of blood on the side of the house.

He caught motion and traversed to find a helmeted soldier peeking around the back corner of the house staring, bug-eyed, at the carnage. The young man barely managed to mouth a curse before Cade's next shot disintegrated his head. He high-crawled to the rear lip of the church roof to get back to the relative safety of the Stryker, silently beratinging himself for having pressed his luck with a second shot as haphazard return fire zipped overhead.

***

Allie turned to notice Tom struggling to unfold the Stinger's boxy, side-mounted cage antenna for identifying friendly aircraft. "You can skip that step, sergeant! You don't need to ping those copters! They're ours, but we're gonna shoot 'em down anyway!" she yelled as she ripped off her tube cover and raised the sight flap.

"You heard her, Sergeant Ngo—get your ass in gear!" Demetrius hollered, scanning the low horizon with his binoculars. "Uncle Sam designed Stingers so an illiterate Afghan goatherd could shoot down a MiG, so you don't have an excuse . . . *targets*! I got targets! Black Hawks, eleven o'clock, skimmin' the treeline! You kids got 'em?"

Allie lowered her Stinger parallel to the ground and quickly spotted their prey—three black blobs flying in a line from right to left, the air around them shimmering in her sights from their hot exhaust. "Got 'em, sir!" Allie and Tom yelled in unison.

"Monahan! You got the lead copter in the stick! Ngo, you got the second! Weapons free! Fire when ready!"

Adrenaline honed Allie's attention to a razor-sharp edge. She forcefully pushed the safety and actuator switch behind the trigger grip down and forward to arm her Stinger, its integral gyro spinning as the battery coolant unit powered it up and flushed the tube with argon. Her pulse raced with the ticking clock—she had forty-five seconds to fire before the battery ran out of juice.

CHAPTER 27

Gabe sprinted to grab the sergeant lying wounded in the middle of the road and drag him by his MOLLE vest to safety behind the house adjoining their cornered enemy.

"It's not bad—you're gonna be OK!" Gabe loudly reassured over the thunder of suppressing fire their comrades across the street were pouring into the home occupied by the dismounted squad. He slapped the field dressing from the screaming soldier's first-aid kit on the bloody channel ripped through his calf by a bullet before grabbing his hand and forcing him to put pressure on it.

Gabe rose to a crouch to face the two young men and one young woman staring back at him, bug-eyed with fear. "Who's in charge?" Their silence answered Gabe's question—he was.

"We're gonna finish the job!" Gabe yelled, yanking the soldiers into a huddle. "The Stryker's comin' back to unload a bunch of thirty mike-mike into that house! The second it stops, we're charging through the front door and clearing it out, just like everyone rehearsed! Got it?"

"Yes, sir!" the woman barked while the two men nodded nervously with Gabe's reminder of one of the core rules of urban combat—soldiers who wanted to live to see tomorrow followed right behind their fire support.

Pucker factor, Gabe thought, stepping out from cover just far enough to hold out a thumbs-up to Grant and the support team, which had taken position along a line of two houses, their faded siding pockmarked with bullet holes. The distinctive whine of the Dragoon's engine rose above the din as it rolled up the street into view, its turret swiveling and depressing to take aim. The barricaded soldiers had just enough time to scream to bug out through the backyard before high-explosive shells belched out at the rate of one per second to shred the house with loud bangs and flashes.

"Follow me!" Gabe screamed the moment the Stryker ceased fire, galloping across the debris-strewn yard, his weapon at the high ready. He stopped at the edge of the gaping hole where the door had once been, just long enough for the rest of his team to catch up and stack behind him before all three darted inside through growing clouds of smoke.

Jed winced in horror from across the street as a brief but ferocious exchange of rifle fire erupted from inside the house. "Get the fuck outta there, you crazy jackass!" he screamed, red-faced.

The guns fell silent. The crackle of the beginnings of a small fire joined the hum of the Stryker's engine and the buzz of Max's drone overhead. "Gabe?!" Autumn called out. A lone gunshot echoed from the house. *"Gabe!"*

"All clear! Coming out!" Gabe hollered with a cough before stepping into the yard, the woman soldier behind him helping one of her teammates, who clutched his left side, his face twisted with agony. "We got two friendly and one enemy wounded!" Gabe pointed back through the thickening smoke. "And we need to put this fire out before we burn the city down!"

The drone tore north to scan for surviving enemy soldiers who may have escaped out back. "Everybody up!" Grant yelled. "Double check that the house is secure before smothering those fires!" He called Cade to take charge as he ran toward the wounded, unslinging his stuffed Special Forces medic bag.

CHAPTER 28

Allie ignored the growing pain in her shaky muscles as she slewed the Stinger's front sight to reacquire the lead Black Hawk after giving the warhead the view of the empty sky it needed—they were running out of time.

High-pitched, grating beeps screeched from the speaker by her ear to inform her she had missile lock. Her left thumb squeezed the uncaging switch on the front grip stock, freeing the missile's gyros and turning the beeps into an ear-splitting buzz letting her know the missile was ready to fly. She raised the tube to track the helicopter in the rear sight, sucked in a deep breath so as not to inhale the missile's toxic propellant, and mashed down the trigger.

A launch motor blew the missile out of the tube with a *ka-pow*, followed by a roar as the Stinger ignited and tore into the sky, staying low on the horizon and hooking left as it homed in on the helicopter's engines. The missile detonated squarely on the Black Hawk's left side with a flash, engulfing it in a fireball that quickly darkened to an oily black cloud; the helicopter broke into a thousand pieces that continued forward for a second until they rained to the ground on trails of smoke. Tom's missile found its mark a second later, obliterating the front half of the trailing Black Hawk—it arced onto its back engulfed in flame, flinging away its blades as it plummeted to earth.

"Good shooting!" Demetrius exclaimed in triumph over the twin *whumps* of both explosions. Allie flinched as Sean opened up with the Stryker's .50-caliber machine gun in a futile attempt to knock down the last Black Hawk before it dove to the treetops to fly nap-of-the-earth. She set down her launcher and tore off her helmet, the cool breeze caressing her sweat-beaded skin. Tom strode to her as the launch plumes drifted away on the wind, his hand raised for a high-five she had to stand on her toes to execute.

Allie looked to the horizon as the chop of the surviving Black Hawk's blades receded into the distance. "Hope we saved that nice radio lady, 'cause we just killed two dozen soldiers who wore the same uniform as us," she said, gesturing at the empty missile tube at her feet. "Besides, those were our only two Stingers."

"Well, now, *they* don't know that, do they?" Demetrius said with a wink. "And those survivors'll be sure to report that we have ADA assets. Job well done, sergeant!"

"Sir, I'm a specialist," Allie responded. Demetrius slapped something in her gloved palm, and she opened her hand to find Velcro uniform patches embroidered with three black chevrons.

"Not anymore you're not, sergeant," Demetrius responded, pointing to the teardrop-shaped specialist rank insignia on the front of her vest. "Lose the sham shield."

Allie smiled, just barely catching herself from saluting Demetrius in what was still a combat zone. "Thank you, sir," she said as she he tore her old rank off her chest with an audible rip. "The E-4 mafia isn't all it's cracked up to be anymore, anyway."

Sean's voice crackled over the radio, informing Miguel of their successful downing of the two Black Hawks. Miguel responded with news of his own—Chewelah was in their hands, and the remaining occupiers were fleeing north out of town in several Humvees and stolen pickup trucks. Tom pointed excitedly westward at the half dozen thin ribbons of black smoke from the helicopters. "That's not even two klicks from us, sir! We could set up a hasty ambush and finish 'em off if we move now!"

Demetrius shook his head. "We got that covered—" he said before being cut off by the distant *boom* of two linked Claymore antipersonnel mines and a cascade of weapons fire. Demetrius, Tom, and Allie stood mute as Colville's surviving residents exacted their revenge.

CHAPTER 29

CHEWELAH

Allie gazed longingly at the foil pouch of chili with beans that Tom pulled out of his MRE. The duo sat, tactical vests unzipped and helmets off, on the ratty, weed-choked lawn of the Chewelah Municipal Building where Demetrius and Rebecca were meeting with city leaders. Around them, their fellow partisans ate or cleaned their weapons in the warm rays of the early afternoon sun.

"Don't bother giving me those puppy-dog eyes," Tom chuckled as he poured water into the military ration's disposable heater to start the chemical reaction so he could enjoy a hot lunch. "I'd sooner eat my boots than trade for your MRE pepperoni pizza."

Allie held up her unappetizing square of food-type substance with disgust. "You mean Play-Doh," she groaned. "Play-Doh covered with 'mozzarella cheese product'—they can't even legally call it cheese." She was ravenous, but her unappealing lunch and Chewelah's ambient stink of trash, decay, and sewage—a nearly ubiquitous odor in the surviving towns of post-collapse America—waged a two-front war on her appetite.

Tom set his warming meal in the weeds and jogged up the open ramp of the Stryker parked across the side street's parking spaces, trotting back a second later with several small silver aluminum cans. "Almost forgot," he said, handing one to Allie. "I managed to snag some liquid refreshment to savor on the field of victory!"

"A Rip It?" Allie said with a laughing grimace as she examined the can of cloying, bowel-loosening energy drink that had attained mythic popularity among servicemen in the Iraq and Afghanistan wars. "Just what I always wanted—end-of-mission diarrhea. Santa got my letter."

Tom cracked his can open with a carbonated *hiss*. "See? I'm not such a bad guy."

Allie coyly smiled. "You trying to win my heart with drinks, sergeant?"

Tom smiled back as their eyes locked. "Maybe a little bit—sergeant." His face cautiously inched toward hers.

"You're gonna have to do better than Rip Its, big guy," she whispered, her eyes fluttering shut as she leaned in. They separated just shy of liplock with the *bang* of Demetrius throwing open city hall's side doors and walking toward them with Sean, Rebecca, and Carleigh in tow.

"How we doin', sir?" Tom asked.

"The city council's gonna let the refugees stay," Demetrius said. "They're not happy about us askin' all the able-bodied adults to join us on our little damned fool crusade, but they'll deal."

Tom tossed him a can. "Have one on the house to celebrate in style, sir."

Demetrius caught it one-handed with a wan smirk. "Thanks, but I'm not in a celebratory mood. I got four soldiers to bury, and two more who'll likely join 'em by tomorrow. Don't even have a way to contact their next of kin, if they even have any left." Rebecca put a reassuring hand on Demetrius's shoulder as he handed the can to her daughter. "Energy drinks are for young people who don't know any better, anyway."

"'A'tomic Pom,'" Carleigh read and cautiously popped the top. "What's it taste like?"

"Pomegranate, expired cough syrup, and the soul-crushing despair of military life, with just a hint of old socks and ass," Allie said.

Carleigh cautiously sipped, puckered her lips, and stuck out her tongue in horror. "That's *vile!*" she gasped, comically staggering into Gabe as he walked past and spilling the sticky-sweet concoction on his chest and rifle. "Oh, I'm sorry!" she pleadingly apologized.

"It's all right, miss—I smell better already," Gabe said. "Piece of advice—stay away from that energy drink crap. It's diabetes in a can." Gabe looked like a walking arsenal with his personal battle rifle across his chest and three newly acquired M5 military rifles slung over his shoulders alongside a rucksack stuffed with purloined gear. The spoils of war for the guerrilla unit not only included equipment from the dead, but also from the vanquished living—unable to incarcerate and care for prisoners of war, the victors settled on stripping them of their weapons and gear and ordering them to walk the fifty miles back to Fairchild Air Force Base, with the stern warning that any of them caught a second time would be summarily executed.

"You lookin' to start a one-man war, or just being greedy?" Sean asked, nodding to Gabe's equipment haul.

Gabe shot a glance at Autumn, who was waving from the bed of a dirt-caked pickup truck on the corner. "My friends are in desperate need of an upgrade," Gabe said, shrugging to adjust his heavy load. "Besides, the poor souls I got these from no longer need 'em—be a shame if they went to waste."

Autumn hopped off the truck next to Jed, who leaned against the back tire staring at nothing in particular; they and the other Chewelah natives were waiting for the OK to visit their homes, or what was left of them. "You really should eat something," Autumn said, gesturing to the unopened MRE in Jed's lap. He grunted, his thoughts dominated by the young soldier who died by his hands, needlessly suffering because of his bad marksmanship.

"I come bearing gifts," Gabe proclaimed, dropping to his knees and laying their new rifles, one by one, onto the grass. He opened the rucksack and pulled out three camouflage-patterned MOLLE vests, complete with high-capacity magazines and first-aid kits; the left side of one of the vests was smeared with rusty dried blood. "One of the Army's new-fangled rifles with ammo, and a proper set of gear, for each of us—although I dunno if I'm ready to put my trusty AR in mothballs," Gabe said, dusting off his hands. "I'll hook up with you both tomorrow morning after we get a good night's sleep so I can give you a crash course and zero your sights."

Autumn gingerly picked up her new rifle to ensure it was unloaded and safed. "Can I ask you a question?"

"Shoot."

"Who *are* you?"

"I'm Gabe," he warily responded. "I spent the winter snowed in with you, remember?"

"No, who are you really?" she demanded. "You've probably forgotten more bushcraft skills than my Brandon knew, and he was born and raised a mountain man. You took to what the Army guys were teaching us about combat tactics like a fish takes to water—like you already knew how to do it! And don't get me started about that action hero stuff you pulled clearing that house—don't you dare tell me you learned all that from reading *Soldier of Fortune* from the gas station magazine rack!"

Gabe broke from her interrogation and stared down the cracked and potholed street, his face suddenly etched with concern. "I'm serious!"

Autumn insisted as Gabe slowly rose to his feet. "Don't blow me off! I want an answer . . ." she said before trailing off upon seeing what had grabbed Gabe's attention. "Dear Lord," she whispered.

A gaunt young woman in tattered and filthy clothes limped toward them, her left arm rocking uselessly in a makeshift sling. Her long blonde hair was ratty and matted, and her face was scarred by acne. Gabe cautiously raised his hands to show he wasn't a threat. "Miss?" The woman's agonizing stride continued unabated, every step a maximum effort.

"Hon?" Autumn ventured. "We . . . we, um, have medics at St. Joseph's, right down the street." *Ohmigod, she's skin and bones.* "We'll take you there. You're gonna be OK."

"I'm looking . . ." the woman whispered through chapped lips before hissing and grasping her left side with her good arm. Gabe and Autumn rushed to steady her as Jed and several of their comrades came running. "I'm looking for Rebecca. Senator Rebecca Stevenson."

"That can wait," Gabe said. "We need to get you to a doctor. Right now."

"You're . . . with the resistance. Take me to her . . . please."

"Make a hole!" Demetrius ordered as he and Sean shoved his way through the cluster of gawking onlookers. Rebecca and Carleigh stopped dead in their tracks upon seeing the young woman; Carleigh's eyes went wide with horror, her hands flying to her mouth.

The woman barely managed a smile that revealed a missing tooth. "Rebecca!"

"Jenn!" Rebecca screamed as James's legislative aide went limp in Gabe's and Autumn's arms.

CHAPTER 30

SANDPOINT

Aunt Maria wiped her eyes for the hundredth time as Alexandra lugged a worn red suitcase down their stone front steps; Paul flung open the squeaky screen door right behind her after finishing one last check of the house.

A dozen armed men and women milled about the front yard, waiting to spirt the duo away to a secure location. While the collapse of the federal government's alphabet-soup menagerie of intelligence and security agencies decimated its electronic intelligence capabilities—and Redoubt Radio's decentralized structure of thousands of participants across hundreds of frequencies made jamming and other countermeasures next to impossible—Olympia's botched attempt on Alexandra's life exposed the safety of the handful of people at the top as the weak link in the chain.

The sun ominously disappeared behind a wall of dark clouds that threatened rain with a thunderclap that echoed through the valley. "Are you sure this is necessary?" Maria pleaded.

"Absolutely necessary," Alexandra said, handing her suitcase to a soldier who unceremoniously tossed it into the open hatch of an armored Humvee. "We're putting you in danger by staying here."

"But . . . aren't we safe now that Idaho declared Cascadia a no-fly zone?" Maria asked. Idaho President Jed Curtis was so incensed by Olympia's attempt to kill Alexandra on Idaho soil that he decreed that, humanitarian efforts aside, any military aircraft heading east within a hundred miles of the border would be shot down. He also made clear to Governor Embrey—in a radio tirade peppered with colorful language questioning her parentage and whether the space between her ears was filled with animal excrement—that the Gem State would consider any future violation of Idaho's territorial sovereignty an act of war.

Alexandra stepped to Maria and Uncle Guillermo, tears welling in her eyes. "We can't take that chance. You're safer if we're somewhere else."

"You know she's right, hon," Guillermo said, draping his arm around his wife's shoulders. "But Alex is bein' her usual modest self. Those *comemierdas* in Olympia aren't interested in killin' two retired *balseros* like us—this ain't about us. She an' Paul have become important to the cause."

Their security detail—a mix of soldiers from the old Idaho Army National Guard and local militia—strolled up to the García family, their boots skittering the gravel of the unpaved driveway. "'Invaluable' is more like it," the Humvee's driver said. "President Curtis said these two are to be protected at all costs."

Maria sniffled. "How're you two gonna keep broadcasting?"

"Sometimes we'll broadcast from established ham shacks like Uncle's—other times we'll set 'em up ourselves in the middle of nowhere and break 'em down when we're done," Paul answered.

The driver nodded to a red-headed, freckled teenage girl who almost looked comical in oversized hunting overalls and a military rifle. "We got the skills, ma'am—you give Rothstein here a coat hanger and a garbage can lid and she'll be able to bounce Miss Chase's show off the moon." The girl blushed at the compliment.

"That's actually a thing, hon—you can do that," Guillermo explained to his wife.

The driver looked to the darkening sky. "Sorry to rush the goodbyes, folks, but we gotta stay ahead of the weather if we wanna get to the site we picked for tonight's broadcast. We're, uh, ready when you two are," he said and walked back with the security detail to slam the Humvee's hatch shut.

The family hugged and cried as another rumble of thunder announced the incoming storm. Guillermo handed Alexandra a faded shopping bag—she opened it and sobbed upon seeing two retort-packed bricks of her tea, a metal strainer, and several plastic bottles of honey. "First time I've ever seen you speechless," Guillermo said, swallowing hard and straightening his flannel shirt. "Can't be the voice of liberty with laryngitis now, can we? We'll both be fine. Go. Your room'll be waitin' when this is all over. *Vayan con Dios.*"

Alexandra and Paul hugged Guillermo and Maria one last time before walking hand-in-hand to the Humvee and the men and women who had pledged to keep them safe. Guillermo pulled the black MURS radio from his belt and let the neighbor on shift at the end of the cul-de-sac know the convoy was leaving. The vehicles revved to life and rolled down the driveway out of sight as a cold, stiff wind began rustling the pine trees.

CHAPTER 31

ARDEN

"Several cracked ribs, numerous bruises and contusions, and a nasty raised scar on her abdomen from what looks like a minor stab wound," the bespectacled, bald doctor said, dispassionately tallying Jenn Maxwell's injuries for Rebecca outside the guest room where James had once clung to life.

Rebecca wrung her handkerchief listening to everything Jenn had endured. She stepped back, almost tripping on the neck of the hall vase shattered by the soldiers who had ransacked the Rands' summer home searching for them shortly after the Chewelah Massacre.

"Your friend fractured her left ulna, and it didn't heal properly—it'll have to be broken again and reset, hopefully once you folks get St. Joseph's in town up and running." The doctor lowered his voice. "She has what I think is chlamydia, and injuries consistent with past sexual assault. Thanks to the supplies your Green Beret medic in there squirreled away, I'm putting her on a course of doxycycline that oughta do the trick. But between that, and other opportunistic infections from months of menstrual cycles without access to sanitary pads, she may not ever be able to bear children."

"Oh, Lord," Rebecca cried into her hands.

"The good news, Senator Stevenson, is that your friend's going to live—she probably wouldn't have lasted much longer. Besides the antibiotics, I'm also prescribing food, and lots of it—she's thin as a reed and needs to put on about thirty pounds. But start her out with oatmeal, bread, potatoes, real simple stuff."

"Thank you," Rebecca sniffled and clasped the physician's hands in hers.

The doctor pushed his gold-rimmed glasses to the bridge of his nose. "Don't thank me—thank your own forward thinking and providence. Without your supplies, I would've been little help to you. My great-grandfather was an old-fashioned country doctor—made house calls and carried his instruments in a black leather bag like you see in those old movies. Like Arthur Clarke once said, he would've considered the advanced treatments I had at my disposal before the collapse indistinguishable from magic. But ironically, if he was alive today, he'd be far better equipped to practice medicine than I am. Without all my fancy gizmos and exotic medicines, I'm little better at healing the sick than anyone else."

The doctor took his leave down the hallway, weaving around the debris that served as a reminder to Rebecca that she and Carleigh were homeless. Governor Embrey hadn't been satisfied with merely ransacking their Kennewick home for clues as to their whereabouts, and ordered it burned down as well; Carleigh had locked herself in her small room of their safe house for two days upon hearing the news. Realizing she was stalling, Rebecca took a deep breath and put on a brave face before stepping into the guest bedroom.

Jenn lay upright in the bed the same way James once did. Grant, dirty and reeking from the fight to liberate Chewelah, silently took his leave as

Rebecca strode to the bed and gingerly hugged her long-lost friend like a rare porcelain doll.

"I heard . . . I heard James got shot," Jenn stammered. "Is he OK?"

Rebecca nodded. "They shot him last fall. The bullet collapsed his lung, and he developed double-bronchial pneumonia that almost finished him off. He's still very weak, and lucky to be alive."

"Just like me," Jenn muttered, gazing at the evergreen-carpeted mountains through the window. The curtains gently flapped on the fresh spring breeze.

Rebecca cautiously took her hand, an IV taped to the back. "Jenn, what happened?" she ventured.

"I messed up. James texted me to drop everything and come here, but I waited a day to wrap up some loose ends. Things were getting bad, but geez, I thought twenty-four hours wouldn't matter. Boy, was I wrong."

Jenn swallowed the lump in her throat. "Olympia was a madhouse—before I even got out of my apartment's parking lot, I had to draw the 9-millimeter handgun James bought me to scare off two thugs trying to get to the supplies in my car. I . . . I tried calling Aidan to tell him I was bugging out, but the cell towers were overloaded, and he hadn't responded to my texts, so I stopped by his parents' house to check on him. Their block was quiet compared to the chaos I saw getting there. No one answered my knock, so I opened the door and stepped in. Aidan . . . he caught the flu. He was lying face-down in his bathrobe in a pool of blood and vomit. The smell, Rebecca, it was . . ." Jenn stifled a sob. "He . . . he groaned my name. I bolted to my car and took off—held the steering wheel with my knee and bathed my hands and face in sanitizer. I left him . . . I left him to die on the carpet."

"There was nothing you could've done for him," Rebecca said. "If you had tried, you'd be dead, too."

Jenn sighed. "With all the major roads hopelessly jammed—and only a handful of ways to get over the Cascades—I pretty much knew getting to Arden was a long shot, especially with every detour extending my route and making finding gas more problematic. I pressed on, figuring I'd worry about gas once I cleared the mountains, but I didn't even make it that far—town after town had set up roadblocks to stop the spread of the flu. I finally found a town that was letting people through, in exchange for a toll of half of whatever they had. So, after handing over half my food and supplies—and letting them siphon half my remaining gas—they let me on my way. I was bawling so hard when I left that I could barely see. I probably made it another mile or two before a baby carriage rolled right in front of me. I screamed and slammed on the brakes—oldest trick in the book, right? Next thing I know, my side window shatters and a gang of masked men yank me out of my car. Stupid me—I kept my handgun on the passenger seat because I didn't like the way it fit on my hip holster, and my shock at the ambush was so total that I didn't reach for it. Stupid, *stupid*!

"They . . . beat me until I stopped resisting. Then they took turns raping me, right on the side of the road," Jenn said, emotionally drained. "They drove off in my car and left me there to die. Miracle of miracles, a passing good Samaritan brought me back to town, where I guess they grew something resembling a conscience and took me to a vacant home to patch me up and quarantine me with a handful of other 'big-city folks' they took pity on—but they said we couldn't stay. I eventually ended up in a refugee camp in Cle Elum, just past the Cascades. The conditions there were inhuman . . ."

Rebecca shushed her and stroked her matted hair. "It's all right. You're OK now. Rest. We'll be leaving soon."

"Where? With James?" Jenn asked as Rebecca covered her with the military surplus wool blanket at the foot of her bed.

"Not yet. We move him around. But we'll keep you safe, just like him."

CHAPTER 32

CHEWELAH

Gabe walked, exhausted, down the broken street toward his house. *Hopefully it's still standing—poor Autumn,* he silently pitied; Autumn's house had burned to the foundation while they wintered in Kaniksu; the hunting cabin she had grown to loathe was now all she had left.

He breathed a sigh of relief as his run-down, mustard yellow, one-bedroom house came into view, and smirked fatalistically at the sight of his beater Chevy Malibu, stripped and propped on cinder blocks by thieves—spare parts and tires in a post-collapse world were worth their weight in gold. He was surprised to find he wasn't the slightest bit angry; he'd almost certainly be dead before he ever got an opportunity to drive again.

Gabe crossed the crumbling, weed-choked sidewalk onto his overgrown front lawn, and froze in his tracks upon seeing that the front door lock was broken. He snapped his rifle to the low ready and swiftly moved to the side of the house so he could enter by surprise and not spend one more second than necessary exposed in the "fatal funnel" of his doorway.

Flinging the door open, he charged inside to come face-to-face with a young black woman screaming bloody murder.

"Ohmigod, don't shoot!" she shrieked, throwing her arms in front of her face.

"I won't if you don't do anything stupid!" Gabe hollered in an authoritative voice. "You got any weapons on you?"

"No! Army wouldn't let us have 'em anyway when they brought us here!"

The *pit-pat* of bare feet from down the small bedroom hallway heralded a young boy who galloped in front of his mother and defiantly threw his arms to his sides to tell the stranger that he would have to get through him to get to her. A wave of melancholy began subduing the adrenaline coursing through Gabe's veins as the boy, who like his mother looked like he hadn't eaten well in ages, brought back memories of places he wanted to forget.

"Just you two here?" Gabe pressed. "Don't lie—it won't turn out well for any of us."

"Just me 'n him."

Gabe pointed his weapon to the floor. "No funny business, no sudden moves."

"I'm guessin' this is your house?" the woman asked. "The photos on the walls from your time in the Army don't show you too good."

"You guess correct. You got a name?"

"Quanice. Quanice Richards." She rubbed her son's head. "An' this here's my five-year-old angel, Deonte."

Gabe took a deep breath of the stuffy house's musty air. "Where you from?"

"Spokane—we fled like ev'ryone else when the shit hit the fan. They kept us in tents at Fairchild for a coupla months, then drove us up here.

Army walked us down the block, busted in yo' door, told us to go on in, and here we are."

Bastards, Gabe thought, silently cursing Chewelah's occupiers. *So much for the Constitution.*

"So, you gonna kick us out?" Quince resignedly asked.

Deonte tore away from his mom and ran back to the bedroom, returning seconds later with a white cylindrical hat with a jet black brim that he lifted up to Gabe as a peace offering.

"Mon képi blanc! Merci beaucoup de le garder en sécurité, mon ami!" Gabe said, plopping the kepi on the boy's head. "Keep it—it looks better on you." The boy lifted the hat high enough to flash Gabe a big toothy smile, minus his two front teeth.

"That don't look like no Army hat," Quanice said.

"It is, just not American. French Foreign Legion, if you'll believe it."

"Didn't think they were real."

"Oh, they're real, all right," Gabe said, slinging off his rucksack and plopping down on his threadbare living room couch. "Uncle Sam wouldn't let me join up on account of one too many teenage run-ins with the law, and I was headed nowhere in the dying logging town I grew up in, so I spent what little money I had on a one-way ticket to Paris on a roll of the dice to see if the *Légion Étrangère* would take me, and they did. Spent time in Afghanistan and West Africa." He nodded at Deonte with a sad smile. "Your boy reminds me of a very precocious but sickly little orphan who hanged around camp in the Ivory Coast."

Quanice's face softened. "What happened to 'im?"

"He died." Gabe exhaled loudly after a pause. "You two can stay. I'm not stickin' around, anyway—my friends and I are heading back out to stir up trouble. If I don't come back, the house is yours. If by some miracle I survive, we'll figure something out. And one day, when this is all behind us, and you and your son land on your feet, you pay it forward. I'll write a note and leave it with my friends, the Taylors. They'll vouch for you."

Quanice wiped a tear from her cheek. "Thank you. God bless you, sir."

"No need to call me 'sir'—name's Gabe. Gabe Culver." He pulled three MREs from his rucksack. "Dinner's on me—you two look like you haven't had a square meal in a while. Sorry it's gotta be Meals Rejected by Everyone—I got spoiled by French field rations. Anyway, in exchange for my generosity, I have one humble request."

"Anything!" Quanice beamed.

"Can I crash on your couch tonight?"

***

Autumn sidestepped Jed so he could unfold his living room hide-a-bed sofa with a grating metallic squeak.

Jed rubbed away the dull, pre-arthritic aches from hands calloused by a lifetime of auto repair work. "You can stay as long as you like. I'll scrounge up some bedding for you . . ." Jed trailed off, realizing he had used the clean sheets as burial shrouds for Mary Ellen and the twins. Pain cleaved his heart like a knife as he stared forlornly at the empty spaces on the walls where family portraits, now safely cached in the woods, had once hung. He grabbed his hunting rifle from the corner and headed for the sliding glass kitchen door, the reds and oranges of the setting sun filling the dusty house with color.

"Jed?"

He stopped without turning around.

"Thank you."

Jed slid the door open and stepped onto the concrete pool deck, his boots crunching on shattered glass from the deck table knocked over by winter winds that had scattered the wicker pool furniture. A waterlogged chair silently bobbed in the brackish water of the half-empty in-ground pool, its blackened cushions floating like filthy rafts. Jed stepped over the fallen shade umbrella and walked the length of the deck, each step becoming more of an act of courage as he descended the wooden stairs leading to his backyard.

He approached the four graves and the large oak tree where God had denied his prayer to die with his family; weather and entropy had not yet claimed the worn tire swing creaking gently with the evening breeze rustling the young spring leaves. Jed leaped with a yelp as something squishy underfoot gave off a piercing squeak; he reached into the shin-high grass and picked up one of Archie's chew toys, a plastic cheeseburger bleached bone white by the elements.

All righty, then.

He righted Mary Ellen's wooden cross and stood silently for what seemed like an eternity before he caught Autumn out of the corner of his eye following the path he had trod through the tall grass, her diminutive frame behind her long rifle belying her skills as a marksman forged by a lifetime of hunting. He nodded a greeting as she stood at his side.

"You had a good family," she ventured, songbirds chirping goodbye to the setting sun as the wind rustled through the grass. "You're lucky to have them here—Brandon's buried along with half the town under the high school soccer field. And you're lucky to have a home—the authorities passed you by and didn't fill your house with big-city squatters who burned it down tryin' to stay warm." Autumn stepped in front of Jed and rose on her tiptoes to look him in the eyes. "You'll see them again—don't you be in a rush, you hear me?"

Jed knelt and set the chew toy on Archie's grave. "We should get dinner and some sleep," he mumbled. "Gabe's comin' over tomorrow morning to teach us how to use those military rifles he got us. I'll get a fire goin' and drain some clean water from the heater tank so's we can get ourselves cleaned up."

Autumn led the way back. "I took the liberty of setting the table so we can eat our MREs like civilized people—but your kitchen doesn't have a 'rock or something' to cook 'em on," she joked, referring to the silly instructions on the rations' flameless heater pouches. She spun around and impishly smiled at the sound of his chuckle. "That's the first time I've ever heard you laugh."

"I'm not gonna make a habit of it anytime soon."

***

Something warm and soft drew Jed from the black of the deepest sleep he had enjoyed in a long time.

He squirmed awake, his mind struggling to process what was going on before a finger settled on his lips. Autumn gazed into his eyes, then lowered herself and kissed him, her black curly hair tickling his face. Jed kissed her back, his hands slipping around her and feeling only bare skin against the gold wedding band he still wore.

"Wait . . ." he moaned in a half-hearted attempt to push her away, kissing her while trying not to. The scents of Mary Ellen's shampoo and body wash were intoxicating.

Autumn gently stroked his freshly trimmed beard. "We're not guaranteed tomorrow, Jed," she whispered. "I don't think we're gonna live through this." She softly kissed him again, feeling him stiffen. "We've lost so much. I don't wanna die alone."

Jed pulled off his shirt as Autumn slid the sheets off of her naked body. Their sighs joined the nocturnal chorus carried on the breeze through the open window.

CHAPTER 33

NEWPORT, WASHINGTON / OLDTOWN, IDAHO

The crotchety proprietor of the sporting goods store on the Idaho side of North State Avenue set the plastic milk crate of ammunition in front of Jed with a jingling *thud*.

"This's all we can spare for youse guys an' gals," said the man, whose gruff demeanor and long white beard made him appear to be the reincarnation of Gabby Hayes. "Hop'fully we'll have more for ya next time—Idaho's also exportin' revolution to southern Cascadia through Moscow-Pullman, and to Oregon—dagnabit, I mean Pacifica—through Lewiston-Clarkston."

Jed sifted through the various calibers—some boxed, others in ziplock bags—under the watchful eye of a man who looked like he'd be more at home cooking beans for a camp of nineteenth-century prospectors than being a poor man's arsenal of democracy. The small store felt like a sweatbox in the July heat; Jed wrinkled his nose and wondered if the funk—a pungent blend of chewing tobacco, body odor, cooked food, and other aromas he couldn't place—was what the old days smelled like before the luxuries of air conditioning and daily showers.

"We'll take anything we can get. Thanks," Jed said and picked up the crate.

The man smiled, his tobacco-stained dentures having replaced teeth that had rotted out long ago. "You can thank me by kickin' your governor's sorry ass. She an' her ilk, an' all their shitty ideas, ruined a perfectly good state."

Jed stepped into the scorching mid-morning sun beaming down from a cloudless summer sky. "Honey, did you remember to pick up a loaf of bread and a gallon of milk?" Autumn teased from the curb.

"Wise ass," he shot back before the duo crossed the street demarcating Oldtown, Idaho, from Newport, Washington. The twin towns, nestled in Kaniksu's southern tip, were a vital supply pipeline for the Cascadian resistance on top of what they pirated from federal forces—their remote location, and their leaders' wise decision at the start of the collapse to seal themselves off, had spared them from the H7N9 pandemic. Partisans milled about openly, thanks to the no-fly zone imposed by Idaho after Olympia's failed attempt to kill Alexandra Chase.

A faded and tattered American flag dangled from a pole in front of a shuttered McDonald's; Independence Day had come and gone the day before with the subdued observation with which one would commemorate the birthday of a departed family member. Several days earlier, the seceded states of Mississippi, Alabama, Kentucky, Tennessee, the Carolinas, plus the Florida Panhandle—the rest of the Sunshine State was nothing but living bandits and dead bodies—had banded together to form the Free States of America. The dark blue flag of Cascadia, a more and more common sight in Newport and other safe havens, flew from an adjoining building.

Jed and Autumn strolled to the parking lot of a former Safeway turned food distribution center where their unit, the First Chewelah Irregulars, had temporarily set up camp. In the two months since mustering after their hometown's liberation, they came to specialize in striking small convoys that dared to travel from Fairchild up the mountain passes of Routes 2 and 395, scavenging what spoils they could while denying their enemy freedom of movement. The unit, which had swelled to thirty members, had returned to friendly lines to split down the middle and create the Second Chewelah Irregulars, which would keep them small and nimble, with the added bonus of driving Olympia's overworked intelligence analysts nuts. Gabe, who was elected as the Irregulars' commanding officer on account of his derring-do in the battle to liberate their town, would stay in charge of the First Irregulars, with Jed serving as his trusted second-in-command.

Jed and Autumn found their comrades in arms chattering excitedly, huddled around a mobile ham radio rig set up by Gus Donovan, the group's silver-haired radio operator.

"What's happening?" Autumn asked Gabe.

"The people of Montana just launched a full-scale uprising to overthrow their asshole governor," Gabe answered. "They're hittin' everywhere, and hittin' hard. Get this—Redoubt Radio's saying the governor and the feds were conspiring to launch some of Malmstrom Air Force Base's ICBMs against the Texas Federation and the southern states to keep 'em from seceding!"

Gus had two receivers going—one tuned to Redoubt Radio, and the other scanning the bands that Montana's guerrillas were using. "Coordinating this big an attack across that huge state without tippin' off the bad guys? These folks had their comms up, that's for sure!" the old man said to no one in particular as Jed muscled his way through the crowd.

"Stick, Actual says Team Romeo needs to get its ass in gear!" a man broadcasted in the clear over the swirl of background static and rifle

fire. *"We need everyone to get to the Capitol Building, ASAFP! His words, over!"*

Jed's jaw dropped. "Sssssssh! Quiet!" he yelled to his teammates, but their chattering continued unabated. *"I said, shut the fuck up!"* he boomed, drawing to his full height and balling his huge hands into fists. The group as one fell deathly silent as he took a knee and leaned his ear next to the radio.

"Stick here! Tell Actual that Team Romeo's enroute! We're moving as fast as we can, but the crowds are getting crazy!" a slightly reedy male voice answered over the revving of a diesel engine. *"Will advise on arrival! Out!"*

Jed jumped to his feet. "He's alive!"

"Who? Who's—" Autumn managed to ask before Jed hoisted her in the air.

"Allan! My kid brother! He's alive!" Jed whooped, spinning Autumn around and almost knocking the radio from its folding wooden table.

"You sure?" Autumn asked the moment he set her down.

"He and his girlfriend bugged out to Montana when everyone started getting sick!" Jed excitedly explained. "He's big-time into ham radio! And 'Stick' was his nickname in school because he weighs a hundred pounds soaking wet! That was *him*! That's *his* voice! *He's alive!*" Jed dipped Autumn like a sailor coming home from war to the cheers of the Irregulars. "Can you clean up that signal, old timer?" Jed asked Gus.

"You bet, sonny!" he answered, quickly turning his attention to the controls.

Autumn playfully nudged Jed's ribs through his tactical vest. "You said you're not gonna make a habit of laughing!"

"I lied!" *Kick ass and take names, Little Brother!*

CHAPTER 34

OLDTOWN, IDAHO

Autumn winced with the loud scream echoing down the street from a formerly vacant storefront. The local dentist, who had managed to acquire the proper tools and supplies—and an old foot-powered drill from a local museum—was back in business.

"Damn, *I* felt that! Poor man," she said, skin crawling. Autumn glanced again at the hand-painted white sandwich sign by the front door advertising dental work in exchange for "precious metals, non-perishable food, produce, or any other item of value," and silently promised to brush her teeth more. "I hated going to the dentist back when we had grid power, novocaine, and bubblegum-flavored tooth polish. You couldn't pay me enough to step foot in there—I don't care how much pain I was in."

Gabe rose from his uncomfortable seat on the wreckage of a prefab garden shed in what had once been a small sales lot. "Don't be so sure," he said, pulling back his left cheek to expose a gap where an upper premolar had been. "It went rotten three years ago, and I couldn't afford to go to the dentist, so I downed three shots of Jack and did the honors myself with a pair of pliers. Lemme tell ya—JD is great for killin' the pain when your girl runs off with the mailman, but it doesn't do shit for do-it-yourself oral surgery. I would've loved to find a dentist that charged canned goods."

The dentist's hapless patient screamed again. "Then again, maybe not," Gabe quipped as Jed absentmindedly paced past him on the crumbling sidewalk just over the Idaho side of the state line. "Jed? *Jed!*" Gabe called out, snapping Jed back to the present. "You're gonna carve out a canyon pacing like that, buddy."

Autumn stepped into Jed's arms, their M5 rifles clacking together on their chest harnesses. "It's OK to be anxious," she said, stroking his beard. "I'm—we're—genuinely excited and happy for you."

A dusty gray Chevy Silverado crossed the Pend Oreille River bridge and rolled into the small downtown. "I think your family reunion's on as scheduled," Gabe said as the truck pulled up in front of a boarded up hardware store.

Allan Schmidt peeked between the front seats to his waiting big brother as Benny Rodriguez, the member of their survival group who had driven them from Montana, killed the engine. "Ain't too late to change your minds an' come back with us. The group won't think any less of you," Benny said.

Allan smiled nervously as Julie flew out the rear passenger door and enthusiastically waved to Jed. "Thanks, but this is where we belong. Washington—Cascadia, now—is our home. This is our fight."

Pete Mick, Benny's alternate driver, hopped into the truck bed and tossed Allan's and Julie's rucksacks and a stuffed olive-drab military surplus duffel bag to the sidewalk, almost tripping backwards over the metal diesel fuel cans strapped upright for the journey back to their survival retreat in the woods outside of Helena. Their two-day trip through the Rockies to the Idaho Panhandle had been uneventful, with Benny's huge collection of country and Tejano music from his pre-collapse career as a long-haul trucker helping pass the time.

Benny rounded the front of his cousin Manny's favorite truck to Allan, his cowboy boots clicking on the pavement. "Your brother stands out in a crowd, *ese*—big sumbitch," he said, squinting into the setting sun at Jed and his entourage from underneath the brim of his ten-gallon hat. Benny's lower lip quivered with Allan's silent nod. "Damn, I promised myself I wouldn't do this . . ." he croaked before the foursome collapsed into a group hug.

"We'll, uh, try to keep in touch the best we can," Julie said, wiping her nose on her sleeve.

"We'll be listening for you," Pete said, holding up his pocket New Testament, "and praying every day for your safety."

Benny sighed and thumbed back the way they came. "Well, kids, we gotta move if we wanna get to the RV park in Sandpoint before it gets dark." Sandpoint, like many towns along the thoroughfares of the recovering northwest, offered travelers safe haven at night for a small fee payable in silver, ammunition, or barter—between dwindling banditry and broken roads choked with stalled cars, fallen trees, and boulders, wise drivers didn't travel after sunset.

"Good luck, amigos. Don't get dead," Benny said as Pete hopped into the passenger seat and pointed his .308-caliber rifle to the floor.

Julie slipped her arm around Allan's waist. "Safe travels, and tell everyone we miss them already."

Benny revved the engine to life and blasted Midland's "Mr. Lonely" from the stereo before tipping his hat and wheeling into a u-turn; Allan and Julie waved until their friends disappeared from sight to begin the long drive home.

Jed's walk quickly became a run as the trio collided into a hugging, crying heap, Jed grunting with surprise at his kid brother's unexpected strength.

"I'm . . . I'm so sorry about . . ." Allan sobbed.

"Me, too, buddy. I'm so glad you're here," Jed sputtered, putting a meaty hand on Allan's and Julie's shoulders to get a good look at them. Allan wasn't spindly anymore. He stood straight, paying no mind to the weight of his rifle, MOLLE vest, and rucksack, and his eyes burned with purpose—Jed sadly thought about how Mikey would have looked if he had joined the military. *You finally grew up, Little Brother.*

"C'mon—I got some friends I want'cha to meet before we take you to the rest of the team," Jed said, hoisting Allan's and Julie's shared duffel bag on his shoulder. "Gotta say, it's weird seeing you two totin' military rifles—you two were cream puffs, even with the survivalist double life you both were leadin' behind my back."

"For the record," Julie said, patting her .308 Winchester rifle, "Allan and I learned to use these long before you did."

Allan did his best to disguise the awkwardness he felt as he smiled and shook Autumn's hand. Jed had told him during their most recent ham radio ragchew that he had met someone—and Allan had meant it when he said that he was happy if Jed was happy—but he admitted to himself that part of him would, unfairly, consider Autumn an interloper. Gabe visibly chafed when Jed introduced him as "a gas station manager and suspected former special forces commando."

The gaggle crossed the street into Newport; some brave soul had managed to scale the traffic light bar to spray-paint "CASCADIA" on the overhead Washington state welcome sign. A four-person community security patrol crossed past them into Oldtown; the two towns pooled their resources, the notions of jurisdiction and municipal fiefdoms having died along with the former United States. Volunteers, their shirts drenched with sweat, ended their work for the day at the darkened Safeway, which was guarded by a squad of armed local militia. Jed got hot just thinking about the one time he stepped foot inside seeking resupply for the First Irregulars—it was like walking into a sauna. The supermarkets that had replaced the friendly neighborhood corner stores of old were great in a world of reliable grid power and climate control, but without it, they became dark, musty caves that were hotter than ovens in the summer and colder than freezers in the winter.

"The rest of the Irregulars are camped out at the old US Ranger station," Jed said as they walked into the reddening sunset. "We're here for another day or two to rest and refit before goin' back out. And you," Jed said, poking Allan in the arm, "are gonna have your hands full familiarizing yourself with Gus's ham rig, God rest his soul." The Irregulars' easygoing radio operator had died in his sleep the night after pulling in the radio chatter from the Battle of Helena.

Autumn waved to a middle-aged couple locking up their gun store turned post-collapse trading post that many of the Irregulars frequented to swap the spoils of war for needed items and desired luxuries. An armed guard cradling a double-barreled shotgun waved back. Two teenage boys rounded the corner pulling a two-wheeled wooden cart, stopping just long enough to dump a nearly empty curbside trash can inside their nearly empty cart before moving on at a trot; in a scarcity economy, things were thrown away only if they couldn't be reused, repaired, or repurposed.

"Starting tomorrow morning, we'll teach the both of you our unit SOPs, which'll probably be different in some ways from whatever your survival group used," Gabe said. "If you don't mind me asking, you two know what you're about?"

"Does the name Stu Magnuson ring a bell at all?" Julie asked.

"He's that tyrant ex-governor that Montana's gonna hang, right?"

"We charged into the Capitol Building and took him alive. Lost two of our best friends doing it. Sorry we haven't had time to update our LinkedIn profiles."

"Got it. Shutting up now," Gabe blurted.

CHAPTER 35

Demetrius savored the cool high desert wind caressing his face in the dead of night after a day spent baking in the scorching Palouse sun.

He shifted his weight, lying prone in the small copse of trees tucked into a draw along the winding road near the top of Lewiston Hill. The quarter waxing moon glinted faintly on the roof of a compact car resting in a nearby ditch, the two desiccated mummies inside staring, hollow-eyed and jaws open, at the twin towns of Lewiston, Idaho, and Clarkston, Washington, two thousand feet below in the valley carved out by the confluence of the Snake and Clearwater rivers. For whatever reason, Clarkston on the Snake River's west bank had power, but Lewiston, on the opposite bank, was dark.

Like Newport and Oldtown to the north, the two border towns had banded together for mutual survival early into the collapse, barricading themselves from the outside world with the help of what was left of the Idaho Army National Guard's 145th Base Support Battalion in Lewiston. However, despite their distance from major population centers, H7N9 found its way in and cut a deadly swath—courtesy, rumor had it, of a lone refugee from Walla Walla smuggled in by her family. The military had occupied Clarkston on Governor Embrey's orders, drawn by its port and its agricultural riches—and left almost as quickly after finding itself embroiled in a guerrilla war with the remaining residents of both towns. Clarkston enthusiastically supported Cascadian independence, and the twin cities served as a pipeline for whatever help the Free State of Idaho could spare for Cascadia and Pacifica.

Those are some hard-core survivors down there—just like the man we're waiting for, Demetrius mused before briefly checking his black wristwatch. "It's 0230 hours—your friend's late," he grunted just loud enough for Sean to hear.

"He's never been late to anything in his life. He's here somewhere," Sean whispered. "Watching us and waiting for the right time—"

"You're both dead," came a muted, raspy voice from behind Demetrius, who leaped up as if someone had poured ice water down the back of his shirt.

"Jee-zus!" Demetrius hissed, a lifetime of military discipline saving him from screaming like a child in a haunted house.

"—to show himself," Sean finished with a grin as he rose to hug the silhouette rising from the black. "How you doin', colonel? Damned good to see you!"

"Can't complain. I'm still breathin'—for now, at least," the man answered in a Southern accent as he pulled off his camouflage boonie hat, the moonlight shining off his gray, flattop crewcut and rough face. "Nice to see time's treated you well, Sean," he said before turning to Demetrius. "An' I'm sorry for makin' you fill your britches, son—go 'head and send me the dry cleanin' bill."

Demetrius shook his hand. "No worries. Your reputation precedes you, Colonel—"

"If you don't mind," the man interrupted, "I'd rather y'all call me by my *nom de guerre* rather than my Christian name—I'm not seekin' to get in the history books."

"'Animal' it is, then," Sean said. "Or, if you'd like, we had a bunch of names we called you behind your back from the hell you put us all through on the Special Forces q-course."

Animal sipped water from his CamelBak's plastic straw. "So, both y'all got an exfil plan, or are we just gonna jawbone 'till we end up like those two stewed prunes in the car over there?"

***

The blackness of night had just begun to turn deep purple with the rising sun as the trio pulled up to the safe house just outside the small Idaho town of Genesee—the twenty-mile trip had taken three hours driving with night-vision goggles on ATVs.

The matronly homemaker handed Animal a tin cup of instant coffee. "I wish I had something a little more top-shelf, but we ran outta whole-bean coffee a long time ago," she said, setting down a small plastic container of powdered non-dairy creamer. "We didn't stockpile the stuff—I never drank more than one cup a day, or I'd end up dancing like a jitterbug."

"This'll do just fine, ma'am, bless your heart," Animal said, glancing around the living room of the cozy farm home. "Thank you for your hospitality—you'd have made a great Southerner."

Demetrius dumped a spoonful of creamer into his cup and nodded toward the blue paraffin oil lamp casting a warm glow from the coffee table. "The coffee's fine, ma'am—besides, it looks like you stocked up on the stuff that matters."

"Yup—I'm a very popular lady at the weekly barter faire in town. Who'da thunk that lamp wicks and oil would make you rich as Croesus one day? And don't thank me, gentlemen—thank you for what you're doing. Just leave the cups on the table for me when you're done," she said and left the room.

Demetrius stifled a yawn and sipped his coffee. "Animal, I do wanna talk to you about how you organized all those separate survival groups and militias into a fighting force that liberated the entire state of Montana. I need all the pointers I can get." He leaned back in the plush leather chair, fighting a losing battle against its call to slumber. "You shoulda heard Sean and his fellow pipe hitters when they first caught your name listening to one of your battles on the shortwave—they hooted and hollered like you hit a walk-off slam to win the World Series."

"We got Cade Laine and Doc Grant from Second Batt," Sean told Animal. "We also got a comms sergeant you never met, Miguel Lopez, who was in Fourth Batt." Sean took a pull of his coffee, unnerved by his mentor's expressionless quiet. "So, um, how's the family? Jo and the girls don't mind you playin' soldier in retirement?"

"Dunno," Animal curtly replied, his steely gray eyes suddenly leaden with pain. "The three of 'em went to spend a month with Jo's mother in Portland right before things went to hell—I told 'em to beat feet back home, but Jo's just as bull-headed as I am. Next thing you know, Antifa and the rest of Portland's merry band of freaky-freakies start burnin' the place down, the damned flu hits, the cell towers and internet go down, and that was that."

"I'm so sorry," Sean said after a long and respectful pause.

"Aren't we all," Animal muttered and set his mug on a hand-painted coaster. "That brings me to the bad news I come bearin', Sean. I ain't stickin' 'round to help you out—I'm just passin' through on my way to Portland to find out what happened to 'em. They're my mission now."

"I know better than to talk you outta something you've set your mind to, old man, but Portland's gone—just like Seattle and every other major city."

Animal sighed. "I know I got a snowball's chance in hell of findin' even a piece of them, but I gotta try. You never got hitched, Sean, but lemme tell ya, Jo was one in a million. Gave me two beautiful daughters, and pretty much raised 'em solo 'cause I was MIA as a father on account of gallivantin' around the world fightin' stupid-ass little wars for a country that doesn't exist anymore. I feel guilty as hell 'bout that. I owe 'em this." Animal turned to Demetrius. "Besides, y'all are in this for the long haul. You wanna know how we won, Cap'n Mathers? We won 'cause we were up against a rabble of misfits and fuckups who were ate up as a soup sandwich and led by a dipshit who couldn't count his balls and get the same number twice. You poor bastards, on the other hand, are fightin' the United States military. Yeah, it sure ain't what it used to be, and their morale's been flushed down the commode, but it's still the United States military. Unless you got some super-secret plan for knockin' 'em out with your ragtag outfit, you're lookin' at years and years of fightin'."

"Funny you should mention a plan," Demetrius said and nodded to Sean, who skulked to the kitchen archway to ensure their gracious hostess was out of earshot. The sky transitioned from purple to the pink of dawn as Demetrius and Sean laid out their idea.

Animal leaned back, knitting his fingers behind his head. "Gentlemen, given the assets you got and what you're up against, your plan is insanity—grade-A, homogenized, USDA-certified organic insanity."

A madman's grin stretched across his leathery face. "I like it."

CHAPTER 36

CHEWELAH

"Are you *kidding*, Mom?" Carleigh fumed, storming ahead of her mother as they walked through downtown on the sunny afternoon to the small gym where Grant was supervising Jenn's physical rehabilitation.

"Honey, I need you to go with Grant to check up on James—you know, see how everyone's doing since they moved to the new safe house," Rebecca pleaded; like a pre-election debate, she mentally cued up her daughter's anticipated arguments for sticking around. "Besides, Diane and the kids absolutely adore you, and they haven't seen you in months."

Carleigh spun on her mother in front of a boarded-up corner pharmacy just shy of their destination, prompting Miguel and the four-person security detail escorting them to halt and scan their surroundings for danger. "I don't have a problem visiting them—it's the 'until further notice' part that pisses me off! I'm nineteen, Mom! I'm an adult, and I don't need to be babysat! I wanna stay with you—we're smack in the middle of the safe zone!" Repeated and successful partisan attacks, with the help of new resistance cells that had arisen following the Battle of Chewelah, had turned much of Cascadia east of the Columbia River

into rebel-held territory, save for the ruins of Spokane and the en-
clave of Fairchild Air Force Base.

"It won't be forever, Carleigh—I'd love to be in your shoes and get
away from all this for a while," Rebecca said, holding up one of her
brunette locks. "I found my first gray hair in the mirror this morning,
thanks in no small part to this job."

Carleigh threw her hands in the air the way young adults do when
parents just don't get it. "It's not about getting away from it all! I
hope that gray hair of yours is the first of many, 'cause that would
mean you'll grow old, and I worry more and more that that's not
gonna happen. I don't wanna leave you, Mom, because . . . because
Dad's dead, and you're all I got left."

A drifting cloud covered the midday sun. "You don't know that,
hon."

"Yes, I do, Mom. He's dead. I feel it," Carleigh said, choking up.
"Southern California's one big mass grave. If the flu didn't kill him,
he died in the riots, or the fires, or from all the diseases the radio said
were running rampant with millions of unburied bodies rotting in
the sun . . ." Rebecca hugged Carleigh tight as her daughter racked
with sobs. "Dad's gone, Mom. You're still here. But . . ." Carleigh
sniffled loudly. "But now you're putting yourself out there leading a
war against people who want you dead."

"They want you dead, too, honey—remember the wanted bulletin
I showed you right after James got shot?" Rebecca said, stroking her
daughter's hair. "That's why we need to keep you safe. Please go with
Grant. OK?" Carleigh silently nodded her acquiescence, wiping her
eyes with her finger and thumb as Rebecca fished a handkerchief
out of her pocket. "It's tough being a woman in a world without
Kleenex," she joked.

Her daughter blew her nose loudly. "But Mom, I don't want you taking any chances. You're not sending me away on a goof—it's because you're all cooking up something big." Carleigh's hand shot up before Rebecca could respond. "Don't patronize me—I wasn't born yesterday. I don't wanna know, because the less I know, the better. But whatever it is you're gonna do, you stay out of harm's way," she demanded. It was Rebecca's turn to nod her acquiescence.

Miguel opened the door of the run-down gym as Rebecca returned the wave of a young woman strolling down the other side of the street, her daughter leading the way on a squeaky red tricycle. They passed a brick tavern, its front door propped open to receive a small delivery of bottled beer from the bed of an old white pickup truck—the first civilian vehicle Rebecca had seen in days. *Like tiny fireweed shoots sprouting from the blasted moonscape of Mount St. Helens,* Rebecca told herself. *Life's coming back.*

The steady bass rhythm of electro-pop music pumping from a black Beats speaker greeted Rebecca and Carleigh as Jenn, her left arm in a pink cast, finished twenty-five one-arm burpees under Grant's watchful eye. "Never took you for a Billie Eilish fan," Rebecca teased Grant, smiling as she remembered Carleigh's youthful obsession with the singer, and the Seattle concert she took her to for her sixteenth birthday.

"This is Cade's PT mix, actually," Grant said with a grin and killed the music.

"I'm gonna tell 'em you said that," Miguel said. "One day, *Mamá Oso,* if you an' Grant are walkin' and his head suddenly explodes, you know why."

Jenn, her blonde hair tied in a ponytail, grabbed a small towel hanging from a nearby barbell. The ugly purple bruises had disappeared from her ribs, which themselves were barely visible after Jenn had been fed back to a respectable weight. Her complexion had cleared up, and her cast was covered with autographs from townspeople, soldiers, and partisans. Grant, when he wasn't away, had taken a personal interest in nursing her back to health; he had paid for a lifetime membership at the gym with a Glock 9-millimeter handgun and one hundred rounds of ammunition; finding workout clothes and running shoes for her, on the other hand, had been much more challenging.

"You look great!" Carleigh beamed.

"Thanks to Grant," Jenn answered more tiredly than she looked. Rebecca knew that fixing her body would be the easy part; fixing her soul would be a much longer journey.

"Don't thank me—you're doing all the work," Grant said, picking up the speaker. "So, Carleigh, you packed up and ready to go?"

"I will be. When do we leave for James's new digs?"

"First light Sunday morning."

Jenn practically leaped out of her skin. "You're going to see James?" she anxiously blurted. "Where is he?"

"Safe with his family," Rebecca said, patting Jenn's sweaty shoulder. "Don't you worry—once Doc Grant here clears you for travel, and James is healthy enough, we'll reunite you two. He and Diane were so happy to learn you were alive."

"Hope this isn't an all-day trip," griped Carleigh, who got carsick easily. "Where are they now?"

"A safe house in the woods just west of Ione, and no, the drive won't be bad, even by post-apocalyptic standards," Grant said, grabbing his rifle, tactical vest, and medic bag leaning against the cracked mirror wall. "We'll head east out of town and then off-road it north up the power line easement running alongside State Route 20. No problem."

The group moseyed for the exit. "Um, Grant?" Jenn meekly said. "I've never said . . . you know . . . thanks."

"All part of the service," Grant replied, holding open the door.

SNOQUALMIE PASS

The two soldiers padded silently in their black wool socks across Billy's hardwood living room floor toward the front door, combat boots in their hands.

"Your turn to babysit our friends across the lake?" Billy asked from his lounge chair.

"Roger that, sir," Luis, a twenty-something Hispanic man answered, almost unrecognizable under his face paint and the green ghillie suit draped over his head and shoulders. "Eight hours countin' everything military either guardin' the I-90 bridges or crossin' 'em," he said, thumbing at the similarly dressed white soldier, "with only this waste of space here to keep me company."

Billy turned down the radio on the lamp stand where his CB base station had been before he and Olivia had received their ten temporary house guests. "I wasn't no officer, so don't call me 'sir'—I worked for a living. And thank you both for following Olivia's Fourth General Order," he said, pointing to their hand-carried boots. The Army had three general orders, dealing with posting guard and performing duties in a military manner, that every soldier had to know by heart; Olivia imposed the fourth—no footwear in the house—after a thoughtless private tracked mud across their Persian rug.

"Least we can do. Your lady's home cookin' beats the hell outta MREs," Luis answered as he opened the front door to relieve the duo finishing their eight-hour shift further up the hill. The early afternoon sun filtered through the trees and into the living room.

"What's the challenge and password again?" the white soldier absent-mindedly asked. "'Destiny' and what?"

"No, *pendejo*, 'destiny' was yesterday's challenge! It's 'lemonade' now, and the password is 'ocelot'! *¡Eres un pinche idiota, David!*" he admonished as the door shut behind them.

It had been a week since the recon team appeared at Billy's doorstep, bearing gifts of food and ammo in exchange for using the home as a base of operations to keep a twenty-four-hour watch on the I-90 avalanche bridge—actually two bridges for the eastbound and westbound lanes on the far shore of Keechelus Lake. It was Billy's reports on the bridge's traffic that had brought him to the attention of the Cascadian resistance as an invaluable intelligence asset, but the sergeant first class leading the team told Billy in no uncertain terms that his days of broadcasting CB updates to Redoubt Radio were over—the gruff middle-aged man said it was a miracle that Governor Embrey's goons hadn't triangulated them and thrown them behind barbed wire. Billy had worried at first that having soldiers running around soldiering would cause his PTSD to worsen, but their presence—and the stories he shared with them, and them with him—had turned out to be therapeutic.

He turned his radio back up in anticipation of Alexandra Chase's show that was set to start any moment. He longed for the day that Cascadia would be able to split off and join the fledgling Union of Free States, which stretched from the two new states of Pacifica and Jefferson east to the Dakotas, and south to Utah, Wyoming, and what was left of Colorado. Emboldened by Montana's foiling of a plot by a rogue faction of what was left of the once mighty federal government to nuke fellow Americans, the seceded states of Kansas, Nebraska, Iowa, Missouri, and

Minnesota—plus northern Wisconsin, northern Michigan, and a newly independent Upper Peninsula—had just banded together to form the Heartland Confederation.

The enticing aroma of apples and cinnamon wafted through the living room as Olivia came in through the kitchen screen door holding two pies, baked with their home-canned filling, from the backyard wood-burning oven. Their temporary house guests looked forward to Olivia's desserts, often baked with the help of the soldiers themselves, who rotated KP duty.

"Am I late?" Olivia asked, sauntering into the living room, her apron dusted with flour.

"Just in time, babe," Billy said with a smile as Alexandra's voice began to fill the room. He rose on wobbly legs to join Olivia on the couch and slide his arm around her shoulders. Something big was coming, and Billy was playing a small but important role. *Maybe Cascadia, and liberty, have a shot after all,* he contentedly said to himself.

CHAPTER 37

PULLMAN

Military and partisan leaders from across Cascadia made their way to their seats in the dim and musty Jones Theatre under Sean's watchful eye.

They had descended on Washington State University's campus in dribs and drabs, many of them through the relative safety of neighboring Idaho; US Route 95, which skirted the border on the Idaho side, had become the resistance's equivalent of the Ho Chi Minh Trail, given that Olympia's forces couldn't touch it. Vehicles that looked like they were plucked from a *Mad Max* film lined the roads and the pedestrian walkway around the theater, all of them facing east so they could flee across the border at the first sign of trouble to Moscow, four miles down State Route 270.

Sean, keeping his imposing and conspicuous vigil at the edge of stage right, greeted Animal with two fingers raised from the butt of his chest-mounted rifle—the storied special operator had bummed a bumpy, turbulent ride on a puddle jumper the night before with Sean, Demetrius, and Rebecca. "Surprised you're still here, old man," Sean said without taking his eyes off the growing assembly.

"Me too—if I eat another lentil, I'm gonna come unglued on all y'all," Animal retorted. Pullman had food, thanks to its location in a breadbasket tended by university students who were allowed to stay, provided they worked as farmhands—but survival meant eating lentils, sprouts, and wheat bread for breakfast, lunch, and dinner. "But don't you worry—I ain't gonna stick around long enough to watch these folks string you up by the balls when you let 'em in on the suicide mission you maniacs cooked up."

"With *your* helpful hints—we'll be sure to blame you if the mission falls on its ass," Sean shot back. "You're gonna miss a hella good scrap, boss."

"Yes, I will. Headin' out first light tomorrow, and I'll be over the border into Pacifica by sundown," Animal said—the eastern half of Oregon had just won its independence. "Then I'll make my way west an' pull a plan outta my fourth point o' contact to sneak into Portland."

Sean nodded a greeting to a middle-aged woman who led an all-female unit he had linked up with several weeks prior to hijack a fuel truck. "I'll swallow the little pride I got left that you never managed to devour—we sure could use your help on this one, Colonel."

Animal watched partisans in the audience shake hands and make small talk, and let the memories flood through him of the band of blooded, fire-breathing Montana patriots he had led on a suicide mission of their own to topple a despot and create a new republic. The siren song of yet another adventure beckoned to him like an oasis calling to a thirsty desert traveler.

"Right after I retired, not long 'fore the shit hit the fan, we went out to catch Kelsie's high school fall play," Animal tiredly told Sean, not taking his eyes off the warriors milling about. "The theater in Helena looked a lot like this one, minus your audience of rifle-totin' ass kickers who stink like a cow pasture on a warm day. I treated everyone to ice cream after the show at this old-fashioned malt shop in Last Chance Gulch when the damnedest thing crossed my mind—I couldn't remember for the life of me if I'd ever taken Kelsie and Marie out for ice cream before." The old warrior stared forlornly at the exits, his face belying a bottomless despair for a lifetime of things left undone and words left unspoken. "Kelsie's play was called 'You Can't Take it With You.' No truer words outside the Gospel have ever been spoken, and it only took me thirty years, a Distinguished Service Cross, two Silver Stars, four Purple Hearts, and a chocolate egg creme to figure it out. Sorry, old friend, but I got a family to find." Animal pulled Sean into a bro-hug. "And when I do, I'm takin' em out for ice cream every day 'till the Good Lord calls me home," he said over Sean's shoulder. "If that malt shop ain't standin' anymore, I'll milk a cow and do the honors myself."

Sean stepped back and slapped Animal's shoulders. "God be with you, old man."

"With you, too. See ya in hell, Billy Yank," Animal said, stepping down from the stage and starting up the carpeted wall aisle.

"Colonel Edmunds?" Sean called out.

Animal stopped without looking back.

"It was an honor serving with you, sir."

"Yes it was, wasn't it?" he quipped with a smile and disappeared through the squeaky metal fire door.

***

Demetrius smiled warmly as Rebecca laughed herself silly in the ratty backstage lounge chair.

"I can't imagine you doing that!" she howled, clutching her abdomen. "And your *name*! Captain . . . Captain . . ."

"Captain Midnight," Demetrius finished her sentence, causing Rebecca to convulse into another round of guffaws over the story of the night that he got rip-roaring drunk and jogged through the streets of Kaiserslautern, slathered in green glow stick fluid and naked as a jaybird except for his protective mask and a cape.

"Took me forever to wash that crap off while my buddies mopped up the glowing trail I left in their barracks," Demetrius continued, his exaggerated deadpan making Rebecca snort. "When I got back to Vincenza—true story—an MP my buddies know emailed me the police report describing their futile attempt to capture the 'glow-in-the-dark black man' terrorizing K-town." He drained the last of his cold freeze-dried Nescafé from the cap of his battered Thermos—a cup of coffee they had shared shorty after he first pledged his forces to Rebecca had become a weekly tradition the duo worked hard to keep.

Rebecca flopped back, spent, in her chair. "Thanks. I needed that," she gasped.

"The story of Captain Midnight's ride is like the family china—I only break it out for special occasions."

Sean poked his head through the stage door to get their attention. "Like now," Rebecca said, smoothing her shirt with both hands. "Showtime."

They walked to the peeling gray door. "For what it's worth," Demetrius said, breaking a brief and awkward silence, "our coffee klatches are the highlight of my week."

Rebecca smiled. "It's worth a lot—and I feel the same way." She shoved down the push bar and threw the door open. "You first, sniper bait."

The two hundred people sprinkled throughout the theater's front rows shot to their feet and applauded as Demetrius and Rebecca walked onstage, the dim overhead lighting casting weak shadows on the Masonite floor. "Thank you and good morning!" Rebecca warmly replied, gesturing for her audience to be seated—a life of military service and elected office allowed her to be heard without a microphone. "For those of you who don't know me, I'm Rebecca Stevenson, and I guess you can call me the temporary leader of our little independence movement."

"Rebecca Stevenson's seven feet tall!" a younger man belted out with an awful imitation of a Scots brogue.

"We know who you are! And we're with ya!" a woman hollered, turning the smattering of laughter from the man's joke into exclamations of approval.

"Thank you, because we have a plan to end this war once and for all, which is why we took the risk of this gathering," Rebecca said, snuffing out the celebratory chatter. "It's a straightforward plan, but it has a lot of moving parts and not a lot of time for your units, or the many others that couldn't send representatives here, to prepare."

She introduced Demetrius, who stepped forward, all business. "Don't write any of this down—if any of you get caught and Olympia gets wind of what we're up to, we're all dead," he admonished as a laptop projector on a rusted metal table sprang to life with a click of Sean's remote. A groan arose from the veterans in the audience as the Microsoft Office logo appeared on the mildew-stained white screen behind them. "Don't worry, we're not gonna subject you to death by PowerPoint," Demetrius said—the software was reviled throughout the military for enabling officers to inundate soldiers with useless information in hours-long briefings delivered in soul-crushing monotone. "It'll be on just long enough to reveal the broad strokes of what we're calling Operation Ripley."

An ominous disbelieving silence fell across the audience with the next slide.

"And the objective of Operation Ripley, ladies and gentlemen," Demetrius said with a dramatic pause, "is to simultaneously destroy bridges at all three of the year-round passes through the Cascade Mountains, cutting off the bulk of Olympia's forces from resupply and reinforcement, and then suing for peace."

CHAPTER 38

IONE

Carleigh opened the black plastic trash bag between her legs, stifling a gurgle as her Humvee rocked like a sailboat caught in choppy seas.

"We're almost there—stay with me, kiddo," Grant said right before driving into another rut in the power line easement that cut north through Colville National Forest. "This is Demetrius's favorite Hummer, so don't blow chow, OK?"

The rear of the lead pickup truck a hundred meters ahead of them bobbed sharply, announcing their next stomach-churning dip. "Ohhhh," Carleigh moaned, "why couldn't we have taken the road?"

"Roads are for people who like to get ambushed," the former Airborne Ranger manning the Humvee's cupola-mounted M240B machine gun yelled down from above. The convoy's route followed the easement, which ran parallel to Route 20 at the edge of the narrow Pend Oreille River valley. Driving down a wide open strip—a "linear danger area" in military parlance—carried its own risks, but Grant felt it safer to avoid the road and the prying eyes in the towns dotting it. Also, the easement offered a straight shot to the safe house where the resistance had relocated James Rand and his family.

Carleigh stuck her head out the window and gulped in the muggy air, the noontime sun accentuating the yellows and reds of easement scrubland kept short by eastern Washington's arid climate. A lone bull moose grazing at the woodline's edge cautiously eyeballed the convoy as it crept past, bringing back a memory of the first, and last, time Carleigh's father had taken her hunting. She silently wished the moose well with an almost childlike innocence—Redoubt Radio was filled with accounts of hungry survivors in what was left of the Midwest and New England denuding the forests of every last living creature just to keep from starving to death.

The moose bounded back into the woods, ending the life of a sapling with a loud *snap* that cut through the droning of the Humvee's diesel engine. Carleigh straightened in her seat, rustling her empty plastic bag. "So, Grant, what do you think—"

The lead truck disappeared in a violent explosion that tossed it in the air like a child's toy. Carleigh screamed and covered her ears, the heat of the fireball stinging her exposed skin as if a hot iron had been pressed to it.

"Shit!" Grant hollered, hooking hard right and flooring the accelerator to mow through the ambush zone while the Ranger laid down a stream of machine gun fire into the woods, further hammering Carleigh's tortured eardrums. "Get *down!*" Grant yelled, roughly shoving Carleigh's head between her knees before his vise-like grip went slack with a loud metallic *ka-thunk* and the crackling of glass. Carleigh looked up to see Grant slumped forward over the steering wheel, the dashboard and shattered windshield sprayed with gore from the softball-sized exit wound ripped out of his chest body armor. She screamed again, fumbling for

the door handle as the Humvee slowed to a crawl, the cab growing uncomfortably hot as it crept toward the engulfed pickup truck.

The machine gun fell silent. Carleigh kicked the door open and rolled to the ground with the thunderous report from the sniper rifle that had killed Grant and the vehicle gunner.

CHAPTER 39

Demetrius circled his laser pointer around the flashing red X marking I-90's serpentine route through Snoqualmie Pass. A photo of the interstate curving along a pine-covered cliff above pristine blue water popped onto the corner of the screen.

"This is Objective Hackman—the primary target we're committing the bulk of our forces against. The bridge—actually two parallel bridges carrying the eastbound and westbound traffic—isn't in the pass itself, but several miles southeast, hugging the eastern shore of Keechelus Lake," Demetrius said. "This is Olympia's jugular vein—reinforcements and fuel flow east, and the food and resources they plunder from Cascadia flow west. The large force they've garrisoned at the ski resort several miles west at Hyak, plus the fact that those thousand-foot-long bridges are built like brick shithouses because they're designed to withstand avalanches passing under them, have lulled our enemy into a false sense of security. Unbeknownst to Olympia, we're able to bring both bridges down, which we'll elaborate on when we break into smaller groups."

Two more red Xs appeared north and south of I-90 on the map of the Cascade Mountains. "Now, this isn't to say that Objective Caine and

Objective Connery—the small bridges on Route 2 at Stevens Pass and Route 12 at White Pass—aren't important. But as long as I-90 remains open, our enemy has the ability to fight. At the same time we intend to hit these objectives, every remaining uncommitted unit in Cascadia and Old Washington will attack every target of opportunity they can to throw our enemy off guard and conceal our true intentions."

Rebecca stepped beside Demetrius. "Which brings us to the whammy—we attack in four days." Obscenities and the Lord's name taken in vain exploded from the audience. "With that, we'll open the floor, but please keep your comments rated PG-13 or better." Rebecca called on a fighter sitting in the front row. "I remember you—Chewelah, right?"

"Yes, ma'am," Gabe Culver said as he rose to his feet. "I wanna know the name of the dispensary where you scored the edibles you all got blasted on before coming up with this craziness," he said over the nervous laughter of his fellow partisans. "I'm glad you chose the actors from *A Bridge Too Far* as the code names for our objectives, because those four words sum up my misgivings quite well. Why not throw everything we got at I-90? You said it yourselves that that's their main resupply route."

Sean flipped back to the Objective Hackman slide. "Because all we'd be doing is buying time until they either repair the bridge or clear the debris and lay down a new road along the shore. In the meantime, they'd dig in tight as a tick around Connery and Caine to keep 'em safe. With Idaho's no-fly zone robbing them of air superiority, their only true force multiplier is their armor, and if they can't get it over the Cascades, it's game, set, and match," he said. "The only way a force like ours can beat the former US military is by making 'em want to leave. We need a knockout blow to do that, and going big is our only shot."

The middle-aged woman Sean had teamed up with for the fuel truck heist stood up the moment Gabe sat back down, dual bandoliers of shotgun shells crisscrossing her ample chest. "Hawk—Sean—I agree with the ponytailed fella here; this looks like a very risky roll of the dice. The soldiers we've been killin' and the vehicles we've been stealin' or blowin' up ain't bein' replaced, and that doesn't count the stuff they hafta sideline from a lack of spare parts. Won't we make 'em wanna leave just by keepin' doin' what we're doin', like they did in Pacifica?"

Rebecca exhaled loudly, steeling herself to share the scenario that played out in so many of her nightmares when it allowed her to sleep at all. "The problem with that approach is that attrition and entropy don't take sides; they hurt us and them equally. A lot of our logistical support—ammo, fuel, the occasional vehicle—comes from what we capture, plus the trickle from whatever Idaho, Texas, and other free states can spare. Olympia is refining its own fuel, and more and more pre-collapse military stocks seem to be making their way to them, so the pendulum of supply is actually swinging in their favor."

She looked around the room and swallowed hard. "But that's not the main reason we've gotta end this fight, and end it now—we're facing a winter die-off of biblical proportions if we don't."

IONE

Carleigh scrambled on all fours to flee the brief but ferocious deluge of gunfire that peppered the trailing pickup truck and butchered the rest of her security detail. She cramped up and vomited as the Humvee rolled into the burning lead truck with a dull *thud*.

Furiously wiping her mouth on her sleeve, Carleigh remembered Grant's instructions to run like hell for the woods if they were ambushed and overrun. She took a deep breath and sprinted for all she was worth toward the forest before fear could cow her into fatal inaction. Tiny crimson pine saplings killed by the unforgiving climate crunched under her boots as the safety of the woods drew closer with each stride.

Carleigh hurdled a fallen tree just shy of the woodline, which suddenly came alive with half a dozen camouflaged soldiers rising simultaneously to intercept her. She screamed as a dozen gloved hands seized her and wrestled her violently to the ground.

"No . . . dammit!" Carleigh yelled as her wrists were roughly pulled behind her back and tightly flex-cuffed. "Let me *go*!"

Two soldiers yanked Carleigh to her feet and spun her around as an Army captain wearing the shoulder scroll of the Second Ranger Battalion out of JBLM strode toward her. She struggled in their arms until the captain grabbed her jaw and held a laminated color photograph of her next to her face. With his affirmative nod, the Rangers marched her down the easement to a perpendicular side clearing, their hands clamped on her biceps like vise grips. She cried, squinting to protect her eyes from the white-hot glare of the fire engulfing the Humvee and consuming the bodies of Grant and the machine gunner; oily black smoke from the burning convoy billowed to the staccato of ammunition from Carleigh's deceased guardians cooking off in their weapons and magazines.

Purple smoke belched from a canister grenade lobbed by a soldier into the clearing to mark their pickup zone. Carleigh thrashed in terror against her bonds as the sound of helicopters rose from the distance—they were going to take her far away.

An ungodly roar suddenly rose out of nowhere to drown out all else before coming to a sudden stop with with a blinding flash of light. She violently twisted away from her captors to see a huge explosion pummel the foothills west of Ione.

Where James Rand and his family were in hiding.

"Noooooooooooooooooo!" she screamed before the ear-splitting sound of the blast tore through the valley.

CHAPTER 40

PULLMAN

Sean switched slides to a list of problems facing Cascadia's survivors, the murmurs of the audience growing more agitated as they read it.

"To put it bluntly, we're running out of food. Don't let our gracious hosts' hospitality paint a rosy picture—Pullman's the exception in Cascadia, not the rule," Rebecca said. "Farmers are growing a fraction of what they did pre-collapse for lack of fuel, fertilizer, and pesticides, and much of that—as well as the dry grains stored from previous years' harvests—is being seized by Olympia to feed their soldiers, and refugees from Seattle and Spokane."

The projector unexpectedly, but serendipitously, shut off with a flickering of the dim overhead lights. "That brings us to our next point," Sean said as the projector restarted with a whir. "While Washington and Cascadia are blessed with an abundance of hydroelectric power, it's not like either side is sitting on a mountain of spare transmission wires, transformers, and all the other stuff needed to deliver it. It doesn't matter that both sides have had a tacit agreement not to damage the power infrastructure—sooner or later, equipment failure and Mother Nature will turn off the lights for good."

"Add in the lack of heating gas, and no medicine to be found any-where, and what's left of Cascadia will go into this second post-collapse winter even colder, hungrier, and sicker than the first," Demetrius said. "If the estimates the feds have put out in their propaganda broadcasts are true, one American in three has died. Everyone in this room has lost someone special to them," he said, unwittingly glancing at Rebecca. "To the pandemic, or lawlessness, or disease . . . or that first winter. We'll end up losing more. A lot more."

The woman who had asked the question quietly sobbed; her three adult sons never made it out of Seattle, and her teenage daughter had committed suicide after her psychiatric meds ran out. Sean watched her and offered a silent prayer that Animal would find his wife and daughters.

"We've gotta end this, or this winter could make last winter's die-off look like a Sunday picnic," Rebecca said. "Other states are picking up the pieces. They're refining gas in Texas, and ethanol in Nebraska. Biotech and pharmaceutical companies in Texas and Alabama are retooling to manufacture antibiotics and medicines again. Interstate commerce is resuming."

Rebecca caught sight of Demetrius making a beeline backstage toward Allie, who nervously pulled him just out of sight of the audience. "That, um . . . that can be us, ladies and gentlemen," she continued. "James Rand saw Cascadia's tremendous potential long ago. Pacifica, Jefferson, and Montana broke their shackles and sent their tyrants packing. We can, too—and we can't spend the next decade waging a guerrilla war while the people we're fighting for starve to death." Rebecca's face softened. "You're all free militia, and can come and go as you please. But we're asking you—begging you—to help. We can do this. Because we have to do this. Every day we keep fighting means more lives, more children, lost

to starvation and disease. We end this now, or we go down swinging."
Rebecca broke out in gooseflesh at the square-jawed, determined faces
staring back at her. "Any more questions?"

Silence.

"Good. Now, pardon my language, let's kick ass so we can all go
home."

The audience rose and stretched with the brightening of the battered
stage lights as Tom and several other soldiers took to the aisles to brief
each individual group on their particular piece of the operation; they
had a while before everyone would be released to rejoin their units under
cover of darkness. Rebecca was about to step down and personally thank
as many people as she could when Demetrius grabbed her arm, her blood
running cold as his haunted eyes met hers. She followed him backstage,
her heart pounding harder with each step.

"The safe house missed its regular radio check," Demetrius blurted the
moment the fire door clacked shut. "A ham operator in Ione reported an
explosion west of town so big that people thought it was a nuke. We can't
raise them."

"Ohmigod—ohmigod ohmigod ohmigod . . ." Rebecca sputtered, her
hands flying to her mouth. "Carleigh and Grant?" she barely managed
to whimper.

"We can't raise them either."

CHAPTER 41

CAMP MURRAY

General Westman stared with a mix of triumph and sadness at the picture of a bedraggled Carleigh Stevenson, her eyes bloodshot from crying and her brunette hair a rat's nest from the helicopter's rotor wash. A pair of olive-drab gloved hands from one of her unseen captors clutched her head still for the photo. *Was that necessary?* Westman silently lamented with a shake of his head.

Westman glanced around the cavernous emergency operations room as soldiers, airmen, and civilian emergency management personnel were relieved for the 1600 shift change; morale had increased considerably with the decision to billet EOC personnel and their surviving family members in on-post housing at neighboring JBLM. The governor herself had relocated from the spartan and sterile facility to a new governor's mansion on the opposite shore of Budd Inlet from the scorched state capitol.

He had just finished briefing a jubilant Alicia on the resounding success of Operation Cromwell, which had crippled Cascadia's leadership by neutralizing James Rand and capturing the daughter of his heir apparent. Just as importantly, Washington was back in the air superiority game with the acquisition of a full fighter squadron cobbled together from remnants of wings from Luke, Nellis, and Eielson Air Force bases; they had blasted the Ione safe house with an AGM-158B standoff cruise missile launched by an F-16 Falcon far outside Idaho's no-fly zone.

Westman's attention returned to Carleigh, who bore a resemblance to his only daughter—Kara was his world after they lost her mother, Patricia, to pancreatic cancer during her freshman year in high school. Kara had been studying finance at the London School of Economics when the collapse started, and Westman had moved heaven and earth—calling in every favor he was owed in US European Command—to get her on the last transport leaving RAF Lakenheath as the H7N9 strain cut through the United Kingdom like a scythe. He tried like hell to get Kara all the way to McChord, but she only made it as far as Scott Air Force Base, Illinois, before a lack of fuel and pilots grounded her. The base, and its skeleton remnant of airmen who hadn't gone AWOL or gotten sick, stood no chance against the hordes of rioters, looters, and refugees swarming from nearby St. Louis. The terse email she managed to send was seared on his soul: *There are no flights left. We have to get out of here before the looters come. I'll try to get a hold of you when I'm somewhere safe. I love you, Dad.*

And now, Westman thought with self-contempt, *I've taken someone else's little girl. Kara and Patricia would be so proud.*

Westman had fancied himself and the soldiers under his command as keepers of the torch of American liberty, preserving some fragment of the shining city upon the hill in a world gone mad until order could be restored and the flame rekindled. That was how he justified what they were doing, even as it became increasingly obvious with each setback, each defeat, each newly seceded state, that the nation he had dedicated his life to defending had become just another once-great empire unceremoniously dumped onto history's burn pile.

What was it Santayana wrote? His precious Kara, wise beyond her years, had given him a copy of *The Life of Reason* for his birthday before leaving for college. *Something about a fanatic being someone who doubles down on his efforts when he's forgotten his goal? Is that what we're doing here?*

"Textbook operation, wouldn't you say?"

General Kett's unsolicited opinion snapped Westman's attention back to the present. "Neutralized our ace of spades, courtesy of our new friends in the Air Force, captured an HVT that'll bring us the head of the snake, and sent a dozen right-wing hillbillies to hell, all without losing a single soldier." Kett's smile slowly melted away with Westman's stone-faced silence. Westman's dislike of Kett had devolved over time into genuine loathing; he was competent enough, but served to Westman as a constant reminder of the latest generation of flag officers who would say and do anything to please their political overlords and get to the next rank, their oaths to the Constitution nothing more than lip service. Like many traditional officers who actually prioritized fighting and winning wars over politics and whatever the woke flavor *du jour* was on Capitol Hill, Westman decided to keep quiet and go along to get along—the Pentagon had become very eager to put old-school senior officers out to pasture in favor of the ones who wouldn't resist turning the Armed Forces into one big sociology experiment. As such, Kett also served as a constant reminder to Westman that he had chosen practicality over principle.

Counting down the days until I could retire with a big fat general's pension and end up making a gazillion dollars more on some corporate

board or working for the defense industry, Westman thought sardon-
ically. *Great plan, high-speed—your pronouns are "sucker" and "fool."*

"General Westman, sir? Do we transmit the governor's ultima-
tum?" asked a dapper young Air Force lieutenant standing in front
of the row of radios staffed by a mix of military and civilian personnel. Westman shoved Carleigh's picture into a manila folder before
she and Santayana could appeal to his conscience, or what little the
collapse and the Machiavellian politics of climbing the officer ranks
had left of it. He cleared his throat and straightened his camouflage
blouse with a sharp tug.

"Send the message," he ordered, silently asking his family's forgiveness.

CEDONIA

"Halt! Identify yourself!" yelped the anxious young sentry as Jed
shambled up the mountain outcropping to the hasty perimeter the
First Chewelah Irregulars had set up.

"It's me," Jed wheezed in annoyance; he was spent from their
chaotic retreat, and in no mood to play Army with a kid who could
see good and damned well who he was in the afternoon sun.

"Advance and be recognized!" the young man recited by rote
from behind a large tree, his rifle trembling in his hands from the
adrenaline of the day's events.

Jed slung his rifle and continued his trudge up the rocky slope. "Save
it, boy. If you think I'm one of the evil lizard people disguised as Jed
Schmidt, then go ahead and shoot me," he panted, legs aching with each
lumbering step. "But if you're gonna make me recite the damn challenge
and password 'cause that's what the book says, I'm gonna shove the

goddamn book so far up your ass that you'll hafta pick your nose to turn the page."

Autumn darted past the sentry before he could respond and tried to grab one of Jed's tree-trunk arms to help him along before he waved her off. He swung his rucksack to the ground and dropped to his knees by a large boulder in the center of their perimeter.

"Everyone else make it? Allan and Julie?" Jed tiredly asked before guzzling one of his belt-mounted canteens.

Autumn grabbed his camouflage-painted face and kissed him hard. "Yes. You were the last one, slowpoke."

Jed leaned back on the lichen-splotched boulder with a groan. Everything had gone so well. The three-vehicle convoy that the locals said patrolled the small towns along State Route 25 had arrived right on schedule. It obligingly slowed down at the tight bend in the road just east of the tiny hamlet of Hunters—smack in the middle of the Irregulars' kill zone—and the guerrillas rained fire from the high ground before the enemy knew what hit them. Jed was about to lead them down to strip the dead of everything from the rifles in their cold, dead hands to the boots on their feet when a flight of military helicopters—three Black Hawks escorted by two Apache Guardian gunships—tore overhead, spooking them back to their objective rally point in the mountains outside the small town of Cedonia.

"I knew doin' this was a mistake while Gabe was away at that little resistance pow-wow," Jed grumbled, ripping off his helmet as Allan and Julie squatted in the rocky dirt next to him. "How the hell they call in those 'copters in so fast?"

"They didn't," Julie said. "They were just passing through."

"How do you know?"

"Because we're not dead," she nonchalantly answered. "Army helicopters have FLIR—forward-looking infrared radar—that can spot human heat signatures, regardless of time of day, weather, smoke, you name it. If they were coming for us, they would've picked us off one by one for sport. They were doing their own thing—transporting something or someone important, if I had to guess."

Jed silently cursed missing out on scavenging the convoy to supplement their meager stores; while many of the Irregulars had equipped themselves with the Army M5 rifle that had replaced the ancient M-16 platform that served the military from Vietnam through America's forever wars in Iraq and Afghanistan, its special 6.8-millimeter round had nowhere near the plentiful civilian availability of the 5.56-millimeter and .223 Remington ammunition of old. He briefly considered going back to plunder the destroyed convoy for supplies—as well as search for C4 or any other explosives for which resistance leadership had inexplicably developed an insatiable appetite—but concluded it was far too dangerous in the event that a survivor managed to radio for backup, or the helicopter pilots had a change of heart.

Allan held out his hand to help Jed to his feet, an almost comical gesture given their differences in size, before reaching back to pat the portable ham radio stuffed in the top of his rucksack. "I should report the ambush and the copter flight," he said, pointing above the treetops to a small mountain several kilometers away. "Let's head over yonder—I highly doubt Olympia's able to intercept VHF, but I'd rather play it safe and put that mountain between us and them after what happened to those dipshits in Wenatchee." A partisan cell inspired by Alexandra Chase had decided to start their own pirate radio station to broadcast into occupied western Washington, but with no thought to staying mobile or hopping frequencies. Their venture barely lasted a day before a battery of the Seventeenth Field Artillery Brigade permanently revoked their nonexistent broadcast license with a barrage of MGM-140 missiles from an M270 Multiple Launch Rocket System—reverently nicknamed "the finger of God" by soldiers for their ability to lay waste to entire one-kilometer grid squares. A fragment of antenna, and a boot with a severed foot still in it, were the only pieces found of the would-be disc jockeys.

Jed ordered the Irregulars to their feet, leaning on the boulder to stretch calf muscles that had already begun to stiffen before hoisting his rucksack onto his back. The Irregulars tiredly lined up single-file behind Julie, who waved her hand forward to move them out. A ribbon of smoke twisted into the cloudless sky from the direction of their ambush; Jed hoped they hadn't started a brush fire that would endanger any homes.

"Thank God we had nothing to do with whatever those copters were up to," he muttered to Allan.

Allan shrugged his rucksack higher on his shoulders and wiped his brow with his dusty sleeve, rubbing off a swath of his sweat-faded camouflage paint. "Don't be so sure, Big Brother."

"Whaddya mean?"

"One thing I learned back in Montana is that, to quote those Marvel Comics Universe movies Julie loved so much, it's all connected. Whatever they were doing, I'll bet you a bottle of your favorite rum that we'll be ass-deep in it before you know it."

Jed shuddered as they began their march over the dry scrub and into the mountains.

CHAPTER 42

CHEWELAH

Rebecca's heavily augmented security convoy sped away from the run-down city airstrip shortly before midnight, their headlights barely cutting through the late August storm angrily dumping sheets of rain across northern Cascadia.

She stared into the black, struggling to hold it together for Carleigh's sake. Her only child had been captured, Grant and the rest of Carleigh's protection detail had been ambushed and slaughtered, and a smoldering crater was all that was left of James Rand and his family. Rebecca desperately wished Demetrius was with her, but he was busy coordinating with the volunteers and Ione locals combing through what little remained of the Rands' safe house.

The Escalade's wipers rhythmically thumped over the convoy's radio chatter. "I still think we should drop you off with Demetrius at the police station," Sean muttered from the driver's seat, his eyes glued to the broken road and the lights of the van in front of them. Cade, sitting behind him to Rebecca's left, concurred with a grunt—he had traded his Barrett sniper rifle for his SCAR-H for the close-quarters job they were heading to do.

Rebecca swayed in her seat as the convoy swerved around the road-block guarding Chewelah's northern city limits. "I'm coming with—especially if what you're alleging is true," she insisted in a trembling voice.

"Fine, but you stay your ass in the car. End of discussion," Sean shot back. "We gotta learn where they took Carleigh, and the person who ratted us out is our only lead. We're not gonna be askin' her nice." The convoy turned hard left off Route 395, the boarded-up downtown strip immediately giving way to run-down homes as Miguel barked orders to the convoy from the front passenger seat to secure the perimeter upon arrival, and to avoid deadly force at all costs so that their target could be captured alive.

"Are you sure she had something to do with this?" Rebecca whimpered, grasping the roof handle to keep from slamming into the SUV's door with another hard left turn.

"Jenn was standin' right there in the gym when Grant blabbed to Carleigh where the convoy was goin' and when—we didn't even tell the drivers themselves 'til right before step-off," Miguel said. "No one else knew 'cept us an' Demetrius. It's the only explanation that makes sense, *Mamá Oso*."

"Don't call me that—I don't deserve it!" Rebecca snapped. *This isn't happening*, she cried out to herself. *Oh my God—my God!*

The lead van's brake lights flared crimson before snapping off a second later. Sean threw the SUV in park and left the engine running, the Escalade's headlights briefly illuminating the soldiers bursting from the van before going dark. Rebecca darted past the soldier assigned to guard her and ran after the trio of former Green Berets moving silently, weapons at the low ready, up the lawn toward the front of the dilapidated house, which like the rest of the residential block was dark as pitch. Cold rain dripped down Rebecca's back in icy tendrils amplifying the rush of adrenaline and the despair of loss—and, if her guardians were right, betrayal—that threatened to consume her.

Sean whirled on Rebecca the moment she appeared by his side at the lead of the line stacked up by the front door of Jenn Maxwell's temporary home, the night-vision goggles lowered over his eyes making him appear almost robotic. "What the *fuck* do you think you're doing?" he quietly growled in Rebecca's defiant face over the rainwater gurgling through the home's mildewed and battered gutters. "You think this is a fucking *game*, lady? You think you can just order whoever's inside not to shoot you if this goes south? We just lost James! You die, and it's game over!" He grabbed Rebecca's winded guard one-handed by the straps of his MOLLE vest, almost yanking him off his feet. "Take Senator Stevenson back to the car, over your fucking shoulder if you have to, and keep her there!" He turned back to Rebecca, his demeanor softening slightly. "I can't imagine what you're going through right now, but you gotta use your head, OK? We can't afford to lose you."

Rebecca stood silently for a second before walking—defeated, cold, and soaked—back to the Escalade, her temporary chaperone in tow. She was about to reach for the rear environment panel to crank the heat when she jumped in her seat with the report of the shotgun blast shattering the aluminum front door's lock; her hands flew to her mouth as Sean kicked the door open and bolted inside, weapon at high ready, with Cade and Miguel following right behind.

One minute turned into two, then three. The heavy rain intensified into a summer downpour that hammered the Escalade's roof.

"Coming out!" Sean hollered to the soldiers outside. Rebecca leaped out the door and sprinted through the rain, Sean's edict be damned.

"Rebecca . . ." Sean said, grabbing her by the shoulders to stop her.

"Where is she? Is she gone?"

Sean blew out a long breath. "No. She's here."

"I wanna see her."

"That's not a good . . ."

"I *said*, I wanna see her!" Rebecca shrieked, breaking free and darting past Cade and Miguel through the unhinged front door into the dark house. She flipped the wall switch out of habit and swore when nothing happened—light bulbs were a scarce commodity two years into the collapse. Fishing a small flashlight from her pocket, Rebecca shined it around the darkened living room, settling on the door to the garage flung open at the end of the small adjoining hallway. Dust specks danced in the narrow beam as she crept forward, her pulse racing as her waterlogged socks squished in her shoes with every hesitant step.

Rebecca rounded the corner into the doorway, and almost dropped the flashlight before slumping against the door frame, too spent to scream. Jenn's lifeless body dangled from the cord lashed to the garage's wooden ceiling beam, feet dangling over the stool knocked to the oil-stained concrete floor.

***

The swirls of flowers and hearts along the lavender stationery's edges gave Jenn's suicide note a surreal, self-loathing feel.

I had no choice, Rebecca numbly read for the hundredth time. *They discovered who I was in the refugee camp. They had my Mom and younger sister and said they would do all sorts of horrible things to them and kill them both if I didn't agree to infiltrate the resistance and give them you and James. Liz is only seventeen—I couldn't let her die. This guilt is more than I can bear. I hope you find it in your heart one day to forgive me for what I've done, Rebecca, because I can't.*

Rebecca dejectedly examined the tiny Morse transceiver built into the inconspicuous mint tin that Jenn had left atop the note as evidence of her guilt. People can be taught Morse code in a matter of days, Miguel had told her—Rebecca didn't want to think about how Jenn had smuggled the transmitter. She wrapped an itchy military wool blanket around her damp clothes and resignedly slid another handwritten note across the table, its all-caps wording hastily scrawled by the radio operator who transcribed it a stark contrast to Jenn's confession.

WE PROPOSE A PRISONER EXCHANGE AT A TIME AND LOCATION TO BE DETERMINED. IN EXCHANGE FOR THE SAFE RETURN OF CARLEIGH STEVENSON, WE DEMAND THAT YOU STAND DOWN YOUR FORCES AND SURRENDER YOURSELF TO FACE TRIAL ON CHARGES OF TREASON AGAINST THE UNITED STATES OF AMERICA UNDER ARTICLE III, SECTION 3 OF THE U.S. CONSTITUTION. YOU HAVE UNTIL 2400 HOURS PDT (0700 HOURS ZULU/GMT) AUGUST 2 TO ACCEPT, OR ELSE YOU WILL BE TRIED IN ABSENTIA AND YOUR SENTENCE CARRIED OUT ON YOUR DAUGHTER.

Demetrius crept into the small city hall conference room with a push of the creaky wooden door, with Sean a step behind. He stopped himself just shy of asking how she was doing—*she's doing shitty, you moron,* he chastised himself—before Rebecca's tortured eyes met his.

"Let's hear it," she groaned.

"They, uh, found a body about two hundred meters from what was left of the safe house," Demetrius awkwardly said. "A young girl, clutching a stuffed pink bunny rabbit. Nothing else but, um, bits and pieces of the others."

"Emily," Rebecca croaked—she had long run out of tears. "She never went anywhere without her stuffed rabbit. What was . . ." she gasped, glancing out the windows at the first rays of sunlight coloring the morning sky through the breaking storm clouds. "I can't . . . I can't remember its name."

"Mister Fluffy," Sean whispered with a sad grin. "His name was Mister Fluffy."

"Rebecca," Demetrius said as he pulled out a chair, "I hate to ask you this, but—"

"*No!*" Rebecca exploded, slamming her hand on the table and scattering both notes. "Like I've told Sean, Cade, and everyone fucking else, no, I didn't tell Carleigh about our plans! And it doesn't matter, because Operation Ripley is hereby fucking *cancelled*!" She shot to her feet, her blanket falling to the floor. "Tell them I agree to their terms."

"Rebecca—"

"*I am not going to sacrifice my only daughter!*" she shrieked, hands balled into fists. "I didn't even want to *do* this! This was James's crusade, and now he's dead! And don't you two *dare* say you understand, because you don't have kids! You have no fucking *idea*! The choice of whether Carleigh faces a firing squad or I do is the easiest decision I've ever made in my *life*! Now send the goddamned message or I'll do it myself!" Rebecca screamed, grabbing the Morse transmitter and hurling it against the wall.

Demetrius paused and cleared his throat. "Rebecca, I need you to hear us out for a minute. There's something we'd like to show you," he cautiously ventured as Sean rolled out a map of eastern Washington on the table. Half a dozen blue dots denoted times and sightings reported through Redoubt Radio of a low flight of military helicopters curving southwest from Ione, giving Chewelah and its nonexistent Stinger missile battery a wide berth. A thick black line connecting the dots ended in Yakima, where two handwritten lines summarized a report of a young woman matching Carleigh's description being carried from a Black Hawk at the airport and bundled into a Humvee headed for Yakima County Jail.

"We know where they took her," Sean said. "We can bust Carleigh out."

Rebecca looked up from the map, a tiny ember of hope kindling in her eyes. "You think . . . you think we can?"

"I've done it before," Demetrius answered dryly.

CHAPTER 43

CHEWELAH

"We're moving out at sundown and spending the next two days creeping along the backroads to Snoqualmie Pass," Jed told Mary Ellen and the twins, the early afternoon wind rustling the tall grass surrounding their graves. "Our job's gonna be to shoot any bad guys we see 'till other folks with a lot more firepower and brains than us shut the pass down. Gabe says it could end the fighting for good."

A black-billed magpie fluttered to a landing on the tire swing hanging from the shade oak and gave a brash, laughing *ka-ka-ka-ka-ka*.

"Then I'll come home. Live the rest of my life in peace, here with you . . . and Autumn," Jed said, uncomfortably gazing at the small, fluffy clouds drifting across the sky. "I . . . I hope you understand." He took a step back and thumbed at the tents of the First Chewelah Irregulars farther up the hill in their backyard. "I'll, um, be back before you know it."

Ka-ka-ka-ka-ka, the magpie sang and flew off.

Jed strolled along the narrow path worn through the grass toward the smoke from the backyard fire pit where they had just finished serving lunch. Most of the Irregulars had retreated to their tents to catch some sleep. Low moans from one tent came to a sudden stop with Jed's plodding footfalls, and resumed several seconds later. A couple in another tent made no attempt to keep quiet. *This keeps up, in eighteen years, we'll have enough bodies to field the Third Chewelah Irregulars,* he said to himself.

Reaching the fire, Jed eagerly accepted a bowl of moose stew from Autumn and sat on one of his homemade wooden chairs next to Allan and Julie. "This is delicious—thanks, hon," he said with his mouth full. "How's the family?"

"Good," she answered curtly, having just returned from bicycling into town for a brief visit with her twin brother and his family. They were doing well, except for their stern refusal to let their son, Ronan, join the fighting—they had twice caught him attempting to run away.

Jed wolfed down his lunch while Allan and Julie silently watched the fire in each other's arms. "I think this is the longest I've ever heard you two go without speaking," he quipped.

"Just thinking about the last time we sat waiting for the big climactic battle, praying we'd all be in one piece at the end," Julie said without looking away. "The Battle of Helena was the scariest thing I ever did—I can't tell you how many times I barely missed being shot. Two of our friends weren't so lucky." She pulled Allan closer.

Jed set aside his empty bowl, anxiety killing any appetite for seconds. "That reminds me, Allan," his voice dropping to match the gravity of what he was about to say. "In case . . ."

"No, dude, we don't get the house if you die, because you're coming back," Allan interrupted. "You and Autumn both. And that's enough of that talk."

Autumn slipped her arms around Jed's huge frame. "That's an order."

Jed kissed the top of Autumn's head. "Fair enough. But in the event Autumn and I survive the war only to succumb to some rare disease or freak accident, I left you and Julie everything. Mom's six-digit birthday is the combination to the basement safe with the papers makin' it official. And don't try to honor my memory with a pool party, because the winter freeze cashed it."

Allan smiled. "I love you, Big Brother."

Jed leaned forward and mussed his hair. "Right back at 'cha, little buddy."

Gabe sauntered to the fire and ladled himself a large helping of stew once he was certain that everyone else had eaten their fill. "Brings back memories of the hunting lodge, doesn't it?" he said, squatting on a nearby log and blowing on a spoonful. "Hard to believe we'd be able to look back at being cooped up through that godawful winter as simpler times."

Autumn lifted her head from Jed's embrace. "Hey, Gabe? Seeing as how we're gonna be boldly riding into the mouth of hell, could you finally cut the bullshit and—"

"French Foreign Legion."

"*What?*" she exclaimed as all eyes shot to Gabe.

"Second Foreign Parachute Regiment," Gabe said matter-of-factly. "Gabe Culver is my real name, though—didn't care much for the one they gave me under *anonymat*."

Autumn's jaw dropped. "Well, I'll be damned," she said incredulously.

"You mean to tell me we've been takin' orders from a cheese-eatin' French surrender monkey?" Jed asked in mock indignation. "Allan, never mind what I said about who gets what, 'cause we're all dead anyway!"

"*Va te faire enculer, sale fils de pute,*" Gabe responded, hoisting his canteen in a salute.

***

Rebecca awoke with a jolt to the muffled *pop-pop-pop* of blank rounds from half a dozen rifles echoing down the school hallway. She realized with a groggy glance at her watch that she had managed to nod off for a full five minutes—*when I should've been eating dinner*, she said to herself before unenthusiastically picking at the meal that had been slapped in the plastic tray in her lap.

Over Sean's vociferous objections, Demetrius acquiesced to her demand to be part of the strike team to rescue Carleigh, so long as Rebecca acquiesced to his; she would train with them, over and over, until she puked—and then train some more until she could clear a building blindfolded. The hand-picked team of forty soldiers and partisans—enough to field a four-squad infantry platoon—had taken over Chewelah's vacant junior and senior high school to rehearse. Aside from answering nature's call at a line of vile portable toilets near the athletic field, they were forbidden from leaving the building to prevent tipping anyone off that something was up.

"This seat taken?" Demetrius asked, sliding down the wall next to Rebecca without waiting for a response. "You're drooling, by the way. Power nap?"

Rebecca muttered a curse and wiped the corner of her mouth with the sleeve of the Army OCPs that Sean had managed to find in her size. Demetrius dug into his grilled elk, wheat berries, instant mashed potatoes, and hard bread dabbed with elderberry jam. "You need to eat," he told Rebecca.

"I'm hungry, just not in the mood to eat. Does that make sense?" Rebecca asked and nibbled at her bread.

"Perfect sense. Been there a hundred times myself. But fasting isn't gonna bring Carleigh back—we're gonna do that," Demetrius lectured, gesturing at the two squads of men and women lining both sides of the hallway shoveling down their chow. "You owe it to all these people who volunteered to risk their lives for you to be operating at peak efficiency, so please put some fuel in your tank, OK?"

"Yes, sir," she said with a mock salute and dug into her wheat berries with a grimace.

Tom and Allie zipped into view down the hall, crouching with their weapons at the ready on opposite walls. They rose and began scrolling forward, followed by the other two squads, who were practicing how to secure a T hallway intersection under Sean's watchful eye. The strike team's SOPs for movements, techniques, and hand and arm signals were cobbled together from the best practices of the veterans' various units, Sean's Special Forces training, and from a former member of the Washington State Patrol SWAT team. Sean briefly paused the exercise to dress down two soldiers who kept hugging the walls, reminding them that bullets had a peculiar tendency to skip along walls like a flat stone on a pond.

"I really like Tom and Allie—they're good kids," Rebecca said. "They dating?"

"Major Burns and Hot Lips Houlihan over there, you mean?" Demetrius snorted. "They think they're being discreet, but they're not fooling anybody."

Rebecca choked down her last mouthful of wheat berries. "Did I just say 'dating'? Wow—talk about normalcy bias! Like they could do dinner and a movie somewhere."

"Makes all that COVID-19 crap with the masks and social distancing seem trivial by comparison," Demetrius said.

Rebecca swigged from her canteen to wash away the food's slimy texture. "Remember how everyone thought 2020 was the worst year ever? Everything locked down under a bunch of arbitrary guidelines where government picked winners and losers, our jobs under a Damoclean sword . . . and worrying every day about Carleigh's education because that 'remote learning' nonsense didn't work. That's when I knew America was living on borrowed time—that it would go the way of Rome sooner rather than later. That's how James and I ended up becoming close. I realized the worst was yet to come, and that I owed it to Carleigh to take steps to keep her safe." She paused and sighed. "Did a real good job, didn't I?"

"Yes you did," Demetrius admonished and turned to face her. "When this whole mess started, especially when I was rotting in that jail cell, I felt lucky as hell that I didn't have a family to worry about. But seeing you and Carleigh, I catch myself wondering what all I've missed."

"If you don't mind me saying, I'm surprised you never married," Rebecca said.

"Came close once, but it didn't take—was married to the Army, I guess." Demetrius set his empty tray off to the side. "Why does that surprise you?"

"Well, this is gonna come out awkward, but you're amazing. Women tend to snatch men like you up."

The loud *clunk* of a metal canister hitting the vinyl tile floor echoed through the hallway before Demetrius could respond. "Gas, gas, *gas*! One thousand *one*! One thousand *two*!" Sean bellowed as his two-squad element closed their eyes against the simulated tear gas attack and ripped their rubber M50 protective masks out of their thigh pouches. "One thousand *nine*! Stop what you're doing—hands down!" About half of his soldiers had managed to don, clear, and seal their masks in the nine-second Army standard time limit.

"We're attacking a jail, boys and girls!" Sean yelled. "Those guards are gonna have tear gas, pepper spray, and other shit to incapacitate people! If you can't get this down, one gas grenade could end us." He stabbed a five-finger point down the hall. "After we clear this hallway, masks on, we'll break for chow like these goldbricks sittin' here."

Demetrius shot to his feet and plopped his helmet back on his head. "You gonna take that shit from him?" he yelled to his two squads. "Finish your chow—you can taste it later!" He flashed his rifle's mounted flashlight with three clicks of the rubber button wired to the front handle. "And check your batteries, 'cause we're goin' hard once the sun sets."

CHAPTER 44

CHEWELAH

A battered black pickup truck, its lights taped to glowing slivers to avoid becoming beacons in the early evening twilight, hit a rut in the fallow farmland and bounced the dozen soldiers crammed in the bed with the groan of suspension that had seen better days. The men and women hopped to the ground the moment the truck stopped inside a thick strip of woods between the field and the lonely country road west of town.

"Aaaand that makes forty. Gang's all here," Tom said to no one in particular, slapping a mosquito on his neck as he fell in behind Demetrius. They silently followed the gaggle through the dried wheat stubble from the previous year's harvest toward the strike team forming a school circle around Sean and Rebecca; behind them sat a stick of four idle Black Hawk helicopters, their sleek silhouettes black against the remnants of sunset's glow.

"I'll keep the Knute Rockne speech short," Sean told the soldiers around him. "You've trained your asses off nonstop for two days, and you're as ready as we can get you. We're gonna swoop in, save the senator's daughter, and then fly straight to Objective Hackman to help

drop-kick these fucksticks outta Cascadia for good! We trackin',
everyone?"

The strike team barked in unison.

Rebecca, outfitted in full battle gear like the rest of the team,
stepped forward, her soul leaden with the knowledge that some of
them—a number of whom were barely older than Carleigh—would
not be coming back. "I only have one thing to say—thank you. From
the bottom of my heart." She looked to the cluster of pilots, co-pilots,
and crew chiefs who stood out in the crowd thanks to their flight
jumpsuits and bulbous helmets. "And thank all of you, and the Republic of Montana for loaning you to us."

The lead pilot from the former Montana Air National Guard
stepped forward. "I have a special message to relay," the woman
boomed. "President Karina Jacobs, the Hero of Malmstrom, asked
me to tell all of you—and these are her exact words—to *kill every last
motherfucker who had anything to do with this*! You think you can do
that for her?"

"*Hoo-rah!*" the strike team roared, pumping fists and rifles in the air.

"Let's go!" Sean barked. "Load up by chalk! Team leaders, make
sure everyone's weapons are unloaded—we're not landing hot!"

Demetrius was about to call out for Tom and Allie, who were
with him on his chalk, when he almost backed into them locked in
a passionate embrace. His eyes met Rebecca's in the crowd.

Rebecca glanced back toward the second helicopter in the stick.
"I'm gonna shake some hands first—I don't think I can sit still right
now," she chattered.

"We got this—we're gonna bring Carleigh home," he said, catching
himself from putting his hands on her shoulders. *See the hill, take the
hill*, he told himself before saying what he had endlessly rehearsed in his

mind during his rare moments of down time. "Um, I know the timing's lousy, but there's something I need to tell you, in case—"

Rebecca grabbed Demetrius's vest with both hands and pulled his lips to hers, their chest-mounted rifles coming together with a crash of plastic and metal. She let him go before he could slip his arms around her.

"Tell me when we get back," she said breathlessly. "Now let's go get my baby."

"Yes, ma'am."

Sean watched with a flash of anger and, to his surprise, a hint of jealousy that he promptly banished back to the recesses of his psyche from wherever it came. *This ain't the fucking movies, Captain Mathers,* he silently chastised the duo as they headed toward their chopper. *You both better bring your 'A' game, because those kinds of distractions get people killed.*

His scowl melted into an expression of awe as a familiar face materialized from the darkness and marched straight for him. *Then again, maybe this* is *the fucking movies,* Sean said to himself before running to Animal and bear-hugging his old mentor.

"Easy there, Hawk, or ev'ryone's gonna think we're spoken for like Romeo and Juliet over there," Animal said. "Put me in, coach."

"You bet!" Sean beamed. "I know better than to think you're doing this as a favor to me—why the change of heart?"

"I can't walk away while some tinpot despot kills someone's little girl 'cause of who her mama is," Animal said with determination. "Jo, Marie, and Kelsie would want me to help save her."

"Been a while since I've seen you in regular Army OCPs," Sean said, stepping back to give Animal the once-over. "So who's Staff Sergeant Kingman?" he asked, reading the Velcro name strip affixed to Animal's helmet and MOLLE vest.

"I didn't get to know 'im. I needed an official bad guy uniform, and Staff Sergeant Kingman—may flights of angels carry him to his eternal rest—was my size."

Sean slapped Animal's shoulder. "Works for me."

Rebecca hoisted herself into her Black Hawk, ignoring the proffered hands that shot out as one to help her, and plopped down in the rearward-facing, metal-framed seat closest to the exit. The crew chief leaned in through the open door to help her fasten the seat's complicated five-point harness, but she spun her rifle muzzle down and expertly snapped herself in as if she had ridden in Black Hawks her entire life. "Miss Stevenson," he said, nodding his head in respect, "I genuinely pity the sons o' bitches who end up in your sights."

Animal passed by and slapped Demetrius on the back. "Glad you could join us!" Demetrius called after him before grabbing a burly machine gunner's hand to pull himself inside the helicopter.

"Was that who I think it was?" Rebecca asked incredulously.

"Roger that—heavy artillery," Demetrius answered, buckling himself in. "We're in business now."

The crew chief stepped over to help a young man across from Rebecca who was nervously struggling with his harness. "First time flyin', son?"

"No, sir," the boy sheepishly answered while the crew chief clicked his straps into the correct slots and tugged them tight.

"Just sit back an' enjoy the ride," the crew chief reassured him, spitting from the huge wad of Levi Garrett chew in his mouth. "You're lucky—the rear right forward seat is the best seat on the bird."

"Really?"

"You're gonna love it," he said with a poker face. The crew chief duck-walked through the crowded helicopter, his boots clanging on the aluminum floor as he checked every passenger's harness before clicking in his safety tether and easing into his seat behind the pilot. Rebecca crammed foam plugs in her ears and nervously clutched Demetrius's hand.

The four Black Hawks whined to life as one in the dark, their dual General Electric T700 turboshaft engines steadily rising to a roar as their rotor blades reached takeoff speed, battering the half dozen teenagers left behind to watch the trucks with dust and wheat straw. They lifted into the sky in order, buzzing the treetops and blowing the Stetson hat from the head of the boys' gray-haired chaperone before heading southwest into the darkness.

PART THREE

Deep in his heart, every man longs for a battle to fight, an adventure to live, and a beauty to rescue.

—John Eldredge

CHAPTER 45

YAKIMA

"**S**ergeant Woj?" Captain Nathan Yawkey called from the darkness over the distant din of helicopter rotors.

Air Force Senior Master Sergeant Ed Wojciech grimaced as the baby-faced, lanky officer made a beeline for him and the platoon boarding a column of three Strykers just south of Yakima Air Terminal's main building. *Just great*, he groused.

Yawkey barely bothered to return Ed's salute. "These soldiers here who just got off those Black Hawks—who do they belong to?"

"Hell if I know, sir," Ed lied. "All I know is they got business in town."

"We got a problem, master sergeant," Yawkey said, stepping into the coal-black shadow the trailing Stryker cast from the main terminal's lights. "I just got orders to ramp up security to one hundred percent 'cause some bigwigs are about to fly outta here," he said, pointing to a white aluminum storage building that had been repurposed into a barracks for the airport garrison. "But I can't muster even half that 'cause the goddamn cooks gave my whole company food poisoning!"

Or maybe because the mess sergeant and I put enough laxatives in their chow to uncork an elephant, Ed silently retorted as Yawkey prattled.

"We need to borrow this unit for a bit," Yawkey told Ed as a tall black captain approached from the lead Stryker. "Excuse me, captain, are you—" Yawkey managed to say before realizing he was standing face-to-face with the maniac who had punched his lights out in front of his platoon and killed three MPs when he escaped from the county jail.

Yawkey's decision to grab for his radio rather than his rifle was the last mistake he ever made. Demetrius slammed his helmeted head into the Stryker's armor, disorienting him long enough to step behind his leg and knock him to the ground. He straddled the hapless officer and punched him repeatedly in the throat until he heard a wet *pop* that he felt through his gloved fist. Yawkey clutched his darkening neck, bug-eyed with horror over the realization that his airway was swelling shut, before Demetrius wordlessly put him out of his misery with a boot stomp that crushed his neck and windpipe with a spine-tingling *crunch*.

"Of all the shitty luck!" Demetrius hissed, looking around to see if anyone had spotted him before grabbing under Yawkey's armpits, motioning with a frantic jerk of his head for Ed to grab his feet.

"If we're still alive by the end of the day, you're gonna hafta tell me what in the actual fuck that was all about!" Ed exclaimed with disgust as the duo tossed the corpse into the Stryker to the gasps and curses of the living.

"We're outta here," Demetrius breathlessly told Ed. "On my signal, unleash hell."

"Yes, sir," Ed said. "Bring that girl home. By the way, this is two you owe me after hiding you back in Kennewick—three, if I count being an accessory to murder just now."

"Relax—if the Army's so desperate that they're promoting twerps like this to captain, we'll do just fine," Demetrius said over the whine of the Stryker's rising ramp.

Demetrius made his way to the commander's seat, offering a silent prayer of gratitude that Rebecca was riding with Sean and didn't witness his barbaric act. He yanked the handheld SINCGARS radio from Yawkey's tactical vest and ordered one of his soldiers to search the still-twitching body for any list of frequencies or passwords Yakima's soldiers were using. The frightened young man nodded and took a knee by the corpse, his face beet red and dotted with welts from being battered by the hurricane winds of the helicopter's rotor wash and the straps of his harness during the flight to Yakima.

"So, how'd you like the Black Hawk's bitch seat?" Demetrius asked.

"Fuckin' crew chief—'best seat on the bird,' my ass," the man groused as the Stryker lurched forward.

Ed watched the convoy roll away and checked his watch—he had about fifteen minutes before the strike team let slip the dogs of war at the county jail. He trotted west toward a section of tarmac repurposed as a motor pool, the chop of rotors fading as the stick of refueled Black Hawks—*the getaway cars*, Ed mused—flew east to the strike team's pickup zone at an abandoned industrial lot on the west bank of the Yakima River. Ed rounded a white government fleet transport van and dodged just in time to avoid being brained by a frightened Asian man wielding a large wrench.

"Jeez!" Ed yelped, thrusting his hands in front of his head. "Hitoshi, it's me, Sergeant Woj! For fuck's sake!"

"Gomen nasai," Hitoshi Hamada nervously apologized and lowered the makeshift bludgeon as three of his fellow countrymen, who like Hitoshi wore the dark green spotted fatigues of the Japanese Ground Self-Defense Force, hesitantly emerged from their hiding places behind other vehicles. Ed pitied the detachment of Japanese soldiers who had arrived at the Yakima Training Center as the advance party for the an-

nual Rising Thunder joint exercise right before the collapse. The final order they had received before the entire Tokyo metropolitan area went dark was to do whatever the Americans told them to do; given that the people of rural Washington would have lost their minds if they found themselves policed by foreign troops, the soldiers were delegated to guard duty and doing whatever shit work needed to be done.

Ed pointed to two menacing Apache Guardian attack helicopters dimly lit by a lone portable utility light pole, Sidewinder air-to-air missiles attached to the tips of their stubby ordnance wings. "If we don't knock those out, my pal's gonna have a real short trip. You guys good to go?"

"We're ready," Hitoshi assured in slightly accented English—he had lived in Palo Alto until he was ten, when his father's job took the family back to Osaka. He held up a cheap black plastic FRS radio. "Give the word, and we're—how does the saying go—'off to the races.'"

"Close enough," Ed said, patting a silver aluminum tube discretely tucked into the side of his tactical vest. "And this green star cluster flare is the alternate signal to go in case the radios go tits-up." Hitoshi's request for an explanation of the ribald colloquialism was cut off by a call from the late Captain Yawkey's executive officer. A high-pitched ascending whine in the distance signaled the starting of a large, twin-rotor Chinook cargo helicopter.

"I can't raise the captain, and I got a two-star screamin' on the horn about security to keep him an' his prisoner safe!" the exec griped. "You seen 'im, over?"

"Negative," Ed replied, cringing at the memory of Yawkey's untimely demise. "Wait—did you say 'prisoner,' sir? It would help immensely if I knew what in the Sam Hill was going on, over." Ed pressed his plastic

SINCGARS headphone to the side of his head and jammed his finger in his other ear as the Chinook's engines powered up.

"Prisoner exchange! General Kett and the governor's chief of staff are headin' here straight from the jail and flyin' her to Fairchild to make the swap, over!"

Ed's blood turned to ice water. He turned to see the pilots and gunners of both Apaches trot from the terminal toward their birds.

"Who's 'her'?" he demanded.

CHAPTER 46

"**B**ack to the airport! *Now*!" Sean radioed the Stryker's driver.

"Why?! What's going on?" Rebecca yelled from the seat behind him.

"Lando says they're moving Princess!" Sean hollered to Animal over the engine, the glow from the commander's station screens giving him a ghostly pallor. "They're flyin' her out early!"

"What do we *do*?!" Rebecca cried.

"We improvise!" Animal roared and turned to Sean. "Remember that armory job at Camp Shorabak?"

"That shitshow?"

"It was a shitshow that worked—and seein' as how we got their radio freqs an' passwords courtesy of that officer Demetrius just whooped, it'll work again. If you got a better idea you can pull outta your ass with T-minus zero minutes to go and a strike team nervous as all get out about poppin' their cherries, I'd love to hear it."

Sean mentally allocated his time: sixty seconds to hash out a new plan with Demetrius over the radio, ten seconds to tell the strike team that the plan they had relentlessly rehearsed had gone FUBAR, then another thirty to brief them on the new one. Animal dug his Special Forces, Ranger, and Airborne tabs and Special Forces unit patch from a side pocket and hastily slapped them on his left shoulder.

"Just remember what I repeatedly pounded into your thick skill from the first day we met, Sean," Animal lectured as he rakishly donned his green beret for the first time since his pre-collapse retirement. "If it's stupid but it works . . ."

". . . it's not stupid," Sean finished.

****

The Chinook's crew chief finished his pre-flight inspection walk around the bird and had just started reeling in the long cable connecting his helmet-mounted radio to the cockpit when he spotted a lone figure walking toward him, barely illuminated by the helicopter's cavernous lighted interior bay.

Hitoshi?! What the hell you doin' here? the crew chief wondered. "Chopsticks?" he called out more for his own benefit, knowing full well Hitoshi couldn't hear over the Chinook's monster rotors. He waved his arms to get the Japanese solider's attention and again hollered the nickname he had always assumed—very incorrectly—that Hitoshi didn't mind. "Hey, Chop—" the crew chief managed before Hitoshi expertly drew his Heckler & Koch SFP9-M handgun and put two rounds in his chest and a third between his eyes. Hitoshi padded up the rear ramp of the helicopter; seconds later, six reddish-white flashes burst from the darkened cockpit like a strobe light.

****

"Whaddya *mean*, the Chinook's not responding? It's right down the runway!" Yawkey's exasperated executive officer barked into his radio.

Ed nervously glanced past the gaggle on the darkened tarmac to watch for the returning convoy, his heart racing like a misbehaving boy waiting for his father to step through the door. A four-man security detail of Army Rangers from Second Battalion flanked an infuriated General Kett, an impatient David Hampton—and between them, a disheveled and handcuffed Carleigh Stevenson, her orange jumpsuit a bizarre contrast to Kett's immaculate fatigues and Hampton's gray business suit.

"Lieutenant, I swear to Christ, if you don't get us in the air right now, I'll have you busted down to e-zero!" Kett threatened, the darkness masking his crimson face. "We're standin' out here waitin' for a damn bird we set up hours ago, your ate-up CO is MIA, and you can't even give us a proper perimeter because your soldiers all have the GI shits!"

A set of Stryker headlights sliced through the night from beyond the terminal. "Sir?" Ed interrupted. "I think that's the security detail Captain Yawkey ran out to get!"

"You told me you hadn't heard from the captain," the exec said, puzzled.

"Yes, sir—I mean no, sir," Ed stammered as the convoy sped straight for them. "The, um, last thing he told me before he went out of contact was that he had a line on some outside help—maybe he's with 'em."

"I guess we'll find out—you gentlemen have no idea the depths of the shit you're in," Hampton haughtily said. *That makes two of us*, Ed said to himself, taking advantage of all eyes watching the Strykers wheel to a nearby halt to clandestinely raise his FRS radio to his mouth.

Soldiers thundered down the Strykers' ramps to form a semicircle around the entourage as a menacing older Green Beret strode to the general. The four Rangers crouched and readied their weapons as they tried to process everything going on around them.

"You're all in danger—no time to explain!" Animal yelled, ditching his Dixie drawl for a standard American accent. "We gotta get you outta here!"

"What in the hell's going on?!" Kett demanded.

The executive officer's radio squawked to life. "All stations this net, all stations this net, Code Delta! I say again, Code Delta! Oh, God, it's starting to smoke—it's gonna blow!" Tom Ngo screeched hysterically on Yakima's radio frequency from inside one of the Strykers.

"Code Delta! Someone's found a bomb!" the executive officer breathlessly explained to Kett.

"I know!" Animal hollered. "That's what I'm trying to—"

"Holy shit!" Ed yelled and pointed, silently cheering Hitoshi's impeccable timing. A thermite grenade's blinding heat pierced the dark, illuminating the distant Apache it was placed on in chalky white light as it started burning through the armor toward the fore fuel tank. A second grenade ignited moments later on the other Apache, briefly spotlighting the crews frantically bailing out of their cockpits.

Yawkey's exec and three of the Rangers were focused on the fires, while the fourth spun to check out the commotion coming from the moaning, incontinent soldiers evacuating the distant barracks over the bomb threat. Animal made his move, kneeing Kett squarely in the groin—relieving him of his holstered Sig Sauer M18 sidearm on the way down—and drawing his rifle with lightning speed on the executive officer. The Rangers drew on Animal only to find themselves hopelessly outgunned by the platoon of soldiers, their laser aiming lights dancing like fireflies on their chests.

"There's forty of us, and five of you—six if you count the soyboy in the suit who's never been laid," Animal yelled, his accent back with a vengeance. "We're not here for you—do what you're told and you'll live to see sunrise!" He ordered the Rangers to slowly unload their weapons and hurl their rifle bolts and handgun slides into the darkness—he wasn't about to have his green troops attempt to disarm elite soldiers.

Animal pointed his rifle at Hampton's head as strike team members tossed the Rangers handcuffs and ordered them to secure their own ankles and hands. "Poindexter, please unlock the cuffs on the young lady, if you'd be so kind. And no sudden moves, unless you want me to pop you a new asshole in your forehead. You're up, Mama Bear, and make it quick, 'cause we just pissed on the anthill."

Carleigh eagerly thrust her cuffed hands to Hampton, who shook so badly that it took him several tries to shove the key into the hole. Rebecca strode toward him, rifle in her grip and murder in her eyes, the burning Apache helicopters behind her giving her an almost demonic appearance.

"Mom?!" Carleigh screamed incredulously and ran toward her, only to stop dead in her tracks with Rebecca's outstretched palm. Hampton's mouth flopped open.

"I have a message for you to take back to Alicia," Rebecca growled before viciously shattering the chief of staff's jaw with the butt of her rifle. Hampton screamed and fell to the ground, hands shooting to his mangled face, before she followed up with a blow to the side of his head. "And this is for Jenn and Grant, you son of a *bitch*!" she yelled, kicking Hampton's left kidney and sending several of his teeth skittering on the tarmac.

Friend and foe alike ducked with the bright flash and rolling *kaboom* of one of the sabotaged Apaches flying apart on a glowing mushroom cloud. "It's time to leave!" Demetrius hollered. "Saddle up! By teams, back on the Strykers—let's go!"

Carleigh turned to see that her mother hadn't heard, or was choosing to ignore, the order. "Mom!"

The sound of the Black Hawk helicopters coming to spirit them away began echoing across the darkened airfield. "On second thought, Dave," she growled, clicking the safety off her M5 rifle and cavalierly aiming it at his chest, "I think I'll deliver the message to Alicia myself."

"Mom!" Carleigh screamed as Hampton pathetically whimpered, raising his bloody hands in an attempt to gurgle a plea for mercy. Carleigh grabbed her arm and yanked her away, praying she wouldn't make her pull the trigger—Carleigh would remember the wild, feral look in her mother's eyes for the rest of her days. "He's not worth it! We gotta go!" Rebecca nodded wordlessly, safing her rifle and following Sean as he violently shoved a flex-cuffed General Kett up the ramp of his Stryker.

Ed sprinted to Demetrius and snapped a salute. "Good luck, sir!"

"You're not comin' with us?" Demetrius asked in disbelief. "You can't stay here after all this!"

The duo flinched with the thunderclaps of the Apache's 30-millimeter high-explosive chain gun ammunition beginning to ignite. "I can't just leave those JDF guys high an' dry after they risked their asses to help us!" Ed exclaimed. "I'm gonna round 'em up and we'll bail together!"

"You're a good man, master sergeant!" Demetrius yelled, shaking his hand.

"This makes *four* you owe me!" Ed said and bolted into the night.

Tom raised his Stryker's ramp just high enough so that it would't drag, and Demetrius rolled off the corpse of the late Captain Yawkey with a kick the moment the convoy made a beeline for the hastily arranged pickup zone at the far southeast corner of the airfield. Demetrius clicked down his night-vision goggles and spotted the incoming Black Hawks moving across the stars, the static generated by their rotors spinning in circles like glowing hula hoops. He leaped off the moment Tom slammed on the brakes, almost rolling his ankle hitting the ground, and counted off each passenger as they exited, with Tom and Allie bringing up the rear. The strike team expertly scrambled into their assigned single-file lines for their boarding chalks—it was the first and only task they executed that evening from their endless rehearsals in Chewelah.

Rebecca thrust Carleigh behind Demetrius and slapped her daughter's hand in a death grip on his MOLLE vest. "Follow Captain Mathers to the door, and whatever you do, don't let go!" she screamed into her daughter's ear as the Black Hawks hovered low, battering them with their rotor wash. Rebecca grabbed Carleigh's shoulder from behind and dug in her boots like a sprinter waiting for the starting gun. *Come on, come on, come on*, she chanted to herself.

Demetrius speed-walked for the lead Black Hawk, grabbing Carleigh by the waist and throwing her to the crew chief, who harnessed her into a seat while the rest of the chalk clamored aboard. The machine gunner bringing up the rear had just climbed in when Demetrius caught a flash out of the corner of his eye and heard the *crack* of small-arms fire. "Contact left! Ten o'clock to our direction of flight, one hundred meters!" he hollered to the gunner before grabbing the crew chief by the lapels. "All present! Go, go, go!"

The gunner brought the bulky M240B machine gun to his shoulder and loosed a long burst of covering fire as the helicopter lifted off. Carleigh screamed, slapping her hands to her ears as the machine gun hammered away in the cramped compartment, the gunner walking the red-hot glow of his tracer rounds into the dismounted roving patrol in the night-vision scope mounted to his gun rail.

Rebecca clutched her daughter tightly as the Black Hawk nosed up sharply to clear a line of derelict Alaska Airlines Boeing 737s at the edge of the airfield before speeding for the relative safety of Ahtanum Ridge.

CHAPTER 47

YAKIMA

Animal glanced down at the lifeless face of General Kett—lying on his back in the grass after being inadvertently shot by his would-be rescuers—as he yanked Sean aboard the Black Hawk moments before it tore into the sky to bring up the rear of the stick, small arms fire pinging off its skin. Sean nearly slipped on the blood-slicked floor before throwing himself into his seat and furiously buckling himself in.

"Shit!" Sean cursed at the three empty seats that had been full at the start of the mission.

"Don't beat yourself up 'cause Lady Luck abandoned us at the PZ," Animal yelled. "Your mission was to rescue the senator's daughter. You got 'er done."

"But—"

"They were volunteers who knew the risks," Animal cut him off. "They're heroes."

Sean slumped back in his seat. "Would've been nice to bag the general," he yelled to Animal over the roar of the Black Hawk's rotor. "Bet he would've sung like a canary. I hope his last thought was the realization that his own men shot his ass."

Animal slapped Sean's knee. "You did good. Real good. For what it's worth, Sean, you've always been my—"

The Black Hawk jinked wildly, violently shaking its remaining passengers like ice cubes in a cocktail shaker. A blaring rhythmic alarm from the cockpit was drowned out moments later by the *whoosh-whoosh-whoosh* of the helicopter's tail flare dispensers blasting their glowing countermeasures past the open doors into the night sky, too late to fool the proximity fuse of the Stinger missile that their enemies had loosed at them. Animal had just enough time to watch a chunk of shrapnel punch through the floor and cleave Sean open from crotch to neck before the left side of his face and his left arm erupted in searing, white-hot pain. Animal's last coherent thought against the agony wracking his body was to beg his wife and daughters for forgiveness as the mortally wounded helicopter spiraled toward the ground with its screaming, helpless passengers.

SKYKOMISH

A chain of explosions snapped the pillars of the Route 2 bridge over the south fork of the Skykomish River, their deafening booms shattering the eerie nighttime quiet of the river's namesake valley. The rust-spotted, pea-soup-green trusses groaned and popped as the entire three-hundred-foot span buckled and collapsed in a thundering cascade into the waters below. Seconds later, a smaller flat-top bridge over the river bend a mile to the east suffered the same loud and spectacular fate.

A small band of partisans cheered from their nosebleed seats on the rocky summit of Beckler Peak as the distant explosions flashed and sparkled, followed by the symphony of tons of of steel, concrete, and asphalt crashing to earth. A young woman, her makeshift radio antenna already set up, excitedly reported that Objective Caine was down, and that the garrison at the large, shuttered ski resort at Stevens Pass to the east was now cut off from Olympia and resupply.

The partisans linked up an hour later with the exhausted squad of Army combat engineers who, almost a year after changing sides following the bombing of Colville, got their chance to blow something up for a just cause. They skirted a derelict campground scattered with the shredded, weathered remnants of brightly-colored tents—and the bones of Seattle-area refugees long picked clean by foraging animals—and trudged north up the Beckler River Valley into the protective shroud of Mount Baker-Snoqualmie National Forest to hide until the heat blew over. If it didn't, they would make their way to the Idaho Panhandle or Canada before winter descended on the mountains to snuff them out like candles in a stiff wind.

Cascadia's all-or-nothing gamble had begun.

CHAPTER 48

CAMP MURRAY

"We *had* her! We could've ended this!" Alicia screamed at General Westman, angrily crumpling the report detailing what little they knew of Carleigh Stevenson's rescue and throwing it to the floor. "How the *hell* did this happen?"

Westman shot a disdainful look at Alicia, who stuck out like a sore thumb in the busy EOC; she had dressed to the nines, complete with the scarce post-collapse luxuries of a professional hairdo and makeup, in anticipation of Rebecca Stevenson being delivered to her in irons in exchange for her only daughter. Instead, the resistance not only saved the senator's daughter, but also killed General Kett and destroyed several Apache attack helicopters. Westman stifled a smirk as he pictured Rebecca smashing in the face of the arrogant little shit Alicia called a chief of staff.

"Madam Governor, I learned very early on not to underestimate our enemy's ability to gather intelligence. A number of people spotted the helicopters from the Ione raid and called it in to that radio network of theirs, and it looks like the resistance connected the dots and made some lucky guesses." Westman stared up at the state map on the EOC's main flatscreen as a harried sergeant blew by, slapping him with a whiff of Alicia's cloying perfume. "But to be blunt, ma'am, that's the least of our problems right now."

Color-coded dots indicating partisan raids by location and type had spread across eastern Washington like a pox, faster than the EOC's flustered staff could tally them. Westman nervously noted the disproportionate number of yellow dots indicating attacks on tanker trucks and fuel infrastructure until his eyes went wide with a red dot that sprang up on Route 12, just west of the garrison at the former White Pass Ski Resort.

The general grabbed an iPad and called up the report—a platoon dispatched to investigate a massive explosion discovered that the bridge over Dog Lake and Clear Creek had been destroyed. The moment he finished skimming the report, two more red dots winked into existence over the Route 2 bridges east of Skykomish.

"God-*damn* them!" Westman growled, slamming the iPad to the table with enough force to crack its screen as the resistance's primary goal dawned on him.

"This is a lot of effort to cover the girl's escape," Alicia said in disbelief at the map display.

"No, you blithering idiot, this is all a diversion so they can destroy the mountain passes and cut us off from our forces!" Westman growled, charging for the radio bank and barking orders left and right before Alicia could admonish him for the insult. "Get every last soldier at Snoqualmie Pass outta their racks and onto those bridges—they're weapons free to kill anyone within three klicks of it! I also want every available unit to converge on Snoqualmie Pass to back them up!" He whirled on an Air Force captain. "Get McChord on the horn, right now!"

SNOQUALMIE PASS

The middle-aged commo sergeant stared at the hazy white band of the Milky Way arcing above the forest canopy. "When they comin'?" he asked.

"First light," Miguel whispered.

The sergeant nervously glanced at the dim green readout of his SINC-GARS radio sitting next to Miguel's. "Then it's all over?"

"It's over when it's over, soldier. Now keep quiet—" Miguel said before he was cut off by an incoming SALUTE report—a summary of an enemy unit's size, activity, location, unit identification, time spotted, and equipment—from the small observation team he had deployed to the ridge overlooking the Hyak ski resort turned Army garrison west of the bridges.

"Size—fifteen, that's one five, Strykers," the young woman nervously squawked. "Three of 'em are SHORADS." The news of the three short-range air-defense Stryker models, armed with Stinger surface-to-air missiles, tied Miguel's stomach into a knot.

"Activity—moving east on I-90, about two-zero miles an hour, straight toward Objective Hackman."

"That ain't good!" the sergeant fretted.

"*Sssssh!*" Miguel hissed.

"Location—crossing the Gold Creek bridge . . . *fuck*!" The distant sound of automatic weapons and vehicle-mounted cannons reached the command point several seconds later. "We're taking fire!" the woman yelled. "We gotta—"

Miguel turned to the sergeant, his special forces photographic recall thumbing through a mental list of callsigns. "Tell Bravo Two Three to take out those SHORADS, or this whole thing falls on its ass!" he ordered, muttering a Spanish curse and punching the frequency to order what little armor Cascadia had to roll west on I-90 to meet and bottleneck the enemy at point-blank range. What had started as a clandestine operation, dependent on stealth and guile to succeed, was about to become a full-on donnybrook pitting armor and infantry of the former United States Army against insurgents.

BRAVO TWO THREE

The bulky Javelin missile launcher bounced on Luis's shoulder as he galloped from his recon unit's cache site in the woods to the nature trail skirting Keechelus Lake's western shore.

He dropped to a knee at the water's edge and set the missile tube's command launch unit to night mode, waiting for it to warm up as he listened for the distant whines of the Strykers rolling down I-90 on the other side of the lake. The three hours since the squad had left Billy and Olivia's cozy home—apologizing profusely for waking them with their racket—had been a blur of ranger-filing in the dark to their cache and digging up the anti-armor missiles for the part of the job they had never revealed to their gracious hosts.

Luis traversed the interstate with the Javelin's two-handed vertical grips the instant the foam-padded thermal sights came to life, and almost immediately found the convoy, glowing white hot against the cold face of the steep wooded cliff behind it. He locked onto the lead SHORAD, its boxy turret-mounted Stinger launcher distinguishing it from its immediate neighbors.

"*Ya te chingaste, güey,*" Luis taunted and sent the missile on its way with a *ka-pow*. He cheered in triumph the moment his sights whited out with the explosion announcing that the Javelin had found its mark, then snapped his night-vision goggles back down over his eyes and sprinted a hundred meters down the darkened trail to where his buddy David was waiting with another missile. Behind him, a Javelin from the unit's other launcher tore after the next SHORAD in the convoy with a glowing *whoosh*.

Luis slid into the dirt next to David and immediately went to work popping the launch unit from the spent tube. They couldn't fire missiles from the cover of the thick woods, and didn't have time to dig defensive positions, so they had to shoot from the open, their body heat advertising their location to the enemy armor's thermal sights like neon signs.

"Let's go, let's go, *let's go!*" David anxiously chanted, glancing at the two burning hulks across the lake and slapping a fresh battery coolant unit in Luis's hand. "We're totally fuckin' exposed, dude!"

"I know, I know! Hold it still!" Luis yelled as he snapped the launch unit onto the fresh missile tube. He had just pulled the pin to release the missile tube's cap when an explosion lopped off his arm at the shoulder—he had two seconds to scream before the follow-on shells from a Stryker Dragoon violently dismembered both young men. Moments later, a Javelin fired by the surviving missile crew slammed into the Dragoon's top hatch, a fireball announcing the kill before the recon unit's survivors tucked tail and retreated. They made it twenty meters into the woods before return fire from the convoy blew them to pieces.

CHAPTER 49

The steep forest ridge overlooking I-90 and Keechelus Lake erupted into dozens of firefights in the early morning light between partisan units and the dismounted infantry tasked with clearing it.

Allan fired blindly at the muzzle flash from a machine gun that had pinned down the First Chewelah Irregulars, then quickly dove behind his cover of a fallen pine tree as a long burst of 7.62-millimeter return fire showered him with bark and wood chips. The machine gun fell silent a second later with the *boom* of a .50-caliber sniper rifle.

"They're falling back! Pour it on!" Gabe screamed, firing at the retreating soldiers from behind an evergreen.

Allan popped back over the log and peered through his M5 rifle's advanced scope, waiting for any survivor of the machine gun crew to pick up the weapon. A blurry figure, glowing under the scope's infrared, stumbled to his feet with the bulky M240B in hand, and Allan shot him twice before the weaker recoil of the second shot informed him that his magazine was empty. He dropped back down and hastily reloaded as his fellow Irregulars and the withdrawing soldiers exchanged fire, the smell of cordite giving way to the nauseating smell of the smoke grenades the enemy had hurled to cover their withdrawal.

Cade materialized from the woods like an apparition and crouched next to Gabe, his bulky green ghillie suit making him look like a rifle-toting Sasquatch in the sepia of morning light just starting to filter through the woods. "You got it from here? I got other places to be."

Gabe nodded vigorously. "We can do this all day!"

"Out-fucking-standing," Cade said, pointing to an Air Force joint terminal tactical attack controller chattering into a radio at the cliff edge, eyes on the dual avalanche bridge spans. "Guard him with your life, 'cause if he goes down, we're done." Cade bolted past Allan, who blurted out a lame thanks for killing the machine gunner as he ran by.

"Hey, Frenchy!" the controller called to Gabe, who had acquired the nickname after coming clean about his mysterious past. "I need your radioman on me, pronto!"

Allan sprinted to the controller, his left toe catching a root and slamming him to the ground. He rose on all fours with a groan, peering downhill as an enemy Stryker trying to maneuver around the smoldering hulks of burning armored vehicles blocking the eastbound bridge took an anti-armor shell to the engine block and exploded. Allan shook his head to clear the ringing in his ears as the Cascadia M1228 Stryker that scored the kill with its monster 106-millimeter turret gun scooted in full reverse to take cover around the bend.

"You any good with those radios, high-speed?" the controller asked Allan, nodding at the handheld ham radio and the handheld model SINCGARS strapped to the chest of his MOLLE vest.

"The best!" Allan shot back.

The controller held up his hand for silence. "Eyeball One," a distant voice echoed from his headset, "Skull Banger One coming in, heading three five zero."

"Skull Banger One, you are cleared hot," the controller radioed back with the calmness of a bored teenager taking an order at a fast-food drive-thru before grabbing Allan's arm and pulling him close over the sounds of battle. "Glad to hear it, Sparky, because you got about three minutes to tell every friendly within nine hundred meters of those bridges to pull back before they get turned inside out."

CHAPTER 50

Rebecca alit from the Black Hawk the moment its tires touched the wide, overgrown grass airstrip in the abandoned small town of Easton, and lunged with one hand to stop Carleigh's futile struggle to undo her seat harness.

"Get her back to Chewelah!" she hollered in the crew chief's face as the rest of the strike team followed Demetrius off the bird. "If we lose, take her back to Helena with you and keep her safe!"

"Mom, *no!*" Carleigh shrieked, yanking her harness buckle in futility, the helicopter's blood-red interior night light intensifying her crazed face. *"I love—"* she screamed before the crew chief slid the helicopter's side door shut.

The Black Hawk tore into the sky, its rotor wash pelting Rebecca's back and helmet with dust and small rocks as she hustled away at a crouch to join the strike team's survivors. Her heart, already heavy with Sean's death, sank deeper upon seeing the noticeably smaller group. A man rubbed the back of a young woman hunched down and sobbing uncontrollably—*her brother*, he silently mouthed to answer Rebecca's mournful stare.

A convoy of Strykers burst from the woods surrounding the airstrip and drove straight for the team, almost invisible in the darkness, their drivers relying on the vehicles' sophisticated vision enhancement systems. The lead vehicle rolled to a halt and its commander's hatch flew open, the dim interior lighting revealing a chiseled black face with captain's bars on his helmet.

"Cap'n Midnight! Long time, no see!" Deion Carver yelled down to Demetrius.

Demetrius smiled ear to ear at his former executive officer, now promoted to Battle Company's commander. "Glad you got my invite to the party! What'cha bring?"

"Taco dip, a case of Heineken, and eight Strykers full of eleven bravos wantin' to get their kill on," Deion answered. "And there's more where we came from—Alpha and Charger companies came over to our side, and they're roarin' up I-82 from Yakima to link up! Where you want us?"

Demetrius knifed his hand west down I-90 toward the chatter of gunfire. "The FEBA is straight shot down the highway! Drop your dismounts two klicks down the road to reinforce the ridge, then press forward to back up the little armor we have—they're gonna be happy as hell to see you!" Rebecca shuddered with the realization that they'd be driving headlong into the thick of it; *FEBA*, she remembered from her officer days—*forward edge of the battle area.*

A loud twin-engine howl overhead quickly rose to drown out the battle, followed by a brief but deafening *brrrrrrrt* that reflexively forced hands to virgin ears.

"What the hell was that?!" a young man screamed.

Demetrius grinned savagely. "A big flying can of whoop-ass."

***

The Free State of Idaho announced its official entry into Cascadia's war for independence with a bang.

The A-10 Thunderbolt from the 190th Fighter Squadron at Gowen Field lined up on the bottlenecked Olympia armored column and let rip with the massive seven-barreled GAU-8 Avenger cannon built into its nose, its depleted uranium rounds slicing through four Strykers in one pass like a hot knife through soft cheese. A second later, a Hellfire anti-armor missile launched by his wingman polished off the column's lone remaining SHORAD before both fighters banked hard left over Keechelus Lake.

Idaho President Jed Curtis had personally promised Rebecca the air support following Carleigh's abduction and the death of James Rand and his family, both of which violated the no-fly zone he had imposed over eastern Washington. The Thunderbolt—affectionately nicknamed "the Warthog" by American grunts on account of its ugly appearance compared to sleek modern fighters—was essentially a ground-attack fighter built around a huge tank-busting Gatling gun. Arguably the greatest close air support plane ever built, the Warthog could deliver an obscene amount of air-to-ground ordnance while taking an ungodly amount of punishment.

Moments after the Warthogs cleared the area, a pair of F-15E Eagles from Mountain Home Air Force Base dropped two GBU-24 Paveway III laser-guided bombs that hammered the eastbound bridge within a second of each other. Hardened for penetration, the two-thousand-pound warheads punched through the concrete base to the steel support beams before exploding. Three hundred feet of the 1,200-foot span came crashing down as the force of the tandem blasts snapped back trees at the cliff's edge like toothpicks and tossed the hulks of destroyed Strykers in the air like pieces on a board game hit by a petulant child. A rockslide loosed by the blasts battered the thick concrete pillars of the westbound bridge, which defiantly remained standing.

***

Allan and Julie helped each other to their feet, heads pounding and spinning from the dual blast waves that had washed over them.

"Was it good for you?" the controller ribbed with a grin.

Julie was about to tell the controller to shove his radio into a very undignified and uncomfortable location when she gawked at the sight of the demolished bridge through the thinning smoke and dust in the morning light; silence had briefly settled on the battlefield, as if the bombs had pushed the pause button on the fighting. She pointed to the eastbound bridge as Gabe, Jed, and Autumn trudged up behind them, shaking their heads and holding their noses to pop their ears. "I figured those explosions would've taken out the other one, too."

"Those sons of guns are built to withstand everything Mother Nature can throw at 'em, which in the Cascades is a lot," the controller answered. "Tell you the truth, I'm amazed the bridge actually went down on the first try."

Allan pressed his radio headset into his ear to better hear the sudden burst of chatter. "Well, dude, I hope to Christ your flying friends brought more bombs, 'cause there's a second, larger armored column—this one with Apaches—heading this way!" The *brrrrrrrt* of a Warthog's main gun engaging the new targets echoed from the valley as if to emphasize Allan's statement.

The controller scanned the intact span with his binoculars. "They did, and if we got this timed right, your war's gonna be over in a couple more minutes, give or take. You all may wanna hug some earth again, 'cause we got another delivery coming . . ." the controller warned before agitated squawking from his radio interrupted him.

Autumn gasped as a blossoming explosion overhead announced the fiery death of one of their F-15s at the hands of an AIM-9X Sidewinder air-to-air missile. Early morning sunlight flashed off the wingman's fuselage as the pilot jinked away, dumping a scattering path of white-hot flares to avoid befalling the same fate.

CHAPTER 51

SNOQUALMIE PASS

"Where the hell did they come from?" Demetrius yelled in disbelief as the mishmash air wing loyal to Olympia fanned out to engage the surviving Idaho F-15s.

"Does it matter?" Miguel shot back just before the roar of jet engines tore through the woods. *"Everybody down!"*

Demetrius instinctively tackled Rebecca, who screamed into the dirt and pine needles against the ear-splitting pain of an A-10 pilot tearing over the treetops in full retreat—the Warthog and its four-hundred-mph top speed was no match against air superiority fighters. "Get her out of here!" he ordered Tom and Allie as he yanked Rebecca to her feet and practically shoved her at the duo. "We'll buy you as much time as we can!"

"Like hell! I'm staying!" Rebecca argued, yanking free from Tom's grip.

Tom and Allie glanced at each other. "Us, too!" they barked in unison.

"Are you *kidding me*?!" Demetrius screamed over a loud explosion. "You got minutes, tops, before their armor breaks through! This isn't a game!"

"I *know* it's not a game!" Rebecca shrieked, charging at Demetrius and getting in his face. "The last man who said those very words to me died this morning saving my daughter! This is bigger than me, or anyone else! I'm done running!" she yelled, her face crimson under the sweat-streaked camouflage paint she had hastily slathered on her face in the Black Hawk. "If you all are going down fighting, so am I!"

Small-arms fire grew louder and closer. "Fine!" Demetrius growled. "As for you two clowns," he seethed, his angry glare flicking to Tom and Allie, "get Molly Pitcher here across the overpass so we can make our last stand!"

"Molly Pitcher was a fucking amateur!" Rebecca yelled and ran after them.

***

Olympia's armor—a mix of Strykers from the Second Infantry Division and the 161st Infantry Division of the Washington Army National Guard—immediately exploited its sudden change in fortune.

The lead Stryker rammed aside the blackened remains of a gutted SHORAD and crashed through a crumbling section of median into the westbound lanes. Its main cannon barked, sending a high-explosive round streaking down I-90 to blow apart the Cascadian Stryker that had inadvertently led Demetrius's reinforcements into a rout with the arrival of Olympia's air power. The attacking Strykers dashed across the surviving bridge to pursue the Cascadian armor retreating up the sloping interstate hugging the ridge high above the water's edge.

An Apache Guardian gunship darted ahead to engage the Cascadian armor withdrawing around the bend, only to be blotted out of the sky by a Stinger launched from Keechelus Lake's far shore. Another

Apache swung around to hose the launch site with a salvo of folding-fin antipersonnel rockets from its dual wing-mounted cylindrical launchers as its mortally wounded wingman plummeted into the clear blue lake with a splash.

Above the fray, Air Force fighter jets that had once defended fifty United States together whirled in an intricate and deadly dance to kill one another. For the first time in more than half a century, American pilots found themselves locked in a full-blown furball against equals, rather than the one-sided turkey shoots to which they had become accustomed since the First Gulf War.

BOVILL, IDAHO

Alexandra Chase listened in disbelief to the unfolding disaster, feeling the anxious gazes of her crew drilling into her.

A cautious optimism kindled by Carleigh Stevenson's rescue and the near simultaneous destruction of the bridges at White and Stevens passes had grown more and more infectious as report after report came in of partisans rising up in revolt throughout Cascadia. The cheers that had echoed throughout their sweltering aluminum pole barn with the destruction of one of the Snoqualmie Pass avalanche bridges had fallen silent with the news of Olympia's fighter reinforcements as if a giant vacuum had sucked the air from the room.

Paul grabbed a rag from his jeans pocket and nervously mopped his brow—the rising summer sun added to the oppressive heat building up from the bank of radios lining both sides of the unventilated prefab. "We might wanna think about pullin' up stakes and relocating, babe. They don't need some NSA supercomputer to triangulate our signal—they know exactly where we are, and with Idaho officially enterin' the war, the gloves are off."

"We're not going anywhere," Alexandra said, turning to face her husband and her crew. "I'm going on—as many bands as you can. Make it happen."

Paul dashed to an adjacent transceiver, almost tripping over the myriad cords snaking out the side door to noisy and noxious diesel generators and field-expedient antennas of every size and shape. Alexandra donned her headphones and scooted her cheap folding metal chair across the concrete floor, her finger stabbing the microphone's transmit button the moment Paul's hands finished darting across the controls.

"If you live in Cascadia, ladies and gentlemen, and you can make it to Snoqualmie Pass, liberty needs you. Right now. And if you happen to be President Curtis of Idaho, President Beckstead of Utah, or you just happen to have a fighter jet in your garage or know someone who does, liberty *really* needs you . . ."

Alexandra's loyal cadre of operators looked at one another and darted for their stations to relay the message to as many ears as they could reach.

CHAPTER 52

SNOQUALMIE PASS

Rebecca nervously stroked her rifle's safety with her thumb as she counted down the final minutes of her life.

She blinked stinging sweat from her eyes and peered into her rifle scope through the evergreens dotting the forward slope of the hill into which she had dug in, next to the few spare forces Demetrius and Miguel could muster. Smoke from burning vehicles and fires started by the battle had begun darkening the sky to the sound of small-arms fire growing closer and closer as their enemy advanced. Morning light danced on the lake beyond I-90's sharp curve around the ridge—at any moment, the shattered remnants of Cascadia's armor would come barreling around, with Olympia in hot pursuit.

Rebecca trembled in her hasty firing position—a human-sized trench barely scraped out of the rocky earth—as her pulse bounced her sight picture like she was riding a horse. Down the hill to her left, two soldiers carrying their few remaining AT-4 anti-armor rockets hustled across the large earthen nature overpass built so wildlife could safely cross the interstate—and which presented the last and best opportunity to bottleneck the enemy armor at its two concrete tunnels through which I-90 ran.

Demetrius radioed their two Javelin teams to remind them that the first Strykers would be friendlies, and to order them not to engage the enemy until right before they reached the overpass. The first friendly Stryker peeled around the bend, followed by a second, its blackened and smoking cannon askew at a 90-degree angle. *Thank God their magazine didn't cook off*, Rebecca thought a moment before a Hellfire missile slammed into its side and exploded.

"Deion!" Demetrius screamed as a stream of .50-caliber fire from the woods scared off the Apache gunship that had popped over the ridge just long enough to kill his friend.

The lead enemy Stryker burst forth moments later from the acrid smoke billowing from the demolished vehicle, followed by another, and another, and another. Rebecca slowly thumbed off her safety, knowing full well that her rifle would be as effective against armor as throwing rocks, and sighted on the lead Stryker still out of range, discipline over-riding her pulse and steadying her aim on the thick ballistic glass of the driver's window slits.

I wish I would've said goodbye to Carleigh, she thought before the Stryker in her sights flew apart in a violent explosion—she screamed and buried her head into the dirt as another explosion announcing the death of a second Stryker stabbed into her eardrums like icepicks.

"Goddammit, you assholes!" Demetrius screamed at his distant Javelin crews, hurling his radio to the ground. "I said wait until they reach the overpass! We had one chance to bottle 'em up, and *you fucked it up!*"

"Those weren't our Javelins! That was somethin' else!" Miguel yelled.

"Yeah! Like reinforcements!" Allie whooped, pointing at the sky.

***

"*Tally tally tally!* Bandits, one o'clock, angels eleven! Weapons free, Red Group!" Lieutenant Commander Callie Harman announced to the three other F-35C pilots in her formation as the stealthy fighters prepared to announce their arrival to the Air Force pilots flying for Olympia.

The F-16 fighter boxed in a lock in Callie's sophisticated helmet visor didn't stand a chance. "Red One—fox three!" she yelled, thumbing the red release button on the top of her stick. Her left weapons bay popped open just long enough to loose an AIM-120 AMRAAM radar-guided missile that closed the distance in moments and disintegrated the Falcon into a flaming ball.

"Splash one!" she triumphantly announced. *That was for you, Kurgan!*

A distant flash announced that Red Three, the leader of her other two-fighter element, had likewise scored his first kill. "Make that splash two, Amazon!"

The icons representing the downed Falcons disappeared from Callie's tactical situation display, which was populated with air and ground targets fed to her on-board computer from all sixteen fighters the Warhawks had brought to the fight, courtesy of Captain Fitzgerald's decision to stop sitting on the sidelines and throw Kitsap's weight behind Cascadia. The enemy armor wasn't her concern; her half of the squadron was tasked with clearing the skies. Green squares highlighting every fighter not from Idaho filled her visor; the Warhawks had to shoot down as many as they could before they closed the gap with air superiority fighters that could give the F-35, designed to ambush by stealth from a distance rather than dogfighting, a run for its money.

Red Three and Four peeled off to engage their next target. "Red Two!" Callie called to her wingman. "Keep up with me, and keep 'em off my ass!"

"Right with you, boss!"

***

Partisans pumped their rifles in the air as a pair of F-35s dispatched four more Strykers with their deadly GBU-53B StormBreaker precision-guided bombs, forcing the remaining enemy armor to wheel back around the bend as fast as they had arrived.

Tom gave Allie a high-five. "I never thought I'd say this, but thank God for the Navy!" he cheered before tipping his helmet to Rebecca. "No offense, ma'am."

"None taken!" she said, excitedly craning her neck to watch Olympia's air force scatter before the Warhawks.

"Let's hope those fast movers brought iron to drop on that last bridge!" Demetrius said. "Miguel, can you try and raise 'em . . ."

"We may not need to!" Miguel's commo sergeant interrupted, jerking his head up from his radio. "We still got one of our Warthogs in the air, and she's packin' Paveways!" he yelled, stabbing his SINCGARS frequency preset for their Air Force ground controller. A *boom* overhead announced another Warhawk kill as Demetrius gave the order for their surviving armor to advance to contact while staying at least a kilometer from the remaining bridge span.

CHAPTER 53

CAMP MURRAY

General Westman watched from the roof of the EOC while the Navy handed him his ass.

The fighter wing that he and the commander of McChord Air Force Base had cobbled together from surviving units all over the western half of the former United States had been preparing to launch a second wave to finish off Snoqualmie Pass's attackers when they were jumped by F/A-18 Super Hornets from the *Stennis*. Two carrier fighter squadrons—VFA-14, "The Tophatters," and VFA-41, "The Black Aces"—tangled with Olympia's air force in the skies above JBLM and the blackened ruins of the Seattle metro area, while the Warhawks and their ultramodern F-35s had punched sonic to rush to Cascadia's aid.

"Sir?" Lieutenant Torres timidly ventured from behind. "Governor Embrey ordered us to raise Kitsap, but they're not answering."

"Of course not—why would they? Alicia's always full of good ideas, isn't she?" Westman quietly muttered.

Black geysers of smoke and dust, followed by a chain of *cr-rumps*, heralded a Super Hornet cratering McChord's runway with a string of Mark 82 bombs. Westman's mind wandered to his many deployments to Iraq and Afghanistan, and all the times his unit called in air support to rain death on hapless al-Qaida and Taliban insurgents.

"So this is what it feels like."

"Sir?" Torres ventured.

"That'll be all, lieutenant, thank you," he said, eyes still transfixed on the air battle.

A flash of blue from below caught Westman's eye, and he glanced down to see a pudgy figure, wearing his emergency management polo shirt and khakis, hustling through the EOC checkpoint, backpack slung over his shoulder.

"Hey, Tony!"

Emergency Management Director Antonio DiBernardi froze in his tracks and slowly turned, nervously looking around until he spotted Westman on the roof.

"I dunno where you think you're gonna hide—your signature's right beside Alicia's on every shitty order she ever gave," he called out, voice dripping with contempt. "They're gonna find you and string you up right alongside the rest of us."

DiBernardi tucked tail and ran for the motor pool, huffing and puffing for about fifty feet before slowing to a power walk. *Good luck surviving five minutes outside the wire, you fat fuck*, Westman said to himself, giving DiBernardi a sarcastic wave goodbye before following Lieutenant Torres back through the roof access door.

CHAPTER 54

SNOQUALMIE PASS

The roar and the overpressure from the Paveway bomb that slammed into the surviving bridge did its best to pop Jed's brains out through his ears.

He rose with a grimace and shambled back uphill on shaky legs with the rest of the First Irregulars, praying that the surviving Warthog had brought down the remaining span. The Air Force controller laid prone on the hill crest behind the tripod-mounted Joint Effects Targeting System he had hastily set up to "paint" the westbound bridge with a laser to guide the smart bomb because the Warthog had taken a bullet to its underslung targeting pod. The lake breeze slowly cleared the smoke to reveal a hole blown through the leftmost lane, but the bridge still standing and its remaining two lanes usable.

"If this is some kind of a joke, I don't think it's funny!" Autumn shouted over the Irregulars' howls of disbelief.

"Bridges are tough nuts to crack," the controller lectured, slewing the cereal box-sized JETS module to find a spot to target the next bomb. "I remember hearin' 'bout a bridge in Iraq that took four sorties to bring down. But seeing as how we don't have three more tries to spare, we're just gonna hafta do it right the next—"

A burst of rifle fire sliced through the controller's chest and shattered the JETS unit, peppering Allan's face with metal and plastic fragments. Allan dropped to the ground, screaming and clawing his face, as Julie grabbed him by his tactical vest and dragged him to cover while the rest of the Irregulars hit the dirt and indiscriminately returned fire into the woods in the general direction of their enemy. The *whoosh* of surface-to-air missiles streaking after *Stennis*'s F-35s from further down I-90 announced the arrival of even more enemy reinforcements heading for the bridge.

***

Cade safed his sniper rifle with his latest kill—a young soldier readying a Stinger to fire at a passing F-35—and prepared to relocate to another position when Miguel's agitated voice buzzed in his earpiece.

"Not now, Caracara—displacing to an alternate hide. Call you in a few mikes," Cade responded, glancing nervously in the direction of a firefight that sounded close.

"Yes, now, Eagle!" Miguel shot back. "We need you to get eyes on I-90 and find our Stryker Dragoon—the one you and Grant stole back in Chewelah. The Air Force controller on loan from Idaho just got zapped, and that Stryker has our one remaining JETS designator. We got the bombs to finish the job but no way to paint the remaining bridge! How copy, over?"

Cade hugged the earth with a curse and scanned the interstate through his rifle scope as fast as attention to detail allowed—every second he remained in his old position increased his odds of being detected, and proportionally decreased his odds of dying of old age. He located the Stryker, knocked on its side and its front end blackened and smashed, but its passenger compartment, still marked with the painted black chevrons from the Battle of Chewelah, relatively intact. Cade reported its location as a long burst of glowing red tracers from a machine gun darted into the Olympia-occupied section of woods. "Let me guess—this is my primary field of fire to cover the poor saps you're gonna send on a suicide mission to snag it."

Miguel paused. "Roger that. We need you to displace somewhere you can cover 'em, over."

"That 'somewhere' would be right fucking here! I'll be sure to tell Sean and Grant when I see 'em that you said hello! Out!" Cade growled, shifting under his ghillie suit into into a stable firing position to await the final act.

CHAPTER 55

"You're lucky you wear glasses, or the shrapnel would've blinded you," Carol Price, the former St. Joseph's nurse turned First Irregulars' combat medic, told Allan as she wrapped his head with gauze to hold a sterile pad on a deep gash over his left eye. "Nothing I can do about your ugly mug, though—I wouldn't count on a career as a face model when this is all over."

Allan fingered his shattered lenses, head pounding, as his gaze uncomfortably shifted to the bloody poncho covering the Air Force controller's body. "Coulda been worse," he murmured.

The rest of the Irregulars knelt around Miguel as he taught a crash course on operating a JETS designator with the mangled, blood-spattered remains of the old one. Their mission was straightforward and dangerous—make a mad dash down I-90 to grab the designator from the Stryker Dragoon and bring it back. Miguel's impromptu class left unspoken the worst-case scenario—pinned down and unable to return, the Irregulars might have to call in the airstrike on themselves.

Behind them, Tom and Allie hurled speedballs—sandbags stuffed with their remaining ammunition and refilled canteens—out of the back of their Stryker to runners ferrying them to the various units scattered along the ridge. The cacophony of small-arms fire grew more intense—with the Navy handling the enemy's armor, Demetrius had ordered every last foot soldier to the ridge to be in a position to give the First Irregulars as much covering fire as they could.

The Irregulars rose, scared to death over what they had been asked to do, as Gabe began shepherding them to a steep and narrow deer path that would take them to I-90 and a waiting Stryker—the sole surviving vehicle of Demetrius's former company. "Why can't those Navy pilots do this? Why's it gotta be us?" a thirty-something Irregular nervously groused, his eyes darting among his comrades for some sign of support.

Gabe pointed up through the forest canopy at a crippled fighter jet—he couldn't tell if it was friend or foe—trailing smoke across the sky. "Luck of the Irish. Navy didn't bring bridge busters to the party, and we're the nearest unit to the objective that hasn't been chewed up."

"Not yet, anyway," Carol quipped and swallowed hard. "Got a bad feeling that's gonna change right quick."

Julie smacked the bottom of the thick plastic Magpul magazine seated in her rifle. "Not if we do our job and do it right—so the sooner we get to the bridge and grab this thing, the better." She moved to fall in at the rear of the Irregulars' column before Jed's large hand fell on her shoulder to stop her.

"Wait, Julie," Jed said, waiting until the rest of the Irregulars walked out of earshot before continuing *sotto voce*. "We need you to stay here with Allan and step in to work the radios if he's not up to it."

"*What?!* Whaddya *mean*, stay here?" Julie stammered. "You're gonna need every live body you can get!" She angrily spun to Allan, who slowly rose to his feet, head spinning. "Did *you* put them up to this?"

"No, he didn't, hon," Autumn said like a mother trying to console a child processing tragedy. "This was our idea."

Julie looked over Autumn's shoulder to Gabe, who solemnly nodded his blessing to the decision. "But—"

"You and Allan used up all your luck back in Montana. You've done your part," Autumn said, a nervous smile crossing her face underneath her helmet and faded camouflage paint. "If the worst happens, someone's gotta live, Julie. We'd like it to be you two."

Jed pulled Julie and Allan into a hug. "I miss Mary Ellen, Mikey, and Beth like you wouldn't believe. They haunt me every day. But you both got my word that I'm not lookin' to fulfill some sorta death wish," he huskily said before pushing them away. "You're both stayin' here, just in case. Understand?"

The duo nodded in unison and winced with the not-too-distant explosion of a 40-millimeter rifle grenade hitting its target. Allan stepped forward and hugged Autumn. "Shoulda done that when we first met. Sorry," he sheepishly said. Autumn bit her lip and grabbed Jed's hand.

Jed lightly slugged Allan in the arm. "You turned out all right after all, Little Brother," he said with an approving nod before he, Autumn, and Gabe ran to join the rest of their comrades in arms.

Gabe darted to the front of the single-file line making its way down the path. "Come on, you apes!" he yelled, picking up speed. "You wanna live forever?"

"You damned fuckin' bet we do!" Carol retorted, helmet flopping on her head and medic aid bag bouncing on her diminutive frame as the Irregulars quickened into a double time.

CHAPTER 56

CHENEY

The pitiful convoy of two Light Medium Tactical Vehicles—both still painted desert tan from some previous Mideast war—rolled off the Eastern Washington University campus in defeat.

"See ya around, kids!" Derek Nealon sarcastically called after them, standing atop a surrendered Humvee and cradling a newly liberated M5 rifle as the rising sun peeked over dilapidated campus buildings. "Don't let the door hit ya where the Good Lord split ya!"

The end of Olympia's occupation of Cheney, after months of cloak-and-dagger plotting by the town's two resistance cells, was comically anticlimactic. Within hours of receiving the coded message over Redoubt Radio that the big attack was on, the partisans crept out after curfew, armed themselves at a weapons cache buried under the front porch of the Alpha Phi sorority house, and with the help of a platoon that had defected, got the drop on the other two garrisoned in town with only a handful of shots fired. The only casualties were a wounded soldier and the resistance's token sad sack, who had managed to shoot himself in the foot.

Sergeant First Class McGreavy strode to the Humvee, which was parked next to the small pile of surrendered weapons in the Roos Field parking lot that had served as the refugee chow point during the first months of the collapse. "You'll be happy to know my men just locked up your quisling mayor and police chief—what you do with 'em is your call. But you let everyone know that anyone who's got any bright ideas about fuckin' with the refugees is gonna hafta deal with us." Derek nodded his agreement—while his feelings toward Cheney's remaining displaced persons had softened, other townspeople were chomping at the bit to "kick the goddamn city people out on their asses," or do worse.

The platoon sergeant rolled himself a smoke and lit up with a *click-clack* of his Zippo lighter. "I'm orderin' everyone to prepare for counterattack, but they ain't comin' back." He took a deep drag and sighed contentedly. "Believe me, they're happier'n you are that this is all over."

"Provided them folks at Snoqualmie Pass can get 'er done," Ty called out from the Humvee's passenger seat, a black Grundig radio pressed to his ear. "From what the lady on the radio's sayin', it ain't soundin' too good."

CHAPTER 57

SNOQUALMIE PASS

Jed tried his best to keep his heart from leaping out of his throat as the Stryker carrying the Irregulars tore down westbound I-90's long incline toward the damaged but standing bridge. The clatter of the raging battle—their friends laying down covering fire, and their foes firing back and hopefully not paying any mind to the lone armored vehicle on a suicide run—intensified through their protective armor shell the closer they drew to their objective.

"Watch out for—" the anxious NCO in the commander's seat yelled before the driver hooked around a smoldering vehicle hulk. Autumn's fingernails dug into Jed's muscular arm like talons as the frightened Irregulars swayed in their seats.

"I got eyes, sergeant!" the driver shrieked, fear driving her voice to a shrill pitch. "Stop fuckin' backseat driving!"

Gabe almost pitched forward into Jed with another sharp swerve, swallowing his panic as the rollover-prone Stryker rocked back and forth on its wheels before straightening out. The man who groused about why the Navy couldn't blow the bridge looked to his teammates, bug-eyed with batshit fear as sounds of the outside fighting intensified. "Y'all don't hear that?! We're drivin' straight into that shit!" he screamed.

"*Can* it, goddammit!" Gabe snapped. "Let's get what we came for!"

"Get ready!" the NCO bellowed without taking his eyes from his periscope display screen, giving scant warning before the driver slammed on the brakes, violently pitching the Irregulars into one another. The sergeant stabbed a button launching sixteen smoke grenades from the Stryker's four turret-mounted countermeasures dispensers in a wide, sweeping frontal arc to hide them from the slopes full of enemies trying to kill them.

"Let's go!" Gabe screamed before he was cut off by the deafening hammer blows of 20-millimeter rounds punching through the engine block and the driver compartment from above.

***

A young black man in Army OCP camouflage bearing the three chevrons and rocker of a staff sergeant slid in the pine needles next to Rebecca. "Where you want us, ma'am?" he breathlessly asked, nodding back to his nine-man squad and three-man machine gun team sheltering behind whatever cover they could find; additional reinforcements of partisans and defecting soldiers had been arriving in a growing trickle.

Rebecca knifed her arm dead ahead into the trees to the northwest. "Just follow the shooting! If they're wearing the same uniform as you but facing this way, they're bad guys!"

"Situation normal—all fucked up!" the squad leader retorted with a growl and ordered his squad to advance to contact by fire teams. His four-man alpha team had just leaped up to dash forward to cover when the overhead scream of an F-16 and the buzz of its M-61 Vulcan gun forced them back to the dirt.

Allan screamed from a nearby fighting position, helplessly watching through binoculars as the Stryker carrying his brother and their fellow Irregulars got peppered by the fighter jet's strafing run. Smoke billowed from their mortally wounded armored vehicle, mixing with the white tactical smokescreen to create a greasy gray smear across the interstate.

"Can we get any of our new armor up the road to extract 'em?" Demetrius yelled, slamming his fist into the dirt in frustration. Miguel violently shook his head—Alpha and Charger companies from Yakima had their hands full slugging it out with enemy armor that had crossed the bridge in a desperate effort to take Cascadia's forces from behind. The distant *pow* of a Stryker's anti-armor cannon was followed by the much closer buzz of the newly arrived machine gunner laying down fire—Olympia's infantry was edging closer.

Julie shook Allan's arm without taking her eye off her rifle scope trained on their friends. "They're OK!"

Gabe hopped from the door hatch built into the Stryker's raised ramp, stumbling and almost losing his balance after dropping three feet to the ground. Jed followed a second later, smoke puffing from the top of the hatchway in belches as he grabbed Autumn by the waist and helped her down. The former Legionnaire waved his arm forward and sprinted across the lanes to the destroyed Dragoon, with Jed and Autumn in tow under cover of the thinning smoke. Gabe fell to his knees in front of the commander's top hatch next to the blackened turret, its dented cannon pointing skyward like the limb of a dead bird, and yanked out the severed upper half of the former commander before diving inside.

CHAPTER 58

Callie pulled into a tight turn to pursue the F-16 that had just strafed the Irregulars' exposed Stryker, the legs of her anti-g suit inflating to press into her flesh like large blood-pressure cuffs to prevent the blood in her head from pooling to her feet.

Her prey—sporting the unique green, black, and tan paint scheme of the Eighteenth Aggressor Squadron at Eielson Air Force Base in Alaska—hesitated for a critical moment before trying to jink her off his tail, and that mistake, like many made in combat, would cost the pilot his life. Too close to loose her last air-to-air missile, Callie shot down the Falcon with a burst from her fighter's underslung GAU-22 gun pod, which burned through its pitifully small 220-round magazine to make the kill. Callie barely had time to savor the victory before her flight computer warned that a heat-seeking surface-to-air missile had locked onto her.

She banked hard and dove for the earth, grunting against the g-forces threatening to squeeze her unconscious like a wrestler trapped in a head-lock. Her fighter's sophisticated onboard computer automatically dispensed flares to throw the Stinger off, correctly deducing that Callie was too busy to do it herself—but luck, which more often than not decided who lived on the battlefield and who didn't, had sided with the missileer hiding somewhere in the wooded mountains below. The Stinger wasn't fooled by the flares or the F-35's stealthy design minimizing its infrared signature, and detonated just behind the fighter. Shrapnel peppered the fuselage, and the force of the explosion hammered Callie as if a giant had punched her in the back.

"Eject! Eject! Eject!" the computer wailed.

"Oh, shi-i-i-i-i-it!" Callie gurgled, g-forces throttling her, as she yanked the yellow and black pull handle between her legs, her fighter coming apart around her.

CHAPTER 59

Autumn's flashlight cut through the darkness of the shattered Dragoon, illuminating Gabe's and Jed's frantic search through debris slathered with human remains.

The stench of burnt plastic and rubber stung Jed's eyes and nostrils as he stumbled over a seat back, his hands shooting out into a cool, slimy pile that he realized with a pass of Autumn's flashlight had been someone's intestines. He dry-heaved a disgusted curse and wiped the entrails on his pant leg as Gabe shot straight up to yank at a tan sack wedged between two sheets of metal, freeing it with a rip on the third try. He tore it open and pulled out the JETS unit, his heart skipping a beat before it purred to life undamaged.

"We're in business!" he hollered, inputting the four-digit pulse code to guide the Warthog's next Paveway to the bridge before stuffing the unit and its attached laser designator back in the sack. A nearby explosion rang through the Dragoon like the inside of a metal can hit by a steel rod. "Let's get the hell outta here!"

"How? Our ride is toast!" Autumn yelled and snapped off her flashlight, her kneeling frame silhouetted against the morning light from the open hatch.

Gabe stumbled to Autumn at a crouch, the sack tucked under his left arm. "We hoof it! There's a spot back the way we came, where the forest slopes down to meet the highway! That's our exit!"

"Are you nuts?!" Autumn yelled in disbelief as Jed crawled up to them. "We'll be fish in a barrel!"

"No choice! We'll haul ass under as much covering fire as our friends can give us!" Gabe replied, stabbing his finger at the dismembered lower half of the vehicle commander. "We stay here, and we'll be adding our guts to the pile!"

The trio scrambled out the hatch and took cover behind the Dragoon. Gabe looked over at the rest of the Irregulars, similarly huddled behind their smoldering vehicle, as he radioed Allan to tell the soldiers on the ridge to start pouring it on. "Listen up!" Gabe bellowed at the top of his lungs over the invigorated covering fire. "We gotta make a run for it! There's a place . . ." He knifed his hand back down I-90 over the hammer blow of an F-35 pounding a distant enemy position with a precision-guided bomb. "About three hundred meters from here—that's a thousand feet—where the woods come down to meet the road and we can climb back up the ridge!" Cade held out the JETS sack with both hands. "If I go down, the next person grabs this and keeps going! This has to get back in one piece! You understand?!" The Irregulars gave a unified, terrified nod.

Gabe glanced skyward and begged God for mercy as two F-15s whirled overhead, locked in a deadly *pas de deux*, the sun glinting off their fuselages as they tried to kill one another. "We go on three! One! Two!" Gabe hunched down like a sprinter, clutching the JETS tight to his abdomen and realizing that he was covered in gore from the Dragoon's hapless passengers.

"Three!"

The First Chewelah Irregulars made it twenty feet before the world exploded around them.

***

The gunner behind the tripod-mounted Mark 19 automatic grenade launcher only got off one burst at the Irregulars before Cade turned his head into pink mist. The assistant gunner dove behind an evergreen tree in a futile effort to avoid his buddy's fate before Cade's next thumb-sized .50-caliber bullet violently skewered him from shoulder to tailbone.

Cade dispassionately traversed and blew open the chest of the third man on the launcher crew in a desperate effort to prevent anyone else from finishing the job on the brave partisans who had volunteered to make a desperation run for the JETS designator. He hastily slapped in his sole remaining magazine loaded with Raufoss high-explosive rounds, settled his breathing, and laid his crosshairs on the boxy, short-barreled launcher's receiver just below the feed tray cover. A pull of the trigger turned the Mark 19 into inoperable junk with a bang and a shower of sparks.

He was long overdue to displace to an alternate position, but the Irregulars were counting on him to pick off threats—he already had added a dozen kills to his tally before spotting the Mark 19's bright muzzle flash as it unleashed. His earpiece hummed with Miguel's frantic efforts to coordinate some sort of rescue for the First Irregulars as he scanned the woods for more targets.

Cade knew his luck had finally run out with the twin booms of 81-millimeter mortars echoing through the valley. The jumble of small units slugging it out along the ridge had prevented Olympia's forces from employing indirect fire out of fear of hitting their own soldiers, but some patient enemy had managed to spot him, and came to the very smart realization that killing an ex-Special Forces sniper was worth the risk of fratricide. Cade had just enough time to take a shot at a first lieutenant before the mortars splashed around him.

He mercifully never felt a thing.

CHAPTER 60

Allan's pleading voice, and searing pain, yanked Jed up from the black of unconsciousness.

Jed shook his head to clear his blurred vision, the dull throbbing of his temples exploding into excruciating pain as if someone had jammed icepicks into them. He found himself sitting upright against the rear of the Dragoon, howling with agony with his attempt to move his mangled left leg. His howl devolved into a mindless shriek the moment he saw Autumn lying nearby, face down on the pavement in a pool of blood, her left forearm hacked off at the elbow.

The rest of the Irregulars were sprawled before him—some where they had been struck down, others, like him, flung by the concussive force of the Mark 19's grenades. Being the slowest member of the Irregulars had saved Jed's life, but just barely. He followed his little brother's hysterical pleas to the radio attached to Gabe's eviscerated body, his lifeless eyes staring at Jed like marbles from his pale, exsanguine face.

Jed fell to his belly, white-hot pain burning through his leg, and pulled himself toward Gabe's corpse, and the bloody JETS sack he was still clutching in his arms.

***

"*No*, you big palooka, I didn't say expose yourself!" Allan screamed into the radio at his brother, his leg leaving a bloody trail as he dragged himself to Gabe and ripped the laser designator from his grasp. "*Stay where you are!* Help's coming!"

Allan winced with the *pop-pop-pop-pop* of an F-35's air-to-ground munitions hammering enemy positions elsewhere down the line and retrained his binoculars on his big brother, who had hurled the sack and Gabe's radio to the rear of the Dragoon before making a determined beeline for Autumn. Carol Price had managed to struggle onto all fours, bloody limbs shaking under the weight of the medic bag on her back, before two rounds sliced though her with puffs of red and knocked her back down to the pavement.

"*Fuck you!* She's a fucking *medic*, for Christ's sake!" Julie screamed at Carol's faceless executioner, shifting aim toward the enemy and indiscriminately emptying her clip in anger as as Jed grabbed the back of Autumn's MOLLE vest and pulled her to cover.

Jed propped himself back up on the Dragoon with a groan, laying Autumn's head onto his good leg and ripping the lightweight JETS unit out of its sack. Finding it undamaged, he set it in his lap and grabbed Gabe's radio handset. "We got the laser, Little Brother. We can end this."

"Okay, now *stay put!*" Allan yelled, tears stinging his eyes. "We're trying to get an APC out to reel you guys in! Just hang on!"

Autumn coughed up blood with a gurgle, the rivulet running down her mouth and further darkening her crimson-stained chin. Jed gently popped the strap to her helmet, which fell to the concrete with a hollow thud. "Allan . . . put the honcho on the horn who's talkin' to the planes."

Miguel ripped the radio from Allan's hand before he could say a word, easily holding the lanky young man at bay with his forearm. "I'm here, sir. What'cha got for us?"

"Our one and only chance," Jed answered, hissing as pain shot through him. "The laser pointer's working, and set to the pulse frequency you gave us. And I'm staring at a nice big fat crack running all the way across the bridge." Autumn spasmed and spat up more blood. "Call that Warthog driver an' have him deliver the air mail. I'll guide it in."

Allan screamed and clawed at Miguel as Demetrius helped pin him down. "Good copy," Miguel said. "It's vital you keep that designator on, an' pointed steady, right in the center of the span. Your fast mover's gonna be inbound from the south." Miguel paused. "Thank you, sir."

"Don't mention it," Jed said with a sardonic grin, his heart starting to race. "Tell everyone who doesn't wanna meet Saint Peter with us to haul ass."

"Fall back!" Demetrius hollered, leaping off of Allan and repeating the order to Miguel's assistant radioman, who chanted it into his headset as he picked up and ran.

Rebecca helped Julie pull Allan to his feet as he snatched his radio back from Miguel and frantically tried to raise his brother. "Jed would want you to make it!" Julie yelled hoarsely. "It's time to go!"

"Jed?! *Jed!* Goddamn you, *pick up*!" Allan screamed into the handset as Julie shoved him in the back to get him moving.

Rebecca spun to Miguel, who was relaying instructions to the A-10 pilot from the SINCGARS stuffed in his rucksack. "That means you, too, Caracara!"

"Negative, *Mamá Oso*," Miguel said, not taking his eyes off the bridge. "I gotta keep eyes on the objective an' make sure there's nothin' tryin' to shoot the Warthog down. I'll be OK—deaf as a fuckin' post, but OK. Get outta here! Scram!"

Rebecca stared forlornly downhill through the trees at the distant man and his fallen friends before Demetrius gripped her arm and pulled her along, the *zip zip zip* of incoming rounds snapping tree branches above their heads as they dashed for cover.

CHAPTER 61

J ed silenced Allan's wails with a click of the volume knob and tossed the radio off to his side.

Autumn's gurgling had stopped. Jed put two fingers to her neck and felt no pulse. He kissed her forehead and reached up to gently close her eyes and caress her cheek with his thumb. *Thank you, Autumn. For everything.*

Jed barely flinched as a stray round pinged off the side of the Dragoon. "You're not stoppin' what's coming, you sons of bitches—day late and a dollar short," Jed groaned as he grasped the JETS, its black carrying strap looped around his right hand like an old-time camcorder. He picked a spot smack in the middle of the fissure in the bridge through the black rubber eyepiece and lazed it, the readout informing him that nothing was blocking the beam—*because I'm only thirty feet away*, he thought.

Jed struggled against the dizziness that began washing over him, either from blood loss or the realization that he was about to die; he fought to steady his trembling arms to keep the laser where it needed to be. He smiled haggardly with the thought of seeing Mary Ellen and the children again before he snuck a quick glance at Autumn's face. *It woulda been nice for us to have had more time—*

The Paveway slammed into the bridge deck, its thunderous explosion ripping the span down the middle. Weakened by the earlier bomb strike and the collapse of the eastbound bridge, the entire central third buckled, crumbling to the earth with a tremendous roar that gave way to an oppressive silence punctuated by debris and dust falling like a light spring rain.

CHAPTER 62

The dirty white bedsheet tied to the thick branch in Tom's grip flapped in the steady summer mountain breeze.

Demetrius, Tom, and Allie cautiously trudged down an old gravel US Forest Service logging road that followed the spine of Keechelus Ridge; ahead of them stood the two-man Olympia delegation waiting for them, their own white flag waving in the wind. The trio passed the smoldering remains of what had once been a beautiful, secluded mountain home toward the burned husk of an up-armored Humvee; Allie stared with morbid fascination at the charred body of a partisan who had been shot after successfully setting it aflame with a Molotov cocktail.

Demetrius stifled a smirk upon recognizing the full-bird colonel who came to parley an end to the conflict, now that the bulk of his forces were trapped with the destruction of the bridges. "Been a while, sir," he said, snapping a salute.

Robert McAndrews returned the courtesy. "Yes, Captain Mathers, it has been."

"Congratulations on the promotion—you were a major when you had me locked up at Yakima and promised to have me shot," Demetrius said. "Speaking of our old stomping grounds at the county jail, we started our day rescuing Senator Stevenson's daughter before your betters could execute her for her mother's politics. You work for some real up-standing human beings, colonel."

"You must be loving this," McAndrews said with a scowl.

"No, sir. I hate it. I've hated every minute of it. So let's talk about ending it."

"Fine by me—you've wasted enough of my time already," McAndrews growled. "What are your terms?"

Demetrius pointed northwest. "You and your men lay down your arms, walk I-90 back to Seattle, and never come back. We keep your weapons and your vehicles—that includes everything you still have at Hyak and the ski resort, but we'll let you have enough non-combat stuff to transport your wounded. Once you reach the King County line, or should I say Cascadia's sovereign border, you all can keep walking the hardball to what's left of Seattle, arrange for pickup, go AWOL, whatever you wanna do—you just can't do it here."

"That simple?" McAndrews asked.

"If you want, sir, we can pen you all up like animals in a makeshift POW camp, but we don't have the resources to feed and care for prisoners, thanks in great part to the wholesale plundering you've done on Olympia's orders. We're not nearly as good at violating the Geneva and Hague conventions as you've become, but we're willing to learn," Demetrius shot back before forcing himself to keep his cool. He nodded at a pair of F-35s orbiting overhead. "Do you accept these terms, or do we tell our new friends to resume the turkey shoot?"

McAndrews glanced skyward. "If it hadn't been for the Navy saving your bacon, I'd be dictating *you* terms right now."

"No, you wouldn't. We would've melted into the mountains and kept on fighting—on and on and on, without end. You know that."

Demetrius paused and took a deep breath. "We were all Americans once. Let's stop the bloodshed, colonel—right here and now."

McAndrews resignedly nodded his acceptance, standing silently as Demetrius dictated how his soldiers would be disarmed and released. The two officers shook hands and saluted before heading back the way they came.

"Hey, colonel!" Demetrius called out a minute later. McAndrews stopped without turning around.

"Told ya I was smarter than you!"

Allie chided Demetrius with a *tsk-tsk* as they casually strolled back to friendly lines under the watchful eyes of a hundred unseen partisans in the woods. "That wasn't very nice, sir."

"Felt good, though," Demetrius said, grabbing his radio to relay the logistics of the surrender while trying his best, with growing trepidation, to mentally tally how many people he had left. Tom lowered the white flag and cheerily carried it on his shoulder like a hobo carrying his meager possessions in a bindle.

The trio strolled into a small clearing and made a beeline for a group of soldiers and partisans huddled around Miguel, the rucksack with his olive-drab SINCGARS perched on a moss-covered stump. "Just in time, amigo!" he beamed with a mischievous smile, handing Rebecca the black plastic phone; resting in the pine needles at Miguel's feet was a small booklet of Olympia's frequencies and passwords, spattered with the blood of an enemy radiotelephone operator who no longer had need of it.

Rebecca shot Demetrius a wink and keyed the thick rubberized talk button. "Well, Alicia, you wanted me—here I am!"

"This isn't over!" Alicia stormed, the tinniness of the speaker amplifying the rage in her voice.

"You and I must not be looking at the same battlefield," Rebecca retorted. "I know you never liked leaving Seattle to visit us rednecks in the backwater provinces, but you really oughta check out the view here—the crystal-clear lake, the bridges we just blew to hell, your army slinking away with their tails between their legs . . . Bob Ross couldn't have painted a nicer picture."

Demetrius and several older guerrillas stifled a laugh. "Who?" Allie asked.

"Later," Demetrius whispered.

Rebecca grinned at the crowd. "Anyway, Alicia, you're done. This is a courtesy call to let you know Cascadia's free. Leave us alone, and we'll leave you alone. You can keep Seattle and the 'burbs. They're *aalllllllllll* yours."

"I'll be damned if I ever, *ever*, let that happen!" Alicia snarled.

"Well, it just did—I'm not asking for permission, least of all yours, because we don't need it. Oh, and suffice it to say that if you *ever* show your ugly mug this side of the mountains, or you're stupid enough to let me get my hands on you after what you did to Carleigh, I promise you'll have a noose around your neck before you know what hit you, and I'll personally yank the lever to send you off to hell. Now order the rest of your forces off our soil—it's over."

"How about you try and move them yourself, Becky? See if you and your hick army can keep rolling lucky sevens? Go fuck yourself!"

"Stand down, Alicia—there's no way you're gonna win," Rebecca tried to reason without sounding pleading—the governor was more right than she knew. Alicia didn't reply.

"Alicia?"

Silence.

"Goddammit!" Rebecca snarled, spiking the handset to the ground.

"This is Major General Jack Westman, Commander of Forces in Washington," a voice blared from the speaker a second later. "Senator Stevenson, are you still there, over?"

Rebecca dove for the phone like an offensive lineman saving a fumble. "Yes! I'm here. Where's Alicia, over?"

"The governor has been removed from office," Westman dryly replied. Rebecca, slack-jawed, angrily waved her free hand to hush the swearing and muted anticipatory cheers of her audience. "Senator Stevenson, I can agree to your terms, provided you can promise me, on your oath as a former military officer, that your forces will allow my men and women safe passage. Can you give me that assurance, over?"

Rebecca looked at Demetrius and Miguel, both of whom nodded vigorously.

"Wait a minute!" a middle-aged partisan angrily blurted. "Sorry to stick my oar in, ma'am, but we're gonna let 'em all go? Some of these monsters did some really despicable things—like the soldiers who kidnapped your daughter, and the ones who burned down my house with my wife an' kids in it. Can't we slow-release these bastards so we can pick out the war criminals and hold 'em over for trial, or something?" he asked to grunts of approval.

Rebecca removed her helmet and shook her head. "I'm so sorry for your loss, but hear me out. The reason my friend James and his far-right caucus in the Senate never got anything done was because they couldn't compromise—it was their way, or no way at all. They forgot that perfect is the enemy of the good." She looked around at the men and women circled around her. "Believe it or not, this war was the easy part. We have a new nation to build, and we have to work very hard, very fast, to keep everyone from starving to death this winter. We're gonna have to leave vengeance to the Lord, as the Good Book says." The man sadly fell silent while the assembled warriors around him silently nodded consensus.

Rebecca raised the handset to her lips and took a deep breath. "You have a deal, general. Your troops have forty-eight hours, not one second more—I can't guarantee their safety after that. In exchange, I demand you release all prisoners your forces are holding, military and civilian alike. Do we have a deal?"

"Wilco—I'll immediately issue stand-down orders to all forces statewide," Westman responded. "Thank you—and good luck to you, ma'am."

The crowd erupted in cheers, pumping fists and rifles into the air as Rebecca grabbed Demetrius's face with both hands and kissed him. "We did it," they blurted at the same time, laughed, and kissed again to hoots and hollers.

Demetrius dispatched the idle partisans to the two points—the Forest Service road and I-90 just east of the demolished bridges—where surrendering soldiers would report to be disarmed. The skies above the clearing became busier with the arrival of fighter reinforcements from Idaho, the *Stennis*, and thanks to Alexandra Chase's plea, Hill Air Force Base in Utah. They were late to the dance, but a welcome sight that would give their vanquished foes second thoughts about changing their minds.

"Remind me when I have time to breathe to thank Captain Fitzgerald at Kitsap," Rebecca said, gazing at the orbiting fighters as she slipped her arm around Demetrius. "The Navy more than made up for Colville."

Demetrius snapped his fingers. "That reminds me!" he exclaimed, patting down the Velcro pockets of his MOLLE vest with one hand and grabbing Rebecca's left hand with the other while Tom and Allie exchanged conspiratorial grins. Rebecca squirmed uneasily as Demetrius produced a ring and slid it on her finger.

"Captain Mathers, you're moving a little fast for me here . . ." she said until the sight of the Annapolis ring she had hurled into the falls when they first met rendered her speechless. "How—where did you . . ." she blurted, examining her hand in disbelief.

"We were up near Colville right after the spring thaw to check on the survivors, and in a blatant and grotesque abuse of my authority, I granted myself and my trusty sidekicks here a twenty-four-hour pass to go back to the falls and pan through ice-cold muck like gold prospectors."

Rebecca stood on her tiptoes to kiss him again. "So," she asked Tom and Allie, "how long has he been pining for me like a pathetic little puppy dog?"

"Pretty much at, 'Hi, I'm Rebecca Stevenson,'" Tom laughed.

Demetrius shot him and Allie a comic scowl. "You're both busted back down to private."

"Nope," Allie smiled, shaking her head. "You can't demote us, 'cause we both quit."

Tom put his arm around her shoulder. "I like bein' in an army where you can give two weeks' notice, don't you, dear?"

"Absolutely—why didn't anyone think of that before?"

Their grins evaporated when Demetrius's faux scowl melted into genuine hurt. "We're not leaving just yet, sir—we'll have lots of time for a proper goodbye," Tom reassured and gazed into Allie's eyes. "We've been talking it over, and we're heading to Alabama." His parents and siblings had not only survived the collapse, but also managed with re-emerging commerce to reopen their restaurant. "I'm gonna introduce my Irish lass here to what real food tastes like—maybe even open a restaurant of our own someday."

"We'll do Vietnamese-Irish fusion—we'll make spicy, exotic cuisine and then boil it for six hours 'til it's soft," Allie joked. "In all seriousness, we'll also be closer to what's left of Indy, and we can try to find out what happened to my family." She turned to Miguel, who hoisted his heavy Special Forces rucksack onto his back with a grunt. "What about you, big guy? What're you gonna do with your life?"

The former Green Beret looked down at Allie and grinned sadly. "Well, kid, seein' as how all my friends are waitin' for me in Valhalla, my first order of business'll be gettin' wasted."

"I think they'd like that," Rebecca said.

Miguel's face softened. "There's more to the story, *Mamá Oso*. Our first night at the Rands' house, right before you an' Carleigh showed up—the last night you could sleep without havin' one eye open—the four of us an' James hit his basement bar. We all got pretty lit. Even let James Jr. have his first beer—Mrs. Rand was *pissed*." Rebecca chuckled sadly at the mental picture of friends and loved ones forever absent.

"Anyway, James pulls out this bottle of real expensive scotch his law firm bought 'im for winnin' some huge case. Says he'd been savin' it for a special occasion, an' figures the end of the world was as good a reason as any, but suddenly, in a moment of drunken clarity, decides we should cache it for the last survivor. James was one smart hombre—he knew a fight was comin'—but who woulda thought it'd only take a year to get to the last man standin'?" Miguel sighed. "Rebecca, Demetrius, once we get back and I dig it up, I'd be honored if you two'll get drunk an' disorderly with me to honor their memories. Hope you two like your Glenfiddich neat, 'cause I ain't climbin' Mount Rainier to chisel you off some ice cubes."

Demetrius slapped his shoulder. "It'd be our pleasure. And if you wouldn't mind, I'd like to belt a few back in honor of Battle Company—they came here out of loyalty to me, and . . ." He paused to fight his quivering lower lip. "And I don't think many of 'em made it."

"We'll polish off the bottle," Miguel said sadly. "And, *Mamá Oso*, as long as we're talkin' 'bout our futures, I got nowhere to go, an' I'd rather not wander the wastes as a Puerto Rican *ronin*, so if it's all the same to you, I'd, um . . . like to stay on as your an' Carleigh's guardian, if you'll have me."

A tear rolled down Rebecca's cheek. "You sweet, sweet man," she said and gently put her hand on Miguel's bearded face. "I wouldn't want it any other way."

"B'sides," Miguel said, stabbing his finger at Demetrius, "you're gonna need someone to protect you from this shady motherfucker." The distant eruption of gunfire from further up the ridge cut their laughter short; Miguel, suddenly all business, ordered Tom and Allie to find their Stryker and drive it back to their position, and barked to a nearby cluster of soldiers to form a loose perimeter around the senator. "I need you to stay put 'till we know it's safe," he told Rebecca as he flung his rucksack to the ground to access his radio. "Sounds like some *cabrónes* didn't get the memo that the war's over—lemme see what I can do."

Tom and Allie sprinted for the logging road. Rebecca curled up in Demetrius's arms and began shaking uncontrollably.

"You OK?" he asked.

She laid her head on Demetrius's chest. "A very dear friend once told me that courage was doing what you had to do and getting scared out of your wits later," she said, teeth chattering. "I guess it's officially later."

The couple held each other, listening to the wind rustling through the evergreens and the hum of fighter jets prowling overhead.

CHAPTER 63

SNOQUALMIE PASS

Allan held his knees on the buckled interstate and sobbed like a lost soul.

Julie rubbed his back, glancing for the hundredth time through the thinning dust and smoke at the gaps where the massive concrete avalanche bridges had once stood, the edges of the surviving sections a tangle of gnarled and twisted steel beams and rebar. The interstate's lanes were strewn with debris and the bloody, charred pieces of what had once been human beings; because the First Irregulars were at ground zero of the final Paveway explosion, neither Allan nor any of their next of kin would ever have a body to mourn over.

The highway was the surrender point for enemy troops caught on the far side when the bridges fell. Soldiers anxiously waited in line on the shoulder to hand over their weapons and night vision gear before being allowed to slide down the embankment and tread across the debris at the lake's edge to begin their trek back to Washington. Cascadian partisans, augmented by machine gunners in the cupolas of two armored Humvees, kept a menacing vigil, ready to turn the surrender into a mass execution if anyone tried anything stupid. A five-man work detail loaded the growing pile of confiscated weapons, ammunition, and gear into a waiting truck.

"Gone . . . they're all gone," Allan bawled, rocking back and forth. "Why are we still here? *Why do we get to live?!*"

Julie coughed, wincing in pain from a throat burned raw from yelling and screaming. "It wasn't our time," she hoarsely whispered, arms wrapped around his shoulders. Anguish radiated from him in waves. "*Ssssssh.* It wasn't our time. It's gonna be OK," she lied, knowing in her heart that Allan would never be OK again.

"Miss Eddington?" a scared young voice timidly croaked from behind.

Julie turned to find Max, the teenage drone pilot who had ended up in the Second Chewelah Irregulars when the group split in two back in Newport, trembling before her. His clothes and military-surplus web gear looked like he had been fed through a shredder, his face barely recognizable under a mask of dirt, dust, and blood from which pierced wild, bloodshot eyes. Behind him, the weapons detail stopped one by one to gawk.

"Oh, thank God!" Julie said, leaping to her feet before stopping cold as Max shrunk back as if she was radioactive. A black handgun shook in his quaking hand.

"I . . ." he stammered. "I saw . . . I—I've seen . . ."

Allan slowly rose, wiping his nose on his sleeve and dislodging the sweat-soaked, filthy, bandage around his head. "I know, Max. We lost Jed and . . . everyone else."

"So . . . we're it?"

Allan nodded sadly. "Think so," he answered, voice catching in his throat.

The boy took another step back, eyes bulging, as he slowly brought the gun up to the side of his head.

Julie raised her hands and took a cautious step toward him. "Please don't, Max. Please. It's over. We won." The gun shook in Max's hand like a sapling in a hurricane. Julie crept toward him until they were face to face. "You have your whole life ahead of you. It may not seem like it right now, but you do. Please don't throw it away."

Max's lower lip quivered for a second before he flung himself into Julie's arms. Allan darted to him and gingerly safed the gun before prying it from his hand.

"I got no one," he cried into Julie's shoulder.

"Yes, you do," Julie said, coughing again. "You have us."

Allan yelled to the nearby weapons detail to find a medic, and a young Asian man peeled off and galloped down the highway as Julie sat Max down. "I'm sorry about your brother," Max whimpered to Allan. "I know how it feels, man. I got nothing."

"You don't know that," Julie said, stroking his mussed hair. "You said the Army drafted your brother and took him away, right? He could very well be alive somewhere. Let's find him together."

Max sniffled loudly and looked at Julie, a flash of hope flickering in his pained eyes. "How?"

She looked up at Allan and smiled as the young partisan jogged back with an Army medic plucked from the surrender line. "With the help of the greatest radio operator who ever lived."

Allan stared at his girlfriend consoling the disheveled boy and re-membered the endless hours he had spent since the collapse listening to surviving hams trying to reunite families. He had desperately wanted to do his part to help, but the strict radio silence imposed at their Helena survival retreat, at his insistence, had kept him from pitching in, and he had been way too busy in Cascadia fighting the war. Allan decided he would make it his mission to help Max find his brother; and when he did, he'd make it his purpose in life to help the people of Chewelah—or anyone anywhere who asked—find their loved ones.

It saved him.

CAMP MURRAY

The smell of cordite gave way to the stink of urine as the EOC's ventilation system filtered the gun smoke from the air.

General Westman stood over Alicia's body, face down in a pool of blood that had already started coagulating where it followed the seams of the laminate tiles. He realized with a start that he was still holding his handgun and quickly sheathed it in his belt holster, part of him morbidly wondering whether Alicia had pissed herself the moment he drew his gun, or after she died.

"It's done, sir," Torres reported from the radio bank, deliberately averting her eyes from the grisly sight. Westman's terse order had been relayed to all subordinate commands: immediately cease all military operations and leave Cascadian soil within forty-eight hours. Soldiers had the option of reporting to other surviving military authority or going on indefinite leave until their ETS dates.

"General, sir?" a freckled young Air Force sergeant piped up from a nearby station. "Fairchild and JBLM are on the horn asking, and pardon me for quoting directly, just what in the fuck is going on."

"Don't respond to JBLM—if they can't figure it out after the Navy ripped 'em a new asshole, they're too dumb to live, anyway. Tell Fairchild they got two days to get out of Dodge before the natives roast 'em on a spit, so they'd better start packing." Westman slowly eyed the handful of remaining soldiers and airmen who hadn't fled with the civilian staff the moment he shot Alicia. He drew a deep breath and issued the final order of his long and, until recently, distinguished military career. "That includes all of you. You can choose to report back to what's left of JBLM, or steal whatever supplies you can and take your chances—make your way to Cascadia, the Union of Free States, the Texas Federation, or wherever, and live long and happy lives." Westman swallowed the lump in his throat. "It's been an honor serving with all of you through these horrible times."

The soldiers and airmen shot to their feet and saluted as one, chairs rolling and squeaking on the tile as Westman smartly returned the courtesy. "Dismissed," he huskily said and headed for the exit, the footfalls of his boots echoing throughout the cavernous and silent room.

He stepped into his spartan quarters and locked the door; Westman rarely made it back to his comfortable home at JBLM, the demands on his time from Washington's humanitarian crisis and the Cascadia rebellion a convenient excuse to avoid a house full of memories of his dead wife and a daughter he knew in his heart didn't make it. The general donned his dress green uniform, every medal and badge placed with painstaking precision, and stepped to a wall mirror to scrutinize his appearance like a young soldier about to appear before a promotion board.

Westman sat at his wall desk, picked up the stack of papers detailing every lead regarding Kara's whereabouts—all of them dead ends—and unceremoniously dropped it in the metal wastebasket. Unbuttoning his dress coat one-handed, he picked up the framed picture of the two of them at her high school graduation and slid it next to his heart.

I did the best I could, honey, Westman thought, silently begging his daughter for understanding and forgiveness as the frame warmed to his temperature. *At least you won't have to live with the shame of your father going down in history as a villain. It's nothing less than I deserve.*

With that, he shoved his handgun in his mouth and pulled the trigger.

CHAPTER 64

SNOQUALMIE PASS

"One day," Callie hissed through clenched teeth as Billy poured moonshine on the gash running down her right thigh, "someone's gonna invent an ejection seat less deadly than the bandit who's trying to kill you."

The downed pilot sat on a threadbare folding tailgate chair next to Billy and Olivia's bountiful vegetable garden, the beauty of the mountain morning a stark contrast to the demolished bridges and burning vehicles across the lake. Billy, red-faced with embarrassment, gingerly reached into Callie's ripped flight suit to wrap her bare leg with clean white gauze. "You're lucky we were out here day drinkin' and watching Cascadia tell the Wicked Witch of the West to fuck off once and for all," he said. "We wouldn't have seen your 'chute otherwise."

Olivia sipped her moonshine, shading her eyes with her free hand from the morning sun as she stared at the fighter planes swarming over the pass. "They comin' for you? You got . . . hey, Billy, what's it called when they rescue downed pilots?" she asked with a tipsy slur.

"Combat search and rescue—CSAR," Billy grunted, easing his broken body into his lounge chair.

"Ya got see-sar comin'?" Olivia asked their guest.

"Negative—I officially resigned my commission by shooting my transponder," Callie said, wincing with pain. "I just turned a hundred-million-dollar fighter into modern art, and I don't see Lockheed building any more of 'em anytime soon, so I figure I'll give civilian life a try. I don't mind being remembered as having sacrificed my life for Cascadia—just make sure when they name a high school after me that it's Harman with an 'a'."

"Home of the Fightin' Amazons," Olivia said.

"Damn straight." Callie gasped and grabbed her leg. "God-*damn*, this smarts!"

Billy stopped Olivia from handing Callie moonshine for the pain. "She's lost a decent amount of blood—booze isn't a good idea," he said before pulling a large joint and a Bic lighter from the pocket of his flannel shirt. "I ain't no stoner—it helps with my PTSD, and I was gonna light this candle anyway to take the edge off after watchin' the fighting. If you're not gonna be pissin' in a cup for urinalysis anymore, ma'am, you may as well celebrate in style."

Billy got the joint started and handed it off to Callie, who took a long drag. "Thank you both for your hospitality," Callie said with a cough. "You have a wonderful home."

"Looks like we'll get to keep it now," Olivia murmured, pleasantly squiffed. "We spent the past decade worryin' about gettin' priced out by all the rich dickheads from Seattle and California buyin' up all the land." She took another sip of moonshine. "Looks like that problem's solved, but at what a cost."

Billy accepted the joint back from Callie. "Well, lieutenant commander, as they told me at Walter Reed, today's the first day of the rest of your life. What'cha gonna do with it?"

"Find my husband. Dylan."

"Where is he?" Billy grunted with a lungful of smoke as he leaned over to pass the joint. "Where was your squadron stationed?"

"Naval Air Station Lemoore, south of Fresno."

Olivia spewed a mouthful of moonshine in a fine mist as Billy halted the handoff. "You wanna go to SoCal? This shit got right on top of you, lady," he said. "I hate to harsh your mellow, but southern California's gone. All of it."

Callie grabbed the Mason jar of moonshine from Olivia and knocked back a gulp, the risk of bleeding to death be damned. "You look like you got one hell of a woman."

Billy smiled at Olivia. "I woulda died a long time ago if it wasn't for her."

"I found one hell of a good man, too," Callie said, staring out onto the water and waiting for the rotgut and the pot to numb the physical and emotional pain. "Put his career on mothballs so I could live my dream of being a naval aviator. Dylan was always there for me through thick and thicker, deployment after deployment. Now it's my turn to be there for him."

"And we're gonna help you," Olivia said, nodding at Callie's bandaged leg. "You're gonna be our guest until you're fit enough to travel. Then we'll take you to the barter market where we get our 'shine and his weed, and find you a ride to get you on your way."

Callie squeezed Olivia's hand. "God bless both of you. Once I find him and we're in a position to . . ."

"You don't owe us a damn thing," Billy cut her off. "Treasure in heaven, ma'am."

A distant fireball and a fountain of sparks heralded the ignition of one of the smoldering Strykers' ammunition stores. The *boom* rolled over the lake several seconds later.

"You think our boys are OK?" Olivia asked, voice cracking over her concern for their young houseguests who had run off in the middle of the night to join the fighting.

"I sure to God hope so," Billy said, taking a deep drag of marijuana to hold the horrors of past war at bay.

Billy and Olivia left the soldiers' gear where it lay, haphazardly strewn about their living room, in the hope that the young men would return to reclaim it. They waited until New Year's Day to gather it up and solemnly trundle it through the snow to their storage shed, where it stayed until they died.

CHAPTER 65

KENNEWICK, REPUBLIC OF CASCADIA

The Columbia River chilled Allan's bare feet as he gently set the white paper lantern honoring Jed's memory onto the water.

He barely had time to whisper a prayer for his older brother before Julie lit the tea candle in another lantern for Jed's beloved Mary Ellen, followed by another honoring Autumn Nielsen, Gabe Culver, and the rest of the First Chewelah Irregulars who had sacrificed their lives. Allan couldn't hold back the tears any longer with the lanterns for Mikey and Beth, whose rooms in the home Jed had willed Allan and Julie served as a constant reminder of everything they had lost.

One by one, Allan set the lanterns afloat, gently nudging them to join the flotilla already bobbing on the gentle waves, their sparkling luminescence growing with the setting sun. A family of entrepreneurs did brisk business walking the Sacajawea Heritage Trail along the river, pulling a squeaky Radio Flyer wagon filled with pre-made lanterns and tea lights.

Julie stepped into Allan's arms, watching with the hundreds of other survivors lining the shore and clutching candles in silence; some stood, while others sat exhausted from months of inadequate calories, their threadbare pre-collapse clothes hanging on them like tents. Allan wiped his smudged glasses with his undershirt, which like the rest of his few sets of civilian clothes had seen better days. Julie had taken to Mary Ellen's hobby of sewing with gusto, and had hemmed and trimmed some of her clothes to fit her—besides enlarging her wardrobe, Julie hoped the sewing machine would mean a steady income in barter or silver, given that her days as a software coder likely were over forever.

The five surviving members of the First and Second Chewelah Irregulars had come to the Tri-Cities to witness the historic vote by the Interim Congress to split the Republic of Cascadia from the corpses of Old Washington and the United States, and join the Union of Free States. Legislators had convened in neighboring Richland, at the federal building which miraculously was spared the fate that befell many federal government facilities at the hands of angry mobs; the city would serve as the interim state capital, and would host the upcoming convention to draft a new constitution for voters to ratify. Concerns that the convention would devolve into a red-versus-blue brawl where both sides would squabble to hard-wire their political beliefs into the new constitution evaporated in an unprecedented spirit of cooperation—survivors were sick and tired of that nonsense and were starving for a fresh start. Borrowing an idea from the Republic of Montana, only people who had fought for or aided the Cascadia rebellion, and had no pre-collapse ties whatsoever to Olympia or Washington, DC, could serve as convention delegates.

Interim President Rebecca Stevenson had urged the people to mark the birth of their new nation with solemn remembrance of those who had died since the collapse. The idea of floating lanterns spread like wildfire on Redoubt Radio and other reemerging media, and waterways throughout the towns and hamlets dotting Cascadia were ablaze with light on this first night of the republic.

Melancholy swept over Allan as he watched the sea of glowing lanterns hugging the shore of Kennewick, as well as the City of Pasco on the opposite side of the river. Part of him yearned to return to the Montana survival retreat where he and Julie had weathered the collapse—and had first shed blood to overthrow another tyrant—but he knew he would feel even more out of place in Helena than he did in Chewelah. Allan was the family's sole survivor; a traffic accident took away his parents, the flu took Jed's family, and then the war took Jed. The spindly weakling who had been content before the collapse wasting his talents and drifting on the winds was the one whom God spared—and who God cursed with an overwhelming burden of guilt that he wore around his soul like a millstone.

"Annie?" a little girl asked, her voice cutting through the silence.

"Yes, dear?" a young woman answered.

"Are you sure they can't come back?"

"No, sweetheart. They can't."

"Never ever?"

Annie stroked the girl's brown hair. "No, honey. Never ever."

Julie stepped away from Allan and knelt in front of the child. "Hi! What's your name?"

"Molly," she shyly volunteered.

"That's a pretty name. I have a very important job for you, Molly." Julie unzipped her backpack and pulled out one of Beth's stuffed animals they had brought to donate to a church collecting toys for Cascadia's many orphaned children. "A good friend of mine would've wanted you to have this. Could you take care of her for me?"

"Twilight Sparkle!" the girl squealed with delight and snatched the My Little Pony stuffy into a bear hug. "We had to leave her at home when the bad things started!" She tried to dash toward the river's edge before Annie grabbed her arm. "Mommy! Daddy! Billy! Aubrey! Look! It's Twilight Sparkle! I got her back!" she screamed, jumping up and down, at the sea of memorial lights.

Molly looked up at Annie, the candlelight dancing in the wide eyes of youthful innocence. "Which ones are theirs? There's so many."

"They heard you, honey. They heard you," Annie said, kneeling down to hug Molly and her new toy, mouthing *thank you* to Julie.

Allan took a deep breath as Julie returned to his arms, savoring her random act of kindness that, temporarily, beat back the demons he knew he would wrestle the rest of his days. "We're gonna be all right," he said.

"We're gonna be great—I'm pregnant."

"Wait, what?" Allan blurted with a jolt.

"You're gonna be a daddy."

"That . . . that *is* great!" Allan exclaimed, dropping his tapered candle and whirling Julie around to the muted congratulations of the mourners within earshot. Allan kissed Julie and set her down. "No more staying out all night, young lady," he joked.

"And you've gotta find a job," she fired back.

Allan pushed his glasses up to the bridge of his nose and sighed raggedly. "I have a request, if you don't mind—it's all right if you say no," he said, voice shaking. "If it's a boy . . ."

"Jed's a great name for a son," Julie finished his thought. "He and Mary Ellen would be so proud of you, and everything you've become."

"I hope so."

"I know so."

They watched as the lanterns lazily floated downriver like thousands of fireflies defiantly shining with the promise the future held.

RICHLAND

Alexandra admired the beautiful colors painted by the setting sun, lost in thought over the history she had just witnessed with Cascadia's vote to go its own way.

Surviving townspeople and members of the Interim Congress lazily strolled across the tall, unkempt grass of John Dam Plaza's open-air community stage toward the Columbia River, candles in hand, to honor their lost. No one recognized her—*the perks of a career in radio*, Alexandra mused as she savored the rare moment of solitude; Paul and the crew were packing up so they could convoy back to Idaho in the morning. The legislators would be staying in town to finish setting up the interim government and to start working on the thousands of problems facing the new republic, from preventing a winter die-off—a crisis worsened by a new influx of refugees fleeing Old Washington following its defeat—to finding the resources to continue cleaning up the radioactive Hanford Site nearby with the federal government gone.

A tap on the shoulder snapped Alexandra out of her reverie, and she leaped to her feet from the plaza's mold-stained bleachers upon seeing Rebecca greeting her with a friendly wave. Cascadia's new president, along with Idaho President Jed Curtis and Montana President Karina Jacobs, were flanked by Rebecca's personal bodyguard Miguel Lopez, and a security detail of troopers from the former Washington State Patrol. Not that Jacobs needed the protection—the former Marine drill instructor, elected as Big Sky Country's first head of state for stopping a plot by its illegitimate governor from launching Malmstrom Air Force

Base's nuclear arsenal against seceded states, wore an AR-15 rifle across her back.

"It's a pleasure to finally meet you," Rebecca said, shaking her hand. "I just wanted to stop by and thank you for everything you did for us."

Alexandra grinned sheepishly. "I just did my part like everyone else, Madam President."

"Nonsense—we wouldn't have won without you. I hope you realize that." Rebecca excused herself to greet a handful of commissioners from the southwest counties of Old Washington, who attended as observers in defiance of threats of imprisonment from the "Emergency Committee" of surviving Seattle-area lawmakers who took power following the death of Alicia Embrey.

"Well, Alexandra," Curtis said, stifling a yawn, "we're all gonna be busier than a one-legged man at an ass-kicking contest for the foreseeable future. What about you? You got plans?"

"Yup. I'm heading back to Sandpoint, and a big plate of my uncle-in-law's legendary *ropa vieja*," she said, waving to Paul and the crew as they walked back from the former federal building across the street. "If it's the rest of my life you're asking about, I'm gonna keep doing what I've been doing—I don't think I can go back to playing Bon Jovi and Hootie and the Blowfish for people who wanna piss away this new beginning pining for the way things were. We're gonna blast our show across the Union of Free States—all over the former USA, actually. Let people know they can trust the news again. No bias, no nonsense—just the facts." She took her leave and ran at a sprint into her husband's arms.

Rebecca returned hand-in-hand with Demetrius, who had just come back from his nightly radio check with Tom and Allie. The young newlyweds—Demetrius had served as Tom's best man for their quickie ceremony—had stopped for the night in Pocatello; they had left for Alabama three days prior, and Demetrius already missed them terribly. He was dressed in mufti, having turned down the Interim Congress's offer to command Cascadia's military on account of the conflict of interest posed by his impending marriage to the commander-in-chief. He jostled a reusable shopping bag filled with floating candles to honor James Rand and his family, Deion Carver and the heroic dead of Battle Company, and the memories of Sean, Cade, Grant, and Animal.

Demetrius smiled sadly at Jacobs, who he learned had belonged to Animal's personal survival group of ex-military members in Montana before he disappeared shortly after its fight for independence ended. "Small world, isn't it? At least you and the rest of Montana finally know what happened to him."

Jacobs glanced to ensure Alexandra was out of earshot. "Actually, I think I'll keep this to myself—keep his legend alive. Besides, pardon my candor, I'm calling bullshit on Animal being KIA—he's way too hardcore to get his ticket punched by his copter going down. Feel free to float that candle, though." Jacobs glanced at her watch. "Time for me to shove off," she said, shaking Rebecca's and Demetrius's hands one last time. "Good luck to you."

"To all of us," Rebecca said. "A republic."

Jacobs nodded. "If you—we—can keep it."

CHAPTER 66

THE DALLES, PACIFICA REPUBLIC

The menacing bouncer sized up Animal to the wailings of a horrible garage band in the beer garden massacring "Mustang Sally."

"What happened t' your face?" he asked in a deep voice, glancing at the burn scars covering Animal's left cheek and arm.

"Your old lady sat on it."

Although the bouncer stood a full head taller than Animal, he let the wisecrack slide—the customer looked like a man who could more than hold his own. "Never seen you here before, stranger," he grunted.

"Ya probably won't see me here again with that lead singer stranglin' a cat on stage," Animal quipped, jerking a thumb in the direction of the fenced beer garden.

The bouncer cracked the briefest of grins. "Ain't that the truth—Ted can't carry a tune in a sack, but he owns the joint, so I gotta listen to his shitty music an' smile, or I'm outta work." He lifted a tattoo-sleeved arm from his chest-harnessed semiautomatic rifle and pointed at a crude hand-painted sign leaning against the cinderblock wall next to a yellow weapon clearing barrel planted in the dirt by the bar's entrance. "The rules. Know 'em and love' em—or else. Please drink responsibly."

Animal examined the sign with detached amusement, sidestepping just in time to avoid an inebriated patron staggering out the door and tripping on the crumbling sidewalk.

WELCOME TO THE WRETCHED HIVE!

RULE 1: CLEAR AND SAFE YOUR WEAPONS IN THE CLEARING BARREL BEFORE ENTERING. YOU FIRE OFF A ROUND INSIDE, YOU DIE.

RULE 2: AMMO, FUEL, ASSWIPE, BATTERIES, AND SILVER COIN ACCEPTED AS PAYMENT. OTHER BARTER CONSIDERED ON A CASE-BY-CASE BASIS. GREEN PAPER CRAP WITH DEAD PRESIDENTS ON IT WILL **NOT** BE ACCEPTED.

RULE 3: HOLD YOUR LIQUOR. YOU START A FIGHT, YOU DIE.

RULE 4: YOU TRY TO SKIP OUT WITHOUT PAYING, YOU DIE.

RULE 5: NO DROIDS. WE DON'T SERVE THEIR KIND HERE.

Animal dumped the magazine from his SCAR-H, ejected the chambered round and dry-fired into the clearing barrel, and then did the same with his holstered Glock 19 before stepping inside the dimly lit watering hole. His adventures had taken him to dives that smelled worse, but not by much—the odors of sweat, stale beer, and piss, all made worse by the stuffiness of the room, would have made a pre-collapse health inspector turn green and gallop back outside for fresh air. Animal walked to the sparsely populated bar, his boots crackling on the sticky tile, and slapped the 7.62-millimeter NATO round from his rifle on the wood.

The sultry young bartender studied the round in the glow of the remaining ceiling lights and the neon beer signs festooning the back wall. "Oooh . . . big spender," she purred. "This'll get you two bottles of the local beer and a shot of 'shine."

"Just a beer, thanks—you can have the other one an' use the rotgut to strip this nasty-ass floor. I'm just passin' through."

The bartender reached below the bar for two unlabeled brown bottles, the unbuttoned top of her bodysuit leaving nothing to the imagination, and popped Animal's cap with a satisfying *hiss*. "I'll be needing that bottle back when you're done, sweetheart. And thanks for the drink," she said, cracking open the beer Animal bought her. Animal took a long pull of cold beer and nodded with satisfaction—if there was one thing the Pacific Northwest did well, it was suds. He headed for the side door to the beer garden, where the band was wrapping up an ear-splitting rendition of "Sweet Home Alabama."

"Sir?" the bartender called after Animal. "I've seen a lotta people like you come through since the shooting stopped. I hope you find whoever it is you're looking for," she said, respectfully lifting her bottle to him.

Animal silently saluted back with a hoist of his own before stepping into the refreshing open air of the beer garden, just as the band announced it was taking a break between sets. He pulled a rickety stool up to a long wooden table covered with the usual crude anatomical engravings and other nuggets of bar wisdom, as well as more recent contributions from patrons boasting that they had survived the pandemic, the collapse, and the war. He muttered a silent toast to Sean and the many other soldiers he had outlived, and took another cautious sip of his beer.

A middle-aged man dressed like a B-movie extra eased onto the barstool across from Animal, a beaten skipper's hat askew on his head and a bandolier draped over an ample, suntanned belly jutting out of an unbuttoned Hawaiian shirt. "If you're lookin' for the Jimmy Buffett tribute concert, the Keys are 'bout three thousand miles that-a-way," Animal said, nodding southeast past some rough-looking men and women playing bags with rifles slung on their backs. "Seein' as how ev'ryone in Florida outside the Panhandle is deader'n a doornail, you shouldn't have trouble findin' a good seat."

"You 'Animal'?" the stranger asked.

"Who's askin'?"

"The guy who can float your crazy ass down the river an' sneak you into what's left of Portland—unless, of course, I'm talkin' to the wrong smartass who got his face an' arm all burned up. I'm not gonna ask why the fuck you want a one-way ticket into that deathtrap, but if you got the money, you got yourself a boat."

Animal discretely scanned his surroundings—a man with money in a frontier society who wants to live to see tomorrow doesn't flaunt it—and slid over a small sack of silver coins. "Steep price, friend."

"For a reason, friend—you wouldn't get within twenty miles of Portland on your own. They'd have you boilin' in a stewpot the moment you crested the Cascades. That ain't no joke." The skipper pulled a silver Canadian Maple Leaf from the sack and flipped it from the bust of King Charles III to scrutinize the tiny anti-counterfeiting laser etch on the leaf side. "Most of the fee pays me an' my crew. The rest pays any tolls we come across."

"When can we leave?"

"Soon as you finish your beer. Ship's tied up at the marina across the interstate, and your limo's parked out back." The skipper gestured toward the sun, which had just ducked below the Wretched Hive's roof. "We'll shove off once the big yellow bitch sets and prying eyes are too busy adjustin' to the dark to spot us."

Animal polished off his brew and wiped his mouth on the back of his wrist. "What do I call ya, skip?"

"Folks 'round here call me Cap'n Barnacles," the sailor said, beckoning Animal to follow him out of the bar.

"Pleased t' meetcha," Animal said, dropping his finished bottle in the collection bin by the exit. "There a story behind that name?"

"My grandson, Jackson, really loved this old kids' show and books about a gang of cute animals explorin' the ocean. Barnacles was the leader. He used to call me that on account o' my boat," he said with a sad smile as Animal tossed his rucksack in the back of a dusty green Jeep guarded by two of the captain's hired hands. "The name's how I honor his memory. Jack-Jack died of strep fuckin' throat, of all things—we survived everything fallin' apart, and we miraculously didn't get *la grippe*, but we lost 'im to something we used to be able to fix with a prescription. Welcome to the New Dark Ages."

The driver gunned the engine and hooked into a three-point turn, barely avoiding a blonde woman animatedly negotiating with a balding man sitting on the bed of a Ford pickup truck.

"Lemoore Naval Station's in Cali?! You're certifiable, lady—there ain't nothin' or no one left down there 'cept the gangs!" the man exclaimed as the Jeep sped away for the marina. "Tell ya what—we got a truck leavin' tomorrow morning for the provisional state capitol in Medford. Lemme see what I can do . . ."

The Dalles's location in the Columbia River Valley made it strategically vital during Cascadia's and Pacifica's wars for independence, given that the small city commanded one of the few bridges over the river along the state line east of Portland. With the wars won, the bridge intact, and the nearby 1.9-megawatt Dalles Dam on the Cascadia side providing power, The Dalles became a vital hub for reemerging trade, and a waypoint for survivors hoping against all odds that they would find their loved ones alive. Its importance would increase further if air travel ever returned to the Columbia Gorge Regional Airport just across the river.

The city was much cleaner and more orderly than the Wretched Hive's seediness implied, Animal noticed as the Jeep circled a roundabout for the I-84 overpass to the marina. Its residents were doing well for themselves, and enthusiastically supported the fledgling Pacifica Republic and the Union of Free States which its legislature had voted to join. *If there's two things that real Americans love, it's second chances and clean slates*, Animal mused, taking in the breathtaking view of the valley and snow-capped Mount Hood dominating the southwest horizon. He swelled with contentment with what he and his comrades had helped accomplish in Montana and Cascadia; this wasn't Russia, Iraq, or the innumerable nations throughout history where people let their brief moment of liberty flicker out because they didn't know what it was or what to do with it. All these new nations forged from the old United States would turn out just fine.

The Jeep pulled into the marina entrance, guarded by two rifle-brandishing men even more imposing than the bouncer Animal had dealt with, and rolled to a stop at the edge of the walkway. "It's gonna be a two-day float," Captain Barnacles explained as Animal slung his rucksack over his shoulder. "We're movin' only at night so's to avoid pirates and toll collectors—a lotta riff-raff and tinpot mayors figured out that chargin' for passage is a great way to make money. Once Pacifica and Cascadia get their shit together, they're gonna hafta shut 'em down or wipe 'em out so's we can have access to the ocean, lemme tell ya—we and the rest of the Union o' Free States won't do very well landlocked."

The captain waved to his daughter standing on the bow of a white 1966 Chris Craft Commander tied up at the nearest bay of the visitor moorage. He turned to Animal and warned him over the din of seagulls whirling overhead to keep his hands off, and not to bring up her little Jackson under any circumstance.

"Pretty lady—your ship, I mean," Animal said as they stepped from the metal walkway to the pier. "Whaddya call her?"

"Well, I never liked the name when I inherited her from my old man, appropriate as it is, but changing a boat's name is bad luck, or so I've heard," Captain Barnacles said, ushering Animal to the rusted metal boarding stairs. "She's called *Tenax Propisiti*—that's Latin for 'Tenacious of Purpose.'"

Animal patted the boat's port side. "Just like us. I think her an' me will get along just fine," he said and climbed aboard.

The *Tenax*'s engines coughed to life twenty minutes later and Captain Barnacles eased her out of the marina and westward into the open river under the pristine cloudless beauty of nautical twilight. A lack of diesel fuel had almost sidelined his business until a steady supply from the ascendent Texas Federation became available for the right price—the ethanol coming from Nebraska and the Heartland Confederation would've killed his engines and his fuel tank, he explained to Animal.

"Runnin' at night on the river is like cookin' ribs—we go low and slow," Captain Barnacles continued, grabbing a pair of older-generation night vision goggles hanging on the bridge's sedan-finish wall and slipping them, one-handed, onto his head. "We got our navigation lights off for obvious reasons, so we gotta assume anyone else out here is doin' the same. Good news is, we don't gotta worry about stayin' clear of the shipping lanes 'cause there's no more fuckin' shipping."

The outside world became black as pitch as the sun finally set and the lights of The Dalles faded behind them, the ship's dimmed instrument panel providing their sole illumination. "Our biggest threat is anything floatin' in the water that could put a hole in the boat or wrap 'round the props. We got off easy—the Big River here didn't get choked with debris and corpses like other places, given that there ain't a lotta civiliza-tion upstream. So, what's your plan for gettin' out of Portland, if you don't mind me askin'?" Captain Barnacles cautiously ventured—Animal hadn't spoken since the *Tenax* set sail.

"I'll cross that bridge when I get to it."

The skipper nodded—he knew the moment he laid eyes on Animal that he was searching for family, but also knew not to press the issue. "Tell ya what—I got Katie mindin' the watch up on the fly bridge, so how's about you help by headin' up to the bow and puttin' that fancy-dancy space rifle o' yours to good use?"

Animal nodded and left the bridge, carefully making his way around the port side to the bow, where there was just enough room for him to lie prone and unfold his rifle's bipod. With a click of his AN/PVS-17A night vision scope, the black of darkness gave way to the shimmering green beauty of stars twinkling overhead and the woods and mountains of the high desert slowly scrolling by.

He soaked in the soothing, hypnotic sound of the lapping water and the engine astern, feeling an instant kinship with his illustrious predecessors who cruised the rivers of South Vietnam, El Salvador, and other hellholes—sometimes to bring order to chaos, other times to inflict chaos on order. He wondered if any of the new nations born from the freedom he had helped win would continue the tradition of special operations units, tracing their lineage back to the former United States the way the Army Rangers had traced theirs back to Rogers' Rangers, of Seven Years' War fame. Animal hoped the men and women who came after him wouldn't be sacrificed by faceless politicians and swivel-chair generals in useless proxy wars no one would ever hear of—as the late United States proved endlessly in the Middle East, Afghanistan, and elsewhere in its sunset years, squandering the treasury on military adventurism to keep the weapons plants humming and war correspondents employed was a sign of the beginning of a nation's end.

Animal realized he was woolgathering at the expense of keeping watch, which is how people get killed. *Yeah, I've gotten too old for this shit*, he told himself. *It's time to hang up my green beret—for good, this time. It's time to live life.* He settled behind his rifle scope and allowed himself one more selfish thought before focusing like a laser on his final mission.

Jo, Kelsie, Marie—I'm coming for you. We can be a family again. Alive or dead, we can be together.

CHAPTER 67

SPOKANE

Allan deployed the roof solar panel of his Tesla Model Alpha sport utility vehicle with the push of a button on the cloudless summer day; it made no sense to feed a coin into the recharging pole at his parking space at James Rand Stadium when the sun would do the honors for free during the baseball game. He stepped out of the driver's seat and locked the car, scratching a well-trimmed beard that covered most of the scars from the target designator that had shattered in his face two decades prior, save for a menacing one crossing over and under his left eye.

He and his fifteen-year-old twin sons, Jed and Raider, hustled to catch up with Julie and his eighteen-year-old daughter, Cheyenne. The twins were already taller than their father and were a force to be reckoned with on Chewelah's varsity football and wrestling teams—just like their uncle had been. Cheyenne was the spitting image of her mother, down to her fiery red hair. All five wore the red, blue, and beige of the Spokane Indians baseball team, with Cheyenne showing a little more skin than her overprotective father would have liked.

Alternating banners mounted to the parking lot light poles advertised the holiday match-up against the arch-rival Helena Slammers, and commemorated the twentieth anniversary of independence from Old Washington, which Cascadia celebrated every August 25—the day of the Battle of the Three Bridges and Rebecca Stevenson's fateful call to Alicia Embrey. And, Allan sadly thought, the day his older brother and far too many good people paid for freedom with their lives.

"Hey, Jed!" Raider called out. "Whaddya gonna have for lunch?"

"I think I'll have a *sandwich*!" Jed answered on cue as the twins plowed into their hapless father from both sides. Allan staggered, laughing at his sons' serendipitous reminder that he had earned his brother's sacrifice by living a good life.

Julie waved to Rebecca and Demetrius, who were waiting at the front gate with Carleigh and her son, Grant, who was Cheyenne's age. In the decade since professional baseball resumed, the Schmidts had come every Independence Day as the honored guests of Cascadia's first president and her first gentleman, who despite looking every bit their age were still spry and full of life.

"Damn, Allan, what'cha been feeding these two?" Demetrius marveled, mussing the twins' hair. "You boys ready for some baseball?"

"You bet!" they chimed simultaneously to Demetrius's amusement.

"Let's get moving—we don't wanna miss the flyover," Demetrius said, beckoning the group through the gate with a wave of their tickets. The ballgame would start with a fighter flyby from the USS *Stennis*, which had just returned to Naval Base Kitsap after a month patrolling the seas around the Kingdom of Hawaii; the constitutional monarchy had a defense agreement with the four nations carved from the former United States, in exchange for the use of Pearl Harbor for their shared Navy. At Puget Sound Naval Shipyard, the keel had just been laid for the new carrier, the USS *Manuel Landero*s, that would eventually replace the aging *Stennis*.

"You excited for the game, young lady, or are you just along for the fresh air?" Rebecca asked Cheyenne.

"I'm just here to read—I'm a basketball girl myself," she replied, brandishing a hardcover book.

"Well, then, you sure picked the right college to attend," Rebecca said. "Oh, wow—Gonzaga starts soon, doesn't it?"

Julie put her arm around her daughter. "We'll be back down here in a few weeks to move her in," she said and bit her lip—she wasn't handling her firstborn leaving the nest well. Gonzaga had reopened only five years prior; Spokane had been slow to rise from the ashes, in great part because of a massive decentralization trend. The exodus from big cities had started before the collapse, courtesy of the COVID-19 pandemic and the crime and unrest that had roared across the former United States in its final years; the survivors of the economic crash and the H7N9 pandemic saw little benefit in returning to the practice of cramming themselves on top of one another. While the city continued to rebuild, mostly along the Spokane River, much of it was abandoned and slowly returning to nature. In the unlikely event Spokane ever did return to its prewar size, Cascadia's presidency was decided via an electoral college system to ensure that it would never run roughshod over the wishes of rural residents the way that Seattle, Chicago, and New York City once did.

The steady stream of passersby wanting to meet Rebecca and Demetrius made their walk to the VIP section slow going. Allan glanced up at Cascadia's navy blue flag, which flew proudly in the breeze above the flag of the Union of Free States; the practice of flying the state flag over the federal one served to remind the Union Congress at the national capital of Boise that the independent states, not the minimalist central government, wore the pants in the family. The wind was blowing toward the infield, Allan realized with a touch of disappointment—there wouldn't be very many runs scored.

The Union's blue and white flag had added an eleventh star with the admittance of the Alaska Republic, where survivors of the collapse and the unforgiving climate eventually petitioned for membership. Cascadia had grown as well, after the southern counties of Old Washington had finally rebelled against Olympia and joined up; it now reached the Pacific Ocean, and the addition of two deep-water ports along the Columbia River gave the fledgling republic's economy a significant boost. The pathetic remnants of the old state government evaporated shortly thereafter, and the entire Seattle metro area, from the ruins of Olympia north to Vancouver, remained a dangerous no-man's land, the cost of cleaning it out and rebuilding far outweighing any remaining value. Aside from tiny, scattered hamlets hanging on by their fingernails, the sole pockets of civilization in Old Washington were Cascadia's enclaves of Naval Base Kitsap, and the two vital petroleum refineries at Anacortes.

Allan gripped the railing to the concrete steps leading to their seats. "I know you won't take it, Rebecca, but I'll make my annual offer to pay for our tickets."

"And I'll give you our annual rebuttal of thanks, but no thanks," she answered. "It's the least we can do to honor your older brother."

"The Indians just raised their ticket prices, honey—maybe we should take him up on it," Demetrius joked—after ten years, the admission cost had increased by twenty-five Cascadian cents. All of the Union's member states had adopted a bimetallic currency standard, with money redeemable for gold and silver on demand, which all but eliminated inflation and simplified rates of exchange.

"I remember when the cost of everything went up, year after year, because the Federal Reserve kept making trillions of dollars out of thin air—it's one of the main reasons the old USA collapsed," Allan lectured his children.

"We know," Cheyenne groaned, rolling her eyes. "You tell us every time we buy anything, and because you pounded it into our heads as kids with those Tuttle Twins books you made us check out from the library over and over."

"Your dad's a pain about it because we don't want you or your children to go through what we went through," Julie said. "Or lose what we lost."

"You tell us that every time, too," her daughter retorted as the family stepped from the cool stillness of the concrete stairwell into the hot summer sun. Allan raised his eyebrow at the two uniformed state troopers—one from Cascadia, the other from Montana—standing vigil on both sides.

"We invited some friends to join us—hope you don't mind," Demetrius nonchalantly said before Allan's and Julie's eyes went wide at the sight of Montana's president and first lady waiting for them in the stands.

"Glad you could pry yourself away from your ham radio for a few hours, Stick," Manny Landeros ribbed his old friend.

Manny barely managed to raise his beer over his head to safety before Allan charged into him with a running hug. Their children kept a respectful distance as their parents reunited with the couple who owned the Montana retreat where they and their survival group rode out the collapse, and fought to topple a despot who had proclaimed himself governor.

"Oh my, the kids have gotten big," First Lady Carmen Landeros said in awe as they sat back down. "Then again, it's been a while—we haven't seen you since . . ."

"The funeral," Allan said—the survival group's mechanic, Jay Kowalsky, had died of a stroke five years prior. "So, Mr. President, what brings you to Cascadia?"

"Wrapping up some official business, and then tomorrow we'll be flying into Kitsap to see how Junior's doing," Manny said.

Julie laughed at his nickname for the new flattop. "I think it's awesome the Navy decided to name an aircraft carrier after you. You earned it."

"You and Allan, and everyone else, were right by my side, every step of the way. Don't see why I'm so special," Manny said, sipping his beer.

Carmen ran her hand through Manny's graying hair. "We do."

"Also, Mr. Modesty, you failed to mention that tiny little thing ten years ago when the former secretary of state crawled out from under a rock and tried to reunite the old USA by force," Julie said. "You played an oversized hand in making sure we didn't all end up glowing in the dark, if I remember correctly."

"All right, all right, I get the point," Manny groused. "Carrier probably won't ever get used, anyway." While the four independent American nations shared a Navy, Air Force, and strategic nuclear arsenal, they didn't inherit the former USA's desire to throw their weight around and get involved in never-ending little wars, living instead by Theodore Roosevelt's maxim to speak softly and carry a big stick.

Allan admonished his kids not to break the bank as they flagged down a food vendor walking the aisles. "Beg pardon, Manny, but catching a ballgame doesn't seem much like 'official business' to me."

"Guilty as charged. This is probably my last trip as president, and I decided to let my hair down a bit," Manny said—he was serving the final year of his second term, and was term-limited under the Montana Constitution. "Rebecca told me about the fella the stadium's named after—sounded like my kind of guy."

"I never met James Rand, but my brother, true story, was standing not twenty feet away when he was shot. Jed and his friends joined the resistance shortly thereafter."

Manny looked Allan in the eyes. "So, seriously, man to man—you holdin' up OK? I know it's hard for you sometimes."

"I'm doing all right," he answered, gesturing to his family. "They give me purpose."

Carleigh leaped out of her seat at the sight of a tall, silver-haired man climbing the steps to their row of seats with the help of a hand-carved wooden cane. "There he is! My hero!" she theatrically proclaimed with open arms and planted a kiss on his cheek to the mortified embarrassment of Grant, who had been trying with futility to impress Cheyenne since they sat down.

Demetrius rose to shake Ed Wojciech's hand. "Hold that thought," Woj said and got the vendor's attention. "A dog and a beer, young lady." He slapped Demetrius on the back. "And this handsome fella's payin' for it."

"You said I only owed you four," Demetrius jokingly grumbled, reaching for his wallet to repeat a ritual he had performed many times over in the two decades since Ed risked his life to help rescue his stepdaughter.

"Yes, I did," Ed said, leaning his cane against his seat and grabbing his order. "And I decided the moment I got shot in the ass crawlin' under the fence at Yakima Airport that one of the four would be drinks on the house for life, with Demetrius Mathers bein' the house."

Carleigh elbowed her stepfather in the ribs. "You heard him—pay up! I'm worth every penny!"

Rebecca helped Ed ease himself into his seat. "So, Rebecca—speaking of Yakima, I heard on *The Alexandra Chase Show* that the little cocksucker whose face you rearranged got denied parole again—pardon my French." She nodded and snuck a cautious glance at Carleigh—the imprisonment of David Hampton, the former governor's chief of staff, was a bit of a sore spot between mother and daughter. While Carleigh believed he had been punished enough for his role in her kidnapping, Rebecca would testify every time he came up for a hearing that the thirty-year sentence handed down by Cascadia's old war crimes commission for her abduction, as well as for abetting a litany of other crimes against humanity, was just and appropriate; the Mother of Cascadia's opinion still carried a lot of weight.

"Pardon my French again, but fuck that guy, Mama Bear," Ed said. "He's lucky he didn't hang."

While Allan had always found baseball as exciting as watching paint dry, the innings flew by as he caught up with Manny and Carmen. Their daughter, Luisa, had become chief of surgery at St. Peter's Hospital, and had given them three grandchildren, who her poor husband was corralling while she was on a mission trip to the Republic of Yucatan-Chiapas. Manny and Carmen filled Allan in on the mundane lives of the rest of their group's surviving members, almost all of whom had decided to settle down around Helena.

Allan cleared his throat. "Any news about Liam?" he ventured—the young man had left their survival group after the Battle of Helena to find his girlfriend and parents in Billings, which like Seattle was a charnel house. He hadn't been heard from since.

"*Nada*. Fell off the face of the Earth," Manny said in a tone Allan knew meant he was done talking about it.

The crowd burst into loud cheers as the next batter walked to the plate. "Let's go, Tailwind!" Julie screamed just as Chewelah native Deonte "Tailwind" Richards connected with his first pitch—scant seconds later, he was standing on second base, kissing his fingers and pointing to the sky.

"So the nickname isn't just marketing, then—guy's fast," Manny said.

"He's a great human being, too," Julie added; one of the first things Deonte had paid for with his baseball salary was a proper memorial to the First and Second Chewelah Irregulars. "He and his mom were refugees from Old Spokane—super humble kid who wants to pay it forward and make a career out of representing us on the team."

"Well, maybe the collapse and a guerrilla war—or in your case, two guerrilla wars—will have been worth it if it means the end of free agency," Manny joked and sipped his beer.

The proud mothers passed their phones around to show off pictures—Cheyenne and the twins, Luisa and her children, and Carleigh's adult stepson, who was an officer in the First Kennewick Lightfoot. His militia unit was serving a voluntary one-month rotation to the State of Jefferson to help patrol its newly expanded southern border against marauders out of Old California, which still presented problems more than two decades after what historians had come to call the Unraveling. Smart phones had returned with domestic manufacturing and reliable satellites; private enterprise in the Texas Federation and the Free States of America were leading a new and friendly space race borne from a need to replace the communications and GPS satellites that had ended their operational lives or drifted out of orbit.

"We could've done without those damned things coming back. I don't care about all the laws forbidding clandestine data collection—I'm never touching a smart phone again as long as I live," Allan griped to Manny, pointing to his twin sons watching the game, and his daughter setting her book down to briefly acknowledge Grant's existence. "I can't tell you how glad I am that my kids aren't pissing away a perfect summer day staring at those stupid little screens—give me ham radio any day of the week." Cheyenne and Jed cared little for their father's hobby, but Raider had taken to amateur radio with a passion; he had recently added Scotland, Flanders, Catalonia, and the newly independent Republic of Khabarovsk to his list of successful country contacts.

"Allan Schmidt shunning high-tech gizmos? I've seen it all!" Manny laughed.

"War changes people," Allan said, helping himself to a handful of Raider's roasted peanuts, fresh from the Georgia Free Republic—he found them a very acceptable pairing with his Whistle Punk hefeweizen. He drained the last of his beer and ordered another.

Manny nodded with satisfaction. "I remember when one pint of Roger's homebrew woulda knocked you on your ass."

"War changes your liver, too, I guess."

Manny ordered himself another as well. "We missed you and the family at the reunion," he chided Allan—their survival group held a bash at his home every August 1 to celebrate Montana Independence Day. Allan started to respond, but Manny raised his palm to cut him off. "And no, calling in on the radio isn't the same. It'd mean a lot to us if you'd visit, especially now that Old Man Time is starting to come for us."

The crowd roared in anticipation as the Indians' batter slugged one that looked like it would go all the way. Deonte rounded third and dashed for home plate, but the Slammers' left fielder made an off-the-wall catch to end the inning.

"I know, I know," Allan said as they sat back down to the chorus of disappointed groans. "But I hope you understand—it's really hard going back to places that bring back memories. They do their best to overwhelm me. We almost came to the reunion last year, but . . . it's complicated." Allan had gotten into metal detecting after Autumn's twin brother, Bruce, passed away and his widow gifted his detector to Allan in gratitude for locating her surviving relatives in what was left of South Korea. One day, he prospected in the woods at the top of the hill behind his home and came across a big hit that turned out to be Jed's cache of family photos and mementos. Allan cried for two days straight as he, one by one, pulled out priceless treasures he thought were gone forever—he was a wreck and in no condition to leave the house, much less drive to Montana.

The sun hid behind a passing cloud, giving the crowd a brief respite from the heat but having the odd effect of leaving Allan slightly chilled. "Sometimes, I walk into my kids' rooms and see them the way they were when my niece and nephew were alive. There are days when the only thing that gets me out of bed and keeps me going is that Julie and the kids need me." Allan took a long pull of his beer. "You know, Manny? You were right all those years ago."

"About what?"

"Right after the Battle of Helena, you told me I was too elated and tired to feel the pain of loss, and that it would hit me later. It did. With a vengeance."

Rebecca's soft hand rested on Allan's shoulder. "I'm sorry for listening in, but you're not alone—the collapse took something from everyone. We deal with it every day. I was forced to lead a cause that, however noble, cost thousands of lives. I led a lot of good people to their deaths." She looked over at Demetrius, who was posing for a picture with Ed and Carleigh. "I asked Demetrius shortly after we got married how many men he thought he had killed, and he broke down and bawled like a baby. The only way we can cope is to live every day to the fullest, and hope God understands when we face Him for judgment. I like to think He will, because He wants us to be free, and where true liberty thrives, so does God."

Allan smiled and slid his hand over Rebecca's, only to have his moment of zen shattered by his sons' loud and tandem belch. He died laughing as Jed and Raider stood and bowed to scattered applause. Cheyenne smacked the duo with her book the moment they sat back down.

"We can't take you two anywhere, can we?" Julie asked resignedly over Allan's guffawing.

"Go easy on 'em," Demetrius said. "It's the seventh inning and no runs scored—that was the most exciting thing that's happened so far."

Allan pulled off his glasses and wiped his eyes. "I needed that, boys, even though it was weak. Your Uncle Jed, now—he had belches that could rip the bark off trees."

"I think Jed and Mary Ellen may actually have heard them just now," Julie said.

"OK, Manny, OK. I give," Allan laughed with a shrug. "We'll be there next year."

Carmen bolted ramrod straight in her seat. "Really? You mean it?!" she squealed, clapping her hands.

"Anything to get your husband off my case. Besides, I can tell my grandkids that I stole towels from the President of Montana's house."

"Road trip!" Raider and Jed yelled in unison to everyone's laughter.

Julie grabbed Allan's arm and pulled him to his feet as the announcer introduced the singer for the seventh-inning stretch—some young heartthrob starring in some new television show he had never heard of; Cheyenne's mindless screaming told her father that she was quite familiar with it indeed.

"Lemme hear ya, Spokane!" the man's voice echoed through Rand Stadium. "A one! A two! A three!"

The sun returned from behind the cloud. Allan closed his eyes and welcomed its rays on his face with a smile as he belted out his off-key contribution to "Take Me Out to the Ball Game."

It's so good to be alive.

Thank you for reading *Cascadia Rising*! If you liked it, it would mean the world to me if you take a short minute to leave a heartfelt review on Amazon (and Goodreads, if you have an account). Your kind feedback is very much appreciated, and very important to me.

Acknowledgements

The key to writing good post-apocalyptic fiction—or in my case, somewhat passable post-apocalyptic fiction—is realizing that there's a little bit of Walter Mitty in everyone.

Mitty, of course, is the protagonist in the famous James Thurber short story about a boring little man who, while going about his meaningless life, daydreams about achieving brave and spectacular things. No, I didn't just call you boring or your life meaningless, but each and every one of us daydreams once in a while about kicking ass and taking names. Everyone at some point fantasizes about being a Rebecca Stevenson or a Demetrius Mathers or an Allan Schmidt—someone who has greatness thrust upon them and becomes a hero.

I had the honor of serving in the Army with some real, honest-to-God heroes, although they would be the last people in the world to allow themselves to be called such.

Some of my most cherished teenage memories include watching war movies with my dad in our basement—he had never served in the military, but he sensed my fascination with military history and, like any good father, cultivated it the best he could. In one of those many movies, *The Longest Day*, RAF Flying Officer David Campbell—played by the incomparable Richard Burton—was drinking a beer in honor of his wingman who didn't make it, and lamented that the worst thing about being "one of the few" was the way that they kept getting fewer. I dedicated this novel to my mentor and friend, Command Sergeant Major Steven Krause (Ret.), who survived Afghanistan only to die of cancer way too young. Unfortunately, as I continued to hammer out *Cascadia Rising*, we merry few, we band of brothers, indeed became fewer—so to First Sergeant James Reddick, Sergeant Ricky "Coach" Rachal, and Specialist Christian "The Dome" Earl, I pray that you and Steve save a stool for me in whatever dive bar you all found in Valhalla.

With two books under my belt, I've discovered that the number of people I need to thank has increased proportionally—not only for helping with *Cascadia Rising*, but also for helping launch my first novel, *Big Sky Fallen*.

Thank you to the book reviewers and advance review readers who selflessly spent some of their precious time to read a debut novel from some nobody—I especially would like to thank book blogger Sandra Jeanz Richardson for her early and enthusiastic support. Besides the constructive criticism, thank you all for catching the handful of boo-boos that somehow managed to survive my umpteen edits, rereads, and revisions.

Once again, thank you to the immensely talented Christian Bentulan for designing yet another book cover for me that knocks it out of the park. Visit his website, www.coversbychristian.com, and follow him on Facebook and Instagram, to check out his amazing and awe-inspiring work.

Being an independent author means that you also become a marketer, an accountant, and take on a whole bunch of other roles that give you precious little time to actually write. As such, I owe no small debt of gratitude to fellow indie authors who publish how-to videos and articles that helped me avoid some of the mistakes they made starting out (so I could make a whole bunch of new mistakes of my own). Thank you to

Mandi Lynn, Bethany Atazadeh, David Chesson of Kindlepreneur, and M.K. Williams, among others.

As always, thank you to my beautiful wife, Kristin, who now has to put up with my droning on and on about running a business on top of never shutting up about what I'm writing.

Thank you as well to Emily St. John Mandel, whose novels, besides being excellent reads, won me over to the idea that a bunch of smaller chapters is much better for story flow in this day and age than twenty or so long ones.

Finally, thank you, the reader, for making this adventure possible, and for the love and the wonderful reviews you left to help get *Big Sky Fallen* off the ground. For those of you who expressed hope that you would read the continuing story of Eric, Susan, Manny, and the other main characters in future books, rest assured that you will, and soon. I promise.

Kevin Craver

May 2024

Historical Note

RIPLEY, John Walter, USMC, Col. (Ret.); born June 29, 1939, Radford, Virginia; died October 28, 2008, Annapolis, Maryland); on Easter morning, 1972, under unrelenting enemy fire, then-Captain Ripley dangled under the Dong Ha bridge in South Vietnam for an estimated three hours, hand-walking along the beams in order to attach five hundred pounds of explosives to the span, ultimately destroying the bridge and thwarting the advance of more than twenty thousand enemy troops. His gallantry was honored with the Navy Cross, the nation's second-highest decoration for sailors and Marines who distinguish themselves through extraordinary heroism in combat.

About the Author

Kevin Craver had a comfortable childhood devoid of zombies, post-atomic mutants, or cyborgs trying to kill him before he could grow up to lead the human resistance to victory. He turned a side hustle of drawing a nihilistic comic strip for his college newspaper into a living as a token conservative in the world of newspaper journalism, earning eighty state and national writing awards over his twenty-year career. Somewhere along the line, he realized that his life didn't suck enough, and spent fourteen years and two deployments as an infantryman in the Army National Guard.

When he's not writing about the end of civilization or hoarding cans of bacon in his basement—because the living will envy the dead in a world without bacon—he caters to the whims of his wife, daughter, son, and Ragdoll cat. He enjoys Mexican food, German beer, and frequent trips to the gym to work off both.

Visit Kevin's website at www.kevincraver.com to sign up for e-mail updates on upcoming releases.

facebook.com/AuthorKevinCraver

instagram.com/kevinpcraver

goodreads.com/kevincraver